"A winning wartime tale....
Fresh and compelling."
—KATE QUINN

*A Novel*

# COURAGE,
# *My Love*

KRISTIN BECK

# Praise for *Courage, My Love*

"A winning wartime tale set in the snake pit world of Mussolini's Rome. Single mother Lucia and polio-crippled Francesca make appealing heroines, flowering slowly from reticent bystanders to fierce resistance fighters as the Eternal City comes under German occupation. Kristin Beck's debut is a fresh, compelling read."

—Kate Quinn, *New York Times* bestselling author of *The Huntress*

"An extraordinary debut set against the backdrop of the Nazi occupation of Rome, *Courage, My Love* is historical fiction at its finest. With evocative and compulsively readable prose, Beck weaves a gripping tale of love, loss, patriotism, and courage. Powerful, poignant, and timely, *Courage, My Love* is a must-read."

—Chanel Cleeton, *New York Times* bestselling author of *The Last Train to Key West*

"Fans of Elena Ferrante and Kristin Hannah will relish this gritty tale of perseverance and resistance set in the Eternal City during World War II. I learned a great deal about the Italian front, and the tangled web of friendship and romance kept me turning pages well into the night. A bold and gripping debut."

—Kerri Maher, author of *The Girl in White Gloves*

"A profound anthem to the tremendous courage that transformed two ordinary Italian women into extraordinary heroes during the harrowing days of Mussolini and Hitler. A powerful story, powerfully told!"

—Stephanie Marie Thornton, *USA Today* bestselling author of *And They Called It Camelot*

"Kristin Beck transports us right into the heart of war-stricken Rome and creates a riveting story about brave women who will stop at nothing to protect the people they love. A tale of resistance, resilience, and friendship—this is exactly the type of historical fiction we need right now. Brava!"
—Elise Hooper, author of *Fast Girls*

"*Courage, My Love*, is a moving story about how ordinary people can do extraordinary things when working together for good. Beck crafts a tale of both heart-pounding intensity and deep emotional resonance, with characters who will stay with the reader long after the pages are closed. Poignant and beautiful."

—Erika Robuck, national bestselling author of *The Invisible Woman*

"Powerful and immensely moving, Kristin Beck's debut novel plunges readers headlong into the dark days of WWII-era Rome. A beautifully written story of women at war, *Courage, My Love* will linger with you long after you turn the final page."

—Bryn Turnbull, author of *The Woman Before Wallis*

"Francesca and Lucia are two magnificent women. How could anyone not admire their bravery, their strength, their compassion, and their fierce determination to do whatever they could to protect both those they love and the people of Rome from the Nazis sweeping through their beloved city? *Courage, My Love* is a beautiful story of female friendship, and the unheralded but hugely important resistance work the women of Rome undertook, in the face of grave danger, during WWII. It's a fascinating, nuanced, and impeccably researched tale."

—Natasha Lester, *New York Times* bestselling author of *The Paris Orphan*

"In *Courage, My Love*, a deeply moving novel of Italy in the Second World War, Kristin Beck plunges the reader deep into the lives of Lucia and Francesca, two women united at first by circumstance and eventually by friendship. It illuminates, often to heartrending effect, the uncertainty, upheaval, violence, and viciousness of the Nazi occupation of Rome; and it portrays, with sensitivity and profound empathy, the many ways in which ordinary people confronted evil with selflessness and true valor. In this wonderful novel, Beck brings a lesser-known chapter of wartime history to vivid life with settings that are perfectly observed, down to the smallest detail, and with characters so imperfectly real they all but jump from the page. *Courage, My Love* is a beautiful and breathtaking book. It is certainly one of the finest works of World War II historical fiction I have ever read."

—Jennifer Robson, *USA Today* bestselling author of *The Gown*

# COURAGE, MY LOVE

KRISTIN BECK

BERKLEY
New York

BERKLEY
An imprint of Penguin Random House LLC
penguinrandomhouse.com

Copyright © 2021 by Kristin Beck
Readers guide copyright © 2021 by Kristin Beck
Penguin Random House supports copyright. Copyright fuels creativity,
encourages diverse voices, promotes free speech, and creates a vibrant culture.
Thank you for buying an authorized edition of this book and for complying with
copyright laws by not reproducing, scanning, or distributing any part of it in any
form without permission. You are supporting writers and allowing Penguin
Random House to continue to publish books for every reader.

BERKLEY and the BERKLEY & B colophon are registered trademarks of
Penguin Random House LLC.

Library of Congress Cataloging-in-Publication Data

Names: Beck, Kristin, 1979- author.
Title: Courage, my love / Kristin Beck.
Description: First edition. | New York : Berkley, 2021.
Identifiers: LCCN 2020042951 (print) | LCCN 2020042952 (ebook) |
ISBN 9780593101568 (trade paperback) | ISBN 9780593101575 (ebook)
Subjects: LCSH: World War, 1939-1945—Underground
movements—Italy—Fiction. | Women—Italy—Fiction. |
Italy—History—German occupation, 1943-1945—Fiction. |
GSAFD: Historical fiction.
Classification: LCC PS3602.E2694 C68 2021 (print) |
LCC PS3602.E2694 (ebook) | DDC 813/.6—dc23
LC record available at https://lccn.loc.gov/2020042951
LC ebook record available at https://lccn.loc.gov/2020042952

First Edition: April 2021

Printed in the United States of America

1st Printing

Cover images by by Richard Tuschman; boy © Galya Ivanova / Trevillion Images
Cover design by Rita Frangie

*For my parents,*
*Lois and Hugh Judd,*
*with love.*

# PROLOGUE

✿

*Rome, October 1943*

A FAINT WHISTLE RANG out over the hill, like birdsong dying out, and the rumble of a German convoy grew in its echo. Francesca's heart pounded against the dirt of the embankment rising over the road. She lifted her gun. Up the street, at its crest, the first trucks appeared. They bumped downhill, followed by a long line of identical vehicles, their beds packed with everything needed along the front: ammunition, fuel, food. She peered over the gun's barrel.

The convoy gained speed as it traveled downhill. She held her breath. The first trucks in line rumbled directly below her, and on cue, their tires burst. A half-dozen trucks skidded into one another, brakes squealing, and the air filled with the smell of burnt rubber. Uphill, trucks lumbered to a full stop and doors flung open. Drivers slid out, alert. Shouts ricocheted through the street. Not two minutes had passed, and the convoy was no longer going anywhere near the front.

Several dark figures gathered midway up the street, gesturing and spinning on their heels, weapons out. An explosion lit the hillcrest, bright as lightning, and the dirt vibrated under Francesca's stomach. The Germans raised their guns, shouting and pivoting in the shadow of their loaded vehicles.

Another whistle sounded, and a dozen men sprang from hiding. Like spirits slipping from the shadows, slim and swift, they flung grenades and *spezzone* bombs into truck beds. A series of explosions thundered, and Francesca pressed her face to the dirt, protecting her eyes from debris. Ammunition crates caught fire somewhere, popping into a breathtaking crescendo. She glanced up as shards of hot metal rained down over the rest of the convoy.

The cacophony faded into human sounds: shouting and swearing and a few screams. Smoke swam over the street, shifting in the breeze, opening and closing channels. Francesca coughed, staring down the barrel of her gun, aiming toward clear patches, covering partisans. Her pulse hammered, and her eyes darted from figure to figure, but the rest of her stilled, finger poised on the trigger. She traced halos around her people, her mind quieting. It was like watching a field for movement, waiting for a burst of quail to rise into the sun. The same trance fell over her, like darkness.

The smoke shifted, exposing a Nazi as he aimed his pistol. She drew a bead on him and started to squeeze the trigger, but he lowered his arm as a partisan dove behind a truck, out of sight. She shifted her aim as well. She wouldn't shoot unless she had to.

Gunfire sputtered uphill, but she couldn't see it. An engine roared to life somewhere, gears grinding, and died back out. Movement caught in Francesca's peripheral vision, and a tall figure broke through the smoke, a *spezzone* in hand, heading for a fuel truck. He skidded beside the truck, tossed the bomb on its running board, and sprinted away. Across the street, a Nazi lifted his rifle. She adjusted her aim. There was no time to hesitate.

She filled her lungs and fired.

# ONE

ಬಬ

## Lucia

*Rome, July 1943*

I T WASN'T UNTIL Lucia stepped into the streets, with Matteo's hot little palm gripped in her own, that she noticed the leaflets. Squares of paper spattered the cobblestones like windswept petals. One, caught in a breath of air, still drifted. She shaded her eyes and studied the strip of sky between buildings. Allied planes must have flown over Rome, dropping their propaganda, but when? Could she have slept so hard last night, with Matteo curled in her arms, that the sirens failed to wake her? Of course, air-raid sirens failed to rouse most Romans these days. They were used to planes passing over, destined for some other populace. Rome was the Eternal City, home to the pope. It would never be bombed.

She glanced at Matteo, who tugged on her arm so he could snatch up a leaflet. His cheeks were red, his eyes still bright with fading tears. Moments earlier, Lucia had mentioned, unwisely, that he had an appointment with the pediatrician after errands. Matteo had sat down on the stairs, refusing to budge. She'd insisted and then pleaded with him. Their cupboards were empty, and the lines for bread and eggs and flour would stretch with the morning. Eventually, she carried him down the steps and through the door, and now here they were: already exhausted.

"Mamma, what does it say?"

She plucked the leaflet from his fingers. "Did you hear sirens last night, Matteo?" She scanned the printing on the square of paper. He shook his head, sniffing. The final sentence rose from the text and hung, for an uncomfortable moment, in Lucia's mind.

*Italians shall die for Mussolini and Hitler—or live for Italy and for civilization.*

She frowned. "Never mind," she murmured, dropping the leaflet and squeezing Matteo's hand, prompting him to match her stride. The sun was barely up over Rome's rooftops, but her lower back trickled sweat. With her free hand, she adjusted the itchy waistband of her skirt and gathered the hair off her neck, a handful of black curls, savoring the air on her skin. Die for Mussolini? That's exactly what she, and especially her brothers, had been raised to do.

Matteo skipped along in his short pants, his arm yanking on hers as he hopped at random intervals, playing a game with the cobblestones. The message on the leaflet wasn't new. Just the other night, Churchill had slipped through some gap in the state-controlled radio, imploring Italy's people to shake off the yoke of Fascism and secure a separate peace. Lucia puffed air through her lips. Right now, she was more concerned with securing bread.

"Think we'll get some eggs today, *piccolo*?"

He looked up at her and shrugged, blinking under his fringe of curls. He matched her completely, a lighter version of her with his thick hair, nut-colored eyes, and double dimples.

"We need at least four eggs," she said, composing a mental list. "And perhaps we'll find a fish for supper. What do you think, Matteo? Will we be lucky today?"

He wiped his freckled nose. "You have cigarettes for the man?"

She laughed. "Yes, for the *fisher*man." She did have some, saved from her rations, but who knew if she'd catch someone along the Tiber who would make a deal?

They rounded a corner onto a wider street, and Signora Bruno, sweeping her front steps, glanced up. A stripe of sunlight fell over the stoop, brightening the old woman's hair. She was nearly always outside, either pruning the bougainvillea that swept over her ground-floor apartment, or feeding stray cats, or propped in a chair to watch the world trot by.

"*Buongiorno*, Lucia. Why are you out so early?"

Flowers fluttered over Noemi Bruno's head like butterflies. Matteo dropped Lucia's hand and ran to the elderly neighbor, thumping against her belly. He wrapped his arms around her waist, and her arthritic hands patted his back. Lucia followed suit, kissing both of Noemi's papery cheeks before answering her question.

"Just trying to get some shopping done before an appointment." She glanced at a pile of leaflets stacked neatly on her neighbor's step. "I see you, too, heard from the enemy last night?"

Noemi shrugged. "I don't know who the enemy is anymore, *cara mia*. But, by the look of it, they dropped their entire bundle on our neighborhood." The old woman laughed, the map of her face transforming.

Lucia smiled, but her chest tightened like a fist. Nobody seemed to know who the enemy was anymore. Her father, a Fascist official, and her mother, German by birth, were steadfast. Their rhetoric against the Allies was like a wall; every time a plane passed over Rome, they added another brick. But in the streets? There, she heard everything. People whispered in cafés, hoping for a coup d'état and peace with the Allies. Anti-Fascists plastered posters on walls and ran. People blamed the air raids on Mussolini himself, whispering that if he hadn't sided with Hitler, if he'd stayed out of the war, their sons and cities would be safe.

Noemi fingered her silvery bun. "I, for one, think we should break with Germany and stop fighting the Allies. The minute they landed in Sicily, Il Duce lost his war."

Lucia hitched her shopping bag up on her elbow. With the Allies pushing into Italy on one side and the Germans on the other, wasn't every path a gamble? She opened her mouth to say so but stopped mid-breath. Because what did she know? Her mother's voice murmured in her thoughts. *Leave opinions to the men.*

"Honestly, right now I'd rather worry about filling my cupboards than war and politics." She reached for Matteo's palm, but he ducked into the frothy shade of the bougainvillea. She tried to give him a scolding look, but a smile crept in. She'd have to catch him if they were to beat the lines. The stones of the city, wrapping under their feet and over the ancient walls, were heating up. "Can we get you anything from the shops?"

The old woman clutched the broom as if to hold herself up. She shook her head, pursing her lips and squinting at Lucia, caught in thought. Matteo squatted behind her, elbows on his knees, and extended a hand toward a cat as thin as a whisper. The creature eyed him, hesitating from a safe distance.

"Noemi?" Lucia knew Noemi Bruno well enough to know she had more to say.

"*Cara mia.* There's something I need to tell you." She shifted the broom and hesitated, looking up and down the street. Then she beckoned Lucia closer, lowering her voice. "I saw Carlo. Last night."

It was like a rock dropped into Lucia's stomach. She shook her head, whispering, "No. No, you couldn't have." She glanced at Matteo. He hadn't heard, or didn't know what he was hearing, because he was still crouched under the flowers, his hand cupped toward the cat in offering. Lucia shook her head again. "It must have been someone who looked like him."

"It was Carlo." Noemi reached out and gripped Lucia's wrist with her crooked fingers. "I don't want to upset you, *cara*, but I thought you should know."

A tiny cyclone started to spin in Lucia's heart, yet she persisted. "Noemi. It's been six years. Perhaps you've forgotten what he looks like?"

"Few men look like him. And he stood right outside my window, close to where you are now, staring at your street corner. He's back, Lucia."

Matteo rose into a half crouch and tottered a few steps across the cobbles. The cat curved like a fish and darted away. Matteo frowned, scuffing his shoes as he walked over and placed his palm in Lucia's, resigned. "I wish I could pet that cat. Mamma, why was he scared?"

"He's wild, *piccolo*," Lucia said, still holding Noemi's stare. She shook the questions from her mind. "We'd better be on our way. *Grazie*, Noemi. And tell me if it happens again, won't you?"

The old woman nodded, and Lucia tugged Matteo on down the street, her thoughts swimming while doors opened here and there and people spilled into the growing heat. The cyclone continued to spin in her heart, kicking up a swirl of doubt. What was Noemi talking about? Carlo couldn't be back. Back from where? She waved her hand as if arguing with someone. No. Noemi Bruno was old, her memory couldn't possibly be that sharp, and for all Lucia knew, her eyesight wasn't sharp, either. It couldn't have been Carlo.

"Mamma? Can we see Nonna again today?"

Lucia glanced at Matteo. "Signora Bruno isn't your nonna. You know that, *piccolo*." She tousled his hair, but his eyes dropped to the ground, and her heart dropped with them. He was only five— how could he possibly understand such distinctions? He saw Signora Bruno every day, when his real grandmother across town couldn't be bothered to see him.

She stopped, bending to cup his chin. "Listen, Matteo. Let's hurry through everything we have to do. When we get home, we can read stories on the terrace, all afternoon if you like. *Si?*"

He nodded, eyes down, scratching a mosquito bite on his elbow. "Can we read the zoo book?"

"*Certo.*" He met her gaze, and she forced a smile, squeezed his hand, and they resumed walking. If only she could bundle him up and take him home. If only they could hide away, reading and laughing and pretending that the world wasn't descending into chaos. But there was no food in the cupboard. The cyclone expanded beyond her heart as they resumed walking. She didn't want to stand in lines, struggling to buy food. She didn't want leaflets to rain down, whispering warnings from the sky. She didn't want to think about the war, about the approaching Allies and Mussolini and the Germans breathing down Italy's neck. And, more than anything, she didn't want to think about Carlo.

Lucia dabbed the corners of her eyes. She wished nobody remembered him, that his name would never be uttered by another neighbor or friend. Because when Carlo left, he'd destined them to a life that never quite added up, no matter how hard she tried to stretch herself to cover the gaps. It was like pulling a small sheet over a large bed: just when one corner was smooth, another came untucked.

Still, Lucia did her best. She cobbled together decent clothes and styled her hair and went about her days, flashing her dimples at shop clerks and giggling with her son, as if her life hadn't fallen apart, as if everything wasn't a struggle. Through it all, she kept Carlo from her mind. If an object reminded her of him, she threw it away. If someone mentioned him, she changed the subject. When his mother wrote in the beginning, she sent the letters back unopened until eventually they stopped coming. She'd told Matteo, from the beginning, that his father was dead.

Because Carlo had abandoned them. The note drifted through her memory like a leaflet, his last words a mere scrawl. *Lucia, I can't do this any longer. Resume your life, your old life, as if we'd never met. I am truly sorry.*

She inhaled and looked up at a church as they passed, its spires splitting the sky. He'd vanished, but of course she couldn't resume her life as if she'd never known him. Not only because she still loved him, despite herself, but because in the wake of his departure, cells had divided in her womb. Eight lonely months later, those cells became a boy, and war broke out, and the world crumbled, and when Lucia's long days were over, she lay awake into the night. Alone.

IT WAS NEARLY 11:00 a.m. when Lucia and Matteo finished their shopping, just in time for his appointment.

"Why do I have to see the doctor?" he fussed as they boarded a crowded bus, holding on to the handles while it swayed into motion. She lifted her eyes, trying to muster a patient response. But the canvas bag dug into her forearm as the bus swayed around a corner, and her blouse was drenched in sweat. She herself didn't want to travel across town in this heat, only to urge her reluctant child to cooperate while he was poked and prodded.

She glanced at Matteo, tiny where he stood between two middle-aged women, and her heart stirred. "It's just a checkup, *piccolo*."

He scowled, and she chewed the thumbnail of her free hand, studying him. His legs were sunbrowned, scuffed at the knees, and slender as reeds. Was he abnormally thin? And did other children swing a pendulum between coughs, fevers, runny noses, and vomiting? Was it because of rationing, the scarcity of fat and protein? Or—her stomach hollowed—was something wrong with him? She inhaled around her thumb. This was why they had to cross Rome to see a doctor. She needed to know she wasn't missing something, that Matteo was all right. He was all she had.

They stepped off the bus near the train station and started up the street.

"I want to go *hoooome*, Mamma."

His heavy curls plastered his forehead. His face was pale everywhere except the cheeks, which mottled like a bruised apple.

"We will," she said. "And remember? We'll eat and read on the terrace, *caro mio*."

They passed a family playing in the shade of a small piazza. A father kicked a ball toward a boy in a red jersey. Was he nine? Ten? The boy ran, stopped the ball, and lobbed it across the cobblestones. The father pumped his fist, and a pair of grandparents, watching from a bench, cheered.

Lucia smiled, despite the sting in her belly. If only Matteo had a father and cheering grandparents. Uncles. Someone to teach him how to play ball. They turned a corner, walking into the shade of an umbrella pine, and the Policlinico hospital loomed down the street. She squeezed Matteo's hand, and was about to comment on the breeze and the shade and the fact that they were nearly at the clinic, when her thoughts broke apart. Overhead, air-raid sirens wailed to life.

Matteo's eyes flicked upward. Lucia glanced from him to the blue sky, fragmented by branches.

"They're going somewhere else, Mamma?" The first bomber slid into view. It lumbered in from the horizon, heavy as a new bee.

"They always are." A dozen more planes appeared, slicing through the hazy atmosphere over Rome. But they lived in the pope's city, and who would risk the pope? She thought briefly of all those people, in northern cities lacking a Vatican, who weren't safe. They would soon see bombs from these planes. She placed a palm on her heart, as if she could send them strength.

And then a sound like thunder shattered her thoughts.

"Mamma!" Matteo screamed, spinning on the sidewalk. In one

breath she gathered him up, holding his little bird bones tight against her chest, while another thud and explosion hit somewhere nearby.

"What is it?" Matteo sobbed, his voice lost in a third thunderclap. Lucia shook her head, his question rebounding in her mind. Her pulse rushed between her ears, loud as a burst dam, and she couldn't form an answer. Dozens of planes darkened the sky. A string of objects dropped from them, like pills, and the earth jolted under their feet. Matteo's scream was lost in the roar, and Lucia spun around, his legs banging her hips. What was happening? Where should she run? Up ahead, a corner of the Policlinico burst apart, disappearing in a plume of dirty smoke. She scrambled the other direction, emerging from the shade of the pine.

What was happening?

Carrying Matteo, she ran down the street, her grocery bag thumping her hip. Where could they go? Was there a shelter nearby? And it was with this question that the facts solidified amid her racing thoughts. *The Allies were bombing Rome.* Those planes overhead, multiplying with every one of her frantic breaths, were not just passing over the Eternal City.

"Breathe, my love, I have you. I have you," she murmured during an inhale of Matteo's frenzied sobbing. Her heartbeat thumped against his, the drum of her grown body punctuating his swift pulse. She tightened her grip on him, and another explosion boomed in their wake. The air thickened. Where could she run?

She hustled up a narrow alley, her flats slipping, and a woman at the top of the incline waved her forward. The band of sky overhead darkened with planes. One after another shot across the gap in the buildings, and everything seemed to tremble: the air, the cobblestones, the breath in her lungs. Lucia reached the woman, a stout, strong nonna who waved her down a flight of steps. The woman was wordless in the vibrating air, her face set in a determined scowl. Lucia ducked and took the steps quickly, leaving the nonna in the road to flag down other bewildered Romans.

More thuds scrambled her thoughts, and as Lucia sat down on the bench of an old stone cellar, knee to knee with people huddled in the shadows, she choked on tears. She held Matteo on her lap, and he twisted, burrowing his hot little face into her bosom. The bundle of groceries slumped between her shoes. If a bomb fell on the building overhead, would they be buried alive? She put her shaking fingers on Matteo's skull, as if her hand could protect him. How strong was the ceiling? She studied its arch, and the door to the street closed, shutting off the spill of light.

Lucia closed her eyes, resting her cheek on Matteo's head. He jolted with every explosion, and she tightened her arms around his little back. Words tumbled through her mind, unbidden. *God, protect my child. Please, God, protect my child . . . Please, God.*

They sat in the dark for an hour, listening to waves of bombs, before anyone spoke. It started with a woman's voice, murmuring a prayer over and over.

". . . *Santa Maria, Madre di Dio, prega per noi peccatori, adesso e nell'ora della nostra morte . . .*"

"You think anyone listens?" a gravelly voice asked after several minutes.

The prayer stopped, and five explosions in a row shook the city. The stone jumped under their seat bones, and Lucia kissed Matteo's sweaty head.

"*Certo,*" a woman answered eventually. "*La Madonna* listens. God listens."

"He's not listening here, I'll tell you that," the gruff voice countered. "Your *Dio* is blind all over Europe."

"Don't say such things."

Another woman spoke. "Do you think this'll be the end of Il Duce?"

"Yes, *grazie a Dio*," the praying woman answered. Emboldened by the safety of darkness, she added, "I'm sick to death of him."

The end of Mussolini? Lucia rubbed Matteo's back to the rhythm of his breath. "You don't think Il Duce will fight back?" she managed. She'd been trained to defend Mussolini all her life. What would her parents expect her to say?

The gravelly voice chuckled, the laugh of an old man. "Fight back how? The Allies can reach every part of Italy with their bombers." He coughed, and the sound was wet. "Anyway, Mussolini's lost the support of the people."

A boy's voice spoke quickly. "We saw how the Allies took Sicily." A pair of fingers snapped in the darkness, as if the taking of Sicily itself had been a snap. "Next they'll march north—"

"Let 'em come," someone interrupted. "I'd take peace over Mussolini any day."

The old man chuckled again, underscoring a series of distant thuds. "*Ascoltami*, it won't be that easy." He coughed, loud and long. "Nothing's easy in war."

A bomb hit close, rattling the walls in the cellar, and the voices died away.

Lucia bent to Matteo's ear. "It's almost over, *piccolo*," she whispered, but she had no idea if it was true. He snuggled in tighter. She closed her eyes and pictured Il Duce, with his heavy jaw and formidable stare. She'd grown up with a photo of him, astride a white horse, on the wall over her bed. Her father, whose stature and beliefs matched Mussolini's, had hung such a picture in her brothers' room as well. But what good had Il Duce done them? Maybe everyone in this cellar was right. If Mussolini had stayed out of the war, her boy would be safe. Lucia wiped her eyes. Even this private thought ignited shame in her heart, hot and familiar.

A concussion hit just outside, and Matteo shuddered. Lucia whispered in his ear, hoping to distract him. His bedtime story emerged, the words like prayer beads, worn and comforting. *"Piccolo,* a boy once went for a walk in a green and sunlit forest, and he saw so many beautiful things," she began, forcing her voice steady, hoping it would give him a rope to cling to until the planes flew away. "When he saw a butterfly he followed it, forgetting everything to run and chase it, and the forest grew dark. The boy was lost, and he thought he was alone. At first, he was afraid and he wanted to cry." Matteo turned his head slightly to listen, sniffing, and she closed her eyes to focus on the cadence of her own voice. "But then, he remembered the sky. He looked up, and there were the first stars, looking down at him, and he didn't feel alone—"

Again a bomb hit somewhere close, fracturing her voice, and Matteo started to weep. Lucia kissed his hot forehead and rocked him, and his bedtime story dissolved back into her earlier prayer, running over and over through her mind. *Please, God, protect my child.*

Sometime later, the world above quieted. The people in the cellar murmured and shifted, stretching sore muscles, but Lucia was frozen with Matteo on her lap. How would they know it was safe to leave? Nobody said much, but the air, dank and hot, was steeped in worry. Had their homes survived? Were their people alive?

The all-clear siren sounded in the streets, muffled. Someone nearby sobbed with relief, and the praying woman breathed, *"Grazie a Dio,"* over and over again. Lucia bounced Matteo a little, grimacing at the tingle in her feet.

"Mamma? I want to go home," he whispered, his cheek on her shoulder.

Overhead, the door creaked open and light flooded the steps. The old man with the gruff voice, visible for the first time, heaved himself upright. He squinted at Lucia, and a spray of wrinkles deepened around his eyes.

"Take care of that lovely boy, signora."

She stood, still clutching Matteo to her chest. "But is it really over? Where should I go?"

The man scratched his scruffy chin, black eyes contemplative. "Go to the Vatican tonight, *bella*, just in case. Even if the planes return, they won't bomb the Vatican."

He reached out to touch the curve of Matteo's back, and they stood like that for a moment, as if they were relatives instead of strangers, as if the old man was giving them a blessing.

*"Coraggio, signora,"* he muttered through a sigh. *"Coraggio."*

# TWO

### ❧

# Francesca

*Rome, July 1943*

T HE ALL CLEAR had sounded hours ago, but Giacomo hadn't come home.

Francesca knelt by the window, her face pressed against a gap in the shutters. Outside, the familiar view of rooftops and bell towers, jumbled like a mountain range, spread before her. But beyond them, *Dio santo*, the world burned. She wiped tears from her eyes but kept staring, fixated. Smoke and dust rose in plumes from the San Lorenzo district.

"*Madonna mia*," she said, and her voice cracked. She sounded overloud in the tiny apartment, and something about her voice, so alone in the darkening room, pulled her from the window.

She placed her palms on a stool and used it to push herself up to her feet. It was Giacomo's stool, the one he pulled over to the window when he was studying. A sob rose like a gasp, and Francesca folded both hands over her heart, as if she could somehow contain the fear that gusted through her like a strong wind, chilling the blood in her veins. What would she do if Giacomo didn't come home?

When the planes first appeared, she'd been at work in the bookshop. She and the other clerks had hurried into an air-raid shelter, listening to bombs falling across the city, too stunned to talk. Then she'd ridden her bicycle the few blocks home, pumping with such panic she nearly skidded over twice. When she'd reached their apartment, she hustled past her neighbors, who crowded the street and the foyer, to the flight of stairs. Francesca went up as fast as she could, but with each step her heart sank deeper.

Because, somehow, she knew even before she pushed open the door that Giacomo wouldn't be in the apartment. Even before she stared out the window and saw where the bombs had fallen, she sensed that he was out there and still in the middle of it.

Now she wrapped her long hair into a bun, pinning it in place. Perhaps, when you'd known someone forever, you could sense when they were in trouble. And they'd known each other longer than forever. They'd sat side by side in school. They'd run barefoot through the Tuscan hills, stepping in each other's shadows. They'd perched at each other's bedsides, read each other stories, and defied each other's parents until, finally, she followed Giacomo from their village to Rome.

Francesca walked with her uneven gait across the apartment. She sensed that he was in danger now, the same way her grandmother could smell rain on the edge of a cold wind.

Well, then. She nodded to herself as she found the key and her handbag, pulling in shaky breaths. She glanced in the chipped mirror by the door, smoothing her skirt over her angular hips. She hesitated, caught by the reflection of her own haunted green eyes.

She blinked and shook her head, dislodging fear. Giacomo was somewhere, and she would find him. She smoothed a tendril of loose hair behind her ear and locked the apartment.

On the stairs, her hand shook as she moved it along the railing, gripping each time her weak leg swung down a step, careful not to fall. She pursed her lips, her pulse rebounded in her ears, and she thumped down the last flight just as Signora Russo's door swept open. The older woman, tall and even thinner than Francesca, came out with a baby clutched to her chest. Signora Russo always looked tired and startled, on edge as the mamma in a family bursting with children. Her eyes widened when they found Francesca.

"No, *cara*." She said it like an order.

"I have to go find him," Francesca managed. It was difficult to speak around the tightening in her throat, her thudding pulse.

"No. I forbid you to go out there. Your young man is as strong as he is smart, Francesca. He'll come home."

"I have to know he's all right." Tears heated her eyes. "The bombs hit San Lorenzo, Signora Russo. Near the university—I can see it from upstairs."

The older woman drew in a breath and pursed her lips as if she was mustering willpower. She took her hand off the baby's back to swipe at the hair falling from her kerchiefed head. Behind her, a small girl stepped around the doorjamb, wide-eyed.

"What could you possibly do anyway, *cara*? If he's hurt? More planes could be on their way right now. What good will come from putting yourself in harm's way?"

Both women glanced at the girl in the doorjamb. Neither would say what they meant with their small audience, but Francesca knew what Signora Russo was thinking. What good could a crippled girl do out in those streets? How could *she* possibly help Giacomo?

The women stared at each other for a long moment. And if little Gabriella hadn't been within earshot, Francesca would have retorted that they weren't any safer inside anyway. This building could be bombed as easily as the next. Nobody was safe, not anywhere.

Francesca looked to the door, breaking their stare, and Signora Russo sighed.

"You're a good wife. Go, then. And get back as quickly as you can."

Francesca nodded, and then she pushed open the heavy door and slipped into the night, choking on another sob. Because of course Signora Russo didn't know she wasn't Giacomo's wife, not yet. They'd pretended to be married when she came from the village, for decorum's sake. But it sounded so nice, suddenly. She walked down the empty, darkening street and saw the future she'd always imagined. She and Giacomo would be married, they would live a respectable, cultivated life, and the world would be at peace.

The neighborhood of San Lorenzo was unrecognizable. Francesca clutched her handbag and picked her way through a street littered with rubble. She pressed a hand over her mouth, but her throat stung with dust. Ahead, the innards of a tall building spilled into the road like a deer with a slit belly. On its edges, a huddle of children whimpered in the twilight. A spectacled nonno, bent with age, helped a woman dig through stones with bare hands. A boy in a red jersey watched and wept. "*Papà, Papà,*" he sobbed, over and over again.

Francesca hesitated, staring at the boy while he wiped his nose on his collar. He'd lost his father. She swallowed, hard, and turned away, picking a path through the rubble. The weight of his loss, all too familiar, sank into her chest.

It wasn't far to the hospital, but several streets were so choked with craters, rescuers, and survivors that they were impassable. Francesca quickened her pace, and as she neared the hospital, both the destruction and the survivors thickened. People, iced in plaster and dust, gestured and swore and wept. She made her way over a mountain of stone and cracked beams, passing a dozen people digging through the rock with chalky hands. Behind them, a little girl screamed under the waking stars.

Francesca rounded another corner, and there it was: the hospital. She quickened again. The road, newly uneven, made hurrying dangerous. She should have brought her cane. The buildings loomed, a proud complex of medical centers, yet even in the twilight she saw that they had swallowed several bombs. A chunk of the Policlinico was gone, exposing the shells of rooms. Nonetheless, people streamed in, many carrying bloodied bodies between them.

Inside, the shadowy corridor was lamplit and lined with people. Some screamed, some comforted the injured, and others jogged the halls, heading back out. Medical staff crowded the corridor, performing triage right where the patients were dropped. Someone had swept broken glass into hasty piles, and Francesca threaded around them, staring at the cots and stretchers hemming the walls.

She stumbled next to a stretcher bearing a young girl, not quite a teenager, whose chest was bloody and lips blue. Francesca froze. There was so much blood she could smell it. She turned, a palm pressed over her mouth, and nearly bumped into a woman clutching a lifeless toddler. The woman wailed, unseeing, her face white with plaster. Her baby's legs bounced against her belly, loose as a doll's.

Someone put a hand on Francesca's shoulder from behind. She turned, and Tommaso, one of Giacomo's classmates, leaned in to talk over the noise.

"Francesca," he stammered. "What are you doing here?"

She opened her mouth to answer, and the foolishness of it all poured over her like cold water. She'd walked into a war zone for no good reason. "Giacomo," she managed. "He was here for his practicum. I was worried—"

"He's upstairs. But you can't go looking for him. He's performing surgeries, one after another. Are you all right?"

She nodded, stunned. Giacomo was performing surgeries? He was only a medical student. Would he know what to do? She found her voice.

"He's not hurt, then, Tommaso?"

Tommaso shook his head. "Listen. Go outside and wait—it's far too crowded in here. I'll send Giacomo down between patients. He'll only have a second, but I'm sure seeing you will give him strength." Tommaso glanced around the corridor, murmuring, "And he needs it."

A half hour later, the sky had fully darkened, and Francesca stood under it, hugging her arms around her waist. She'd been irrational to come here. Now she wanted to go home almost as much as she wanted to see Giacomo. The quiet apartment, with its shuttered window and hard bed, had never seemed more like home. She watched an old mother and father carry their middle-aged son through the open hospital doors. People were still digging in the craters, searching for loved ones under an expanse of stars.

She leaned against a wedge of crumbled wall, closing her eyes and seeing other stars, from years before. She shivered. Her mind swept her back, offering respite from this night with the memory of another.

Giacomo's face at eight years old appeared in her mind. He'd climbed through her window and sat on the sill, his limbs hanging over the floor, starlight framing his head. She was in bed, as she'd been for a long time.

"I lost my tooth, Mino," she said.

He hopped down and took his place on her quilt, transforming from a silhouette in the window into a boy with wild hair and bright eyes.

"Let's see," he whispered, reaching toward her mouth. She bared her teeth, and he fingered the gap in the darkness, nodding his approval.

"I'll tell you everything that happened in school today." His voice edged out of a whisper. "And then you can tell me the next dragon story. *Sì?*"

"*Sì.*" She gave him a stern look. "But be quieter, Mino."

Her parents murmured in the next room. It was winter, and they sat at the fire long after bedtime, sipping wine or grappa through hushed conversations. If they heard voices and investigated, they'd discover Giacomo had snuck through the window again. And if they made him leave, she didn't know what she'd do. She might simply dissolve into her quilt, her useless limbs melting away. Because Giacomo's visits, and their whispered stories, were all she had to look forward to.

"Francesca," he said, scooting closer. "Today Maestra Pisano asked what we want to be when we grow up, and I know. I know what I want to be."

She stared into his large eyes.

"A doctor. I'm going to be a doctor someday. So I can cure you."

They glanced at her polio-stricken legs, like two sticks under the patchwork quilt, and she bit her lower lip. Giacomo could be a doctor when he grew up. But what would she be?

"Francesca. I'm here."

His voice broke into her memories, and she opened her eyes. Her back was numb against the wall, her legs stiff. The night assembled before her, with its stars and rubble and misery.

She turned, and there was Giacomo. Even in the dark, she saw that he was covered in dust and the blood of other people. His smudged glasses sat low on his nose. Behind them, his eyes found hers. She collapsed into his chest, and he curled over her, wrapping her in his arms.

"I was worried about you," she murmured.

He nodded, and she pressed her head against his collarbone, listening to the rebound of his heart, and breathed him in. Her own heart steadied, like a boat with a sail. She was home.

* * *

SIX DAYS LATER, Francesca glanced at Giacomo where he sat by the window, bent over a textbook, reading in the evening's copper light. It was time to pull the curtains. But she paused, one hand on the knife she'd been using to chop garlic, studying him. Hair fell to his eyes like a black brushstroke, always just a little too long, and his thumb tapped out a rhythm on the book cover as he read. She smiled. All his life he'd been that way: energetic, restless, forever tapping out a beat while his mind moved like the melody.

"Mino," she ventured, reeling him in from his thoughts. He looked up, adjusting his glasses, and grinned as if he'd been elsewhere and was glad to see her. She tipped her head toward the window, and he understood, pivoting on his stool to pull the curtains. The memory of bombers darkening the sky was so fresh, Francesca had barely slept since. She wasn't taking any chances with light.

"I'm not ready for the next exams," he sighed, clapping the book closed and standing.

She scraped the garlic into a pan. "You never think you're ready, and then you get the top score. Come on and eat something."

He strode over to stand behind her, wrapping an arm around her waist and kissing her ear. "I forgot to tell you."

"What?" She giggled. "You realize I'm holding a knife."

He pivoted, leaning against the counter where she worked. "I ran into Lino Moretti today. Remember him? From home?"

She cocked her head. An image of a boy, years older than them, rose in her memory. "The handsome one?"

"Not as handsome as me." Giacomo grinned, and his glasses flashed. "He went off to Rome when we were kids."

Francesca nodded. She hadn't known Lino Moretti, not really, but he and Giacomo had something in common: they were both the smartest boys in their year. But Giacomo, who pivoted to pour two glasses of table wine, was the smartest boy ever to come out of Pienza. And soon, he'd be a doctor.

"Not as smart as you," he said whenever she praised him. She'd roll her eyes, but deep down she knew they were equally bright. She'd always understood things, from schoolwork to the way people navigated their lives, more quickly and thoroughly than most. She hunched her shoulders and chopped the head off a carrot. It didn't matter if she was smart. To take advantage of intelligence, a person had to be brave. Able to step out into the world, without wobbling.

Giacomo handed her a glass of wine. "It was strange seeing Lino," he continued. "He gave me an address and asked if I wanted to come to a meeting. Said I was the right kind of person."

"What kind of person is that?"

He shrugged and reached for two plates on a shelf. "Who knows? I'm not going to get wrapped up in it, whatever it is."

They ate by candlelight, laughing over their plates while the moon rose somewhere outside the blackout curtains. Then they sat on the floor of the dark apartment, hip to hip, and flipped on the radio. The state-controlled broadcast was about to start, and they listened every night, analyzing what was said, and what was omitted, and trying to guess what would happen next. So far, people seemed to blame Mussolini for the bombing. In the streets, they grumbled about Il Duce and the *Fascisti*, and Francesca remained expressionless, shifting between sore feet in queues and hoisting her grocery bag, but inside she burned with satisfaction. Finally, the rest of Italy hated Mussolini like she always had. Finally, something could change. Didn't it have to change, now that the Allies were in Sicily? Now that the Allies had shown that they would even bomb Rome, the Eternal City, if it would nudge Italy away from Fascism?

Francesca twisted her hair into a rope and pulled it over her shoulder, letting her neck breathe. The apartment was muggy, full of heat trapped during the day. The broadcast still hadn't started. Had they turned the radio on too early? She glanced at Giacomo, who sat cross-legged, one of his knees resting on hers. She bumped him with her elbow, and he glanced up. It was often like this: they didn't need to talk. They could simply look at each other, and whole conversations passed through the silence between them. Giacomo closed his hand over hers, and his thumb tapped the floor. They waited.

The radio crackled, then dipped back into silence. What was going on? The broadcast was never late. Francesca cocked her head, listening hard, as if there would be something to hear if she put forth the effort. A full minute clicked by, and Giacomo released her hand to check his watch, squinting in the flickering light.

"It's 10:47. Maybe my watch is off?"

She shook her head, and her stomach hollowed. Something was wrong.

Another minute ticked by. Still, silence.

Giacomo was reaching to fiddle with the dial when the quiet broke. He froze, his hand suspended, and Francesca held her breath to listen.

The announcer spoke slowly. *"His Majesty the King and Emperor has accepted the resignation from the post of Head of Government, Prime Minister Benito Mussolini . . ."* She inhaled sharply, her hand flying to her mouth. *". . . His Excellency has appointed the Marshal of Italy, Pietro Badoglio, as Prime Minister."*

Francesca's pulse gathered strength with each word, quickening and rising to a whoosh between her ears. Had she heard right? She couldn't possibly have heard right. Could it be true? Had Mussolini resigned?

Then Badoglio's voice was on air, affirming that he was head of a new military government. Francesca and Giacomo stared at each other, wide-eyed, while Badoglio declared, *"Italy will be true to her word. The war continues."*

The broadcast dissolved into the Italian national anthem, rather than the Fascist hymn that had closed all broadcasts in Francesca's memory.

Giacomo scrambled to his feet, pushing his hair from his forehead and glancing around the apartment as if looking for signs. She reached up, and he automatically held a hand down to lift her, taking the burden off her weak leg so she could rise.

Together, they listened to the final words of the anthem, tinny over the radio. *". . . the sons of the Fatherland will cover themselves with glory, shouting 'Freedom!'"*

"It's over," he breathed.

"Over?" She said the word as if she didn't know its meaning.

"*Dio santo.* It's over, Francesca. They've removed Il Duce."

He said the words as though they were foreign, as though neither of them could quite grasp the meaning. Mussolini was *gone*? Could peace be on the horizon? But Badoglio had said that the war was to continue. What did it all mean? A wind seemed to blow through Francesca, engulfing her heart and lifting everything in her, everything in the room.

Then Giacomo's arms were around her, wrapping her sapling waist in his own slender muscles. Her feet kicked up as they twirled, her laughter building and whirling with them. The end of Fascism! Il Duce, gone! Could it be true?

Outside, noise hummed in the streets as the news sank in, saturating Rome. Doors creaked and slammed shut, punctuating the shouts and laughter bouncing between neighbors. Francesca, tugging Giacomo's hand, walked to the window. She pulled the curtain back, peering through the shutter slats. The dark city blinked, one house at a time, to life. Nearby windows flickered, lit by candles. In the distance, where the neighborhood climbed a hill, electric lights burned. One by one, window curtains slid back and shutters flung open. Human shapes appeared on balconies in the night air. They all knew there would be no planes tonight.

"Il Duce's . . . gone," she whispered, trying to make the words feel true. "*Dio mio.*"

She pushed open the windows, and a gust of air cooled her. Stars brightened over the tile rooftops. She leaned out, just a little. Below, doors opened, like a chain reaction, and people poured into the streets. Mussolini had ruled Italy for Francesca's entire life. Her father's face appeared in her mind, and she held him there for a moment, with his kind eyes and broad grin. Surely, he, too, was rejoicing somewhere.

Giacomo's arm tightened around her waist as he stood behind her, his body molding to hers while he stared over her shoulder. His heartbeat tapped her back. In the street, someone whooped, and it caught on, contagious, until everyone was cheering and laughing, dazed with joy. Giacomo kissed the tender space under her ear.

When he spoke, his breath was warm. "Our life will be so different now. We'll get married for real, and the war will end, and we can live in Rome and I'll give you everything. Whatever you want. Francesca, it's over."

"But, Mino," she said, her eyes on the street. Her joy faded a little, because it couldn't be that good. She couldn't believe it. "Badoglio said the war continues. You heard him."

She felt him shrug. "That's just talk. He had to say it, because the Germans are listening, too." His voice strengthened in her ear. "Dismantling allegiances takes time, but this is the first step toward neutrality. They'll negotiate, and we'll make peace with the Allies. It's the beginning of the end of the war, the beginning of a new life."

She stared at the boiling crowd, dual sparks of hope and fear igniting in her chest. How could he be so sure? If there was one thing life had taught her, it was to doubt. She put her hand on his and watched the revelry gain momentum in the street. Signora Russo wavered below, wrapped in a robe, and her three oldest, pajamaed children orbited around her. An elderly woman sobbed and laughed at the same time in the arms of a younger woman. A man, with a limp like Francesca's, screamed, *"Abbasso Mussolini!"*

Another man, short and whiskered, grinned and yelled as if in reply, "Out with the foreigners!" People around them held the words up like a torch, chanting both, *"Abbasso Mussolini!"* and "Out with the foreigners," a discordant anthem. The crowd began to flow, dislodging from the neighborhood and moving like a slow river through Rome.

"They mean the Germans," she murmured, half to herself. "Out with the Germans."

Giacomo pulled her in, squeezing her waist. "They'll leave. Their chapter's closing here."

She was about to disagree with his optimism, but he pulled her away from the window to face him. Their chests pressed together, and she looked up into his hopeful gaze.

"Francesca." Giacomo said her name like a decision. "Marry me. Marry me tomorrow."

Her breath stopped. He smiled, hesitant, hair in his eyes. She'd always wanted to marry him. She would absolutely marry him. But now? "Tomorrow?" she managed.

"Why wait? Italy's headed for peace, and we can move on with our lives. Let's make our charade real. I want it to be real, Francesca. When I look into the future, I only see you."

"I only see you, too." She held her breath, waiting for the words to come. *Yes, Giacomo.* It was all she needed to say. She yearned to say it.

But her mother whispered from the corner of her thoughts, like a woman waiting in the hall. Francesca had left her months ago, storming out amid a shouting match. They'd spoken only once since, when her mother managed to call the bookshop after the bombing, her voice thin with fear. Could she get married without her mother there to witness it?

Francesca dropped her eyes from Giacomo's stare. Because one layer deeper, another question whispered. He was a university student, nearly a doctor, but she hadn't become anything. Somehow, she'd always thought she would eventually rise from the shambles of her childhood and, alongside Giacomo, find a calling. But she hadn't. She scoffed at her own silliness. Wasn't being a doctor's wife enough? What else was there for a girl like Francesca?

Still, she met his gaze and shook her head. "Mino. We can't get married tomorrow." She reached up to brush the hair from his eyes, ignoring the glint of hurt in them. "You know I'm yours. But I want the war to end first. When all this is over"—she gestured toward the chaos—"we can have a real wedding." She cleared her throat. "I want my mamma to be there."

He nodded and mustered a lopsided smile, squeezing her hands. "All right. I'd have married you yesterday, but I understand. When the war ends, when the bells ring, we'll marry."

She turned around and leaned her back into his chest. "When the bells ring."

"It won't be long now."

Francesca watched the people below, streaming past in their pajamas, faces wet with joy. She wouldn't contradict him again, but her own hope hardened. Peace wouldn't come so easily.

If life had taught her anything, it was that.

# THREE

ॐ

## Lucia

*August 1943*

L UCIA KNELT ON her rooftop terrace in the dark, staring at a square of oilskin cloth in her hands, folded tight. It was nearly midnight, and Rome spread around her like waves on a black sea. The lights were out again. In the weeks since Mussolini's fall, Allied planes had sailed over the city more than once, tipping their wings in the sun. The people watched, ready to cower, and at night they again sealed their windows.

She glanced from the bundle in her hands to the stars wrapping overhead and the moon, which hung bright as a shell. The question everyone whispered, in every shop and kitchen, rebounded in her mind: *What next?* It was the question that had brought her up here, slinking onto the terrace while Matteo slept in his muggy bedroom two floors below.

She shook herself from her thoughts and picked up the wooden spoon she'd snatched from the kitchen drawer, pivoting to the terra-cotta planter. What if a neighbor heard and came up? She'd better hurry. A stunted lemon tree stretched from the soil, sun scorched but alive despite neglect. She'd once planted it herself, as a younger woman with a chest still full of hope.

An explosion brightened the distance. Lucia glanced up, scanning the horizon, studying the darkness for planes. Was it the start of another bombardment? She listened, but there was nothing more. She swallowed the ache in her throat and began to dig.

Italy was unstable. Her hand shook on the spoon as she worked it around the tree roots, seeking loose soil. Mussolini was gone, Badoglio claimed that the war would continue, the Germans seemed to be multiplying like rabbits, and the Allies were expected to invade. Today, walking through Rome, Lucia and Matteo had seen a crowd gather around a marble bust of Mussolini. The people were shouting, incensed, and Lucia had frozen, her hand tight on her son's palm. Someone threw a rock at the statue, and the people cheered. More rocks sailed through the air, and she'd hurried off, avoiding the fevered eyes of men.

She wiped curls from her sweaty forehead, no doubt smearing dirt on her face. Seeing a mob defacing Il Duce's relics had terrified her, but not for the reasons she would have expected. She'd run away from them, but also from herself. Because, for an instant, she'd had the urge to shed her upbringing and become someone different. She'd had the urge to throw a rock.

She thought of Matteo, his little chest rising in sleep, and she worked faster. Despite the joy in the streets, peace wasn't on the horizon. The Fascists wouldn't give up so easily. And the Germans? They wouldn't give up at all. She knew this, in the curves of her soul.

"But how do you know?" Noemi Bruno had implored her earlier that day, shuffling to peer out the window, her brows tipped in worry. "The Germans will withdraw once we make peace with the Allies, *cara*. Everyone says so."

Lucia closed her eyes now on the rooftop, shaking her head. If everyone was saying that, they were wrong. War would rake right through Rome before anyone gave up.

How did she know? She dug on, remembering.

★   ★   ★

ON A BRIGHT, cold day eight years earlier, Lucia had walked through
the door of her parents' apartment building, grinning at the *portiere*.

"And how were your classes today?" he asked, holding the door
wide.

"Lovely. And how is your wife?" The *portiere* was old, and his
wife had been sick.

Lucia paused, placing a hand on his elbow. "Would you like me
to fetch more cough suppressant for her? I have some upstairs."

He waved a hand, the lines creasing around his eyes. "*Grazie*,
but she's much better, Signorina Colombo. We have a bit of medicine left over, in fact."

"Well, let me know if you run out. *Arrivederci*." She turned up
the wide marble staircase, taking the steps two at a time despite
her heels. Four apartment doors graced each floor, widely spaced,
and she hurried to hers. She wanted to finish her reading as quickly
as possible so she could entice her best friend, Lidia, to join her at
the cinema. She stepped into her parents' foyer, dropped her handbag and coat on a hook, and paused. The lights were off. Was nobody home?

"Mamma?" she called, striding toward the parlor. Her mother
was there, sitting on the sofa, but she didn't raise her head from
where it rested in her propped hand. Her hair, usually pinned in
careful, blond waves, fell in a disheveled heap around her face. Even
stranger, Lucia's father sat in the other corner of the sofa, home
early from work. And across the room, her little brother, fifteen,
glanced up from his chair. Marco shook his head. He wore his
*Avanguardisti* uniform, as if he'd been about to trot off to the Fascist youth club when something stopped him.

"What's going on?" she managed, glancing from person to
person.

Her mother buried her face deeper in her hands, but her father looked up. His cheeks were wet with tears, and he wiped them quickly, as if they stung.

Fear gathered in Lucia's chest. *No.* It couldn't be. Nobody spoke, and Lucia looked from her father to the photos on the mantel. There, Piero's face laughed out from a frame. The picture had been snapped a month ago, before he left for Ethiopia. He'd worn his Royal Air Force uniform but couldn't muster solemnity in time for the flash. She'd teased him that day, saying the outfit didn't suit him. He was too jolly to be a pilot, too gentle to be a fighter.

Lucia's knees gave out, and she sank into a nearby chair. It was as if someone had hit her with something heavy. She couldn't breathe. She met her father's stare, and he nodded.

"Your brother's plane came down in the desert. I'm—" He struggled with the words, dropping his eyes to his knees. "I'm sorry, Lucia."

For a minute, nobody spoke. When Lucia found her voice, it came out in a croak.

"His plane came down? He could still be alive, then. Missing in action?"

Nobody looked at her, but her father shook his head, and her mother choked on a sob. Lucia pressed both hands over her eyes, breathing hard. She heard Piero's laugh in her mind, full and loud, as if he were in the next room. She saw him, with his face that mirrored her own. He was older than she, but her whole life they'd been mistaken for twins. It was as if in making Lucia, God had used the mold of her big brother, and they'd come out the same.

"I don't believe you," she said, struggling to force out words. "He only just left."

"Oh, Lucia." Her mother sniffed. "Don't make this more difficult than it already is."

Lucia shook her head. Could Piero be gone? She felt for him in her soul, like a person looking for shapes in the dark. Surely, he was out there, somewhere. But as she searched, she found nothing. Her pulse beat faster, pumping out grief and something else, small and hot. Anger.

She stood, casting about. "It was supposed to be simple. An invasion. Barely a war." She looked from parent to parent as if they were responsible. "He wasn't supposed to *die* there. How could Piero die a meaningless death? It can't be true."

Her father heaved himself up from the sofa. "A meaningless death?" His stricken face transformed. "How dare you suggest such a thing!"

She crossed her arms, meeting his stare. Like him, she burned too hot at the center. Like him, she found anger easier than grief.

He shook his fist, gaining momentum. "Piero died for his country."

"For his country? He wasn't even in his country. They sent him off where he had no business—he should be here, right now—"

She didn't see the slap coming. Her father took one step across the room, and with an open palm he hit her, hard, across the cheek. She stumbled backward, lifting her hand to her jaw while he strode from the room, boots clicking the marble floor.

Her mother rose, speaking in barely more than a whisper. "How dare you say such things, Lucia?" Her irises were shockingly blue against the bloodshot whites of her eyes. "You don't even know what you're talking about. Il Duce is restoring Italy to glory. Recapturing an empire, making something . . ." She choked on the words. "Something great. Your brother died a noble death. Don't you question it."

Her mother stumbled from the room, treading in her husband's wake, and Marco released a sob from his chair. He sat hunched over his knees, shoulders shaking. Lucia stared at her little brother for a long moment, her hand on her stinging cheek.

He wore his black shirt and blue scarf and fez pinned with Fascist emblems, like all of Mussolini's boys. He'd just graduated from the *Balilla* to the *Avanguardisti*, the next step on the stairs to the military. She sucked in a breath, sickened, and staggered to him.

"Marco," she murmured, nudging him over so she could sit. She wrapped an arm around his thin shoulders, and he sank into her, sobbing. The knobs of his spine poked through his shirt, and pain swelled in her throat. Could Piero really be dead? She closed her eyes, shuddering. She'd drown from the pain.

"The war in Ethiopia won't last long," she said, squeezing her little brother. For the first time, it struck her: how terrifying it was to be a boy in Mussolini's world.

"Marco." Her voice thickened with tears. "You won't have to fight. Please don't be afraid."

Marco stilled. He stared at her, eyes hot and mucus dripping from his nose. Then he shrank away, shaking her arm from his shoulders. "You think that's what I want? To be a coward?" His voice cracked, and he looked like he was seeing her for the first time. "Better a day as a lion than a hundred as a sheep," he said, staggering up to stand.

"Marco, that's just a saying . . ."

He straightened before her, tapping his heels together. And even though mucus dripped from his nose and his Adam's apple bobbed in his neck, he spoke with conviction. "Papà's right—you don't know what you're talking about. I'll fight for Italy, and for Il Duce, and for the new empire. Like Piero."

When he marched down the hall, Lucia was left alone, adrift. She perched on the chair in the center of the room, like an island, and wept.

Now Lucia set down the spoon, gritty with dirt, and picked up the oilcloth bundle. Without thinking, she opened it, fold by fold, to reveal the handful of jewels within. Her grandmother's diamond earrings glittered in the moonlight, a pearl necklace coiled like a snake, and a ring, the humblest object in the bundle, weighted a crease.

Lucia plucked out the ring and held it up. The band caught the moonlight, and her breath hitched. Carlo's face flashed in her memory: clove-colored eyes and a laughing smile. He was the opposite of the man her parents expected her to marry, with his radical, barely concealed beliefs. So why had she chosen him? It was a question she'd circled for years, and the closest she'd come to an answer was that she couldn't resist. She'd risen to him, again and again, like the ocean toward the moon.

She sighed, fingering the ring. But, perhaps, there was another layer to her reckless love, to the way he'd compelled her. Perhaps he'd seemed like a way out.

She shook her head, and her feelings scattered like fish. She dropped the ring in the cloth and refolded it quickly, stuffing the entire thing in the hole she'd carved around the lemon tree's roots. With the spoon, she scraped the dirt back over her most precious possessions, concealing them where nobody would ever look.

She might need them someday.

# FOUR

≈

## Francesca

*August 1943*

FRANCESCA AND GIACOMO stepped onto a bridge spanning the Tiber. The Fatebenefratelli Hospital loomed before them, straddling an island in the river, linked to Rome by bridges on either side. It had been a hospital of one type or another for hundreds of years.

"Who are you meeting?" she asked as they started across, hand in hand.

"Tommaso's here for a practicum. Thought we might catch him at lunch."

She stiffened. They both had the day off and had been out for a walk when Giacomo suggested they stroll by the Fatebenefratelli, the hospital he hoped to work for someday. Tommaso also had his sights set on the island hospital, but he was more hotheaded than she liked. Such conviction worried her, especially with Italy so unstable. She frowned while Giacomo whistled, and they stepped onto the island dividing the river, passing through the shadow of a bell tower.

They turned a corner into a small, shady piazza flanking the hospital, and Giacomo grinned and called out, "*Ciao*, Tommaso!" A pair of young men sat in a patch of grass under a scatter of umbrella pines, eating lunch. Tommaso raised an arm in greeting, and they ambled over to join them in the splash of shade.

"They'd better finish peace negotiations soon," Tommaso's friend was saying, taking a bite of his panino. Francesca lowered herself into the grass, tucking her weak leg under her skirt. She hated meeting new people, especially doctors, whose eyes invariably fell to her withered calf. Their gaze would pause, clinically, while her cheeks burned.

"They'll come to an agreement. Any day now," Giacomo said, jumping right in. The coup d'état had occurred nearly three weeks ago, Italy hung in a state of limbo, and it was all anyone wanted to talk about. This conversation was happening on every street corner in Rome, in every café, in every bar: Would Italy disentangle herself from Germany, strike peace with the Allies, and step aside from the war?

The young doctor chewed, thoughtful. "I hope you're right, because they should have finalized an agreement *yesterday*. Germans are flowing down through Italy like an avalanche from the Alps—"

"But we should be safe here," Giacomo interrupted. "Rome's an open city."

Francesca frowned. The "open city" declaration had just occurred. It was meant to set Rome aside from the war, a neutral bubble in a sea of destruction. But the word "open" only made her think of a void.

Tommaso shook his head, unblinking. "You think the Nazis will respect a declaration? Haven't you been paying attention? Listen. I don't know why they haven't closed the Brenner Pass. But at this point, Badoglio will have to declare war on Germany to get the Nazis out of here." His gaze went from man to man. "We'll have to fight them back into their borders—"

"No. The Germans will retreat," Giacomo interrupted again.

"If we formally surrender to the Allies, Hitler will know Italy's lost. It wouldn't be worth more casualties."

Tommaso smirked. "That's a pretty idea, but we're talking about Nazis. They're already occupying northern cities—"

"Where did you hear that?" the doctor asked.

"Doesn't matter. What does matter is that the Nazis will keep their grip on Italy." Tommaso's eyes narrowed. "They're not going to let us switch sides. We'll have to fight them."

"We?" Francesca ventured. Her voice wavered as she spoke. "Surely, you mean the army and the Allies—*they'll* fight if the Germans don't retreat."

Tommaso studied her for a second, and she resisted the urge to shrink closer to Giacomo.

"I mean *we*," Tommaso said. "Me. Volunteers. Even you, if you feel brave. Personally, I'll fight *Fascisti* the second I get a chance. Been waiting my whole life for it."

Francesca inhaled. She knew it. Heads nodded around her. Giacomo's hand tightened on her knee, and when she met his gaze, there was something in it, like a spark.

Minutes later, they were back on the bridge, and a hive of hornets circled in Francesca's stomach. She glanced at Giacomo. He wouldn't sacrifice himself for a cause, would he?

"You don't intend to *fight* Germans, if Tommaso's right?" They were midway across, and she slowed, examining him.

Giacomo glanced back at the hospital as if he could see Tommaso there, with his dark eyes and infectious conviction.

"I'll do whatever's right. If that means fighting for peace, I'll fight for peace."

"You're not a fighter." She stopped dead on the bridge. "Giacomo. Don't get dangerous ideas. If the Germans don't retreat, real soldiers can force them out."

He hooked his hands into his pockets, scuffing his shoe on the cobbles, always fidgeting. He looked like a boy, but his voice was serious. "If war comes to these streets, I won't hide."

"Mino, look at you—you're hardly bigger than me." Her voice trembled. "You and me, we're not made for revolution. You're a scholar, not a fighter."

"Is that how you see me?" His brows tipped up. "Weak?"

"It's not about weakness. It's about the fact that life can go wrong, Mino. Don't let bravado carry you away."

"It has nothing to do with bravado. What if Tommaso's right, and the Fascists try to align with Germany to regain power? If we don't act when we have the chance, what kind of future will we have?" He held her gaze, earnest.

"We'll be alive—that's the kind of future we'll have."

He stared at her, as if she were a question he didn't know how to answer. "Look," he said after a moment, taking a step forward, speaking gently. "I know this scares you, because of your father. But Francesca, you're the one I'd be fighting for. For us, and our life together."

She spoke without thinking. "Then you're a fool."

He looked like he'd been struck. After a stunned second, he shook his head, murmuring, "I'll walk home." He pressed a bus token into her hand. "See you there for dinner."

"Mino," she called, but he'd already turned and started off in the other direction. She wrapped her arms under her breasts, hugging her belly, and watched him go. Did he really think he could be some kind of fighter? He was as slender as a shadow against the sun.

She drifted to a bench alongside the river and sat. Giacomo knew everything about her, but he couldn't understand her fear. Not completely. She sighed, staring at the Tiber's slow current. He thought this was about what had happened to her father, and it was, in part. But for Francesca, fear was more profound than that.

Its seed had been planted in her soul when she was small, and it had grown roots and branches, spreading further with every loss she'd endured.

That seed of fear had dropped into her life in the middle of a glorious October. She could remember everything about that autumn: the feeling of dew on her ankles, the sun on her cheeks. Her thoughts swept back, catching on a morning when she was seven. To anyone else, it would appear to have been a day like all the rest. But for Francesca, it was the last of so many things. And for that reason it visited her often, unspooling with absolute, aching clarity.

She'd woken up early and was feeding the chickens when Giacomo arrived at the edge of her yard. He held up a hand, smiling under his flop of hair. She dumped the rest of the corn from her apron, leaving it in a hasty heap in the dirt, and smacked the dust from her hands, grinning.

"*Ciao, Mamma! Ciao, Babbo!*" she yelled at the house, hopping through the chickens at her feet. If they wanted to call her back, it was too late. Giacomo was already running ahead, weaving through tall grass in his bare feet. She followed, quick as a rabbit.

They ducked into the olive grove, sprinting downhill under his father's trees. Her knees rose in perfect rhythm, feet pounding the grass, and she was a horse, a dragon with wings, something strong and brave and free. The wind opened her lungs, cool and bright. Ahead of her, Giacomo whooped. A dozen quail burst from a seam of brush hemming the olives. They slowed, elbow to elbow, watching the birds rise into the sun.

"Let's play the survival game," Giacomo panted. He bent over, hands on his knees, catching his breath.

"By the stream," she answered, and he grinned. His nose was freckled, and both of his front teeth had fallen out over the summer. He'd lost one of them down this hillside, ankles in the dwindling stream, biting into an unripe apple. Francesca ran her tongue over her own front teeth. She still had all of them, which at age seven stung like an insult.

She took the lead, crouching through a gap they'd made in a hedge of brambles. A thorn scratched her shoulder, but she shrugged the pain away and pushed through the thicket. She unfolded her limbs on the other side and reached for Giacomo, tugging him out like a cork. Before them, a thin stream ribboned through a wild strip of land between two tended groves. A half-dozen olive trees, ancient and unpruned, hung over the patchy water like umbrellas. Their silvery leaves rippled in the sunlight.

Francesca waded into the water. Her throat burned a bit from running. She cleared it.

"You have a cold?" Giacomo asked, and she glanced at him. He leaned over, his arms draped before him like an ape, and studied the water. He was looking for fish. His dream all summer was to catch one big enough to eat, start a fire, and cook it for lunch. It didn't seem to matter to him that the stream all but dried up in the summer. He could imagine water.

"Just a tickle in my throat." She hoisted her dress above her knees and waded in.

He straightened, studying her. "Hope you can play tomorrow. You're not sick?"

She shook her head and bent, turning over a rock. Giacomo hated it when she couldn't play. Sometimes, she had chores to do, and he had to either help her or wait, listless. Neither of them had siblings, but since they lived next door, they'd found each other long ago. She bit her bottom lip, studying the silty hole left by the stone.

She stood, forgetting her dress, and it swirled around her knees. Giacomo tromped forward and reached for the limb of an olive tree hanging over the stream. He jumped a little, grabbing the branch and hoisting his legs up. He was smaller than most boys their age, with wide owlish eyes and a gentle smile. Her mamma said he was too mild for the rough-and-tumble village boys, and that was why he played with Francesca. She walked against the water until she, too, was under the limb. She sprang up, gripping the bark with both palms and swinging her legs aloft. She hooked her knees over the branch and hung there for a moment, her wet dress flopping down over her face.

She knew her mamma was wrong. Giacomo didn't play with her because he had nobody else. He played with her because they were the same. Together they ran, climbed, and splashed. She pulled herself up onto the limb, straddling it to face him. Together they were knights and kings and dragons and queens. They were wild and brave, and nothing in the world was beyond their invention.

She swayed a bit, dizzy, and tightened her thighs around the tree limb. She must have run too hard down the hill. Giacomo grinned amid the leaves, showing his gap-toothed smile, and she matched it.

Hours later, when it was time to go home, Francesca's sore throat had turned into a fever. Giacomo held her hand up the hill because, suddenly, it seemed very steep.

When they reached her house, he stared at her, solemn. "You're sick. Knew it."

"But I was fine this morning." She held a hand to her forehead, wavering. "See you tomorrow," she murmured, tromping toward the house in a daze.

When she pushed open the door, her father turned from a group of men at the kitchen table, slopping a little wine on the floor. Every man stilled for a heartbeat, then went back to drinking and talking too loudly. Their eyes flashed with something. Was it excitement?

Francesca stepped inside, looking for her mother. She was probably out in the garden.

"Where have you been, *allodola*?" her father asked from the table. "Out playing wild animals?" He called her *allodola*, skylark, as often as her real name. When she asked why, he said it was because someday she would fly.

He grinned, his green eyes teasing. He was older than her friends' fathers, with heavy brows and laugh lines around his eyes. But he was the best of them all. He carried sweets in his pockets, bellowed in laughter if someone was mischievous, and could still throw Francesca up and catch her in his farmer's arms.

She tried to smile at him, but it came out as a shrug. Her stomach swam with nausea, and her head hurt. "Where's Mamma?"

He stood, and the chair scraped across the floor. The sound reverberated in Francesca's head. Where *was* Mamma? She glanced at the table in time to see the nearest man lower his glass, gaze on her. Whenever these men came, two from town and the rest from Siena, her mother vanished in a huff, but Francesca didn't know why. She closed her eyes. She wanted them to leave now so her mother would reemerge and take care of her.

She swayed like a tree in the wind, and then her babbo's arms were around her, capable and strong, and he was bellowing, "Giulia!" through the open front door.

From that moment on, everything blurred.

The next morning, Francesca woke to her parents at her bedside, but nobody was dressed for Mass. She tried to ask if it was Sunday while her mother touched her forehead. Her palm was cool. The room smelled of vomit, but Francesca wasn't sure if it was from her. She sank away, folding into a current of dreams. She drifted in the silt of a riverbed, rising every so often toward the sparkling surface to see and hear things through the water.

"She's burning up. *Mio Dio* . . . what do you think it is?" her mamma said before she floated away. Her mother's words echoed in her mind. What was that in her voice? Fear?

"Stay out, Giacomo," she heard her father say later. "Run on home."

Francesca tried to open her eyes to see Giacomo, to ask him to stay, but again dreams carried her away before the words formed on her lips.

Later, a doctor appeared. His face was pinched, eyebrows low as he studied her. Like a pair of caterpillars, she thought, and then she dropped back into her riverbed of dreams.

When Francesca finally woke from her fever, it was like exploding through the water's surface. Her eyes stung in the air when she opened them, wide for the first time in days, and tried to look around. She wasn't in her own bed. She recalled a car ride, as if from a dream. She'd glimpsed busy streets and buildings while she burned in her mamma's arms.

The room was white and searingly bright. She lifted her neck, and everything hurt: her spine, her arms, her legs. There were other children nearby, lined up in beds.

"Mamma!" she called, and she could hear her own pulse behind the word. Her mother appeared and was joined, a half breath later, by her father.

She tried to sit up, but she couldn't. Her spine was as tight as a strung bow. She could hear her own breath, the whoosh of panic between her ears. When she tried to move her legs, they flopped like a pair of dying fish. She started to sob.

"Mamma," she wept, unable to put words to the questions building like a hurricane inside her skull. She could barely lift her arms.

"Calmati," her mother said, but tears ran down the lines in her cheeks when she leaned over to smooth Francesca's hair, the lights making her a silhouette. "Calm yourself, love."

A nurse floated in the background, glancing up from her chart. Her father cleared his throat. He held her limp hand and nodded, as though he knew what to do.

"Francesca," he said. Her mamma put a palm on his elbow as if to stop him, but he shook his head. His eyes were full of sorrow. "It's best to tell her, Giulia." For a long moment, her parents stared at each other. Then he cleared his throat again.

"*Allodola*, you have an illness."

She watched his mouth forming words, unable to ask the questions that swirled faster and faster in her mind. He held her gaze, and his lower lip shook, but he saw that she needed more information. He'd always understood her.

"It's called polio." His voice was gravelly, but he forced it into its normal, slow cadence, as if he were explaining anything. How to slice a seed potato. How to move a pawn in a game of chess. How to calm a pony.

"But what's happening?" she sobbed.

"It can make your body stop working, for a while. It's good that you're awake now, *allodola*. And you're in this wonderful hospital. They will help you get better, my love."

His eyes brightened, and he wiped at them with his sleeve. "You will get better."

FRANCESCA OPENED HER eyes, and it all fell away: the bed with its quilt, her floppy legs, her wide eyes and pounding heartbeat. Her mother. Her father.

The Tiber moved before her, slow and constant. She gripped the arm of the bench to stand, bent as an old lady. But she inhaled and straightened, shaking off the ache of memory.

Behind her, the Fatebenefratelli Hospital rose in the center of the river, separating the slow current. She turned to study the island, with its bridges and stone, as if it were a new adversary in a life full of adversaries. She thought about Giacomo and his huddle of men, young and excited, their eyes flashing with conviction. She'd seen that flash before.

She turned, walking against the Tiber's flow. She'd wind back into the center of Rome. The ancient buildings, thresholds worn from use, would grant her perspective. She inhaled again, stretching her lungs. It would be worth the walk. Because her fears would settle in the shadows of the Pantheon. Her memories would recede before the figures in the Trevi Fountain, their limbs forever frozen.

Then she'd go home. Calmed, she would remind Giacomo of how much she'd already endured, and how much she'd already lost.

She would remind him of another time she'd watched men huddle and plan.

And she would remind him of what had happened.

# FIVE

ஐ

## Lucia

*September 9, 1943*

NOEMI BRUNO HAD been in Lucia's apartment since Eisenhower spoke on the radio.

Lucia glanced at her elderly friend, standing a few feet away in
the darkness, staring through a gap in the blackout curtains. Noemi visibly jolted with each flash of light, her arthritic hands
pressed together as if in prayer. Lucia turned back to her window.
She couldn't think of anything reassuring to say. Artillery rumbled in the distance. It was approaching midnight, and the truth
of it was that they were both terrified. Rome was lost.

Noemi had come over the day before, because Lucia had been
in a mood to celebrate. She'd taken Matteo to the doctor, finally,
while the sounds of distant explosions filtered over Rome. The
Allies were bombing again, somewhere outside the city. With a
pounding pulse, she'd gone anyway. The trek to the doctor paid
off: he said Matteo was thin but healthy enough. When they left
his office, the skies beyond Rome had quieted, and Lucia was so
relieved she'd invited Noemi over. Her elderly friend, a widow
and childless, joined them often, standing in like a steadfast
mother. And so they'd shared table wine on the terrace while
Matteo sat near the lemon tree, drawing animals on a scrap of

paper. Afterward, they flipped on the wireless, and everything changed.

Eisenhower's voice rolled over the airwaves, slow and serious.

*"Italy has surrendered unconditionally."*

His voice was grave.

*"Effective this instant."*

Now, Lucia stared through the window where she'd stood, off and on, for twenty-four hours, watching the wrong army approach Rome. She studied the horizon, where the Germans fought what remained of the Italian army. How long before the Nazis breached Rome's walls? The sky flashed again, exploding like a string of fireworks.

"At least the suspense is over," Lucia said.

"But why aren't the Germans leaving?" Noemi whispered. "The leaflets said the Allies will be here in a week. Won't they retreat?"

Lucia shivered. Leaflets had fluttered down mere hours ago, celebrating the armistice and the advancing Allies. Of course, the leaflets had said nothing about the Germans.

Noemi jolted at another explosion. Her voice was pained. "But if the Allies come, and the Germans have already taken the city— what then?"

Lucia shook her head. Gunfire popped in the distance, chased by more bursts of light. Indeed, what would they do? So far, what was left of the Italian army held the Germans back, but they couldn't last long. Would Rome be occupied, like Paris? Luxembourg? Warsaw?

"Surely, the Allies will protect us, now that we're on their side," Noemi said, unable to let go of the optimism she'd held on to since the coup d'état.

"The Allies are in *Salerno*, Noemi." Lucia couldn't keep the exasperation from her voice. "Nowhere close enough to save Rome."

She thought of the king and Badoglio, and a frustrated puff escaped her lips. They must have mismanaged it, the negotiations and the armistice and whatever strategy Italy should have employed. Because now here they were, a day after the announcement of peace with the Allies, watching the German army approach Rome.

"We're their enemy now," she murmured, half to herself. "And I'm quite sure Germans are in the business of conquering enemies." She glanced at her old neighbor. Noemi trembled like a breath in front of the window.

"I'm sorry." Lucia spoke in a rush. Her heart clenched. What she'd said was true, but wasn't Noemi terrified enough already? She took a sideways step and wrapped her arm around the old woman's frail shoulders. An arthritic hand came up to clasp hers.

A voice piped up from the hallway. "Is it thunder and lightning?"

Matteo stood in the doorway, clutching his stuffed bunny and looking around the dark room, startled from sleep. The southwest horizon flashed and boomed again.

Lucia let the curtain fall and strode across the apartment to her little son. She scooped him up and held him so his face was close. He blinked his thick lashes.

"Yes. There's always thunder and lightning in autumn," she lied. "Don't you remember?"

He shook his head forcefully.

"Well, that's just because you were only four last time the season changed. It happens every year. Nothing to worry about." She smiled as brightly as she could in the darkness, touching her nose to his, never mind the mucus crusting his nostrils from his latest cold. He giggled, as she knew he would, and she faked a chuckle to encourage him. "Shall we go back to sleep? So you're not too tired tomorrow?"

"What are we doing tomorrow?" he asked as she hoisted him to her hip. "Can I play with Niccolo?"

"We'll meet Niccolo and his mamma in the park sometime soon," she said, forcing another smile. In the distance, artillery thundered again. "When the storm has passed, *sì?*"

She glanced at Noemi, still at the window. "I might just go to sleep with him," she said, and the old woman nodded. "Remember the extra blankets in the armoire if you get cold."

Lucia carried Matteo to his bed and laid him down. He tucked into his pillow, brown curls spreading, and she pulled up the blankets.

"Mamma," he murmured, drowsy. "Will you tell my story?"

*"Certo."* She settled on the edge of his bed, and he snuggled closer, waiting for the words he heard every night before sleep. She smoothed the hair from his forehead as she began. "A boy once went for a walk in a green and sunlit forest. He saw so many beautiful things—tiny flowers speckled the ground, a woodpecker tapped out a song somewhere way up high—"

"A *farfalla*," Matteo whispered sleepily.

"Yes, and a butterfly, and it was all the colors in the world. The boy followed the butterfly farther into the forest, forgetting everything to run and chase it, but then the forest grew dark. The boy was lost, and he thought he was alone. At first, he was very scared, and he wanted to cry. But then, he remembered the sky. He looked up, and there were the first stars, looking down at him, and he didn't feel alone anymore. He started to walk, and he knew where to go. And as he walked, he saw the forest was beautiful, even at night. He just had to travel through it to find his way home."

Matteo's eyes closed, and she held his little hand, as she always did, and gave it a squeeze. "Matteo, do you know how much I love you?" she whispered.

"As much as all the stars."

*"Bravo.* And remember: the stars are always with us, always, even when we can't see them."

He nodded slightly, and in a moment his breathing steadied. She paused on the edge of his bed, suddenly tired herself. Should she try to rest? She sank back, still in her dress, surrendering to exhaustion. It was just as well. She could stand at the window all night, watching the sky ignite, but what would come of it? She closed her eyes. Rome was in the crosshairs of disaster, and she could only wait.

What was Carlo doing now? Before she could retract the thought, it multiplied. Was he out there, fighting the Germans as they marched toward Rome? She sighed. Ever since Noemi thought she'd seen Carlo, he'd haunted Lucia's thoughts. Once, she'd even had a strange feeling that he was nearby, watching her. She'd been out walking with Matteo in her neighborhood, and they'd bumped into one of Piero's oldest friends, Angelo. Like her brother, Angelo had joined the Royal Air Force and been shot down over Ethiopia, but he'd survived the burns to come home. It was a joy to see Angelo; she'd known him all her life. He'd kissed both of her cheeks, placing his thick, scarred hands on her shoulders and holding her out as if for inspection. Then he'd picked up Matteo, swinging him around, and that's when Lucia sensed it. It was like pressure between her shoulder blades, as if she could feel someone's eyes on her. *Carlo's.* She'd pivoted, searching the street, and for a second she thought she saw a long shape in the distance. She squinted into the light, Matteo giggling behind her, and studied the people walking under the lowering sun, their shadows rippling over the cobblestones. *No.* None of them were Carlo.

She'd turned back to Angelo and her laughing boy, shaking her intuition away. It was simply her imagination, responding to the power of Noemi's suggestion. Carlo wasn't in Rome. He couldn't be, not after all this time.

Now, gunfire sounded in the south, and she reached for Matteo's forehead, feeling his temperature and smoothing his hair.

And, in the darkness of the unsettled night, she allowed herself to do something she rarely did. She allowed herself to remember Carlo.

LUCIA HAD ONCE been optimistic about her future. She'd drifted through her days at university, talking through lunches and failing, over and over again, to study for exams. But it didn't matter. Wealthy girls attended Università di Roma in small numbers, and they weren't expected to excel. As trained Fascist girls, what they *were* required to do was find a husband.

"Oh, I'm going to have a whole flock of children," she told her friend one morning over cappuccino. She pinched the handle of her ceramic cup, pinky finger out, and sipped.

Lidia rolled her eyes. Winter light fell over her dark hair and shoulders, making her glow. She, too, was a trained Fascist girl, though perhaps not enthusiastically so.

"Roll your eyes all you want." Lucia smirked. "But when you fall head over heels for some boy in chemistry, it'll be me who curls your hair and matches your handbag to your shoes."

Lidia glanced at her shoes, which didn't currently match her handbag *or* dress, and Lucia laughed. Lidia was interested in science—fascinated, really—and she actually wanted to be in university. They couldn't be more different, but their friendship was as solid as the travertine winding through Rome. They'd grown up in adjacent, spacious apartments, playing through childhood in the nearby Villa Borghese gardens.

"Handbags and shoes aren't for me." Lidia laughed. "But really, Lucia, a dozen kids? Il Duce would be proud."

Lucia shrugged. Mussolini implored Italy's women to populate his expanding empire with many children, but that wasn't why she wanted them. She looked out the window, blowing on her coffee to hide her feelings. She'd started to dream of children after Piero died, but she couldn't explain why. Did she think having a flock of kids would ease the blow if one died? Did she imagine her own babies, sweet and soft, staring up at her with Piero's eyes? She sipped her cappuccino and couldn't swallow. He'd been gone for over a year, but the sorrow didn't fade.

Lidia touched Lucia's wrist. "Piero?"

Only Lidia could see such things. With everyone else, Lucia was able to hide her true heart. "I miss him," she managed.

"I do, too." Lidia nodded. "God doesn't make many like your big brother."

Lucia tried to smile, but it fell flat. Lidia regularly brought God into conversations, but faith of any type had never felt more distant to Lucia. Lidia's family was Jewish, while Lucia's attended Mass half-heartedly, their true devotion used up by Mussolini and his state. What would it be like to really believe in something, the way Lidia did?

"All right, Lucia," Lidia said, patting her hand. "You can raise your dozen kids, and I'll be their aunt." Her dark eyes flicked to her watch, and she gulped the last of her coffee. "Andiamo. We're going to be late."

The girls hustled down the sidewalk, books clutched to their chests, handbags swinging. When they'd nearly arrived, Lucia's heel slipped a bit, and for a second she thought she'd fall. But she caught herself and, heart thumping, stretched her stride to follow Lidia around the corner to the university gate. She was wearing the wrong shoes for hurrying. Lidia paused at the building door, beckoning, and disappeared inside. Of course, if it were up to Lucia, she wouldn't hurry. She'd rather just be late than arrive sweaty under her belted jacket.

Someone stepped into her path, and she ran right into him, hard. Books exploded between them, and Lucia scrambled backward, nearly falling again. Before she had time to digest any of it, the man she'd run into was bending, cursing under his breath, and gathering spilled books and papers. He was tall, very tall, and had short, dark hair that swept up in thick tufts. His square jaw needed a shave, and he wore a fashionable suit and polished shoes. She gaped, books around her feet, as he stood to his full height. It was like a romantic novel. Or a film. Everything slowed around her while she stared—he was as tall as Fred Astaire, but handsomer—and next he'd pick up her books, and, overcome by her charm—

"Look where you're going next time. *Gesù Cristo*," he said, breaking into her fantasy.

She crossed her arms, flustered, and mustered a retort. "I could say the same to you. I was simply rushing to class—a *very important* class—and you stepped right in my way."

He met her stare. His eyes were the brown of coffee beans.

"Aren't you going to pick up my books?" She tried to glare.

He cocked his head, and in an instant, his irritation dissolved into amusement. "I don't see any reason why I should. Don't you have a pair of arms?"

Her mouth fell open, and she stared at him for a long, astonished second. "Were you raised by wolves? My goodness!"

He chuckled, bending and stacking her books. When he dropped them in her waiting arms, he cleared his throat. "I apologize. But I really must go. I have an exam and a meeting, both critical. In penance for my rudeness, would you meet me later for a drink? I'll prove that humans did, indeed, raise me." He grinned. "Though wolves worked out fine for Romulus and Remus."

"Not for Remus, actually." She shifted her shoulders back and smoothed her curls, forcing herself not to smile. "Would it really be a penance to have a drink with me?"

He laughed again, loud and genuine. "Seven thirty, at Il Passetto, near Piazza Navona. Do you know it? Will you be there?"

"Only to teach you some chivalry."

"I'll be a good student."

She could no longer smother her smile. They stared at each other, stuck for words but grinning like fools, for a long, strange moment. It started then: the gravitational pull. Carlo the moon, Lucia the ocean.

"I have to go," she said finally, glancing at the building she was meant to be in. *"Santo cielo.* I've never been this late! I don't know what the professor will do."

He chuckled. "Well, then, *in bocca al lupo."*

She shrugged, giving the customary reply, *"Crepi."*

He winked and pivoted, striding away.

*Into the wolf's mouth.* Lucia had always thought it a funny way to say good luck. Before he turned a corner, he pivoted again, walking backward.

"My name's Carlo. What's yours?"

"Lucia," she called. He grinned and turned back around, loping away.

He had awfully broad shoulders. She let her own shoulders drop, striding off toward class. She pictured his face. *Carlo.* Maybe it would be like a romantic film, after all.

LUCIA WOKE TO the sound of gunfire, closer now. She pulled her arm from the warm weight of Matteo's head, stood, and crept from the room. In the parlor, another sound emerged, filtering up through the cool dawn. Noemi slept on the sofa, covered in a crocheted blanket. Lucia bent, smoothing the fabric over the old woman's bare feet.

Gunfire spattered the horizon. Lucia wrapped her cardigan tighter over her dress, crossing her arms. She tiptoed to the balcony door, following the sounds filtering up. She opened it a crack and peered at the street below.

A stream of people wove along the cobblestones. They were

men, mostly, but young women dotted the crowd. Many had rifles slung over their shoulders.

Lucia needed to know what was happening. Inhaling, she stepped
onto the balcony and leaned slightly over. "Where are you going?"
she called, attracting the attention of a middle-aged man on the
fringes.

"To fight the Germans," he called up.

"Where are they?"

He tipped his head in the direction of the closest city walls. His
rifle swayed under his armpit. "On their way here, but we're going to help the army keep 'em out. Rome won't fall to the Nazis,
not today." He grinned, as if he were on his way somewhere fun.

The man was nearly around the corner, swept along with the
crowd, when he turned and sought her out again with his gaze.
He called out once more.

"Stay inside, signora. Rome will be dangerous today."

She watched him vanish, a phrase repeating in her mind: *In
bocca al lupo.*

# SIX

༚༝

# Francesca

*September 10, 1943*

Francesca was awake in bed most of the night, listening to gunfire and explosions in the distance. When she finally closed her eyes, she sank into a troubled doze. Memories rose in her dreams, one after another, like leaves on the wind.

There was her father. The image of his face sailed toward her, his green eyes crinkled as he bellowed in laughter. And there he was again, sitting at the kitchen table, scratching something out with his pen. She fell into this memory, headlong.

She sat opposite her father in a chair, her legs straight and stiff in braces, thirteen years old and angry. Spring light splashed the room.

"When your mamma gets home, we can ask her about new shoes," he was saying. He glanced up, his kind eyes troubled, and she crossed her arms and looked away. Her mamma and nonna were out, and she was furious at them. She was furious at her father, too, and at everyone in the whole world, because her feet hurt and her legs hurt and she had to wear clunky shoes that made the other girls snicker at school.

"I'm not going to school anymore," she spat, staring at the floor as if it were alive. He sighed across the table.

"Francesca," he murmured.

He didn't get to finish whatever he was going to say, because the front door burst open.

She froze. A pair of broad men, wearing Mussolini's Blackshirt uniforms, strode into the house. They were yelling, but she couldn't focus on the words, couldn't think, because one of them grabbed her father and hauled him out of his chair. The other cuffed him, hard, with a gun. Blood burst from his nose, speckling the floor.

Francesca screamed, and they ignored her, yanking her father toward the open door.

She scrambled up from her chair, using it to balance.

Her father looked back at her, desperate and wild-eyed. "Francesca, *amore mio*. I'll be back—tell your mother—"

But before he could finish, the Blackshirts shoved him through the door and into the waiting car.

She stumbled to the doorjamb without her crutch. "*Babbo*," she screamed, "*Babbo, no!*" But she was screaming at a car, closed and sleek, and the engine rumbled into gear.

By the time Francesca tottered out into the yard, wailing, the car, and her father, had vanished.

FRANCESCA SAT UP in bed, gasping. Giacomo glanced over at her.

"The dream?"

She nodded, pressing a hand to her forehead. But it wasn't a dream, not really. It was her life: her father, lost to political exile, like so many of Il Duce's enemies. He'd been sent to a remote *confino*, where he'd died, they were told, most likely of a heart attack. She closed her eyes, pushing the memory from her mind, letting the sound of gunfire replace it.

Giacomo was across the room, packing a bag. Francesca swung her legs off the bed, breathing to clear her head. She looked to the window, squinting through the shutters. The blackout paper was pulled back, the sun barely up.

Reality assembled before her. She stood, shaking her head. Giacomo was sweating, though it wasn't yet hot in the apartment. He stuffed bandages and scissors into the bag.

"Mino." She picked up where she'd left off the night before. "Don't go."

He paused, glancing at her with a roll of bandages in one hand. Gunfire volleyed somewhere in the distance, followed by a roll of thunder. But, she knew, it wasn't thunder.

"It's the right thing to do, Francesca."

She went to him, wrapping her arms around his neck. "It's a war zone."

He cupped his hand on her cheek. "War zones need doctors."

She sighed, stepping back and glancing around the dark apartment. He zipped the bag shut while she walked to the window. Her stomach sickened. "I'm coming, then," she said over her shoulder.

Her words hung between them, and she spotted what she was looking for. She plucked his glasses from the sill and turned.

He stared at her.

"No." He shook his head hard. "No, you can't come. I won't let you take that risk."

She stepped over to him, opening the glasses, and reached up to slide them onto his nose. She tucked a peg behind each ear, never breaking her hold on his gaze.

"I'm not letting you go alone."

"But, Francesca, the fighting's outside the city. It's at least a two-kilometer walk—"

"I can walk that far."

"But what if you need to run?"

"You'll help me." Before he could open his mouth to protest

further, she turned away, looking for her shoes. "Don't bother trying to convince me otherwise. We're equally stubborn."

When she pulled on her first shoe, her hands shook. She pinned her eyes shut and swallowed a swell of nausea. But she wouldn't let Giacomo go out there alone. What if he left and never came back? The thought was more terrifying than the sound of fighting. She'd already lost someone without a trace. She wouldn't let it happen twice. Distant explosions punctuated the silence as they locked the apartment door.

The streets were empty and pale in the early light. Giacomo took Francesca's elbow, and they hurried. His other arm hoisted the bag of bandages, tools, and ointments. They turned up a wider, tree-lined road that snaked toward the city walls, following the sound of fighting.

Cutting through Parco del Colle Oppio, they melted into a cluster of other civilians streaming under rows of umbrella pines and cypresses. The sun broke over buildings on the eastern horizon, burnishing rooftops. The trees swayed in the breeze as if this were a normal day, as if this were any other autumn.

A leathery, middle-aged man fell into step beside Giacomo. He squinted at the bag.

"What's in there? Weapons?"

"Medical supplies."

"Ah." The man nodded emphatically, swinging his gaze ahead. Francesca hooked her arm into Giacomo's, using his momentum to keep up with the long-strided men. He supported her weight, automatically boosting her every time she hitched her weak leg forward.

"Always a need for medics," the man continued. He had a smoker's voice, low and rough. "You served before?"

Giacomo shook his head. "I've had an exemption as a medical student."

"Ah, *sì*. I served on the ground in Ethiopia." The man spat on the path. "Now here we are again, fighting another war Il Duce queued up for us. *Il bastardo*."

They walked on in silence, streaming from the park toward the Colosseum, huge under the rising sun. A flock of starlings dipped over the ancient ruins. How many wars had been fought in Rome since the forum was built? The starlings folded into one another and disappeared over the horizon. Countless. Gunfire ratcheted in the southeast, echoing over the ruins and tightening Francesca's chest. Countless wars.

They made their way to the edge of the city, and her pulse rose into her ears, thudding like a drum. Explosions echoed off buildings, and Giacomo glanced at her, wide-eyed. A whir and a crack rebounded somewhere down the road, and he shrank into an alcove with one knobby elbow over Francesca, as if to shield her. She looked out from under his arm, watching other civilians hurry forward, clutching guns. Ahead, the Aurelian Walls met the Porta San Paolo, an ancient, turreted entrance to the city. Its redbrick shoulders rose in the sky, guarding the start of the Ostian Way. Civilians and soldiers alike gathered at the base of the monument.

"The fighting must be down Via Ostiense," Francesca said over the noise. Porta San Paolo was still behind the front line, if barely.

Giacomo nodded. He took her hand, and ducking under the cacophonous noise, they ran.

"I'm a doctor," he said when they arrived at the wall, speaking to the first soldier who looked like he might know how things were organized. Francesca looked past the *porta* to the Pyramid of Cestius, which stood in its shadow, guarding the Ostian Way. The road snaked into the distance, and not far down was a throng of fighters shooting and reloading from a barricade of overturned tram cars. Was that the front line? It was stunningly close.

A bomb exploded somewhere, and she looked back to Giacomo. The man he'd been speaking with gestured toward a handful of trees beyond the wall. Francesca followed Giacomo past weary-looking Romans, and there they found a makeshift field hospital in the open air. The wounded were lined up in the shade like matchsticks.

Giacomo dropped his bag and knelt next to a boy with a dark bloom across his chest. He breathed with a wet suck. Francesca's limbs trembled like twigs in a storm. Why had she come? A barrage of artillery thundered. What could she possibly do to help?

A hand weighted her shoulder, and she turned, facing an older woman. Steely hair wisped into her firm stare. "These people need water." She pushed a canteen into Francesca's hands. "We're trying to find transport to a hospital, but we've had to move with the fighting . . ." She shook her head, grimacing. "Help out in the meantime. Bind up bleeding wounds until a medic can see to them."

The woman dropped a roll of bandage into Francesca's free hand and shuffled away. Francesca stared at her hands, as if bewildered by the items in them. Machine guns ratcheted down the road. How long could the Italians hold back the German army? Days? Hours? Long enough for the Allies to arrive? Her pulse thudded everywhere in her body. Giacomo was already on his second patient, kneeling in a pool of blood, hair in his eyes, checking a pulse rate. She inhaled and started toward the other end of the long line.

Her first patient was a man around the same age her father would've been. She knelt, ignoring the shake in her fingers. There was a gash across his thigh, and she unraveled a bandage. Again she inhaled, marshaled her hands, and worked the bandage under the leg. She'd tie it above the wound, tightening like a tourniquet, until Giacomo or another medic could see him.

"You don't look like you should be here, *bella*," the man murmured. She glanced at his face, surprised. His pupils rolled beneath half-closed lids.

"Would you like some water?" she asked, hoping to catch him before he dipped back into a stupor. She placed her palm under his neck, lifting slightly, and poured water over his dry lips. He swallowed eagerly, eyes closed. When she lowered his head, he tried to speak again. She had to bend close to hear him.

"You look like a dancer. You know Degas? Ballerinas . . ."

She smoothed drips from his chin. He was adrift, confused.

"Go home, *bella*. The Germans . . ." He sank away for several breaths, then his words rose in a final swell. "The Germans'll eat you alive."

Francesca bit her lip while the man floated off in his mind. She glanced toward the Ostian Way. What was she doing out here? She, who could barely run?

Clutching her canteen and summoning her nerve, Francesca pivoted to the next patient, a boy. She felt his forehead. He didn't move. She studied his face, his long lashes resting on sunburned cheeks, and her breath caught. The air seemed to sharpen around her.

He was dead.

She reached for his wrist and tried to find a pulse while her own pulse galloped. *Nothing.* Her hand moved on its own to press against her mouth, stifling a sob, and her eyes stung in the dusty sunshine.

She sat back on her heels and stared in the direction of the fighting. The boy looked to be about fifteen. Machine gunfire rattled the oxygen in the trees. Why was she surprised? There must be scores of dead people out there. She wiped her eyes. There was nothing to do but move on.

The morning unspooled that way behind the monuments, gaining its own strange rhythm. Francesca, Giacomo, and a handful of other civilians and medics rotated between the wounded and dead, doing what they could. Over and over, she had to pin her eyes shut, drop a wrist with no pulse, and govern her emotions. When the sun hung in the west, hot on her neck, Francesca trudged to the fringes of the makeshift field hospital. Giacomo was there, taking a rare break.

"How are you holding up?" he asked after pulling a long drink from a canteen.

She shrugged. "Just getting through it. I don't even know if I'm helping."

"You are." He caught her gaze. "You're here, aren't you? That's more than many can say. Did you hear about the king? And Badoglio? They fled Rome in the night, the cowards."

"What do you mean? How can they govern Rome if they've left it?"

He narrowed his eyes against the sunlight. "They can't. They saved their own hides, abandoning us to the Germans. One of my patients told me. He had a hole in his belly, had been fighting for over thirty hours with no food, little water. And yet what he couldn't get over was Badoglio and the damned king."

Shouting drifted over the treetops, and they glanced down the Ostian Way. Giacomo handed her the water. "How are our fighters supposed to keep up morale?"

Francesca tried to wrap her head around it. Without the king and Badoglio, Rome was without a government. The Ostian Way exploded with noise. And those who wanted Rome for themselves? They were close.

She took a long drink. When she had finished, her mind sharpened, almost immediately. She stared past the *porta* again, sensing something. The noise was changing.

Giacomo's eyebrows tipped up. He sensed it, too. Men gestured in the shade of the pyramid, and Giacomo pivoted to study the side streets. The civilians ministering to the wounded stood, lowering canteens and glancing toward the Ostian Way. It took a long moment, under the hot September sun, for the situation to crystalize.

"They're retreating," Giacomo said as the first Italian soldiers appeared on the other side of Porta San Paolo. They jogged in loose clusters, eyes wild and weapons slung under their arms. The crowd agitated.

A string of explosions thundered down the road, breaking into the cacophony with a new sound. It was louder somehow. Sharper.

A man in a helmet loped past, and Francesca grabbed his arm. He turned, startled.

"What's happening?" she yelled under the new sound. Was it shelling?

"We're out of ammunition." The soldier shook his arm away from her grip. "It's over, kid—Rome's lost. Get out of here."

He ran toward the neighborhoods, and Giacomo pressed his hands to his forehead, pushing his hair into sweaty tufts. Several soldiers were taking up positions behind the wall, aiming toward the Porta San Paolo, ready to fight to their last breath.

"The patients!" Giacomo shouted into the chaos. He tried to get the attention of a group of soldiers, but they were readying for the Germans. "We have to move the patients!"

The old woman with steely eyes hustled over, grabbing Giacomo's and Francesca's arms. Her hands were like claws.

"Leave them. Get into the neighborhoods. Now. The Germans will leave the wounded alone—they're no threat. We'll come back once they've passed and get them to a hospital."

Francesca nodded. She linked Giacomo's elbow as the Italian soldiers started to fire, shattering the thoughts in her skull. "Mino," she shouted over the noise. *"Andiamo!"*

There wasn't a second to waste. Francesca grabbed Giacomo's hand, yanking hard, and they ran for a side street. He lifted as she thrust her weak leg forward, gesturing to a narrow alley off the main roads. They skated into the shadows of the buildings and crouched, unsure of which direction to run from here. A rumbling grew from the Ostian Way. She listened, frantic. It took her a moment to guess what it was. She looked to Giacomo.

"*Tanks*, Mino. They're driving tanks into Rome."

He nodded in time with an explosion, wide-eyed. They both knew it then: Rome was lost.

"They'll have to take a main road," he sputtered after the shelling. "We should circle back and go home through the forum—"

A barrage of gunfire interrupted him. She knew he was thinking not only about their route out, but also about the patients. Several of their faces, sunburned and pained, flashed in her mind. Was it possible to stay with them? Could they hide, reemerging to save whomever was still alive when the Germans passed?

The noise from the main streets died down abruptly. A few shots echoed, but the Ostian Way dipped to an eerie quiet. Francesca met Giacomo's stare. Perhaps that was it? Had the Germans beaten the last of the Italians? Now they would roll through with their tanks, abandoning this part of Rome for the center . . . Francesca's pulse filled the quiet, the blood pounding in her skull while her thoughts raced.

"Let's wait here," she whispered. "See to the wounded when they leave . . ."

Giacomo opened his mouth to answer but was interrupted by a single shot echoing from the direction of Porta San Paolo. He froze. Another rang out. It was as if they were timed.

"*Madonna*," Giacomo breathed. Shock washed over his face. He dropped her hand, whispering, "Stay here." He scuttled, in a crouch, back toward the Ostian Way.

"Mino!" She glanced around the quiet alley, frantic. What was he doing? They hadn't waited long enough—the Germans were still there. She tightened her fists and slunk behind him, staying close to the buildings down several side streets, until they both stopped in an alcove's shadow. From there, they could see out toward the Porta San Paolo.

Francesca gasped. Beyond the monuments, on the Ostian Way, a column of tanks idled in a long, even line. On their side of the wall, a German officer ambled through the shade, vanishing and reemerging as he stepped past tree trunks. At regular intervals, he lifted his gun, passionless, and shot the wounded.

Time stopped. Francesca couldn't look away. And suddenly, she couldn't hear—not the tank engines, the German shouts, the birds exploding from trees after each shot—all she could hear was the click of the gun followed by a bang. The people jolted when they took the bullets.

Not an hour ago she'd wiped sweat from those foreheads, poured water over those lips, and stoppered the blood running from those limbs. The Nazi ambled to a broad, talkative man Francesca had helped when he came in.

"My mamma's surely beside herself with worry," he'd managed, voice gurgling, hands pressed over a bullet wound in his leg. Now he raised an arm toward the Nazi and was shot mid-sentence, his head jerking apart.

Giacomo bent and vomited. Francesca turned to him, and it was is if a cold wind blew through her brain, stripping her thoughts like leaves off a limb. Only one remained: *We have to get out of here.*

"*Andiamo,*" she whispered, tugging Giacomo's hand. They were far too close and barely hidden. What if someone saw them? "If they catch us, they'll shoot us, too."

He met her stare, nodding as this new reality took shape before them. Hooking elbows, they ran up the shadowed alley just as the tanks rumbled back to life.

Like mice in a maze, they hurried through side streets, choosing routes too narrow for vehicles and avoiding patches of gunfire erupting through the city. Francesca's legs ached. Giacomo held her around the waist, half carrying her, and they spilled onto a narrow street leading to the Colosseum. Shots ratcheted through the neighborhood at their backs, and the amphitheater rose silently over the gap between buildings. Home wasn't far. They could arc along the Colosseum and cut back through the park. The idea of the cypress trees, cool and quiet in the lowering sun, drew Francesca like a magnet.

But as they neared the end of the street, the Colosseum looming, a rumble grew. Giacomo gripped her hand hard, and they stopped, again in shadow, nearly at the intersection of the road circling the amphitheater. The stones shook under their feet, vibrating up into their limbs as a Tiger tank rolled past, so close they could've hit it with a rock. They took a step forward and glanced in the tank's wake. Beyond the Colosseum, on the avenue that straightened toward the Aurelian Walls, a line of tanks and armored cars idled in formation.

Francesca turned to Giacomo, whispering, "Find another way?"

She saw her own bewilderment in his flushed, sweaty face. Before he could answer, someone yelled something indecipherable in Italian. Footsteps clattered down by the Colosseum, and a series of explosions shook the air. Resistance fighters appeared from nowhere, aiming at the German column. Giacomo wrapped his arm around her waist, and again they sank into an alcove, hugging someone's door. Bullets zinged, chipping buildings, and the Tiger tank rolled past again.

For several minutes, Francesca and Giacomo didn't move, unable to leave the safety of the alcove to run. Then the noise died away. Was the skirmish over? They slipped out, tentative.

Scattered across the street circling the Colosseum, Italian men lay on the ground like tossed dolls. One of them lifted his torso onto his elbows and stared at his bloodied leg, anguish across his face. He opened his mouth to scream, inhaling dust and smoke. The whites of his eyes flashed under a helmet that seemed too big for his skull.

The Tiger tank bounced past the Colosseum and down the road, rejoining its column.

"They'll kill him," Francesca whispered to Giacomo. He met her stare, eyes darting behind his glasses as he calculated. The area remained quiet, with only the low movements of the dead and dying, and the German column idling in the distance.

"We could get him, Mino." Her voice was rough in her throat. "We can't just leave him out there."

They stared at each other. How far was the wounded soldier? Fifty feet? Would they be shot as they ran out to get him?

Giacomo nodded. "I'll go."

Francesca was about to protest when he dropped her hand and ran, hard, into the empty street. He ducked and hooked his hands into the armpits of the stunned soldier, dragging him toward the alley. Their shadows dipped and bobbed over the stone. They were halfway to safety when machine guns erupted in the distance and bullets split the air over Giacomo's head.

Without thought, Francesca scrambled from hiding and ran to him, taking the soldier's feet. She could feel the wind of bullets as they missed, zinging in the gaps between their three bodies. She pooled her focus on moving without falling. Gasping, they lugged the soldier into the narrow alley. Where could they go? As if her thoughts had been heard, Francesca saw a building up ahead with a gate for a door, and an enclosed courtyard beyond it. An elderly man stood in the archway, gesturing wildly. They hefted the soldier to the gate, which the old man swung open and shut so they could vanish inside.

"Bring him in, quickly," the man said, ushering them to a door on the other side of the courtyard. They passed an empty fountain, hot in the lowering sun, and then they were inside a dark and quiet kitchen. They hoisted the man onto the table.

The leg needed binding. The young soldier's eyes were wide, but he seemed unable to talk, perhaps from pain and loss of blood.

"I don't have my supplies," Giacomo said, but their elderly host left and came back with a scarf, fetched from a closet. Giacomo tied it into a makeshift tourniquet, pulling the ends tight.

He raked both hands through his sweaty hair, eyes darting. "I have to go back. There were at least two more alive out there. Maybe I can get them before the column comes through." He turned to the old man. "Will you shelter more than this one?"

The man nodded, emphatic. *"Certo."*

"Then I'll be back in a minute to tend to him. He'll be all right for now. Give him water, if you have it."

Everything in Francesca tightened. What if the column of tanks was already moving? What if whoever had shot at them was in the street now, searching? She struggled to speak but knew it was hopeless. There would be no talking him out of it.

"I'll come keep watch," she managed. He nodded, likely aware that she, too, would not be talked out of following him.

They hurried through the shadows, hand in hand, and found the road skirting the Colosseum the same as when they'd left it minutes ago. Empty. Francesca exhaled. They could make it if they were fast. The column still idled down the way, as if whoever was in charge was deciding what to do next. And what *would* they do? Would the Germans really occupy Rome? She shook the questions away. Giacomo dropped her hand when they reached the hem of the shadows. He cupped her cheek, whispering, "Stay here. You promise? No matter what?"

He'd be safer if he didn't have to worry. She nodded. "Be quick."

He leaned in, kissing her lips for no more than a breath, then turned and sprinted into the street like a track runner. His wiry limbs propelled him forward until he slid to a stop beside a body. Kneeling, he checked the pulse, grimaced, and crouch-walked to the next man. Francesca joined her hands in prayer, pressing them to her mouth. Every second he was out there, exposed in the sunshine, was a second someone could notice and take aim. She couldn't breathe. But in another minute he had a man slung over his back, and ducking, he prepared to run.

An engine revved from somewhere around the corner. An armored car appeared from a different alley, bouncing into the road.

Francesca's hands flew to her mouth. She wanted to scream. They'd been waiting for him, hidden. Could he run?

But it was already too late. Giacomo was backing up, eyes wild, while the car careened toward him and lurched to a stop, nearly at his feet.

Giacomo turned, the wounded man still draped across his back, and looked around frantically. Francesca watched him search for an escape that wasn't there. There was nowhere he could go that a bullet wouldn't hit him in the back as he ran. When he glanced in her direction, he widened his eyes and, ever so subtly, shook his head.

She could read his mind. *"Stay hidden."*

Two German soldiers jumped out, boots thudding as they hit Roman ground. One hoisted a gun, leveling it at Giacomo with tired informality. Francesca's blood boiled into her head, and she had to press her palm hard against her lips, pushing back a scream.

"Please," Giacomo spoke quickly. "I'm a doctor. I just wanted to save him. I'm a doctor."

The Nazi gestured with his gun for Giacomo to drop the wounded man, so he lowered the weeping Italian soldier to the ground. The gun fired immediately, and the weeping stopped.

Giacomo remained standing, arms up, his eyes on the dead soldier. His glasses flashed.

"I'm not a fighter. Just a doctor," he sputtered in Italian, his slender arms shaking in the sunlight. *"Sono solo un medico."*

The German leveling his gun hesitated. He looked Giacomo up and down, seeing no weapon. He turned to his counterpart and exchanged a few unintelligible words. When he turned back to Giacomo, the gun dipped slightly.

*"Medico?"* the Nazi repeated, his accent heavy.

Giacomo nodded, emphatic. *"Sì. Medico."* He pointed at his own chest.

The Nazi shrugged, said something to his partner, and both of them stepped forward. Taking Giacomo roughly by the shoulders, they hoisted and dragged him away. His heels pedaled, trying to keep up, as he was lugged toward the armored car. Then they leveled their guns on him again, ordering him in.

Everything in Francesca wanted to scream, to run, and to pull him back to safety. But just as she thought she couldn't resist, Giacomo took a risk and glanced at her. He nodded his head once, sharp and subtle, before climbing into the vehicle.

His thought was a scrap in the wind, sailing past her.

*"Coraggio,"* the wind whispered.

And then he was gone.

# SEVEN

ℜℜ

## Lucia

*September 11, 1943*

IT WAS WELL past midnight, and Lucia sat at her window, listening, hands knitted over her lips in prayer. Gunfire spat here and there, echoing over the rooftops. She glanced toward Matteo's room, willing him to stay asleep. What would she say if he woke? That the Nazis were in the streets, shooting weapons and drinking Roman wine and doing God knows what else? That they'd taken over the city? She closed her eyes, breathing through the cavern in her belly. No. She would let Matteo feel safe for as long as possible.

Footsteps clattered outside, and she leaned forward, peering through a slit in the curtains. Three figures lurched down her little elbow of a street, laughing. One detached from the rest, raised a wine bottle to his lips, and discovering it empty, threw it. The glass shattered against a neighbor's house. Another staggered away from the group, stopping just below Lucia's window. She leaned close, heard the sound of a zipper, and then the spatter of urine on her doorstep.

"*Madonna mia,*" she muttered under her breath. But her irritation vaporized when the third German stumbled to the door and jiggled the handle. She froze. Was the downstairs door locked? Surely, old Signor Bianchi, on the ground floor, wouldn't answer it? What would she do if they came up the stairs? She pivoted, eyeing the rolling pin on her counter. Could it crack a skull, if it had to? No, that was silly. They'd have guns. Boot steps echoed down below, and she peeked through the slit in the curtains. Three shadows lurched away in the darkness.

*Santo cielo.* They were gone for now.

The next day, Lucia stood on her stoop, ignoring the smell of urine in the afternoon heat, and studied her quiet street. Matteo stared up at the door, squinting at the spectacle of a spider building its web in the jamb. She gripped his hand as though someone might snatch him from her threshold. Her heart hammered against her breastbone as she listened to the sounds of her city. What would they find out there? What did an occupied city look like? Was it safe to go out now that the Nazis controlled Rome?

She puffed air through her lips, stepping from the stoop, but Matteo didn't budge.

"Not yet, Mamma. I want to see it catch a fly." His tone was grave, and he scrunched his nose as if something tasted bitter. "That's what spiders have to do."

"We don't have time to watch a spider, *piccolo. Andiamo.*"

She found her stride, and Matteo trotted reluctantly alongside her, glancing at shuttered doors and windows, his eyebrows knitting into a puzzled frown. For two days now, he'd asked, over and over, about the noise in the city, and Lucia didn't know how to explain.

"It's not thunder," he'd insisted when he'd woken up the first morning, staring at seams of light escaping through the shutters, worry glinting in his big brown eyes. She'd known the story of a storm would only last until he saw daylight. From the moment Matteo had learned to talk, he'd peppered Lucia with questions. One query chased another, but he sat very still during the explanations, as if turning answers over in his mind.

She'd decided to give him just the barest facts. "There are German soldiers in Rome," she'd said firmly. "And some people are trying to make them leave. We'll stay inside until it's safe."

He'd flinched at a round of distant gunshots, his shoulders hunching under his pajamas. "When will it be safe?"

"Soon. When the Allies come, they'll make the Germans leave."

Today, they'd woken up to a quiet city, yet they'd hidden in the apartment all morning. Matteo asked Lucia to read his favorite book, about animals in a zoo, at least ten times. Then they'd drawn pictures and played hide-and-go-seek and tried to nap, but it was no use. The kitchen was bare, Matteo was hungry, and they couldn't wait inside forever. Lucia walked quickly now, fingering the ration card in her pocket. Would shops even be open today? There was only one way to find out.

"Mamma . . . I don't like it." Matteo's leather shoes scuffed over the cobbles, and his sweaty grip was unusually tight on her hand.

"What don't you like?"

He studied the unnaturally still curve of their street, struggling for words. "The way my tummy hurts. It feels like . . . like it's prickly in there."

"Well, that's why we're going shopping, *piccolo*. You're just hungry. But first, we'll visit Nonna and Nonno. *Sì?*"

He nodded faintly, clearly unconvinced. It was Saturday. She and Matteo always visited her parents on Saturdays, and hopefully they could tell her what to expect next. She tried to picture them, huddling in their apartment now that war had come to Rome. Would they be terrified? Unmoored? Or would her father have already taken charge, finding an opportunity to thrive as he always had? He, at least, would know all the news.

They passed Signora Bruno's shuttered house, weighing the noise drifting from the next street. Lucia lifted her chin and forced herself into a rhythmic walk, heels clicking, Matteo at her side. If

she didn't feel confident, at least she could look like it. For Matteo.
Another turn, and they came face-to-face with their new reality.

An armored car rumbled between the buildings hemming Via
del Tritone, its machine gun swiveling toward pedestrians. Lucia
pulled Matteo tight against her waist while it passed. Were there
German men inside, laughing at the terrorized faces on the other
side of their gunsights? She humphed, mustering indignance.
Boys, more like. A foursome of infantrymen came from the other
direction, swaggering while Romans spread from their path, and
Lucia fought an irrational urge to roll her eyes even though her
heart thudded fast. They were boys, drunk on power, misbehav-
ing and disgusting.

"*Hallo, Schätzchen*," one called to her as he passed, raising his
blond eyebrows and whistling.

"*Fahr zur Hölle*," Lucia spat, unthinking. Her eyes dropped from
his stunned face to the revolver tucked in his belt. She'd told him
to go to hell, but he could actually send her there in a heartbeat if
he wanted to. She gripped Matteo's hand, hurrying him around a
corner.

"Mamma, who are they?" he whispered, his eyes wide. "They
seem . . . they seem mean."

She bent in the shadow of a building, holding her gentle boy by
the elbows. By God, she'd failed him. She should have prepared
him more. She stared into his chestnut eyes.

"Did the guns scare you?"

He nodded, head bobbing fast. His lips pursed as he tried not
to cry.

She cupped his soft cheek, wiping a tear from his freckles.
"They're scary, I know. But the guns are not for us, Matteo. The
Germans are fighting our friends, the Americans and British."

"They're here? *Gli Alleati?*" Matteo swiveled as if to look for the
Allies.

She bit her lip, thinking. Where *were* the Allies? How long would it take for them to liberate Rome? "They're not here yet," she said, forcing worry from her face. "But they will be."

"Nonna Colombo's German." Matteo's voice wobbled. "What side is she on?"

He looked like he was thinking hard. Lucia reached out to smooth his curls.

"She was born in Germany, *piccolo*, but she's lived in Rome for a long time. You're right, though. She speaks German sometimes. Let's go see Nonna Colombo, shall we? I bet she'll have a cookie for you."

She stood, gripping his hand and thinking hard herself. What side *were* her parents on, now that the tide had turned so dramatically around them? She began to walk as quickly as Matteo's little legs could travel. In about ten minutes, at least a few of her questions would be answered.

They passed shuttered shops. Nothing was open. Tram cars sat where they'd been left in the street, abandoned, and a scatter of Romans walked around with bewildered expressions. Matteo's hand gripped hers ever tighter. *"Madonna,"* Lucia breathed. They should have stayed home. The city was too unsettling. At the next intersection, Matteo followed a passing armored car with his eyes. "They're scary," he whispered.

"But we needn't worry, right? We're just a lady and a boy. Nobody will bother us."

He whispered while they crossed the street, and she had to lean in to hear.

"Maybe they want our house?"

"No, *piccolo*. If anyone tries to come into our house, I'll hit him with a rolling pin."

This made Matteo smile, just a little, despite his welling eyes. He wiped a tear, and Lucia's heart cracked. Why did he have to grow up in such a world? Why couldn't she assure him of his safety, knowing it was true? An image of Piero and Marco, as boys, floated into her mind. They marched in Mussolini's *Balilla* uniform, chins high, army boots stomping. She sickened. If only she could raise Matteo in a world where he'd never have to wear any uniform.

They were a block from her parents' house off Via Veneto when a small crowd appeared, gathering loosely in a piazza where a man rolled a poster over a stone wall. People at the front of the throng leaned forward, squinting to read, while in the back neighbors talked, some in whispers, others gesturing and shouting in disgust.

Lucia nudged Matteo off course, veering into the crowd. They worked their way toward the front, catching snippets of conversation as they passed through.

"We're subject to German Laws of War?" a woman murmured. "What does that mean?"

An old man harrumphed, "How can they prohibit private correspondence? *Bastardi.*"

"I'll trade on the black market if I have to. Laws be damned—"

"Of course you will—how else can we buy enough bread? I've six children at home . . ."

Lucia emerged at the front of the crowd and looked up to the poster, reading the rest of the ordinances. According to German Laws of War, there was also to be no disseminating enemy propaganda, no possessing weapons, no violating the curfew, no listening to enemy radio, and no harboring of fugitives. She scanned the many bullet points.

Lucia pressed a palm to her chest, shaking her head. Then she tugged on Matteo's hand, weaving him back through the crowd.

"What did it say?" he asked, skipping to keep up.

"Just a list of rules. No littering and whatnot. Come along— we're almost there, *piccolo.*"

Thank goodness he couldn't yet read.

*   *   *

LUCIA PUSHED OPEN the door to her spacious childhood home, stepped across the marble threshold, and cocked her head. Music wafted from the parlor. Were her parents trying to drown out the chaos from the streets? Or were they pretending everything was as it had always been for them—safe and prosperous? Matteo glanced up, just as perplexed.

Her mother appeared in the foyer before they could investigate. Her blond hair, streaked with gray, was expertly curled against her long neck. She wore a fashionable green dress and pinched the stem of a glass of white wine.

"Lucia. I wasn't sure if we'd see you today, what with all of this." She flapped her free hand as if indicating a problem with gnats. Her bracelet sparkled.

Lucia dropped Matteo's palm, and he trotted off, heading for her brothers' old bedroom and the toys her mother kept there, like relics.

"We nearly stayed home, in fact. It's terrifying out there. But my cupboards are bare."

Nonna Colombo turned and strode toward the parlor, ignoring the comment about empty cupboards. That's how it always was, week after week. Her mother either regarded her struggles as distasteful or insinuated that they were her fault, a direct result of marrying *that man*. She never said his name.

"You could have done something with your hair, my dear," Nonna Colombo said over her shoulder, drifting toward the sofa. Lucia followed, cupping her fingers to the curls on her neck. Was she disheveled?

"I wasn't thinking about fashion today, Mamma. I doubt anyone's noticing me with all the Germans rumbling around in the streets."

"People always notice."

Her mother lowered herself onto the sofa next to her father.

Lucia glanced away. For years, she'd tried not to let her mother's barbs stick to her, but they did. Like fishhooks.

Her father glanced up from his book, nodded as if Lucia had been there all along, and muttered, "What a day. Sounds like a madhouse out there." He tightened his square, well-shaven jaw in a grimace.

"It won't last for long," her mother said. She took a full-throated gulp of wine.

Lucia perched on the edge of a chair. "Whatever do you mean by that, Mamma?" She glanced toward the window.

"The Germans will set things right."

"The Germans? They're running rabid out there. You think they're going to improve things?"

"Well, our traitorous government certainly can't run the country. Or didn't you hear? Badoglio and King Emmanuel fled Rome in the night. They've abandoned us to hide down south among the Allies, in Brindisi. It's all over the radio."

Lucia gasped while her mother pursed her lips, swirling her wine.

"Don't worry, *Liebling*," Nonna Colombo went on, clearly enjoying Lucia's shock. "Your father was in a meeting all morning. There's going to be an effort to squash the anarchists running loose in the streets. Italy will be restored soon. You'll see."

Lucia didn't know what to say. Italy would be restored? Certainly, her mother didn't believe it would all just go back to the way it was? Not now, with Mussolini in exile, Germany occupying the country, and the Allies fighting up the coast?

Her mother set her glass aside, hinging forward just a little at the waist. She tightened her lips in a conspiratorial smile, and her wrinkles formed a box around her mouth.

"This brings me to an idea I had this morning. An inspiration, really. There are an awful lot of handsome young soldiers in the city now, Lucia."

Lucia hesitated. "You mean the Germans?"

"Of course I do. Not the grunts, mind you. But there are plenty of up-and-coming officers in Rome, for the time being."

"Mamma. From what I've seen, they're hardly gentlemen."

"Nonsense. And don't forget your roots. You're only half-Italian. Your own brother, dear Marco, fights alongside Germans on the Russian front. You must remain loyal to him, and to the greater cause."

Lucia shook her head, stunned. Was that reason enough to remain loyal to the Fascists and Germans? So if Marco died they could all feel good about it? At what point would her parents pull back, hesitating in their conviction? Lucia had been hesitating since Piero's death.

It was too difficult to say all of that, so she deflected. "Mamma, I'm still married."

Her mother rolled her eyes. "That, my dear, is a technicality at this point. Listen. You're still something to look at, especially if you make an effort. Your father tells me that the best of these German visitors will join society while they're here. You have the chance to meet a lovely, single man who might overlook the fact that you have a child. You could end up in Berlin!"

Lucia stared at her, openmouthed. Her father cleared his throat and stood, disappearing down the hall without making eye contact. But Nonna Colombo pressed on.

"This upheaval is an opportunity for you, *Liebling*, to get back on your feet."

"Mother. I don't know what world you're living in. The Germans are not visitors—they're occupiers. Mussolini is gone. The world you've been living in is gone, Mamma. The war is on our doorstep."

"For now." She dropped her voice. "There are those who think Il Duce will regain power. The Germans will rescue him for us and reinstate him. He's not dead, after all."

"Even if that happened, do you think the Allies would just disappear? Because last I heard, they aim to beat both the Germans and the Italian Fascists."

"Don't take that sarcastic tone with me." Nonna Colombo stared at Lucia for a long moment. "And be careful, or you'll sound like that man. That scoundrel."

"You mean my husband."

Lucia marveled at the words coming from her own mouth, and the tone she was, indeed, taking. She never spoke back to her mother.

"Yes, I mean your husband. In fact, you should quit being stubborn and think about him right now. Perhaps then, you'll see that this time you should take my advice. You ignored all my warnings about that man, and look how it turned out."

"I loved him, Mamma."

"You understand nothing of love." Nonna Colombo picked up her glass and drained it. "Anyhow, marry a traitor, and sooner or later he'll turn on you, too. Sooner, in your case. But not soon enough." She glanced toward the room where Matteo played.

Lucia stood. "How dare you!" She pressed her hands together to calm their shake.

"I love your child, Lucia. Don't act so affronted. But you need to face facts: your options are limited. Do you want to live alone all your life, in an apartment your parents pay for?"

Lucia tried to form a retort, but she couldn't get the words out. She knew her mother wished Matteo hadn't been conceived. But to imply as much out loud? She shook her head, speechless. It was excessive, even from her mother.

"Actually, Matteo and I have to be going," she managed. "We need groceries."

Nonna Colombo nodded, eyebrows arched. "He does look unnaturally thin."

Lucia buttoned her lips, turned, and strode to the front door. Her father emerged from the kitchen, approaching her.

"Matteo!" Lucia called. Everything in her was shaking now.

Her father cleared his throat in the foyer. "I've paid the rent on your house, *cara*. Let me know if you need anything."

He'd said the same thing at the door, every week, for six years now. And every week she answered, as she did now through her fury and shock, "Thank you, Papà."

He nodded, pressing some money into her palm, and she tried to smile in gratitude. Their routine never varied.

Nonna Colombo appeared, Matteo's shoulder under her hand, and Lucia adjusted her purse. Did she look as stunned as she felt? She made the effort to close her mouth and nod slightly, though nausea welled in her stomach. Her mother was not only willing to collaborate with the occupiers, she wanted to marry her daughter off to one of them. To wash her hands of responsibility for her daughter and grandchild, at long last. And Matteo was not much more than a bump in the path in her view.

Lucia pivoted, gripping Matteo's hand, and marched through the door.

THEY WALKED ALONG the Tiber, taking a circuitous route home to avoid the city center. Yellowing trees shaded the sidewalk, and the street here was oddly quiet. Matteo picked up a twig and ran it along the low wall lining the riverbank.

"Mamma?" he said. "Why do bees have clear wings?"

Lucia half smiled. "I don't know, *piccolo*."

"And why do they sting?"

"To protect themselves, I suppose."

"Do you know that bees can talk to one another? We just

can't hear them." Matteo gazed out at the Tiber, thinking, his
stick scrawling the wall behind him. "I'd want to be a worker
bee," he murmured, almost to himself. "I'd visit the flowers." He
quieted the way he always did when his imagination took hold.
Lucia listened to the slow rhythm of their footsteps, falling into
her own thoughts. Of all the things her mother had said that
afternoon, one hung in her mind now: *Did* she understand nothing of love? What she'd felt for Carlo had seemed somehow bigger than love. She stared at the river flowing beside them, lost in
thought.

Within a month of meeting Carlo, Lucia's whole world had
melted into his, and his into hers. They were like two currents of
wind colliding, folding into each other and blending into a powerful, beautiful storm.

"Come away with me," he whispered in her ear one night after
dinner. It was nearly spring, and all along the Tiber branches
thickened with the promise of leaves. Some had already burst into
bloom, and petals detached in the breeze, taking flight.

"For the weekend, somewhere by the sea." His breath was hot
against her cheek, his jaw rough. She nodded, pulling back so
she could stare into his clove-colored eyes. She'd go anywhere
with him.

They took the train to the coast and boarded a boat, sailing for
Elba. Carlo knew of a little inn overlooking a beach in Portoferraio where they could stay.

"Napoleon was exiled to Elba, long ago," he said on the boat
deck, grinning while the ocean air gusted around them. His tie
whipped up and over his shoulder.

"Is that so?" she murmured, moving close so he could mold his
lanky body around her. His pull was magnetic, attracting every
pulse of her heart to his warmth, his breath, the resonance of his
voice in her ear. She wanted to exile herself away with Carlo,

anywhere. If they were together, the rest of the world could simply fade into a pale backdrop.

They spent the day eating gelato and walking, hand in hand, through the streets and harbor of Portoferraio. Boats bobbed in the waves, and petals swirled over the cobblestones. They ate *frutti di mare* in a little trattoria by the beach, drinking a bottle of wine and laughing so loud the local diners paused, forks aloft, to look.

"When should I meet your parents?" she asked over dessert. He glanced down, carving off a wedge of fig cake, and leaned forward to place it on her tongue. But when she swallowed, he lifted his eyes and they were serious. His brows gathered.

"Lucia." The candle's flame moved, and his gaze darted to the tables surrounding them. "Sometimes I worry about what you'll think of my family. They're so unlike yours."

She took a sip of Chianti. She knew he was from a small town in Tuscany. She knew they'd been brought up differently. His childhood had included chickens and harvest seasons and too many cousins to keep track of, while hers was full of fine linens and party dresses. And there was an undercurrent of something more, the same current that ran in his handsome face sometimes.

They'd shared some Sunday meals with her parents, and she'd seen how he hardened when they spoke of Il Duce. When her father praised the growing alliance with Hitler, Carlo had gotten up and left the room. When he came back, his veneer was intact, and he apologized for ducking out to fetch another bottle of wine from the kitchen. But her parents had met each other's gazes, and she'd winced inside.

Now she glanced at the nearby tables, checking to make sure nobody was listening. "You know it doesn't matter to me that we were raised with different . . . values."

He looked down, running his thumb along the grid of the tablecloth. "But I haven't told you the extent of it. And if we're serious about each other, about our future, I have to."

"The extent of it?"

Carlo met her stare. "My father was active in the underground for years. He made and distributed newspapers, attended meetings . . . He declined to join the Fascist party. It made things hard for my mother. He couldn't find consistent work. We struggled." He cleared his throat. "He's no longer active, but I've attended some meetings in Rome, Lucia."

She hesitated. "Why?"

"Because I want the future to be different. I want a life that's not controlled by the state, that's not at risk from endless war. I don't want my children to be conscripted . . ."

He trailed off, and she knew he was thinking of Piero. Thanks to Mussolini's war in Ethiopia, Carlo would never meet her older brother. She glanced to the sea outside, watching it roll and ebb, forever moving. Piero had been dead more than a year already, but the ache was sharp.

"Recently, I've thought about my parents, my mother especially," he continued. "How she struggled. So I've backed down from active resistance." His eyes glittered in the candlelight. "Because there's something I want more, and I don't think I can have both."

"And what would that be?" She already knew.

He reached for her hand, pulling her to him over the narrow table, and kissed her softly. When they dropped back to their seats, he held her stare. "I'll always have my convictions, but if you want me to refrain from dangerous work, to be more conventional than my own father, I will."

She nodded, assembling what he'd said into what she knew of his life. None of it was surprising. She'd sensed rebellion in him long ago, like a torch flickering in his soul. For more than a year, she'd suspected the existence of her own torch, tucked in deep. She'd never let it ignite.

"Carlo, I'm not the same as my parents." She flushed, but he didn't react. "I've not spoken this out loud, but I have doubts. Maybe I'd like the world to be different, too. But I've already lost a brother. I don't want to lose anyone else, no matter the cause. Can you live with that?"

He held her stare. "I can live with anything, as long as I live with you."

After dinner, they walked along the beach. Behind them, the sun hung over the hump of the island, gilding the sky. The shore was soft, and Lucia kicked off her shoes, letting them dangle from her fingertips while her feet disappeared in the sand, still warm.

"I'll take you to my village," he said when they'd walked to the edge of the ocean, letting the waves roll in over their toes.

She turned, and the surf splashed her calves. "But we haven't even discussed the most important thing. Will *your* parents like *me*?"

He placed his palms on the small of her back, working his fingers into the waistline of her skirt. "Who could resist you, Lucia?" He leaned in and seemed about to kiss her, but instead he paused, his nose on hers. "You," he whispered, "you are exactly who I've been searching for."

She let his breath fill her lungs. It was like Adam and Eve, but instead of using a rib to create Lucia, God had made Carlo in the exact relief of her heart.

When they kissed, Lucia melted into him, aloft with yearning. The first stars woke in the sky, and she wanted every part of him: his body and soul, his presence alongside her always.

When they pulled apart, he held her gaze. "Marry me." His hands moved up to her cheeks, and he cupped her face. "Marry me, my beautiful girl."

Tears stung and laughter rose at the same time from within, like a spring. She lifted her hands to cup his face as well, and then he was laughing with her, and the wind encircled them, whipping her skirt around his knees and billowing his shirt as her hands found skin under it, warm and solid.

"Yes, Carlo." She laughed. "Yes, I will marry you."

"Can we visit Nonna Bruno?" Matteo asked, breaking Lucia's trance.

She glanced down at him, and the wisps of that night, with the sea and stars and Carlo, vanished. Matteo stretched to catch a leaf on the wind. It was yellow and veined with age.

She cleared her throat. "You know, that's a nice idea." She squeezed his hand, pushing Carlo from her thoughts and restoring the shelter she'd erected around her heart so long ago. "Let's do that, *piccolo*."

Soon they stood on Noemi's doorstep, the bougainvillea fluttering overhead. Lucia knocked, but nobody answered. She stepped over to the shuttered windows, trying to see in, while Matteo rapped the door continuously with his little knuckles. "Nonna Bruno might let me feed the cats," he said, glancing around hopefully for a sign of the strays.

Lucia's chest tightened as she rejoined Matteo on the stoop. Noemi was always home. Was she all right? Could she be sick? Hurt? Unable to get the door?

Just as she was about to shout through the window, the locks clinked. Noemi opened the door a crack, enough for her silvery head to poke through.

"Matteo! I thought that was your knock." She smiled, deepening her laugh lines.

Lucia looked the old woman up and down, seeking a reason for her odd behavior. Why was she guarding her apartment like a bird over a nest? "Has something happened?"

Noemi hesitated, glanced up and down the quiet street, and then opened the door wide enough for them to pass through. "Come on in, but hurry. Hurry through." She slammed the door behind them, fussing with the locks until both the dead bolt and chain had slid into place.

It was dark inside, with all the shutters closed tight, but as soon as Lucia's eyes adjusted to the gloom, she understood. The apartment was tiny, with a bedroom, a kitchen, and a parlor. And in the parlor, where they stood now, three Italian soldiers were laid out on various combinations of pillows and blankets. One had bled into the sofa, where he was still splayed with a leg raised in bandages.

"*Mamma.*" Matteo's whisper was urgent. "What happened to his leg?"

Lucia turned to the old woman, who wrung her hands in the foyer.

"What in heaven's name, Noemi?"

But before Noemi could talk, Lucia bent to Matteo, held his chin until his gaze swung from the soldiers to her, and said, "Go into the kitchen and find something to eat. Now."

Catching her tone, he pivoted without asking more questions.

"I had to take them in," Noemi whispered when Matteo vanished around the corner. "The Italian army's been disbanded. They're fugitives."

Two of the men slept, but the one on the sofa was awake and reading a book in the dim light. He'd lowered it when they came in, and Lucia saw that he was just now regaining his composure. She understood—with a broken leg, he couldn't slip through a window if he had to.

But why was Noemi endangering herself in this way? Fear flapped up into her chest. She had to convince her to move these men, and fast.

"Do you know what will happen if they catch you harboring fugitives? You'll be arrested. Maybe killed. *Dio mio.*" She pressed a palm to her forehead.

"We had nowhere to go," the soldier on the sofa offered, his accent southern. He pushed his hands into the cushions, struggling to sit. "Don't you understand, signora? The Italian soldiers who fought to keep the Germans out of Rome, just yesterday? Well, today we've all been forced into hiding. Those of us who survived, anyway." He glanced at Noemi, nodding with an air of gratitude. "Signora Bruno saw us sheltering in an alcove across the street and took us in. Soon as I can walk, I'll leave."

"This woman is old enough to be your great-grandmother. You're putting her in terrible danger." Lucia felt dizzy. The poster cited the death penalty for hiding fugitives from the Germans, did it not? Would they shoot an old woman? She looked the soldier in the eye.

"Don't you have somewhere else you could hide?"

He shook his head. "I'm from Calabria—I have nowhere else. Signora, the new law demands that Italian soldiers fight alongside the Germans, but I'll never fight for *Fascisti* again, *nel nome di Dio.* If we refuse to join up, they'll deport us to Germany. And I don't know what they'd do with men who were wounded in battle against them." He grimaced, shifting his weight. "Soon as I can walk, I'll get out of here and join the Roman Resistance. I'll repay her for hiding me by expelling those vandals."

Lucia rolled her eyes. Did all men live in fantasy worlds? "And how long before you're going to be walking, much less fighting Nazis? By the looks of it"—she stared pointedly at his leg—"you'll be here a long time." Fear tightened under her angry words. The longer he was here, the longer Noemi was endangered.

Matteo came around the corner, a heel of bread in his hand, and stared again at the soldiers. His wide eyes took in the bloodied bandage, and Lucia blew air through her lips. This was just what she needed—on top of machine guns and Germans all over town, now her five-year-old was seeing an example of what those guns could do.

She held out her hand. "*Andiamo*, Matteo. Let's get home before dark." It was hours until dark. But tonight there would be a curfew—they'd better get used to it.

"Please," Noemi said at the door. "Don't blame me, Lucia. We all must do what we can."

"What you're doing is unwise." She stared into Noemi's small, earnest eyes. What if someone like her mother lived in an adjoining apartment? Nonna Colombo would report violations to the Germans in a heartbeat. Any remaining Fascists, bitter at the loss of Mussolini, might spin their loyalty to the Nazis if given the chance.

Noemi's hand landed on Lucia's, gripping tight. "*Cara mia*, you have a good heart. You must see that they're hunting these boys. If we allow it, who will be next?"

Lidia's face flashed in Lucia's mind, but she shook her head. "We wouldn't allow them to persecute Jews, not in Rome—"

"We already did."

Lucia couldn't look away from Noemi's unflinching stare. Lidia's religion had meant nothing to her growing up. The girls ran together, played together, dreamed together—what did it matter that Lidia went to temple and Lucia to Mass? Jews served in the Fascist government; they'd been welcomed from the start. Lidia's family could trace their roots in Rome for generations, just like Lucia's father could. But that all changed in 1938. Early that year, Lidia fell in love with a Jewish boy from the physics department. They married, and a month later Mussolini copied Hitler and enacted racial laws in Italy. Lidia and her new husband had to drop out of university, Lidia had a baby, and their dreams of careers in science fell away. Lucia and Lidia's friendship fell away soon after. Lucia always told herself that it was because they were busy, that it was typical in this season of life, but in her heart, she'd grieved the gulf between them.

"We were indifferent," Noemi said, pulling Lucia's mind back into the dim foyer.

"I wasn't indifferent about the racial laws. I was furious. And they were wildly unpopular—"

"But nobody stopped it from happening, *cara mia*. And that's because we were indifferent—all of us. Anger alone isn't enough. We have to act."

Lucia sighed, frowning. "I need to go home and think. I'll see if I can do something to help you. But for God's sake, don't give yourself away. Stick to your normal routines. Go outside and sweep the stoop, feed the cats, smile at passersby as if nothing was going on inside this house."

Noemi reached for her hand and gripped it in both of her own small palms, and Lucia leaned in to kiss her cheeks. She smelled like old people do, of soap and cotton and tea.

When Lucia straightened, she couldn't keep the tears from her voice. What she wanted to say was that she loved Noemi, and needed her. She needed her warmth and wisdom and steadfast support—something she'd never found in her own mother. She hated to see her in danger.

"You should let other people take a stand," she whispered instead. "Stronger people."

"That's where you're wrong." Noemi squeezed Lucia's hand. The wrinkles fell from her face, re-forming as she grew solemn. "We can all be strong. And Lucia. *Cara*. We must."

# EIGHT

ଏଏ

## Francesca

*Late September 1943*

FRANCESCA CHECKED THE address and rapped on the door. In her other hand, she held the handlebar of her bicycle, with its special left pedal that Giacomo had rigged with a strap to secure her weak foot. With quite a bit of difficulty, she'd hoisted the bicycle up the short flight of steps after riding across town. It left her breathless, but she wasn't a strong walker—she couldn't risk having it stolen. And with Giacomo gone, she had no choice but to carry it upstairs herself.

He'd been gone for more than a week. She'd spent entire days pacing the apartment, barely sleeping. Hunger twisted her stomach while she stared through the window's shutter slats. She went over everything she could think of—all the questions, all the possibilities. Should she quit her job and return home to her mother? Did she even have a job anymore? The bookshop, like most shops, had been shuttered since the Germans rolled in. But if she left, would she ever find Giacomo? Was he in prison, or had they shipped him elsewhere? She remembered how the Nazi hesitated when Giacomo said, *"Medico."* Perhaps they had need of his skills?

Every time Germans appeared in the street beyond her shutter slats, her heart started to pound, but it was anger that rose in her

throat. Italy had learned on Monday that the Germans had res-
cued Mussolini. German-controlled newspapers declared Il Duce
as leader of Italy again, but anyone could see he was only Hitler's
puppet now. It infuriated her. And it was this fury that made her
remember Giacomo's remark about Lino Moretti.

*I ran into Lino Moretti today,* he'd said that night. She closed her
eyes to recall the conversation. Lino had wanted to reel Giacomo
into some kind of group, something political. She pulled up an
image of Lino as a young man. She could see his face, not because
she'd known him well, but because of one particular Sunday back
home, one she'd tried to forget.

She was fourteen that day, and she and Giacomo were coming
out of Pienza's cathedral after Mass. Sunlight spilled over the piazza outside, gilding the heads and shoulders of people pausing to
chat before walking home. A pair of steps flanked the cathedral's
facade, and a huddle of teenage boys sat on them, whispering and
laughing raucously as their eyes raked the crowd. Francesca stiffened at the sight of them, preparing to be noticed. The boys only
threw words at her, but they bruised, nonetheless.

"C'mon," Giacomo said, eyes troubled behind his glasses. He
was gangly as a colt, with messy hair and a gentle smile. He
reached to steady her as she took a step down the two stairs flanking the church, but it wasn't enough. Her cane slipped off the step's
edge, her clunky shoe skidded, and her leg buckled. Francesca fell
headlong, hitting the ground with a force that rattled her teeth.
Laughter volleyed from the boys, along with taunts she couldn't
make out over her pounding heart and smarting eyes. Adults were
already marching across the square; they'd only make it worse.
Francesca snatched her cane, and Giacomo hoisted her up, glancing over his shoulder.

"Go to hell!" he shouted at the boys, his contemporaries, his
voice cracking. The laughter expanded. And then it shut off, sud-

denly, like a spigot. Someone was striding past the boys, commanding silence, long legs reaching Francesca before the arrival of the dreaded adults.

"You all right?" He swung to a stop before them, and the concerned grown-ups slowed their approach, as if they knew Lino could handle the disturbance better than anyone. "Ignore those *idioti*," he said, smiling affably, and Francesca forgot her humiliation for one dazzling second. The young man was the Moretti boy, who'd gone off to university the year before. He wore a pin-striped jacket and gleaming shoes, like a man who'd stepped in from another world.

"We always ignore them." Giacomo glanced toward the steps, Francesca's palm in his grip, ready to defend her. "Those *bastardi*"— he checked Lino's reaction to his bold language, stifling a self-conscious smile—"they aren't worth our time."

"They're not. Bullies are cowards, as a rule." Lino looked between them, nodding decisively. "You're good kids. I'll have a word with those *bastardi* before I leave town."

Francesca had swallowed at the memory, steeling herself. *Lino would help her.* She'd hurried to Giacomo's books and papers, shuffling through them. If anyone had connections, it would be Lino. Picking up a scrap of paper, she'd squinted, tossing it. No. Didn't Giacomo say Lino had written down his address? Pain gripped her throat as she flipped through page after page of Giacomo's handwriting, the messy scrawl of notes on pathology and anatomy. And then there it was—a paper with an address on it, written by a different hand.

And now, an hour later, she stood in front of that address.

The door cracked open, and a middle-aged man stared through the gap.

"I'm here to see Lino," Francesca said.

"Who?"

She held up the address, written in Lino's own hand, and the door swung wider. The man gestured her inside, glanced around the stairwell, and closed it quietly after she wheeled her bicycle into the foyer.

"*Gesù Cristo!* Is he writing his address down and passing it out?" The man shook his head, his eyebrows screwed low. "Give that to me, signorina. I'm going to burn it."

The man shuffled off, paper pinched in his fingers, and Francesca looked beyond him. The foyer split in two, opening into a tiny kitchen on one side and a dining area on the other. In the kitchen, a tall man, with brown eyes and tufted hair, looked up.

"Welcome," he said cautiously, staring at her for an awkward moment, a steaming mug cupped in one hand. He glanced toward the front door, as if listening for spies, speaking quietly. "Did I hear you say you're looking for Lino? You'll have to excuse my manners, but are we acquainted?"

She cleared her throat. Of course he didn't remember her. "I grew up in Pienza. My"—she cleared her throat again—"my husband is Giacomo Lombardi. You told him to come here."

He nodded, visibly relaxing. "Ah. I remember." He laughed a little, setting down his cup. "Nobody outside of Pienza calls me Lino, and we're all a little tense at the moment. Forgive me for my confusion."

"Oh, I'm sorry—"

He waved a hand agreeably. "It's quite all right. My family called me Carlino when I was little, which became Lino to the rest of Pienza. But when I came to Rome, I reclaimed my given name. Call me Carlo, if you would."

She nodded, replacing his nickname with his grown-up name. Carlo. Carlo Moretti.

"Come and sit down, please." He gestured toward the table. "Would you care for a cup of coffee?"

She shook her head stiffly, and he hesitated, considering her. "And where is Giacomo?"

She had to inhale, filling her lungs for strength. "The Germans took him last week. We were at Porta San Paolo when they broke through."

"*Dio mio.*" Carlo set his cup down and strode over. He picked Francesca's hands up in both of his, squeezing. "I'm sorry to hear it."

She nodded, struggling to respond around the pain in her throat. "Giacomo suspected you to be in the underground. I thought you might have connections. Can you find him?"

Carlo shook his head. "It's unlikely that anyone could find him."

She pulled her hands from his and crossed her arms over her chest, as if she could hold back the anger and fear burning within. "I won't accept that. As long as he's alive, there must be something I can do. Surely, I can find out where they're keeping prisoners."

Carlo frowned. "The trouble isn't figuring out where they're stashing prisoners; it's finding a specific prisoner. The Nazis have our people all over—in prisons and barracks and work gangs. And they're sending Italians to their front lines. But I'll ask around, all right?" He gestured to the kitchen table. "Why don't you sit down? We can talk this through a bit."

She followed him to the table and folded into a chair facing him. It felt good to sit. When she met Carlo's gaze, he was studying her, as if fully seeing her for the first time. Then his eyes widened, and he dropped his palms to the table.

"Wait—I know you. You're Giuseppe Gallo's daughter."

They held each other's stares, mutually surprised.

"You knew my father?"

Carlo slapped the table. "Of course! I do remember you. I remember when you got sick. The whole town talked about it. The rest of our parents lived in terror of us catching it. I was locked inside for a week."

She deflated. It was just the polio he remembered. Did he remember her tumble in the piazza? She pressed her thumbs to the corners of her eyes. They leaked constantly now, as if her interior had sprung holes.

"It's what I was known for. Contagion, leg braces. Pity." Some of the old women in town used to cross themselves, warding off misfortune, when Francesca came hobbling down the street in her braces. It was who she'd been most of her life: the polio survivor.

But Carlo was shaking his head. He leaned forward.

"That's not all I remember. When your father was arrested by the Blackshirts? My family left town after that. We went to my uncle's, by Lake Como, for the entire summer. They used the excuse of mountain air, but it was actually because my father was in the same group as yours."

Francesca dropped her hands from her temples. "He was an anti-Fascist?"

Carlo nodded.

"Did he come to our house for meetings, with those men from Siena?"

"Sì." Carlo's eyes widened as if they were kids, discovering their parents' secrets. "They created underground newspapers together. For years."

"Years?" She shook her head, in awe. "I've tried to piece all of that together since he was taken, but my mamma wouldn't tell me anything. My nonna moved into the house after he left, and they were both convinced that the less I knew, the better."

"Your father was a brave man, Francesca Gallo." He nodded, enthused. "My father still talks about him after a few swigs of grappa. After your babbo was exiled, mine dropped out of the group. He was afraid he might be caught, too. He often mentioned your mamma. And I remember how everyone dropped things by your place after we heard that your babbo died in *confino*. To help."

Her mouth fell open. She'd always wondered why a farmer might stop by with a side of meat, or a box of apples, or why new clothes appeared as she grew. Was it because she was a cripple? Fatherless? Or was it because her father was something of an underground hero?

The new information puzzled into the gaps in her story, those holes her mother would never fill. She shook her head, speechless, but a spark of pride flared in her chest.

"Your Giacomo," Carlo said, and everything in Francesca caved inward again.

He rubbed his jaw, giving her a moment before continuing. "I'm sorry to hear it. I really am. You were married?"

She hesitated and then shook her head, lowering her gaze to the table. "Just engaged, actually."

Carlo waved her confession away, clearly intent on something else. "Listen. I probably don't need to ask how you feel about the Nazis. It's safe to assume—"

"I hate them." She met his stare. The words burned on her tongue.

"I imagine so. Francesca, we're working in the spirit of your father. We're going to fight back until they're gone. Until Rome and all of Italy is free. And we need more people." He leaned forward. "Will you join us?"

She took a deep breath, and her thoughts spun. She saw her father's green eyes shining with fear as he was taken away. She saw Giacomo ducking into an armored car, a rifle at his back. And she saw herself, immobile under a quilt, sobbing over her lost freedom while stars glittered outside of her window.

But really, her freedom was the one thing she hadn't lost—not yet. The fear and grief surrounding her heart broke like an eggshell.

She cleared her throat. "Tell me what you want me to do."

Carlo half smiled. "You're your father's child." His brown eyes gained intensity, like a cat focusing on movement. "What's your schedule like? Do you have a job?"

"I work in a bookshop. But it's been closed since the Germans came—I'm not sure if I have a job anymore, honestly."

"That's happening all over Rome. Will you be all right if you lose your income?"

"For a bit." Wasn't that everyone's situation now? Italians could no longer peer far into the future. Instead, they had to live their lives in uncertainty, bit by bit.

"Tell me this: How are you on that bicycle? Are you able to get around pretty well?"

She shrugged. What was he getting at?

"You'd make a perfect *staffetta*, if . . ." He hesitated.

A *staffetta*? She pictured it, herself as a courier, and the idea immediately hardened. "If I can ride far—is that what you'd like to ask? My difficulty is in my left leg, but I can compensate with my right. I use a cane when I have to walk much. But with a bicycle? I can go anywhere." She held his stare, withholding what he didn't need to know. She could go anywhere, but not without pain and exhaustion.

"*Brava*. You'll be perfect, Francesca. The Nazis will never suspect someone like you."

She straightened, stung, but then she understood. He was right: All her life, she'd moved like a shadow in the company of men. She was small and quiet, with a visible disability, easily dismissed by imperceptive men. What seemed like vulnerability could actually be her strength.

But who was she going to be working with, exactly? It was her turn to study Carlo.

"Does your organization have a name?"

His eyes flashed as he glanced around the room, though there was nobody to overhear. Francesca recognized his wariness. She'd watched her father hush conversations all her life, until the Fascists quieted him for good.

"We're the CLN." He lowered his voice. "The National Liberation Committee. It's a new conglomerate of all the anti-Fascist groups. Our aim is to work together until the Germans are expelled, and to resist Fascism thereafter."

"So, the CLN includes the socialists, the communists—"

He interrupted. "Sì. And the Christian Democrats, the Action Party, the Labour Democratic Party, the Italian Liberal Party— we're all united."

"And in terms of the Allies?"

"Our aim is to work with them. To help them win this war."

She nodded, piecing this new world together in her mind. "When can I start?"

Carlo grinned. "Tomorrow." He stood, turning toward the kitchen and calling over his shoulder, "If you'll stay for a cup of coffee—terrible coffee, I admit—I'll explain everything you need to know. *Va bene?*"

A flame grew in her soul, rising amid the fear and grief that had rained through her all week. Carlo returned with a full cup, sliding it into her waiting palms.

"From now on, you'll call me Gianluca Falco. And you'll need to choose a nom de guerre for yourself. The Nazis are already hunting us, *capisci?*" He paused, holding her gaze with his intent stare. "You understand the danger, don't you? From the moment you start, you'll be risking your life."

Her thoughts curved inward. She saw the Blackshirts when

they came for her father, the fever in their faces. They'd been
hungry to take him. They were following orders from someone
higher in the Fascist hierarchy; they didn't have reason to hate her
father. But they yearned to hurt him, nonetheless.

"I understand." She warmed her fingers on her steaming cup,
finding her voice. "You can call me L'Allodola."

THE NEXT MORNING, Francesca wheeled her bicycle through the
courtyard of Carlo's building, past the mailboxes, her heart pounding with each step. As she approached the door to the street, it
swung open. A man and a teenage boy strode inside. Seeing Francesca, limping along with her bicycle and the oversize laundry
basket fastened to the front of its handlebars, they stepped aside
and held the door. The boy, dark haired and pimple faced, looked
her over. She passed, and the father's gaze fell on the basket, with
its neatly folded linens. He had heavy eyebrows and wary eyes. A
rivulet of sweat tickled her lower back. The door swung shut behind her, and she exhaled, lifting her weak leg over the bicycle's
seat. She gave it a push with her strong leg, and she was off.

The air cooled her lungs, and she pumped faster until the rattle
of cobblestones smoothed beneath her tires, taking on a settling
rhythm. As long as she was moving, she'd be all right. Apartment
blocks slid by as she whirred down a hill, threading between a
sidewalk and a bus.

She thought through Carlo's instructions, delivered an hour ago.

"The contents of this basket are needed in Trastevere. Memorize this address." He'd handed her a slip of paper, tearing it up
after she'd read it. "This load'll be heavy on your handlebars, but
you can manage, sì?"

They were in his bedroom, and he'd bent over, pulling an array
of guns and grenades from under the bed and loading them into

the deep laundry basket. She'd watched, stunned. Carlo whistled softly while he nestled weapons against the wicker, tucking linens around them as one would settle a baby. Then he layered a thick pile of sheets over the stash. The crowning bedsheet was clean, but stained with something that looked like blood.

"For security. Nazis are terrified of contagion." He stood to his full height and smiled. "Bring back the linens, if you would. We'll use them again. In fact, from now on when you visit here, it'll be under the guise of a laundress."

Francesca nodded, but she couldn't locate her voice. She stared at the basket on the floor, pressing a hand over her mouth as if working on a difficult equation. Did this all add up? Could she transport such a basket? What would she do if someone investigated her cargo?

An idea dropped into her mind, immediately calcifying. "I'd like a gun of my own."

Carlo's face fell to seriousness. He rubbed a hand over his stubbled jaw, shaking his head. "We're not giving weapons to women."

She crossed her arms. "That's unreasonable. Are you arming your men?" She tipped her head toward the laundry basket, which was clearly intended to arm a whole group of them. He hesitated, glancing toward the kitchen, which, today, was full of men.

"If I'm going to be a partisan, just like all those boys at your table, I want a gun of my own. I won't fire it unless I have to."

"I'm not worried about your restraint." He lowered his voice. "Do you even know how to use one?"

A memory rose: her father from years before. They were outside in a wild field, and a beam of sunshine broke behind his head. His eyes shone as he regarded her, not yet a teenager, kneeling in the grass. She held a rifle. Somewhere in the field, six quail lay dead, brought down for their supper. Her father had laughed out loud.

She cleared her throat and matched Carlo's gaze. "My father taught me to hunt when I was little. I'm a reliable shot."

He nodded, glancing again at the door, and motioned for her to open her coat. From his own waistband, he withdrew a Beretta. He held it as if testing its weight, then placed it in her hand.

"*Grazie*," she murmured, tucking it inside an interior pocket.

Moments later, Carlo had wheeled the bicycle through the apartment, murmuring instructions. "If anyone stops you, play your role. The gun is only a last resort, *sì*? If they catch you, they'll shoot you or hang you or torture you for information. So, don't get caught."

He carried the bicycle downstairs, glancing around to make sure the courtyard was clear. Then he'd placed his hands on her slim shoulders and met her unwavering stare.

"*In bocca al lupo*, my friend. Remember: you're stronger than they'd ever guess."

Now she pumped up a hill, breathing the smell of cypress warming in the September sun. The Trastevere neighborhood was fifteen minutes away, and she had to cross through the center of Rome to reach it. The streets were quieter than usual, but every passing vehicle carried Germans. They'd begun stealing cars and bicycles whenever one struck their fancy, so now Romans went on foot, tram, or bus.

She tightened her grip on her handlebars, and the laundry basket rattled along over the bicycle tire. She imagined the grenades in there, bumping amid the linens. Could one of them get rattled a bit too hard and blow up? Did that ever happen? She lifted her eyes back to the street and puffed air through her tight lips. No, of course not. Wasn't there a pin that had to be pulled? She glanced over her shoulder, slowing for a bus before veering across the street. It would be best to keep her mind off the basket and focus on riding. This was no time to crash.

Francesca swooped onto a narrow street, barely more than an alley, slowing so her tires bumped over the cobbles and rattled her teeth. She wound down the alley and turned onto another, threading her way through the tight streets that made up the Jewish ghetto. An old woman, taking down her laundry, waved as Francesca passed. She wove the bicycle through a piazza, passing mothers encircled by children, old men chatting in the autumn sunshine, and gaggles of boys kicking balls and whooping. Another turn, and the tree-lined avenue flanking the Tiber spread before her.

She looked at the river. The Fatebenefratelli Hospital straddled its island in the water, a stone's throw from the Jewish ghetto. An image of Giacomo rose in her mind: his head bent over a row of patients in the sun, strong hands binding a leg, sweat speckling his glasses, only hours before he vanished. She pedaled faster, passing the synagogue, veering through the canopy of riverside trees, leaving the Fatebenefratelli Hospital behind. What would Giacomo say if he could see her now?

The Ponte Sisto was a narrow pedestrian bridge crossing to the Trastevere neighborhood. Francesca slowed as she approached it, studying the sprinkle of people moving along the cobbled span. None were German. She exhaled and swung her leg over the saddle of the bicycle, gripped the handlebars, and started walking across the ancient stone arcing over the green water.

"*Ciao*," a voice called from behind her, the accent heavy. Francesca glanced over her shoulder as a young German in a Wehrmacht uniform trotted onto the bridge, leaving a trio of other soldiers who'd materialized across the street. She stiffened as one of them lit a cigarette, staring at her with interest. Her pulse accelerated, like a flood in her chest, and the young German fell into step beside her.

"*Ciao, signorina*," he said again. "Let me take the bicycle across for you, *ja?*" He grinned under his fringe of dark hair. His eyes were the color of stone.

Did he suspect her? She forced herself not to glance at the basket of weapons, which suddenly seemed so obvious under the linens. She smiled up at him, trying to harness her spinning thoughts. What did he want? Would he inspect her incriminating cargo? He motioned for the handlebars, and she shook her head with force, swallowing a surge of panic.

"You wash linens for work?" he ventured, filling her silence with choppy Italian. He eyed the basket, boots clicking with each step. She subdued the flood of fear. *She was nothing but a laundress.* She had nothing to hide. She glanced at the water shifting in the sunshine as it flowed and folded under the bridge, and she marshaled her composure.

"Let me take it for you," he persisted. "I'm pleased to give you a hand."

"You're too kind," she managed. She exaggerated her limp and tightened her grip on the handlebars to keep her fingers from shaking. She sensed the weight of the gun against her ribs. If it were to escalate, could she pull the trigger? If she did, she'd be shot by his friends in the same breath. But at least she'd take one of them with her.

"My friends will laugh at me if you refuse," the German said, trying another tactic.

What did he want? She cleared her tight throat. "I need the bicycle for support, you see."

She dragged her weak foot even more, and he glanced down as if noticing for the first time. Maybe he'd fall back now. Weren't the Nazis intolerant of infirmity?

But he didn't. If anything, his expression brightened. "Polio? My aunt had polio as a child. Much the same, but she died a while back. Do you have pain?"

She nodded, bewildered. But they were more than halfway across the bridge. Perhaps it was safest to chat with him, putting him at ease. "You speak Italian," she managed.

He grinned. "Not well. But I love Italy. I'm so happy to be stationed in Rome."

She could think of no response to that. The bicycle bumped over the final stretch of bridge, and she yearned to climb onto it, to disappear.

"Care to visit longer?" His eyebrows shot up. "Perhaps you enjoy the cinema?"

They stepped from the bridge to the street, and she faced him. "I'm very sorry, but I'm already late. My client expected me some time ago."

The German nodded, glancing once more at the basket on the handlebars, and he hesitated, noticing the stain. "That one doesn't look very clean. Your client won't be angry with you?" He bent close to examine the sheet, touching it with his pale fingers. "Looks like blood."

Francesca's heart beat so hard she was sure he could hear it. But she forced a shake of the head, and he stepped back, resigned.

"Very well. Thank you for visiting with me." He grinned. "You see, we are not all monsters."

"I can see that." She met his gaze and nodded, then hoisted her leg over the bicycle. As she began to pedal, bumping away from him and into the maze of Trastevere, she smiled in response to his final words.

Not a monster, perhaps. But he'd shoot her in a second if he knew what was in her basket.

# NINE

༺

## Lucia

*Late September 1943*

LUCIA AND MATTEO left the apartment, canvas shopping bag in hand, to track down food for the weekend. She planned to seek flour through the black market, and already her stomach boiled with nerves. It was unwise to take the risk, to endanger her little son in this way. But when she glanced at him trudging at her side, so thin the wind blew through him, she gritted her teeth.

Some rules had to be broken.

*"Piccolo,"* she ventured, squeezing his hand, "shall we stop by Niccolo's house after errands and invite him to play?"

Matteo's face brightened at the thought of his little friend. "Can he bring his cars? I want to play cars. And zoo."

She nodded and concealed the sorrow spurred by his hopeful smile. If only she could give him a normal childhood, filled with playmates and joy instead of uncertainty, hunger, and fear.

They rounded the corner, heading toward Signora Bruno's house, and Lucia glanced again at Matteo, taking in the rise and fall of his little legs. But then he planted both feet. Before she could question him, he patted her arm and raised his other hand to point.

She followed his finger to Noemi's house. Lucia took one look and gasped. Without thinking, she scooped Matteo up and hugged him to her chest, holding him the way she had when he was a toddler. She pressed his head to her shoulder.

The front door was flung wide. Beyond the pink bougainvillea a black truck was parked, still idling, its tailgate open. Shouting drifted from the apartment into the street. Lucia adjusted Matteo's weight in her arms. Should she send him home and try to intervene? Something crashed in the house, and sickness rose in her throat. Would the Nazis arrest such an old woman? Perhaps she could convince them that Noemi was senile. Her German was perfect. She'd use it, and her family connections, to stop this. She set Matteo down, bending to stare into his troubled eyes. "I want you to run home—here's the key. Wait for me inside. If I'm not back soon, you can ask Signor Bianchi for help."

"What are you going to do, Mamma?" He blinked, his lower lip trembling, and she cupped his cheek.

"I'm going to help Nonna Bruno. Now go—run home."

Matteo turned and scurried up the cobblestones as instructed, his knees rising over his leather shoes until he vanished around the corner. Lucia glanced up and down the narrow street. It was empty, quiet, everyone's shutters drawn tight. She inhaled the truck's exhaust and raised her chin, setting off. The shouting amplified as she neared Noemi's front door.

She was nearly there when two Germans in uniform trudged out, the soldier with the broken leg slung between them. The soldier was screaming, "We made her keep us. She didn't want to—" when the Nazi at his head cuffed him so hard he lost consciousness, his skull flopping on his neck. They dragged him past Lucia, his limp legs bumping on the cobbles, and threw him in the truck.

Fear spun in her chest, but she overcame it enough to speak. "Excuse me," she said in clear German.

Two of the Nazis ignored her, striding back into the house as if she hadn't spoken. But the one who seemed to be in charge, a young man with dark hair and a pale complexion, paused. "You speak German?"

"My mother descends from Bavaria." She spoke quickly, her gaze darting to two blond Nazis coming through the door again, the remaining pair of Italian soldiers limping before them at gunpoint. "The woman who lives here is my friend. Can you tell me what's happening?"

The Nazi smirked. "She may be your friend, but she's also a traitor. Go home."

Everything in Lucia tightened. "What are you going to do to her?"

He rolled his eyes. "Go home."

As he said it, Noemi came hobbling from the house on her own, an apron still knotted around her waist. She squinted in the bright light. The bougainvillea fluttered over her silvery hair, and she glanced around, her expression more confused than frightened. "Lucia? *Cara mia*, please don't worry. I will talk to them . . ." The dark-haired Nazi took her by the elbow, jerking hard, and Noemi stumbled.

"No," Lucia barked. She grabbed Noemi's wrist, and the two blond Nazis, still moving the Italians toward the truck, turned.

"My father's a Fascist official. We're loyal—he'll vouch for Signora Bruno. She's old—"

All pretense of courtesy dropped from the head Nazi's face. "Get out of here, woman!" He pointed up the street, shouting, "If you interfere further, I'll arrest you, too." His black eyes brightened.

Lucia stepped closer, fury and fear driving her forward. "You will *not* take this woman. Shame on you—"

A scuffle at the truck halted her words. One of the Italians broke loose, while his captor's eyes were on Lucia. He ran up the street with his hand on his waist. All three Nazis raised their weapons. Two bullets hit his back, and he lurched forward, his spine blooming red. He was still falling when the remaining prisoner burst up, grabbing for a raised gun and knocking it from the Nazi's grip. The weapon clattered to the ground, and the prisoner snatched it.

Before Lucia understood what was happening, more gunfire cracked the street wide open. She clutched Noemi and scrambled sideways, pulling the old woman against the building and shrinking under the sweep of bougainvillea. The final Italian soldier's head jerked, and he fell to the pavement, his blood and brains spreading under a haze of gun smoke. The three Germans straightened from defensive postures, unhurt.

*"Gottverdammt!"* The dark-haired Nazi spun in the littered street, irate, and the others holstered their guns. He barked commands at his soldiers, his shouts echoing around the silent buildings. The blond Germans hurried away to collect the first body.

Lucia wrapped her arm around Noemi's aproned waist, hoisting her up while the head Nazi strode toward them.

"Go inside and lock the door," she whispered, voice shaking. Noemi found her stare and nodded, dazed, still clutching Lucia's hand.

*"Cara mia,* I'm so sorry—" The old woman's voice caught in a sob as the young Nazi snapped to a halt before them. He looked from Noemi to Lucia, the anger in his eyes hardening. Then he raised his gun. Before Lucia had time to push Noemi through her front door, he pulled the trigger.

The old woman crumpled on her threshold, a hole in her head, and the world shattered like glass in an explosion. Lucia heard herself screaming. Blood spurted from Noemi's feathery scalp as she rolled off the stoop, her soft body settling on the cobblestones, her bright eyes open, forever startled.

Lucia fell on Noemi, shrieking, her own wail ripping through her mind like an air-raid siren. Was Noemi dead? She couldn't be dead. *No.* How could she go on without Noemi? A figure stopped behind her, she wheeled in her crouch, and fear poured over her like cold water. A name bounded into her galloping thoughts: *Matteo.* She couldn't let them shoot her.

The Nazi smirked, gun raised, his black eyes nailed to her.

"I have a son," she stammered.

"Do you?"

She stared up the black barrel of the gun, unable to breathe. "He has nobody else to take care of him. Please—"

The Nazi leaned forward, pressing the cold muzzle of the gun to her forehead, and she pinned her eyes shut. She felt the circle of metal push on her skull, heard the sweep of her breath, and held an image of Matteo's face in her mind.

A whisper broke into her panic. *"Bang."*

The metal fell away from her forehead, and she opened her eyes, heart in her throat, dizzy with fear. The Nazi laughed.

"Go tell your father, the *Fascist official*, that Italians had better start following the rules." His eyes sharpened, as if he was memorizing her face. "We're in charge now."

He turned on his heel, striding back toward the truck. "Throw all the bodies in the back," he shouted at his soldiers, and they heaved the final Italian soldier up and over the tailgate.

When they came for Noemi, Lucia couldn't move. She knelt over her old friend's body, clutching her arthritic hands, imagining the bullet that had nearly exploded in her own skull. *Matteo would have been left alone. An orphan.* The blond Nazis reached down, one at Noemi's feet and the other hooking her armpits, and hoisted her up. The limp hands wrenched away from Lucia's grip. She staggered to her feet, sobbing.

The Nazis acted as if she were no longer there in the street. They threw Noemi over the tailgate and without ceremony climbed into the cab of the truck.

The engine rumbled, and the wheels began to turn. They rolled through two pools of blood as the truck gained momentum, bouncing up the cobbles and vanishing around a corner.

Lucia stood alone under the bougainvillea, weeping, her heart torn open.

# TEN

## ɷɷ

## Francesca

*Late September 1943*

FRANCESCA SLOWED HER bicycle in front of a long building, peering through barred windows. She was due at Carlo's in an hour. But first, she had to search for Giacomo.

The building, once infantry barracks, was now said to house forced laborers. The Germans were collecting men off the streets. Earlier that week they'd cordoned off whole neighborhoods outside of Rome, seeking able-bodied men to, presumably, build fortifications along German lines. Francesca tamped down a bloom of anger. The Nazis took whatever they wanted—food, men, cities, countries—without a thought. Carlo had learned that the laborers were held in the barracks before shipping off. Could Giacomo be in there, too?

She rolled to a stop on the unguarded back side of the building, finding a window cracked open. "Hello!" she called, studying the gap in the bars. "Is anyone in there?"

A face appeared in the window. "*Sì*, many of us." A man craned his head to see her, thin and in need of a shave. "We've been locked up since Tuesday. I did nothing wrong—they snatched me on my way to work. Will you help me?"

"*Certo*. What do you need?"

"Please send word to my wife that I'm all right. We think we're going to the Eastern Front, to German lines, but don't know for sure. They could also send us south. Will you tell her?"

Francesca nodded, and the man called out a name and an address. She committed it to memory, but before his face disappeared, she called, "Wait! Will you check among the men in there for my husband? His name is Giacomo Lombardi."

"*Sì, aspetta*," the man called back, and his face vanished from the windowpane.

Francesca waited for several minutes, hope and fear dueling in her chest. Was everyone in the barracks from the neighborhood sweep, or could Giacomo be there, too? Her knuckles whitened on her handlebars. An image came to her, and she swallowed a surge of grief: Giacomo, propped on an elbow in bed, sunbrowned arms against white sheets. His lopsided grin and gentle eyes, his hand, rough and warm, gliding down the curve of her back—

"I'm sorry, miss," the man called through the window, interrupting her memories. "There's nobody here by that name. Perhaps he's already been sent off?"

She nodded, but her heart dropped as if through a slit in the pavement. Her yearning—to wrap her arms around Giacomo and sink into his chest—was overpowering.

Francesca cleared her throat, gathering strength. "*Grazie, signore.* I'll send word to your wife."

She pedaled away, shaping her sorrow into a plan. She would come to this window every week, just in case Giacomo somehow ended up behind it. She would ask Carlo if there were other barracks or prisons holding conscripted men. And she would keep searching, no matter how long it took.

"THE GERMANS ARE using these roads to transport supplies," Carlo said to a circle of gathered men and Francesca, the only woman. He pointed to a map, ticking off several roads stretching from the city into the outskirts and, eventually, southern Italy. "They're moving convoys at night, to avoid Allied bombers," he continued, glancing up to catch everyone's eyes. "That's where we come in. We're going to make it impossible to move supplies through Rome, or anywhere near it. We'll push the convoys into the countryside, where the Allies can bomb them. A poorly supplied army fights poorly—we can make a big impact on the front."

"How will we do it, exactly?" Tommaso asked, leaning forward to study the map, elbows on knees. Francesca had been mildly surprised to find Tommaso when she walked into Carlo's apartment; the last time she'd seen him at been at the Fatebenefratelli Hospital with Giacomo, which seemed like a lifetime ago. But of course he was here. He was a natural rebel.

Carlo held up a small tangle of iron, grinning. He passed it around, and it traveled through a half-dozen hands before landing with Francesca. It was a pair of long, thick nails, bent in the center and welded together so all the points stuck out. She handed it back to Carlo, and he tossed it across the floor. It landed, points up.

"No matter how they're thrown, they land perfectly to puncture a tire." He tipped his head to Francesca. "L'Allodola will pick up a basketful and transport them to our target. The Germans have been moving supplies outside of Trastevere, as if the roads were theirs. She's our best chance at getting the nails across the city—the Germans have lost a few convoys south of us, so they're searching people for nails. Fortunately, L'Allodola looks innocuous."

Tommaso glanced up, his hickory-colored hair falling over his forehead. "And when the convoy's stopped, we'll attack it. *Sì?*"

"We'll jump out of hiding and toss grenades and *spezzone* bombs into as many trucks as we can. Our goal is to take out supplies: ammunition, weapons, fuel . . ."

"But won't they shoot at us?" a young partisan asked, glancing around with owlish eyes.

Carlo nodded. "A group working on the north end of the city lost two partisans last week during a similar ambush. Don't participate in sabotage unless you're prepared for the worst, understood? This is battle. You could lose your life."

"Or you could be captured." Tommaso was grave. "Capture means torture, and if you crack during torture, every one of us is endangered." He turned to the boy. "Make sure you're not a weak link. We can always assign you a different role."

Francesca cleared her voice, glancing around the group of pensive men. "You'll need someone to cover you during the ambush. I could do that. If there's a way to watch the road from above . . ."

"There's an embankment," Carlo said. "A place where the road narrows downhill—"

"We're not going to rely on a girl! Really?" An unshaven, wide-shouldered man stared at Francesca, faltering. "To cover us? We need a trained man. A sharpshooter."

"*I'm* a sharpshooter," Francesca said. "I can shoot twice as well as any of you. I'm not your weak link."

"Oh, really? And how will you run away if they see you shooting at them? Tell me, *little lark*." The gruff man barked a laugh.

"*Basta*, Alberto." Carlo spoke in the quiet voice of someone used to being heard. "I have faith in her, and you should, too. Beyond the embankment, there's a strip of woods edged in footpaths. She can take the paths to the hideout. The rest of us will run—"

"I'm with Alberto," another man interrupted. "This young lady is going to be our sharpshooter? We might be a ragtag group, but that's ridiculous."

Even Tommaso glanced at Francesca, shaking his head. She caught his stare and held it, clenching her jaw. But Carlo stood, gathering his map, unconcerned. "Enough. No more questions. We'll meet in three days to finalize the plan."

Francesca watched him clap the shoulders of the men as they left. When the last one walked out, she headed for the door, took down her coat, and pulled two letters from its pocket. One was addressed to her mother, the other to Giacomo's parents. She held them against her chest and turned to Carlo.

"I have a favor to ask. Both my mother and Giacomo's family must be worried sick."

Carlo nodded. "With the phones and post a mess—*si*, I understand."

"I thought perhaps you could find a way to deliver these. With all of your contacts . . ."

He nodded again, thinking. "I have some friends who travel north for the underground. I can't promise that they'll arrive quickly, but I can probably get them there."

She handed the letters over, and he strode away, stowing them somewhere. She hugged her chest, feeling hollow as her scrawled words started their journey. *Giacomo has been taken by the Nazis.* She'd written it twice, hand shaking. *I plan to wait for him here, in case he finds his way back to Rome.* For her mother, she'd added another page. *I'm sorry for so much*, she wrote. *That I fought with you before I moved away, and also that I left you alone. I've been angry and lost for years, since Babbo died. Now, as I grieve for Mino, I see that I never thought enough about your sadness. You didn't deserve my anger, Mamma. I hope you know that I love you. I always have.*

"Care for a cup of something?" Carlo returned, interrupting her thoughts.

"I really should be going."

"Come on," he persisted. "I could stand to chat with a girl from home. Been spending too much time among hotheaded young men."

She smiled. "How do you know I'm not just as hotheaded?"

"Nope, you're not." He moved the few steps to the kitchen, lighting the stove to boil water. "You're coolheaded, *bella*. That's what these men don't understand—yet."

Noise filtered up from the floors below as they sat at the table, their hands around warm cups. "Have you found anything more about Giacomo?" Carlo asked.

She shook her head, her grief smarting. "Nothing. Nobody knew him in the barracks." Another dead end.

"Even if he's not in Rome anymore, they won't kill him. Trust me, Francesca—they wouldn't squander his skills." Carlo waited for her gaze to meet his. "They need medics. They'll have drafted him to the front lines."

"Am I supposed to feel encouraged by this? The idea of Giacomo on the front lines—"

"It's the best possible outcome. He has a strong chance at survival as a medic."

She imagined Giacomo in a field hospital, dark hair in his eyes, glasses flashing over a patient. She fingered her cup, the image searing her soul with hope.

For a moment, neither of them said anything more. The sound of a ball hitting the courtyard wall, over and over, punctuated their sips. Then a woman hollered something from an apartment balcony, and Carlo chuckled.

"Does it remind you of small-town life? I swear, the old ladies pass more gossip between these balconies than they did in the piazza back home."

"Do you ever worry about that?" She took a sip, letting the ersatz coffee burn her throat. "What if they gossip about you, and all the people coming and going from your place?"

"It's a risk." He nodded. "There's a family downstairs I keep an eye on. They're true believers. Fascism as religion. I think the wife's harmless, but the son and father worry me."

Francesca set down her mug. "Dark-haired man? Teenage boy?" She pictured them, with their heavy eyebrows and wary expressions.

"*Sì*. What do you know?"

"Nothing. I've seen them here and there, and there's just something about them. I'm not surprised that they're still trying to follow Il Duce."

"They'll follow him to their own graves." Carlo's brow knitted. "It's a shame. What will happen to them when the city's liberated? People hate them already. When the Allies come, the people siding with the Germans will be persecuted . . ." He trailed off.

"Why should you care, Carlo? They're Fascists."

"Most people were, not long ago. You have every right to hate the people who stole your father, Francesca. But the normal folks, who went with the tide—should we hate them?"

She shrugged, exasperated. What was he getting at?

"Those people downstairs? I don't care about them, not really." He rubbed his jaw. "But a long time ago, I did care for someone. Her whole family was deeply Fascist. True believers. She wasn't, not in her heart, but the rest of Rome would never guess that. And now with Blackshirt thugs resurfacing in the streets, gathering recruits, collaborating with the Nazis? People will skewer anyone with Fascist ties when the Allies come. And I fear what will happen to her if she doesn't distance herself from her upbringing."

Francesca nodded. It was true that an especially vile brand of Fascists had begun roaming the streets, many of them young and violent, all too eager to support the Germans and Mussolini's puppet government. She studied him. "If it concerns you, why don't you talk to her about it?"

He smiled, but his eyes were sad. "No, I could never face her. I saw her once, from a distance, and she was with a man and a little boy, maybe three years old." He shrugged. "They looked happy.

Clearly, she's moved on with her life, and I—" He hesitated, clearing his throat as if words had risen and stuck there. "I have no right to talk to her about anything. I just wish I knew that she'd be safe, when this all shakes out."

The ball thumped the wall downstairs, and Francesca thought while Carlo swirled what was left in his cup. Carlo had been good to her. He'd taken her seriously, given her a job, taken her letters, given her someone to talk to about Giacomo. Maybe she could return a favor.

"Would she listen to me?"

His eyes bobbed up.

"Do you know her address? I could pay her a visit, just to see where she stands. I'd say an old friend wanted to warn her to stay neutral, to distance herself from the Fascists—"

He interrupted. "And to separate her identity from her parents'. You couldn't tell her who sent you, under any circumstances."

"Of course not. I'd say a childhood friend asked me to stop by."

"You would really do this?" His brows lifted. "It would be such a relief to know she might be all right. If you could just find out her positions, and warn her against even the appearance of collaboration—*sì*, it would mean a lot to me. More than I can explain." He stood, suddenly energized. "Let me make you another cup of this shitty coffee, and I'll tell you what you need to know."

He loped to the kitchen, and she watched him fill the kettle. Whoever this woman was, she still had Carlo's heart.

# ELEVEN

᠀

# Lucia

*Early October 1943*

LUCIA HAD KNOWN grief. And here she was again, flooded by sorrow, the pool in her heart so deep she'd surely drown in it. It was late afternoon, Matteo was napping, and she sat at the kitchen table, her hands spread out over the grain of the wood, staring at the wall. Behind her eyes, images flew past, like a newsreel. Noemi taking her hand in a firm squeeze. Noemi laughing on the balcony, her eyes liquid from a half glass of wine, the setting sun tracing her hair in gold. Noemi's cheek when they kissed goodbye, soft as petals. Her steadfast presence. The way she looked at Matteo.

She also saw herself, not a week earlier. *A fool.* There she was, marching up to the Nazis, as if her status and parents and fluency in German could protect anyone. As if the Nazis were rational. Fury and shame burned like acid in her stomach. What if she'd stayed out of it? Would Noemi be alive now? The question festered. Noemi could have survived prison until the Allies arrived. Everyone said it would be any day.

Lucia bent, lowering her head to the table, pressing her skull against the wood until it hurt. She saw Noemi with a hole in her temple, and the horror of it washed over her again, drenching her down to her soul. How would she find the strength to pick herself up when Matteo woke in an hour? How could she carry on as if everything hadn't changed? As if the world weren't broken beyond comprehension?

*You can be the light in all of this.*

The words whispered from some crevice in her mind, drifting like ghosts. Lucia pinned her eyes shut, and a sob escaped with the memory. It was Carlo's voice whispering to her.

He'd said it on a rainy Sunday afternoon in autumn, two weeks after their wedding. They'd been setting up their new apartment with what little furniture they had; their bed still sat on the floor, draped in mismatched blankets, their bookshelves wobbled, and the bare walls echoed with their laughter. Midday they took a break, walking, and then running across town when they got caught in the rain. They arrived at Lucia's parents' house for lunch, dripping and giggling, hands clasped, their new rings clinking together and surprising Lucia, over and over, with little jolts of joy. *She was married.* She glanced at Carlo as they climbed the marble stairs. He met her gaze as if he was thinking the same thing, half smiling as they rounded on the doorway of her childhood home, squeezing her hand twice. *Love you.*

Merely an hour later, when they were breaking bread, the perfection of that day fell apart. Marco sat across from Carlo, almost a head shorter than him and still skinny as a kid, though he was nearly grown now. Lucia stared at her brother as he plucked a piece of bread from the basket and set it on his plate. He chewed on the inside of his cheek, the way he did when he was nervous, and his eyes sparked with something like excitement. She sipped her wine and glanced at Carlo when his palm landed on her thigh under the table, the warmth of his touch seeping from her leg to her belly. But she looked back to Marco, watching him over the rim of her glass. He had something to say. She could feel it. She didn't have to wait long to be proven right.

"I've made a decision," Marco said after their father refilled everyone's wineglasses, sitting back down with a grunt. Marco glanced around the table as it quieted. Their mother lowered her glass, and their father looked up, brows raised, dull interest in his eyes.

Marco cleared his throat, Adam's apple bobbing. "You know my friend Eugenio?"

Their mother smiled helpfully. "That boy with the noisy mother. Claudia, I think."

Marco nodded, grave. "That's him. He was in the class ahead of mine. Last summer, Eugenio volunteered to fight in Spain to support General Franco. He's been flying fighter planes, just like Piero did."

Lucia watched her little brother pause to swallow, gathering his feeble nerves, and all of her own nerves vibrated as if with lightning. Mussolini had sent a volunteer army to fight alongside the Nationalists in Spain, seemingly eager for yet more war. She pinched the stem of her glass so hard she thought it might shatter. Surely, Marco wasn't planning to volunteer himself for Spain? He wasn't a brave boy, though he desperately wanted to be. She took a deep breath, trying to subdue the dread rising in her chest.

Marco managed a smile, visibly caught between nervousness and the triumph of whatever he was about to say. "I've made a decision," he declared again, gaining volume. "And since we're all here today, I may as well announce it. I'm going to volunteer. I'll go as soon as I finish school."

Lucia cut him off without planning it. "You can't do that, Marco. You're just a boy." Heat washed over her face as all eyes shifted to her, but it was the heat of anger. Of fear.

"I'm nearly eighteen." Marco met her stare and lifted his chin slightly. "And *you're* just my sister. You should keep your mouth shut."

Carlo's hand tightened on Lucia's thigh, and her father spoke before she could supply a retort.

"Marco's right. Il Duce has called on us to support General Franco, and it's noble to answer that call. Marco, we'll speak more about it later this evening." Their father's eyebrows sank over his dark, flickering stare, and he glanced around the table as if that would be the end of the discussion.

Lucia found herself standing, moving on impulse. "No," she spat, glancing between the still-living members of her family. She sensed Piero, as though he drifted between them, his gentle soul despairing. "How can you think of going off to fly fighter planes in some other country's war, Marco? Have you forgotten your brother, dead in some desert where he never should have been, his bones bleaching in the sun? Mamma, Papà." She wheeled between them, anger heating her words. "Do you want to lose another son? How can you support this?"

"Enough, Lucia." Her father barked it, his words gravelly, and her mother stared at her wineglass as if she could disappear into its liquid.

"No. I will *not* stay quiet this time—"

Her father stood with a clatter, his broad shoulders rising to tower over her. "Enough!" He shouted it, his anger flaring as quickly as hers. "How dare you speak of our lost son this way? And how dare you speak against your brother, when he's made a man's decision to stand up and fight? Stop talking about things of which you know *nothing*, you stupid girl!"

"I'll ask you not to insult my wife." Carlo stood, his words falling over the table, full of authority, and for a stunned moment, nobody spoke. In the history of their family, only Lucia had argued with Signor Colombo. Now Carlo rose behind her, his chest like a wall at her back, his hand tightening on hers. "You should listen to her," he said quietly. "She's smart, and she's right. Marco, don't die fighting a war that's not your own. Signor Colombo, you underestimate your daughter. But she's my wife now, and I will not sit here while you belittle her. She has every right to remind you of all you have to lose. All you have lost."

The family stared, and Carlo tugged Lucia's hand. She found herself following him away, in a daze, from the table, where her parents swapped looks, murmuring to each other. In the foyer, he helped her into her coat, and then they were out the door, thumping down the stairs and into the rain in shaky silence, her heart fractured by warring emotions.

Back at their own apartment, Lucia sank onto the bed, dripping and wiping at her eyes. Carlo sat and pulled her into the warmth of his chest. His heart beat against her ear, and he smoothed the wet hair from her face with his strong, capable hands. Outside, light filtered through the clouds, lowering as the day aged. Lucia tipped her face up to study her husband. She reached to cup the angle of his jaw, always rough with the shadow of a beard, and he lowered his forehead to touch hers. For a moment, they breathed together, and she felt as if her soul spread from her body, reaching through her skin to mix with his.

"They don't deserve you," he murmured, his voice low.

She found his lips in response, pressing into his warmth and heartbeat and breath. His hands cupped her waist, and he lifted her slightly as they kissed, moving her onto his lap. Then his hands worked slowly up her back, pausing on each knob of her spine, spreading out over her shoulders. He tipped back slightly, looking her in the eye. His gaze was deep in the lowering light, limitless.

"Never stop being yourself, no matter what they tell you." He spoke just above a whisper. "No matter who disagrees. Lucia, you can be the light in all of this. That's who you are. You weren't made to sit quietly by."

She ran her palms over the curves of his shoulders to his neck, hanging on to him like an anchor. "We'll be the light together," she murmured. "You and me."

She sank into him, and he lowered back on the bed, running his hands up and under her clothes, and she shed her fear for her brother, her anger at her parents. She no longer belonged to her family. She was Carlo's now, and he was hers.

LUCIA WAS so lost in memory that she almost didn't hear the knock at the front door. But then it came again, bumping her from the glow of the past. She lifted her head off the table, rubbing at the numb spot where her forehead had rested on the wood, wiping at her eyes, and blinking at the quiet kitchen surrounding her. Matteo was still asleep. She was back in the present, back in her lonely sorrow, with nobody to hold her through it.

Someone knocked again.

Who could it be? She stood, ready nerves nudging the memory of Carlo from her mind. She walked to the front door as a third knock sounded, insistent. Could it be her mother, coming to check on her because she'd missed a Saturday visit? She unbolted the door, leaving the chain in place to peer cautiously out, and her anxiety fell away. A lone girl stood on her threshold.

"Lucia Colombo?"

Lucia nodded, dazed, and unhooked the chain to open the door wider. She didn't recognize this girl, but clearly she was no threat. Willowy and slight, she wore a plain, shapeless skirt, and a curtain of hair hung over one shoulder. She stood at the top of the stairs with a bicycle, of all things, staring up resolutely. Surely, she'd come to this door in error? Before Lucia could gather her questions, the girl brushed past her, wheeling the bicycle right into the foyer. She limped alongside its spokes and leaned it up against the coatrack, nearly toppling the whole thing. Both legs under her knee-length skirt were thin, but one was wasted where it disappeared into her shoe. Polio.

"Who are you?" Lucia managed. "Why are you here?"

The girl glanced up, serious. "Do you mind if we sit down? It was a long ride over." She moved to the table and settled into a chair.

Lucia raised her eyes to the ceiling, suppressing the urge to say something about manners. "Who are you?" she repeated, following her to the table.

"I was asked to come." The girl stared up with startling green eyes. "We have a mutual friend, but I can't tell you who she is. Only that you've known her since childhood, and she's worried about you." The girl cocked her head, her gaze sharpening.

Who would be worried about her? And why couldn't this girl reveal who it was? Lucia touched her face. Perhaps someone had seen her out shopping yesterday? How terrible did she look? She hadn't been able to cry for two days, but her eyes were still puffy. The first three days after Noemi's death, Lucia had locked herself in the toilet off and on, sitting on the cold porcelain to sob. When she came out, Matteo sized her up, wary.

"When will we see Nonna Bruno?" he asked, again and again.

"When she comes back from her trip." She didn't know what else to say. She didn't know if he thought it was strange that Nonna Bruno went on a trip right after the Germans raided her house, though she claimed they'd only taken the soldiers. It was unclear what conclusions he drew while staring at her tear-streaked face. But she couldn't bear to tell him the terrible truth.

"Are you all right?" the girl asked, bringing Lucia back to the kitchen table. She pulled herself from her thoughts. The obvious question rose again before her. *Who was this girl?* They had a mutual friend from childhood? She could only think of Lidia. Had Lidia sent her? Why wouldn't she just come herself?

"I need an explanation." The words left Lucia quickly, and suddenly she felt that her confusion was urgent. Could the Germans have sent this Italian girl? No, that was absurd. But what about the Fascists? "Explain yourself fully, or get out of my house."

The girl almost looked relieved. This must have been what she expected: questions, not a grief-stunned woman who let strangers in. She inhaled sharply, the only sign she was mustering her nerve. "Our mutual friend is aware of the various loyalties in Rome—perhaps more than the average person. The Germans and the Fascists will be expelled eventually, signora. They will lose this war. Our friend is worried that, when they do, openly Fascist people will be persecuted."

Lucia stared, bewildered. "I don't have the faintest idea what you're talking about. Who is this long-lost friend of mine? Why didn't she come here herself?"

"I can't tell you her name. But she's not close by."

"Yet she knows the inner workings of *Rome*? There's more to this than you're telling me." Lucia's heart accelerated as she tried to piece together the puzzle of this girl, sitting in her kitchen, trying to warn her, and an idea took hold. Was it someone who'd been involved with Noemi? Had someone been helping the old woman hide those soldiers? *The underground.*

"Is my friend part of the underground?"

The girl's face was blank for a long moment. She nodded slightly.

Women were part of the underground? Something burned in Lucia, but she couldn't yet say what. If only this girl would reveal who'd sent her. She scoured her mind, pulling up handfuls of faces from her school days. Or could it really be someone Noemi had sent, a liaison she'd set up before she was killed, out of concern for Lucia? The idea quickened her heart.

"Why do you think I'm aligned with the Fascists?"

"I don't, necessarily. Your friend actually has quite a bit of faith in your willingness to rebel from your upbringing. But your father's a Fascist official. Your mother's demonstrably loyal, and German. Their sons, your brothers, fought for Il Duce." The girl glanced around the quiet apartment. "And your husband . . ."

Lucia frowned. "What are you talking about?"

The girl shrugged. "I heard you have a child, so I assume you have a husband as well. Perhaps he comes from a similar family."

Lucia glanced reflexively toward the bedroom where Matteo napped. "My son is asleep down the hall. And my husband is dead."

"I'm sorry to hear it." The girl hesitated, as if knocked off-balance. "The war?"

Lucia nodded. People always assumed she was a war widow.

"Listen." The girl seemed to collect herself. "If the Allies liberate Rome, and you're lumped in with your family, or your husband's family, or if you've helped the Nazis and the Fascists in any way . . . Well, people will hate you, and you'll be in grave danger."

"I would *never* help the Nazis." The words shot out before Lucia could harness them.

The girl sat back a little, folding her hands into her elbow creases. "*Brava,*" she said simply.

"What about you?" Lucia met her gaze. "I assume you're resistance, too?"

"I'm not."

"I don't believe you." She sat forward in her chair. "Here's the truth: Our mutual friend, whoever she is, doesn't need to worry about me. I'm not aligned with my parents. I'm not aligned with the Fascists. I've been sick of them all for a long time." If Noemi was behind this visitor, she'd probably asked her to come after Lucia gave her a talking-to about hiding fugitives. Shame rose in her throat, aching. She forced words around the pain. "I *hate* the Nazis. I'd do anything to see them gone."

"Anything?" The girl sat still, unblinking. She had a thin face and frail figure, but there was something about her eyes. Her gaze was watchful, imploring even, while the rest of her was so subdued. She wasn't pretty, really, but compelling, nonetheless.

The girl dropped her head and pushed her chair back from the table. "*Bene,*" she said, rising and pivoting toward the front door. "I'll tell my friend to stop worrying about you."

Lucia stood, following. "Wait. Why are you leaving so abruptly?" She wanted to talk further, to learn about the resistance. She stepped into the foyer, and the image that had haunted her for days came in a wave: Noemi's head jolting backward, red spurting from her temple. Noemi's startled eyes. Fury flared, consuming her shame and grief.

"Did Noemi Bruno ask you to come? Please tell me."

The girl righted her bicycle, saying nothing.

"I want to do something. To help." Lucia found the words spooling from her lips without forethought. It was only as she said it that she realized it was the truth.

But the girl shook her head. "That's not my role in this." She wheeled toward the door.

Lucia reached for her arm, desperate. "Will you visit again?"

The girl paused, frowning.

"Please," Lucia persisted. "I have nobody else to talk to about any of it—the state of things. I'm very alone now."

They stared at each other for a long, weighted moment before the girl answered. "If you're serious, I'll meet you at the end of the week, the morning of October 8. In Piazza del Popolo. Think about what you might offer us."

With that she wheeled through the door, calling back over her shoulder, "I'll wait by the obelisk."

The door swung shut.

Matteo emerged from his room down the hallway, rubbing his

eyes. He walked right into Lucia, thudding against her waist and burying his sleepy head. "Who was that?" he asked, his voice muffled by her dress.

"Just someone stopping by," Lucia murmured, petting his cowlicks flat. She stared at the closed door, her thoughts buzzing. Carlo's voice whispered in her mind. *You can be the light in all of this.* Maybe she could. Maybe she could stand up for her beliefs, resist, and fight back for Noemi. And for Piero, and even for Marco, forever waging someone else's war.

And that girl could show her the way.

# TWELVE

৵

## Francesca

*Early October 1943*

F RANCESCA WAITED, STANDING on a high, treed embankment over a quiet road. Her stomach, empty of food, soured with nerves. She adjusted the strap of a submachine gun slung on her back and stared at the street below. With deepening dusk, the nails had vanished on the pavement. *Bene.* They were still there, of course. Ready. From here, she'd have a perfect vantage point for the whole thing: the road carved downhill, and she stood above it, blending into the trees on the embankment.

She sucked in air, replacing her nerves with an image of Giacomo. She pictured him a hundred times a day, with his swift smile, his intelligent eyes, and the way he looked at her. His heart continued to beat somewhere, she was sure, in sync with her own. She shifted the gun off her back and lowered herself into the dirt, lying on her stomach just behind a boulder, torso propped on her elbows. It was twilight, nearly dark. If it didn't start soon, she wouldn't have enough light to aim. Was Carlo's information about the convoy correct? She squinted at the trees lining the other side of the street, studying the shadows. Carlo and the rest of his partisans were over there somewhere, hiding. Waiting.

In the trees behind the embankment, Francesca's bicycle leaned against a trunk, basket empty, wheel facing downhill so she could make a quick, if tricky, escape through the woods. Earlier, she'd struggled to pedal, the frame creaking and handlebars weighted with a cache of fifty four-pointed nails. She'd ridden right past a throng of *Fascisti* thugs in the street and wobbled past a Nazi guard on a bridge, frisking a young man. She arrived at the meeting point without having to tap her brakes once. Nobody looked twice at her, a girl with a basket full of laundry.

A faint whistle rang out over the hill, like birdsong dying out, and the rumble of a convoy grew in its echo. Francesca's heart pounded against the dirt of the embankment rising over the road. She lifted her gun. Up the street, at its crest, the first trucks appeared. They bumped downhill, followed by a long line of identical vehicles, their beds packed with everything needed along the front: ammunition, fuel, food. She peered over the gun's barrel.

The convoy gained speed as it traveled downhill. She held her breath. The first trucks in line rumbled directly below her, and on cue, their tires burst. A half-dozen trucks skidded into one another, brakes squealing, and the air filled with the haze of burnt rubber. Uphill, trucks lumbered to a full stop and doors flung open. Drivers slid out, alert. Shouts ricocheted through the street. Not two minutes had passed, and the convoy was no longer going anywhere near the front.

Several dark figures gathered midway up the street, gesturing and spinning on their heels, weapons out. An explosion lit the hillcrest, bright as lightning, and the dirt vibrated under Francesca's stomach. The Germans raised their guns, shouting and pivoting in the shadow of their loaded vehicles.

Another whistle sounded, and a dozen men sprang from hiding. Like spirits slipping from the shadows, slim and swift, they flung grenades and *spezzone* bombs into truck beds. A series of explosions thundered, and Francesca pressed her face to the dirt, protecting her eyes from debris. Ammunition crates caught fire somewhere, popping into a breathtaking crescendo. She glanced up as shards of hot metal rained down over the rest of the convoy.

The cacophony faded into human sounds: shouting and swearing and a few screams. Smoke swam over the street, shifting in the breeze, opening and closing channels. Francesca coughed, staring down the barrel of her gun, aiming toward clear patches, covering partisans. Her pulse hammered, and her eyes darted from figure to figure, but the rest of her stilled, finger poised on the trigger. She traced halos around her people, her mind quieting. It was like watching a field for movement, waiting for a burst of quail to rise into the sun. The same trance fell over her, like darkness.

The smoke shifted, exposing a Nazi as he aimed his pistol. She drew a bead on him and started to squeeze the trigger, but he lowered his arm as a partisan dove behind a truck, out of sight. She shifted her aim as well. She wouldn't shoot unless she had to.

Gunfire sputtered uphill, but she couldn't see it. An engine roared to life somewhere, gears grinding, and died back out. Movement caught in Francesca's peripheral vision, and a tall figure broke through the smoke, a *spezzone* in hand, heading for a fuel truck. He skidded beside the truck, tossed the bomb on its running board, and sprinted away. Across the street, a Nazi lifted his rifle. She adjusted her aim. There was no time to hesitate.

She filled her lungs and fired.

The Nazi crumpled, his rifle clattering to the pavement. One of the others dropped beside him, hollering, and Francesca hugged the earth. A spray of bullets hit the embankment, and she dug her face into the dirt behind the boulder. Abruptly, the air stilled around her, and she fought her own mind quiet, sucking in gritty breaths. Could they see her? *No.* If they could, they would have aimed. Her heart hammered, her trance broken.

Carefully, she looked around the boulder.

Alberto emerged from the shadows, crouching low, his eyes pinned on something up the street. He felt for his gun, and movement downhill caught Francesca's eye. *There.* A Nazi hiding behind a truck trained his gun on Alberto. Again she took aim, waited for stillness, and fired. The Nazi collapsed. Alberto swung around, looking from the fallen Nazi, gun still aimed, to Francesca's boulder on the hill. He stepped backward, vanishing into the shadows.

The smoke shifted, and a cluster of Germans gestured, running up the road as if in pursuit, vanishing from sight. She glanced from them to the truck where Carlo had tossed his bomb, fighting to slow her pulse. *Merda.* The *spezzone* hadn't gone off.

Shouting and gunfire volleyed over the hill, but the street quieted around the trucks with punctured tires. The partisans had scattered, melting back into the darkness, and Francesca's time was up. She sensed it like a shift in the wind. She squinted into the dusk, lifting her gun once more. Before she left, the fuel truck had to go. She aimed at it, scanning what she could see of its running board. *There.* She could just make out a shape that might be the bomb. Was it unstable enough to explode if hit? She pooled all of her focus on the black cylinder, held her breath, and pulled the trigger.

The explosion was deafening. A hot wind blasted the embankment, and Francesca buried her face in the dirt, digging her nails into the earth while charged air rippled over her. Black smoke engulfed her, and she coughed, choking into the dirt. Tears streamed from her eyes as flames leapt from the truck below, growing, heating the embankment.

Forcing herself to move, Francesca scuttled backward into the woods. About ten trees in, she gripped a trunk and hoisted herself upright. Every cell in her body shook, as if in standing she'd knocked herself fully awake, fully aware of the cold danger everywhere. She had to get away. *Now.* She slung her gun over her shoulder and stumbled toward her bicycle.

Shots still peppered the convoy as Francesca dropped the gun in the basket, covered the part that stuck out with a blanket, and positioned a tangle of clothes hangers around it as camouflage. She mounted the bicycle, blinking down the treed hill. It was even harder to see in the smoky woods. But the forest wasn't wide. She just had to weave through it, carefully, and she'd spill onto a footpath on the other side.

"HALT!" a voice shouted behind her, and for a half second, Francesca froze. She glanced back through the strip of trees, thinly separating her from her firing spot. A Nazi stood there now, breathing hard and squinting into the forest, backlit by fire. Behind him, another soldier scrambled up onto the embankment. Silhouettes against leaping flames.

She shoved her strong leg down on the pedal, and the tires lurched forward. A shot cracked the air, and the bullet whistled past her ear. The bicycle bounced over roots and twigs, gaining speed. The air stung her eyes, and she strained to see the dark shapes of trees. Another shot fired, and she jerked the wheel, missing the trunk of a pine and nearly losing her balance. She stayed upright and rocked around another tree, gaining more speed, and the gun fired again. Were they running down the hill after her, taking aim? *Focus,* she commanded herself. If she toppled her bicycle, they'd kill her.

Ahead, the footpath appeared through the forest. It threaded through fields and clusters of trees, winding to the city. She wove toward it, riding in a serpentine, blocking out the shouts in her wake. *Pedal. Steer. Get away.* When she arced around the last tree, skidding onto the gravelly path, her balding tire slid out from under itself, and she flung her strong leg down, nearly capsizing.

A clothes hanger clattered to the path. But she straightened and heaved the bicycle back onto its tires, kicked off, and gained momentum as another shot fired.

Something hit her strong calf. She gasped, and her front wheel wobbled sharply. She jerked it straight, shut her eyes against a throb of dizziness, and two words rebounded in her skull. *Don't fall.* She tightened her grip, and pain pulsed in her leg, roiling up like a wave. Shouts echoed from the forest, but Francesca stared ahead, swallowing nausea and veering around a curve. Had she been shot? She sailed along another hem of forest, and the noise died out behind her. It sank in: she'd been shot in her good leg.

*Madonna mia,* she whispered into the wind.

The footpath hummed under her tires, and she blinked away the tears stinging her eyes, pulling her attention from her shrieking calf. It would have to wait. Because she wasn't finished. She still had to slip into a basement on the outskirts of Trastevere, outside the Aurelian Walls, without being seen. If she was seen, she'd be shot again, this time for good; it was after curfew, and she had a submachine gun in her laundry basket. She clamped her teeth and pedaled on, her mind skimming ahead while buildings appeared around a curve. Could she make it to the apartment? Suddenly, this part of the scheme seemed poorly constructed. They didn't have to pass through the guarded *portas* into Rome, but it was after dark, near an ambush. And every partisan carried a weapon.

Her thoughts hopped, like birds in a cage. She glanced at her hurt leg but couldn't see it rising and falling under her skirt. Fear gripped her so hard she shook her head, as if she could dislodge it. She couldn't lose her one strong leg. And then there were the Nazis in the woods. Had they gotten a good look at her? No. Smoke and dusk and the forest would have confused her features, concealing anything identifiable. She breathed, stretching her lungs past her fear.

Ahead, apartment blocks rose against the dark sky. She slowed, pushing the ambush from her mind. Where the footpath intersected with the street, she scudded to a stop, lowering her throbbing leg to the gravel. The apartment she needed was just down the street and around a corner. It was only three blocks away, and the neighborhood appeared to be empty, everyone tucked inside for the night.

She rolled out onto the pavement, pedaling into the shadow of a building. The rising moon hung heavy, dusting the street with its light. She sailed past an alley and pedaled harder, ignoring her pain. She was nearly there.

*"ACHTUNG!"* The word was like a shot, hitting Francesca between the shoulder blades. She hesitated, glancing back and pulsing her brakes. A pair of soldiers hovered in the road, both of them pinching lit cigarettes. Behind them, the shape of a car sat in the dark alley. She'd rolled past it, her mind on the rendezvous spot around the corner.

*Dio santo.* She bumped to a stop, fear exploding in her chest. What could she do? She touched her jacket pocket, but the Beretta wasn't there. She eyed the blanket flung over the submachine gun, which levered out of the basket among the clothes hangers. No. Killing these soldiers was a bad idea, even if she could pull it off. But they only had to look at the shape of the blanket to guess what was under it. She pinned her eyes shut in the darkness, trying to breathe, and prayed. *Oddio. Send me a miracle.*

All the while, boots hammered the pavement behind her as they approached.

"It's past curfew," one of the soldiers barked, and she turned to look at him, still straddling her bicycle. He was Italian. A Fascist, working alongside a German. Despite her pain and panic, her stomach soured.

"I'm sorry," she said, stumbling over her words. "I was out delivering laundry, and I fell on my bicycle."

Both men glanced at her basket while the Italian translated, but they didn't seem to register the shape of the blanket. She felt the burn in her cheeks, the blood heating them up while she waited for the inevitable.

"Is that why you're bleeding?" The Italian squinted in the moonlight. The German looked at her wounded leg and then her other calf, bone with a strip of muscle, and grimaced. She followed their stares, glancing at her wound for the first time. In the faint light, it looked like a gash, not the hole she'd imagined. Perhaps the bullet had only grazed her? Relief washed over her, unexpected. Perhaps she still had one strong leg after all.

She nodded, struggling to produce intelligible words as fear overtook her momentary relief. She met the German's stare, forcing her attention from the way his hand rested on his gun. What would it feel like to be shot in the chest? He studied her. Or would they hang her?

"I'm very sorry," she repeated, standing straighter. "My tire slipped in the gravel, and a stone gashed my leg. I had to sit down to recover—my other leg is weak, you see." Her thoughts raced. They would have heard the explosions from here. If she didn't reference them, she'd seem suspicious—the whole neighborhood must have heard the ambush. It could be why these guards were here, watching this obscure street.

"And then I heard sounds of fighting and . . ." Francesca thought fast. What would they expect a laundress to say? "I was terrified. I didn't know which way to go."

"That's why you shouldn't be out after curfew," the Italian interrupted. He shook his head, his eyebrows arched in superiority.

She nodded and widened her own eyes. Let him feel superior, if it made him overlook the obvious.

"Get on, then. Get out of here," he barked, and she nodded again. She pushed down on the pedal and wobbled away. Her shoulders, as she gained speed, stiffened. With every revolution, she expected a bullet in her back.

But then she turned the corner and was at the right apartment block, dismounting the bicycle and pushing open the door. Her chest welled as she wheeled inside, letting the door slam in her wake, shutting out the street behind her. How had she made it? She closed her eyes and paused in the darkness, governing her breath and pulse into normal rhythms.

She found the correct door and knocked, her knuckles rapping out a secret code. Had the other partisans made it, or were they hiding in the woods? Her hands shook, and she glanced down while she waited, making out the shape of her fingers in the gloom. That finger, that one on her right hand—it was responsible for shooting two men. Maybe killing them.

The locks turned, the door opened, and an older woman scanned her figure.

Francesca murmured the password, "*Romulus*," and the woman waved her wordlessly down a set of stairs into what looked like a cellar. Candlelight flickered against stone walls below, and Francesca thumped down, the gun slung on her back. In her mind, the Nazis slumped to the street, over and over again.

She scoured her heart for feelings, but none of the ones she expected were there. *She'd killed people.* Where was her sorrow, her guilt, the panic of moral ambiguity? The emotions she'd prepared for were barely there, faint as a whisper.

Instead, she saw Giacomo's quick smile. Her father's green eyes. The way she'd drifted from her mother as a teenager, engulfed in grief. And she felt rage.

She stood on the cellar floor, glancing at the assembled partisans, and someone handed her a lump of stale bread. She tore off
a bite, pulling the gun from her back and leaning it against the
wall.

"You did well."

Francesca turned to see Alberto, shuffling over, rubbing his
bearded jaw.

She tipped her chin up. "You, too."

But he was shaking his head. "I saw what you did up there. You
covered us, cool as ice. Without you, I'd be dead. Carlo, too."

She nodded, stiffening. She'd proven herself, that was clear. But
a knot of anger twisted in her chest. They'd doubted her, because
when they looked at her they saw only a crippled girl. She'd show
them, again and again. She cleared her throat, glancing around.
"Where are the others?" There were less than a half-dozen people
in this room, and Carlo wasn't among them.

"Went to the woods," Alberto murmured. "They'll hide in the
hills tonight." He cocked his head, distracted, and bent, squinting
in the candlelight. "What happened to your leg?" Without waiting for an answer, he turned and called, "Elena!" gesturing for the
only other woman in the cellar. "Take a look, will you? She's
bleeding."

"It's just a graze," Francesca protested, but the older woman
bustled over and knelt, holding her kerchiefed head and a flickering candle close to the injured leg.

"A graze from what? A bullet?"

Francesca nodded, and the woman turned to Alberto. "Get me
some alcohol and my sewing kit. Over there—I brought it just in
case." She flicked an impatient hand toward the cellar corner, and
Alberto hurried away. The other partisans, assembled on circled
crates, glanced over but continued talking quietly. They were disbanded soldiers, men who'd been drafted into the Royal Army

before Mussolini's downfall. Like so many young men, they'd gone underground after the armistice, refusing to fight for Fascism anymore. Now, hiding from persistent draft notices posted by the new puppet government, they fought against it.

"You're right that it's just a gash," Elena murmured, pulling Francesca's attention from the huddled men. "You were lucky. But we don't want infection to set in. Mind if I stitch it closed?" She didn't look up when she spoke, fingering the flesh around the wound instead.

Pain shot up Francesca's leg. *"Per favore,"* she managed, blinking her watering eyes.

A moment later, she perched on a wooden crate, gritting her teeth while a needle punctured her skin over and over. As always, she thought of Giacomo. She'd inquired at every barrack and building rumored to be holding prisoners in Rome, with no luck. Where was he? What if he could see her now, hiding in a cellar full of partisans, a bullet wound in her calf? Only a season had passed, mere months since Il Duce had fallen, and everything was different. Without meaning to, she'd changed with the contours of a changing world.

And she barely recognized herself.

# THIRTEEN

ஐஇ

## Lucia

*October 7, 1943*

LUCIA STOOD ON the rooftop terrace of her building, unpinning laundry from the line with shaking fingers. She'd barely slept all week, and she felt it now, from her brain to her toes. Was she being impulsive? Reckless? She pinched the last clothespin. There had been a break in the rain, enough for the October sun to dry her best dress and the slip to go under it, *grazie a Dio*. She only had an hour to put it on, deposit Matteo with her father, and accompany her mother back into the mirrored halls of her old life.

As she dropped laundry into a basket, she glanced at the lemon tree in its pot, branches reaching toward the sky, roots concealing jewels. A memory flitted through her mind, unbidden: she saw herself, six years ago, gloved and laughing with a trowel in her hand. Carlo sprawled on a near by bench, his brown eyes bright. He cupped a glass of wine in one hand, swirling it.

"Why do you want to grow a garden up here?" He smiled, teasing. "I hear they sell excellent lemons at the market, *amore mio*. Oranges, too."

She'd pursed her lips and moved the dirt around with her trowel. "You won't tease me next summer when you're drinking fresh *limonata*." She picked the little tree up, scowling at its roots, and Carlo laughed.

"Here," he murmured, setting down his wine and taking the trowel. "We'll plant it together. And then someday we'll sleep in its shade and remember when we were newly married and you wanted a garden in the heart of the city."

Lucia hoisted her laundry basket, and the memory disintegrated. Her life was so different than she'd imagined. Nothing she'd planned had come to fruition. Not even the lemons on that stunted tree.

She thumped down the stairs, wondering what Carlo would say if he knew what she was up to. Would he, the anti-Fascist, approve of her now? She used her hip to nudge her apartment door open. Could anyone approve, when she could barely articulate her own plan? It had come to her in a burst of inspiration, but now she worried it was foolish. In an hour, she would go out with her mother to circulate among the German elite. Hate burned in her chest as she imagined them, reclining in hotels after a day spent arresting and murdering innocent people. First, she planned to look them in the eye, never letting them know she saw the devil beneath those uniforms. Then she would listen. For what? She didn't yet know. But if she heard anything that might interest the girl who'd visited her apartment, and the shadowy resistance behind her, she'd pass it along.

It was something, Lucia thought as she shook out her dress over the kitchen table. Matteo looked up from his drawing, solemn. "This is a scary dog," he explained, pointing to the creature on his paper. "See his big teeth? And mean eyebrows? A guard dog."

Lucia sighed, eyeing the movement of Matteo's pencil as he bent to add more teeth. She had to do something. That was all she was sure of now, in the wake of Noemi's murder. She could offer the resistance her position as a daughter of the Fascist elite. She could offer them her eyes and ears. She glanced at Matteo's skinny arms, busy over his paper.

She would find a way to fight for a future where those arms would never carry a rifle.

An hour later, Lucia and her mother crossed Via Veneto. The Hotel Excelsior, immense and glowing yellow in the setting sun, loomed over the street. Lucia followed her mother, curls bouncing, staring up at the cupola gracing the building's corner. The hotel, around the corner from her parents' house, had always been favored by the Fascist elite. This was not Lucia's first time crossing its threshold. Nonetheless, as they passed through the brass double doors into the grand entrance, her breath caught. She paused on the checkered floor, taking in the crystal chandeliers and the people drifting under them, everyone wearing fine clothes, faces bright in laughter. Uniforms, both German and Italian, peppered the crowd.

"Come along, *Liebling*," Nonna Colombo whispered, her smile glittering in the light. "Remember: you're a widow from now on. And you don't have to mention Matteo right away, either."

Lucia followed her mother, the words she held back searing her throat. Matteo was her *son*, her reason for breathing—not a shameful secret. She would indeed keep him secret tonight, but only because she'd keep her boy as removed from the Nazis as possible. She swallowed her anger and smiled at a couple lounging on plush chairs, glasses of wine balanced in their palms. As far as she knew, she actually was a widow. That might be the only truth of the night.

Across the hall, more couples danced to the music of a live band. Everywhere there seemed to be food: *antipasti* circulated, little plates sat on tables, forgotten, and fine cheeses and prosciutto floated into smiling lips. How could there be all this food within these walls, when across Rome the people went hungry? Her anger flared, always reliable.

"Shall we fetch a glass of something, Lucia?" her mother said, jarring her thoughts. She nodded, forcing a smile, and her mother's wrinkles deepened. She placed her thin fingers on Lucia's elbow, digging in as she leaned close with more whispered guidance. "Darling, don't forget to speak German with our guests. Your fluency will elevate you."

Lucia had to look away. Guests? How could her mother think this way? Her eyes fell on a table full of food, and she thought of her purse. Could she sneak something home for Matteo? Some meat and cheese? At the end of the night, she'd try.

Nonna Colombo lifted her jeweled fingers, snapping, and two glasses of wine appeared in their hands. Lucia took a long sip, steadying herself. Her mother recognized a friend, exclaimed in delight, and glided across the room.

The wine, bloodred, trembled in Lucia's glass. She stared at it for a half second before she understood: she was shaking. She took another sip. What was she doing here? Her eyes darted from uniform to uniform. Wehrmacht. Luftwaffe. She was playing the fool again. Who did she think she was? A single mother, that's who. A woman apparently doomed to struggle, no matter how hard she tried. In reality, she couldn't do anything of substance to fight anyone.

She drained her glass and glanced from her mother to the door. She would simply leave, abandon this misguided venture and go back to hiding in her apartment until the world changed without her help, for better or for worse.

She was looking for a place to set her glass when a trio of officers sauntered toward her. *Santo cielo.* Two wore SS uniforms, and one was Luftwaffe.

*"Piacere,"* the Luftwaffe officer said, his accent thick. *"Come sta?"*

The younger of the SS officers chuckled at the halting Italian words, and the taller, older one looked to the ceiling.

"Forgive my colleague's language," the older man said, speaking competent Italian. His eyes, taking her in with unmasked interest, were the weak blue of a winter sky. "Shall I get rid of these young pups?"

Lucia nodded. If only there was a way to get rid of all three of them. She was stuck now. She'd have to play a role until she could excuse herself politely.

The tall officer turned to the others and switched to German. "Go and get us some drinks. A good wine for the lady."

When they'd left, he grinned, but his eyes remained strangely solemn. "I'm Hauptsturmführer Hans Bergmann. You?" He extended his hand.

She hesitated before gripping his fingers and pumping once. *"Ich bin Lucia Colombo."* *Hauptsturmführer*—wasn't that like a captain? She raised her chin, swallowing bitter bile, pretending she was pleased to meet him. "We can speak German if you prefer it." Had he ever raided a home? Killed an innocent citizen?

"Ah, you speak German?" The Nazi sucked a breath of air through his nose, brightening. "You look fully Italian."

Lucia shook her head, and her curls bounced against her neck. "My mother's German, in fact." She gestured toward Nonna Colombo, who was laughing across the room, blond head tipped backward. "Her parents were Bavarian."

"It appears she's enjoying herself," Bergmann murmured. He reached into his breast pocket and fished out a cigarette.

"My mother loves a party." Lucia paused while he lit his cigarette, sucking air until the tip glowed red. She pulled her gaze from the ember to his eyes.

"How long have you been in Rome, Hauptsturmführer Berg-mann?"

"Nearly a month." He still stared toward Nonna Colombo, again taking a quick breath through his nose. "Your mother is here without your father? Doesn't he, too, love a party?"

Was this stranger judging her parents? She placed her empty glass on a tray as it floated by. What did it matter? She judged her parents, too. She shrugged, cocking her head. "He usually accompanies her, but he's been quite busy. He's a Fascist official, you see. Like you, he has his hands full at the moment."

"Ah." Bergmann nodded, blinking his blond eyelashes. "Yes, I imagine your Duce's loyal followers may not be in the mood for revelry at the moment. But they should be, with the excellent news pouring in from the south." He inhaled and the cigarette smoldered.

She watched the ember brighten and fade while he puffed, and something glowed in her own chest. Maybe the idea that led her here wasn't so foolish. She tipped her head, feeling the air on her neck. It had been years since she'd charmed a man, but it was coming back to her. She'd once been good at a party, sociable, able to work herself through a crowd to whatever position she desired. Could she trick this man into divulging secrets? She smiled. What was there to lose? She'd flirt with the devil if it would contribute to his downfall.

"You think the news from the front line is excellent?"

"Certainly. It's only a matter of time before we drive the Allies back into the sea."

"Right where they belong, if you ask me." She laughed. She'd pretend she was the person she'd once been, years ago. Before Noemi. Before Matteo, before Carlo. Before Piero died.

The younger men appeared with fresh glasses of wine. The Luft-

waffe officer opened his mouth to speak, took one look at Bergmann's glare, and beckoned his friend off toward the dance floor.

"Let's toast." Bergmann held up his glass. "To the future of your
country, which is once again in firm hands."

"A tremendous future, indeed." They clinked glasses. "Tell me,
Hauptsturmführer. Where were you before Rome?"

"Oh, Paris for nearly two years, but I'm coming now from a
brief post in the east." He took a long drink, clearing his throat.
"I expect to stay in Rome for the foreseeable future."

"Paris! I haven't been in ages, of course. Such a lovely city." So,
he'd been part of the occupying force in Paris. Now he was in
another occupied capital. What did that mean?

"And what do you do here, day-to-day?" She reached for his
burning cigarette, plucking it from his fingers without breaking
eye contact. Was it a suspicious question? He watched while she
inhaled slowly, filling her lungs. It burned, but she laughed.

"It varies," he said when she replaced his cigarette. "I've been
procuring labor for the war effort, managing subversives—things
like that."

"Subversives. You must mean people foolish enough to break
the law?"

"Some of them break the law. Others simply don't belong. It's
the same role I occupied in other cities, but the job is exceedingly
difficult here. Half of Rome is hiding the other half. I'll have to
outsmart your countrymen, I'm afraid, to make much progress."

"Remember, my mother's people are Bavarian. I consider my
countrymen to be those of my ancestry." Anger spread through
her stomach, hot and nauseating. *Half of Rome is hiding the other
half.* She saw Noemi, propping fugitive soldiers up with pillows
and blankets, tending to their wounds. She flashed a lidded smile,
baiting him. "I do hope you punish these subversives when they're
caught."

He grinned. "With satisfaction."

She snitched his cigarette again, pulling acrid smoke into her lungs to obscure the fury in her eyes. Could she really use this man somehow? Perhaps she was again being foolish, overestimating herself, but she yearned to try. She yearned to spy on this monster and toss whatever she gleaned to the resistance, striking him where he never expected it. She was meeting the girl from the underground in the morning. What would she think of this idea?

"Tell me." She put his cigarette back in his fingers, her eyes watering from the smoke. "How is it that you speak such lovely Italian, Hauptsturmführer Bergmann?"

He inhaled, a quick uptake of air. "I lived in Florence as a student. Years ago, studying Renaissance art, of all things."

"Oh, Rome will astonish you, then. Do you practice art yourself?"

"No. My teachers claimed that I didn't understand it. Perhaps I didn't—it was my mother who wanted me to be an artist. Thankfully, I'm no longer so susceptible to suggestion." His pale eyes met hers. "But I'll enjoy Rome nonetheless, particularly once we've cleaned it up."

She didn't know what he meant by that. "Yes," she said, nodding as if in agreement. "Rome has lost a bit of its luster. Your mother—is she happy to hear you're in Italy again?"

"She's dead." He said it flatly, his eyes on the dance floor.

"I'm sorry."

"It's quite all right. We weren't close."

She looked away, watching couples spin and laugh to the cadence of the live band.

"You must tell me about yourself, Lucia Colombo. You have no . . . connections?"

"I'm a widow." She smiled, nerves gathering. What if he asked about children? She couldn't tell him about Matteo. She glanced around the room. Did anyone here know her, aside from her mother? She'd been out of society for years.

"I'm sorry to hear of your loss," Bergmann murmured. "Did he die a soldier?"

She nodded, leveling her wide eyes on his. "He sacrificed everything to his ideals. But I've been lonely in the years since." She'd gamble: Nobody here knew her anymore. Her mother surely never spoke of Matteo to her friends; her son-in-law and grandson were sources of embarrassment, after all. Lucia would keep her secret.

Bergmann's hand landed on her elbow, and she forced herself not to jolt.

"Would you care to dance?"

"I've been hoping you'd ask."

She set down her glass, and he took her hand.

"I can't tell you how agreeable it is to speak German with an Italian woman. The best of both worlds, *ja?*"

She laughed, her palm moist in his. "The best of both worlds, indeed."

They passed a group of aging women, and her mother caught her eye. Nonna Colombo winked, smiling in approval, and Lucia's heart smarted under her laughter. She hadn't seen anything like that smile in years. How long had it been since her mother had approved of her? Lucia could only imagine what she'd say if she knew the truth of her motives, the wild reason she'd come tonight. She glanced over her shoulder, holding Nonna Colombo's blue gaze for two steps. Then she returned the wink.

# FOURTEEN

ಬಿ

## Francesca

*October 8, 1943*

NINE O' CLOCK CAME and went, and Francesca finished her weak coffee. Piazza del Popolo, spreading from the windows where she sat, was eerily quiet. She'd strategically positioned herself, so if Lucia laid a trap at their meeting place, Francesca could slip through a side door of the café and melt into the neighborhood. But now it was clear that nobody was coming, neither Lucia nor Gestapo. She pushed her chair back, using the tabletop as leverage to stand. Her weak leg ached from overuse, and her good one from the gunshot graze.

She stepped out into the chilly autumn air. It was just as well that Lucia hadn't materialized. The woman had been raised in the lap of Fascist prosperity, which made her less than trustworthy. Francesca had delivered Carlo's message, and that was enough. She righted her bicycle and started pushing it across the piazza, handlebars bumping past the obelisk, now obscured by sandbags stacked high to protect it from bombs. The sky grumbled overhead, heavy with rain.

"*Aspetta!*" The call echoed around the piazza.

She turned, cocking her head. Lucia hurried across the cobblestones, belted coat flapping in the breeze and a small boy hanging from her arm.

"*Santo cielo*," Lucia huffed when she arrived, out of breath. "Sorry we're late."

Francesca glanced around, looking for a Gestapo tail. The piazza remained empty, with only a pair of priests, cassocks swinging, hustling under the expanse of threatening clouds. "I thought you weren't going to come."

"Well, here I am. A little late, but that's just getting out of the house with a child." Lucia tipped her head to the boy. His face was tear streaked and blotchy, and he swiveled to watch a pigeon pick its way across the cobbles.

"Mamma?" The boy's eyebrows knitted as he stared at the bird. "Why are there so *many* pigeons?"

"They like to live among people, *piccolo*," Lucia said, turning from her child to Francesca. "Do you mind if we chat in the park? It would be better for our small counterpart, here."

Francesca nodded and began to walk, uneasiness curdling her gut as she watched the boy run ahead. Carlo had said the child was three, but this boy, though small, seemed older. How much would he overhear and understand? And was it safe to go to the park? What if Lucia had an ambush waiting there? She scanned the terrace overlooking the piazza, which flanked the Villa Borghese grounds, and studied the palm trees and pines obscuring the staircases leading up.

"How old is your son?" Francesca ventured.

"Five. His name is Matteo." Lucia, too, glanced around, furtive as a grounded bird. "Run along, *piccolo*," she called, encouraging him to start up the stairs. "We'll meet you on the terrace. Wait there before heading into the park."

They reached the stairs, and without referencing it, Lucia took the bicycle, hefting it up so Francesca could climb.

"Why did you come today?" Francesca asked, watching Matteo disappear over the top.

"Because I've had an idea." Lucia hoisted the bicycle, breathing hard. "I'll tell you about it when we're alone in the park."

They landed at the top, and again the boy ran ahead, as if he couldn't wait to get somewhere. Francesca took her bicycle, and they crossed the wide terrace overlooking the Piazza del Popolo, heading for paths lined in statues and fountains, still grand despite everything. Trees closed in around them, and the gravel crunched under their shoes as they walked, wordless.

Before they could resume the conversation, a pair of German officers appeared in the path ahead. Francesca's chest tightened. She sensed the weight of the Beretta in her pocket. She glanced at Lucia, testing the air between them for a trap, looking for recognition in the woman's face. Lucia's eyes snagged on the soldiers, and Francesca did see something in them, but it was entirely different than what she expected. *Hatred.*

The officers sauntered by, laughing loudly, and Lucia whispered the second they were out of earshot. "I want to help the resistance, and I have a notion of what I might do. My mother invited me to go out with her, to circulate in 'better society,' as she calls it. Last night, I went with her to the Hotel Excelsior." Lucia's voice shook a little. "I thought I could befriend people there, Fascists and Germans, and listen for information. Nobody would ever suspect me of it."

*Like a spy.* Francesca watched the boy run into a grove of yellowing eucalyptus. A swing sat in a clearing, and he climbed aboard, a scramble of thin arms and legs, and began to pump.

"Why should I trust you?" Francesca asked, glancing at Lucia as they approached a bench by the swing. An oleander, flanking the bench, scratched her back as she sat.

Lucia kept her eyes on her little boy, watching him rise and fall.

"When my husband died, he left me very alone. My parents barely tolerate me. My friends are busy in their lives . . . It's not easy being a single mother. When I was at my most desperate, a neighbor, an old woman, became my closest friend, and Matteo's surrogate nonna. The Nazis shot her last week."

Francesca looked down at her uneven feet. A pigeon hopped out from the oleander, snapping its beak back and forth to stare at them. "And that was enough to change the beliefs you were raised with?" Her heart smarted from Lucia's story; she knew how losing someone could change a person. Still, she scrutinized the woman, testing her for lies.

"My beliefs aren't a problem." Lucia put weight into each word, and her eyes swung with her son, back and forth. "I haven't been a true Fascist for a long time. But I'm a woman, and all the women I know hold back, quieting their ideas. They held back while Mussolini and his men marched us into ruin, over and over again. You mentioned my brothers the last time we met, Piero and Marco? Piero died in Ethiopia. I won't be surprised if Marco takes a bullet, too. I remember watching them as little boys, parading around in *Balilla* uniforms, raising their rifles and shouting as if they had a future, as if Il Duce hadn't stolen it already." Her face hardened. "I'll be damned if that's going to be Matteo's life."

Francesca sat back, breathing in the sweet smell of oleander. If Lucia was lying, she was one hell of a liar. "Why not hide people in your apartment, if you want to help?" she said after a moment. "It would be simpler."

"I cannot hide people."

"Why not, if you're so committed to switching sides? With all the disbanded soldiers trying to disappear, and the Jewish families seeking refuge—you could provide a place."

Lucia looked her in the eye. "If my parents sensed fugitives in the apartment they pay for, they'd turn us all in. It would be utterly foolish. But the Jews are safe in Rome, are they not? All that treachery couldn't happen here."

"Have you not paid attention to what's happening in other occupied cities?"

"Of course I've paid attention." Lucia flushed. "My best childhood friend is Jewish—the deportations make me sick. But it won't happen here. Romans wouldn't allow it."

It was true that the racial laws had been resoundingly unpopular in Italy. But Italians were no longer in charge. Francesca opened her mouth to respond but forced the words back. She wasn't here to argue.

"So you want to be a spy instead. What makes you think you could do it?"

"I wouldn't call myself a *spy*. That's rather fanciful, don't you think? I would just inhabit my old life and listen. Last night, I met a man who said he manages subversives in Rome. I took that to mean people like you. Hauptsturmführer Hans Bergmann is his name." Lucia smirked. "He likes me. I could wrap him around my little finger."

Francesca's breath quickened. Would Carlo know that name? Perhaps she was underestimating this woman. "Don't be so confident," she said, hiding her pulse of excitement. "Your *Hauptsturmführer* is, without a doubt, a cunning man."

"He's still a man." Lucia smiled smugly. "Men have common vulnerabilities."

Francesca found herself nodding. If Lucia was right, this Nazi of hers posed a clear threat to all the partisans in Rome. Could she really get close to him? Use him to help the resistance?

It was a chance worth taking.

"*Va bene*," Francesca said, making up her mind. There was no harm in giving Lucia some time to prove herself. She knew nothing about the resistance, so the risk of betrayal was small. "I'll run this by my contacts, and we can meet again in a week. Next Saturday, on the Lungotevere De' Cenci." Francesca had no idea what Carlo would say. He'd sent her to warn this woman, not to recruit her. And yet, if she really could spy on someone involved in hunting partisans? It was too great an opportunity to walk away from.

Lucia stood. "I'd like to meet in the morning, if you don't mind. Matteo and I will have to get in line for groceries afterward, so the earlier the better." She glanced at Francesca, a smile pricking her lips. "You know, you still haven't told me your name."

"We have code names." Francesca hesitated. "Mine is L'Allodola."

"The Skylark?" Amusement flashed in Lucia's eyes. "*Santo cielo.*"

The little boy hopped from the swing and ran over, his eyes bright over his thumbprint nose, cheeks pink in the breeze. He was achingly thin, but his smile loosened something in Francesca's chest. She thought of Giacomo as a child, sitting in a tree, grinning with gapped teeth.

"Are you finished talking? Who is she, Mamma?" the boy asked. A leaf drifted over his head, like a little sail, and he jumped to catch it.

Lucia smiled at her child, and it was like watching a person unfold. She tousled his hair as the first raindrops fell from the sky.

"She's a new friend, Matteo."

# FIFTEEN

༄

## Lucia

*October 16, 1943*

RAIN DRUMMED THE umbrella over Lucia's head like a percussionist's mallet. Matteo skipped beside her, tugging on her arm as he jumped puddles. L'Allodola would be coming from the other direction—they'd planned to walk along the Lungotevere De' Cenci, this riverside street, until their paths crossed. She had little to report. She'd seen Bergmann at the Excelsior, but they'd spoken only briefly. He had, however, asked her for a true date in two weeks. It was something: the promise of more to come.

"*Basta*, Matteo," she said, frowning at her little boy. His shoes, worn-out and nearly too small, had cardboard soles. She'd asked the cobbler for leather the last time he patched them up, but there wasn't any. Rome was running out of everything: food, cooking gas, electricity, leather, textiles. How much longer would the list grow before the Allies came to their rescue?

She imagined the chill in his wet toes and shivered a bit herself. He would certainly catch another cold if he soaked himself. Just the thought made her tense, because colds so easily transformed into bigger beasts. "*Piccolo*," she said, trying another tactic as both his feet landed in a puddle, triumphant. "How about we play a game? Pretend the water is lava. Your shoes can withstand the wet pavement, but lava puddles? They'd catch on fire! *Sì?*"

He giggled, gesturing to the synagogue rising over the street ahead. "And Mamma? That's the volcano." He widened his eyes for effect, adding, "It's erupting."

She nodded, glancing at the pale building towering over the Lungotevere. It rose at the edge of the Jewish ghetto, mirroring the bulk of the Fatebenefratelli Hospital across the Tiber. A figure materialized in the road flanking the synagogue, and she squinted through the rain while Matteo skipped around puddles, avoiding them now. It was a Nazi, guarding the bridge across from the temple. A bit of dread nudged her interior, but she batted it away. Germans guarded bridges all over Rome. They would continue past him to meet L'Allodola—if they didn't, she had no way to find the girl again.

They were nearly at the intersection flanking the synagogue when the guard, clutching a rifle against his gray raincoat, looked uncertainly at the neighborhood spreading behind his back. He pivoted, striding not over the bridge, but into the ghetto.

She gripped Matteo's hand and tugged him forward, hoping to cross the intersection while the guard's back was turned. They stepped into the street, a shout broke through the rain from the ghetto, and Lucia's breath caught. *Santo cielo.* She stared into the ghetto, her heart accelerating. *Not in Rome.*

A throng of people, mostly women and children, stood in a long line down the street. They huddled at the base of the Portico d'Ottavia, an entry into ruins adjacent to the neighborhood. Rain drove down on them while German soldiers milled, weapons raised, periodically shouting. Behind the crowd, farther up the street, trucks idled.

Lucia shook her head, trying to harness her racing thoughts. The first guard she'd seen now sheltered under an umbrella, bent over a clipboard held by another. What were they studying? They flipped a page and it came to her. *Lists.* The people murmured and shuffled. A woman stood surrounded by teenage children, who clutched soaking pillows and blankets under their arms. A little girl in a nightdress pivoted, bewildered, gripping a bag. An elderly couple clung to each other. The wife, bent with age, had set down an assortment of things hastily gathered: a large pot, a framed picture, a pillow. A puddle formed around her forlorn belongings.

"Mamma?" Matteo whispered, breaking into her shock. "Why is everyone outside?"

She looked at him, her heart spinning like a broken compass. What could she do? They were taking the Jews. "I don't know," she managed, looking from her boy back to the crowd, unable to dislodge her own feet from the pavement.

A pretty woman stood at the edge of the throng, cupping a baby to her chest. The woman's husband milled a few feet away and glanced furtively up an alley. He looked back to his wife, who jerked her head toward the alley and widened her eyes. Rain gusted over them. Lucia stopped breathing. *No*, she wanted to shout. *Don't do it.*

The man inhaled, again met his wife's urging stare, and broke from the crowd in a run. Lucia grabbed Matteo and pulled him into her skirt, covering his head with her coat while the man streaked across the cobbles a few blocks away. He ran as though chased; if he made it to the alley, he'd have a chance. She couldn't let Matteo see. She wrapped him tighter, willing the man's strides—five, six—and then a shot rang out. The man jerked forward and fell, face-first, in a puddle. The woman with the baby shrieked and tried to scramble to him, but her neighbors held her back by the elbows.

Lucia picked Matteo up, dropping the umbrella, pushed his face into her shoulder, and started to hurry away. She'd only made it a few steps when a Nazi officer turned, a dark shape in the rain, and saw them. He shouted, "Halt!" and Lucia froze, clutching Matteo.

*Merda*, she breathed under her shudders. Matteo whimpered on her shoulder. "What happened, Mamma? What was that sound?"

"Nothing, *piccolo*," she whispered, watching the Nazi stride toward them. *Dio santo*. She shifted Matteo, pulling their documents from her inside pocket and whispering into his buried ears. "The guard shot at a bird. It's all right—"

"Why are you here?" the Nazi barked, boots hammering the cobbles.

Lucia shook her head, speaking in quick German. "I have our papers. We were simply walking to the market—"

He squinted at their documents, rain dripping off the end of his long nose. When he looked up, he was impatient, distracted. "Get out of here. Now."

She nodded, hustling away as quickly as she could carry Matteo, leaving her umbrella tottering in the puddles. When she passed under the synagogue, she released a sob, and Matteo matched it on her shoulder.

"Why was he yelling?" he wept. "What will he do to those people?"

She could no longer protect him from the horrific truth. He'd seen the evil wrapping around Rome, but she'd shied from fully explaining it. Now she understood. Maintaining Matteo's innocence was like letting him play in the forest, yet never warning him about the wolves lurking there. She walked two more blocks before setting him down on his cardboard soles. She held his shoulders and looked into his eyes, blinking away raindrops and tears.

"The German soldiers are dangerous, Matteo. Nonno may have told you different things, but now you see. We have to treat them like monsters, understand? Don't speak with them, ever.

Hide from them if I tell you to. If they stop me or talk to me, stay quiet and do exactly as I say. Never trust them, *capisci?*"

He nodded, his lower lip trembling, and whispered, "Monsters. *Capisco*, Mamma. But those people?"

Her heart broke. "I don't know what will happen to them, *piccolo*." She wrapped him in a tight hug, holding back further tears. Over his shoulder, down the road, a figure trudged through the rain. L'Allodola was coming in their direction, limping along with a cane in one hand and an umbrella in the other. She was nearly upon them when a name fell into Lucia's mind.

*Lidia.*

When L'Allodola approached, Lucia reached for her elbow, gripping it too hard. She leaned in, whispering what they'd seen. When she stepped back, the girl's eyes widened.

"You're sure?"

Lucia nodded. "And my oldest friend lives in Trastevere." She swallowed around the clamp in her throat. "She's a Jew. She and her husband have two little girls. Or three? I haven't seen her in a long time." *Oddio.* Her thoughts rattled through her mind like a swift wind. Had the Germans already come for them? Lidia's in-laws lived next door to her, with their widowed daughter and her child.

The girl started to walk, detaching from their huddle without preamble.

"*Andiamo.* We might get to them first."

They hurried over the Ponte Sisto, winding into the maze of Trastevere. *Grazie a Dio*, the streets were still quiet. There were no signs of Germans yet; just a few people plodding under umbrellas. Matteo hurried at her side, his big eyes fearful, and her heart hurt.

The girl's cane punctuated their steps. They turned three corners, and there was the plain wooden door Lucia had visited periodically over the years, bringing flowers or food when a baby was born. She and Lidia had seen each other less as time trudged on. Lidia was immersed in a big family, busy with children and in-laws, while Lucia drifted on waves of loneliness. The last time they'd snuck away for a cappuccino was ages ago, when the war had barely begun, and Lucia had returned home feeling even more alone.

She rapped on the door, praying silently. Because, despite the wedge of years and diverging lives, she loved Lidia. She saw her friend as a child, her dark braids swinging while she ran ahead in the park. And as a teenager, serious, always lugging too many books around. *Please open*, she thought, staring at the door. What if they weren't home? What if they'd gone to the ghetto for something?

But then it swung wide, and the new, grown-up Lidia stared out. She wore slippers, a plain dress, and a baby on her hip. Her hair hung in waves, and the baby gripped a chunk, pulling it to his mouth. Lidia's eyes widened with confusion.

"Lucia? What's going on?"

"Oh, thank God above," Lucia stammered. "We're in time."

Lidia glanced at Matteo, reaching instinctively for him. "Come on in, *bello*. You must be freezing!"

They stepped into the tiled foyer, and a little girl close to Matteo's age appeared.

"Rosa," Lidia said to her, "take Matteo and find a towel. Help him warm up."

Lidia pivoted back, the question clear in her eyes, and Lucia stepped closer.

"Lidia, you have to gather your family and your things. Right now. The Germans are rounding up Jews in the ghetto."

Lidia shook her head as if Lucia's words didn't make sense. She glanced at the rooms spreading beyond the foyer. The apartment smelled of steaming broth, and at the kitchen table a toddler sat in an older woman's arms, playing a clapping game. Lidia's mother-in-law paused her clapping. Wrinkles formed around her eyes.

"I saw it myself, Lidia," Lucia whispered. "They could be coming as we speak. We need to get your entire family out of here. Fetch your shoes and coats."

Lidia glanced at the baby on her hip, and the child reached to touch her lips with a dimpled hand. "Surely, the Nazis wouldn't be interested in us?" Her black eyes flipped up, but her voice was fringed with doubt. "My husband and father-in-law . . . *Dio mio*. Lucia—they went to the ghetto on an errand. A half hour ago."

Lidia pivoted, blanching while her mother-in-law stood, walking quickly across the apartment, the toddler on her hip.

"Grazia," Lidia said. "What should we do?"

"You saw it yourself?" Grazia, the older woman, stared at Lucia.

"*Sì*. We have to go right now."

"I knew it." Grazia's eyes narrowed, and she set the toddler down and knelt before her. Her wrinkled hands shook while she worked a shoe onto the tiny girl's foot, speaking quickly. "Get shoes and coats, Lidia. I told them—I told Enzo and Davide we should hide. But they trusted the rabbi . . . *Oddio*. I have to go and find them. Where's Rosa's coat? Hurry. *Hurry now*."

Grazia dropped a pair of shoes next to Lidia's slippered feet.

Lucia took the baby from her friend, cradling his soft little body so Lidia could wriggle into a coat and shoes. L'Allodola motioned for Rosa to hold out her arms, threading them into sleeves. Matteo looked between the adults, silent.

"What about Papà and Davide?" Lidia took the baby back, hands trembling. "We can't just leave them. What if they return to an empty house?"

Grazia looked stricken, as if this new, terrible reality was hitting her in waves. "I'll go and find them," she repeated, struggling to button her coat.

The baby released a fussy cry as they filed out the front door.

Moments later, they were in the street, along with Lidia's sister-in-law and ten-year-old niece from next door. They huddled under two umbrellas as the rain gusted sideways. They hadn't taken even a second to discuss where to go next.

"My house?" Lucia said. She calculated quickly—there was plenty of room. The baby would give them away to the neighbors, but she'd have to take that chance. Only old Signor Bianchi, downstairs, might care. She'd have to find a way to conceal them from her parents, if they ever came over. But surely, they, too, would protect Lidia? They'd known her all of her life.

L'Allodola bit her lip, shaking her head and interrupting Lucia's speeding thoughts. "It's too far away. We'd have to travel right through the city center, and if we're stopped in the street . . ." She frowned. "We need a closer hiding spot, at least for now while they're out sweeping neighborhoods."

Lidia bounced her baby as he fussed, gripping her lapels. "My parents are safe, sì? Surely, they won't raid Via Veneto . . ." She blanched. "Lucia. We have to get my parents."

L'Allodola shook her head, interrupting before Lucia could respond. "We have to get your family to safety first. Lucia and I can warn your parents afterward."

Lucia thought of her own parents, who lived in the same affluent building as Lidia's mother and father. Would they help, if they understood what was happening? Their neighborhood was filling with Fascists and Germans, and Nonna Colombo was thrilled by it. No—she couldn't be trusted. Lucia swallowed a bead of shame. Her own family was the enemy.

The sister-in-law spoke up, blinking large eyes. Her daughter, a smaller copy of her, shivered at her side. "I have a friend in Centocelle who would shelter us. He's not Jewish—"

"Again, much too far," L'Allodola interrupted. "But listen. The

Fatebenefratelli Hospital is minutes away. I have a hunch they'll help."

Lucia stared at her. "How can you be sure?"

"My fiancé was friends with the younger doctors. Trust me."

Her fiancé? Lucia fit that into what she knew about this mysterious girl. Which, she realized, was nearly nothing.

"But it's right next to the ghetto," Grazia said. "We could be seen."

L'Allodola nodded, her gaze darting while she thought. "We could be seen anywhere. We'll walk toward the bridge to Fatebenefratelli, and you can all hide in an alley while I go ahead and see if it's clear. If it's not, we'll take the risk of walking to Lucia's."

"It's a gamble," the older woman said.

"Everything's a gamble," the girl countered.

Grazia struggled to say her next words. "My son and husband." Grief strangled her voice. "I'll go look for them in the ghetto, once the children are hidden. I have to—"

"*I'll* look for them. The second you're all safe," Francesca interrupted. "But the longer we wait here, the less the odds are on our side. *Andiamo.*"

As if to prove her right, the rumble of a truck echoed somewhere beyond their little alley. Gears shifted, and a motor grew louder, approaching. The women met one another's stares. The Germans had requisitioned most vehicles in Rome. If there was a motor running, it was theirs.

They hurried in the other direction in the blowing rain, the baby fussing on Lidia's chest. Lucia's heart pounded, and she grew lightheaded with fear. Motors growled in the streets behind them, then died. Somewhere in the rainy neighborhood, a shout echoed.

Lucia hurried up to L'Allodola and took her cane and her arm. Supporting the girl on one side and Matteo on the other, they quickened. Their feet slapped stone, impossibly loud despite the rain. The cobbled alley rolled down a hill toward the river, and Lucia led the way while her thoughts tumbled over themselves.

*Please don't let the Nazis see us. Please let the way be clear.*

At the edge of the alley, where the neighborhood intersected with the Tiber, they stopped. L'Allodola met Lucia's stare. She motioned for the adults and children to wait, and she walked out into the street by herself. She swung forward to the rhythm of her cane, striding into what appeared to be an empty, rain-washed avenue overlooking the river. Lucia could barely breathe while she crossed. Then she stood, a silhouette above the riverbank, alone against a backdrop of rain and fog. If someone was looking, they would see her. Lucia's heart dropped, and she realized: that was the point. The girl was testing the street, offering herself like bait to whomever might be watching, tempting them to approach.

L'Allodola stood at the railing under the skeleton of a tree, already stripped of leaves, for what felt like a long time. She looked up and down the river. Then she stared, unmoving, at the hospital looming dark and silent beyond the bridge. Would the doctors inside hide a family?

Finally, she pivoted around her cane, raised a hand waist high, and beckoned them forward. Lucia glanced back at the huddle of women and children. They'd have to walk along the riverside for a block before reaching the Ponte Cestio, which spanned the Tiber to the hospital. For a few minutes, they would be completely exposed. What if they were on the bridge when more Germans came, following their lists to the Jews in Trastevere?

They strode on, silent, trusting the hunch of the girl leading the way with her cane. Even the baby didn't make a noise. Wind gusted, soaking through their coats and rippling the puddled street. Lucia walked with her shoulders back, but inside she flinched with each step, ready for a voice to ricochet off the river, yelling, "HALT!" What would the Nazis do if they caught them?

Would she be arrested? The thought made her stomach drop. What would become of Matteo?

But then they were on the bridge, spanning a river swollen with rain. The hospital hung, ghostly, over the water, its bricks and stone disappearing in the mist. Somewhere ahead, across the island and the arc of the next bridge, lay the besieged ghetto. Shouts and cries drifted over the water. A pair of gunshots cracked in the distance. Lucia hurried faster.

They were halfway across when another engine rumbled behind them. Lucia tightened her grip on Matteo's hand. The engine echoed through the rain, coming from Trastevere.

L'Allodola pivoted and motioned to them. *Hurry.*

They scurried from the bridge to the island, turning into the piazza in front of the hospital. The engine grew louder. Lucia lifted Matteo, and they ran, all of them, moving as one toward the hospital doors. What would they do if the doctors didn't let them in? Lucia's heart pounded against her breastbone, and Matteo's shoes bounced off her hips. The truck's gears ground. In seconds, it would pass the bridge. But L'Allodola was already holding open the door, ushering them out of the rain, and Lucia stepped aside while the children filed in. Lidia and the baby disappeared, the other women followed, and Lucia turned, letting the door fall shut behind them all. Through its crack, she saw a truck rock past, in plain view across the Tiber. A huddle of people stared out from under its canopy.

Then the door closed.

L'Allodola was already at the intake desk, dripping on the floor and speaking quietly to an older doctor with a mustache. He glanced up through his spectacles, assessing the shivering family before him and nodding.

"*Sì, sì,*" he murmured, motioning to a young doctor who appeared in the hallway behind the desk. "We've had several already this morning."

The younger doctor strode over, a clipboard tucked under one arm.

"Francesca?" he asked, scanning the family. "I heard about Giacomo—"

She shook her head, quieting him, and the older doctor stepped closer. "It's another group with Syndrome K, Vittorio. Take them back and fill out the intake paperwork."

Vittorio held up a hand and beckoned the dripping family down the hallway. Grazia paused, whispering, "You'll search?" and both Lucia and L'Allodola nodded. Grazia inhaled, as though forcing her desperation to wait, and walked little Rosa and the toddler down the hall.

Lidia's sister-in-law sent her daughter down after them, but she stepped forward before following. Her lovely, dark eyes rested first on Lucia, then on the green-eyed girl. *Francesca.*

"I don't know how to thank you for warning us."

"There's absolutely no need to thank us," Francesca said quietly.

"My father." The woman's voice cracked. "And my brother. You'll try to find them?"

Francesca's voice was fierce. "I'll search as if they were my own."

The sister nodded. She leaned across the gap and kissed Francesca's cheeks.

Lidia was at the intake desk, speaking quietly to the older doctor as he hung up a telephone. She walked over. The baby was quiet on her hip, yawning, ready for a nap.

"He's sending a runner to my parents' house, Lucia. We tried to call, but nobody answered the telephone. I don't know if it's not working, or—" Tears glittered in Lidia's dark eyes. "*Oddio.* I need my husband. How will I get through this without him? My poor children—" The words seemed to stick in her throat, and Lidia looked away, blinking fast. She smoothed the fine hair around her baby's ears, inhaling shakily, as though she could store her grief for later. "Lucia," she said, "you saved my children."

It was difficult to speak. "You'd do the same for mine," she managed, and Lidia nodded. Lucia reached for her, squeezing her free hand. "As soon as the Germans leave the neighborhood, I promise we'll search for your husband and your parents." Again Lidia nodded, and Lucia struggled with her next words, but they had to be said. They'd nested in her soul for far too long. "Lidia, I'm so sorry. When you were barred from university, ostracized in your own country—I should have been there for you. It was cowardice that allowed me to fall away. It was cowardice that kept me passive while terrible things happened."

"We fell away from each other, Lucia. It wasn't just you." Her eyes glistened. "But you were here for me today." Lidia stepped over and wrapped Lucia in a hug. They held on to each other for a long moment.

Then Lucia watched her oldest friend drift down the hall with the doctor, disappearing around a corner. She turned to L'Allodola, sighing as the knot of fear loosened a bit in her chest. A question hung in her mind.

"What's Syndrome K?"

L'Allodola stared down the hallway. "A fake disease. The doctors are going to tell the Nazis that it's deadly and highly infectious." A hint of a smile brushed her lips. "The K stands for Kappler and Kesselring."

"What's Kesselring?" Matteo murmured, snuggling his face into Lucia's waist.

"A German commander, *piccolo*." She pulled him close, removing his cap to clear the damp hair off his forehead, and swallowed a lump of grief. She'd do anything to protect him. The mothers across the river, being herded into trucks right now, also yearned to protect their children.

Lucia blinked back tears and turned to the girl, Francesca. "I want you to know that I'll do whatever it takes." She covered Matteo's visible ear with her palm, pressing gently and speaking carefully. "I won't stop until they're out of Rome."

The girl nodded, meeting her stare. "I believe you this time." She glanced at Matteo, leaning close to whisper, "I'll tell my contacts about your Nazi suitor. Carry on with your plan."

"I will." Lucia caught her green gaze with her own. "Francesca, *sì?*"

"Keep that between us." L'Allodola crossed her arms, shivering. "Now, *andiamo*. We're not finished yet."

# SIXTEEN

☙

## Francesca

*October 17, 1943*

FRANCESCA PULLED ON her jacket and hoisted a laundry bag full of false identity documents and *Italia Libera* leaflets. She was going to make sure Rome saw the feature article in the Action Party's underground news leaflets this morning. The message, about the persecution and roundup of the Jews, was potent:

*All day long, the Germans went around Rome seizing Italians for their furnace in the north. The Germans would like us to believe that these people are in some way alien to us, that they are of another race. But we feel them as part of our flesh and blood. They have always lived, fought, and suffered with us. Not only able-bodied men, but old people, children, women, and babies were crowded into covered trucks and taken away to meet their fate. There is not a single heart that does not shudder at the thought of what the fate might be.*

She placed the leaflets in the laundry bag, their words seething in her soul. After leaving the Fatebenefratelli Hospital the day before, she and Lucia had gone separate directions, looking for the rest of Lidia's family. Lucia had hurried to Via Veneto to check for Lidia's parents, and Francesca had waited until it was safe to search the ransacked ghetto for her husband and father-in-law. They'd met again on the Lungotevere before curfew, defeated.

The apartment on Via Veneto was vacant, a half-eaten breakfast still on the table. The ghetto was empty, eerie, and there'd been no sign of Lidia's remaining family. Or of anyone else.

Francesca was exhausted from using her body past its limits, but she wouldn't stop. Not today, or any other day. She locked her apartment and headed for the stairs. In a city clamped tight under German law, leaflets spread the news—the real news, not Nazi propaganda. It was worth the considerable risk necessary to deliver them.

She gripped the handrail, thumping downstairs with the laundry bag, and pivoted at Signora Russo's ground-floor apartment. She knocked. A week earlier, Signora Russo had seen her wrestling her bicycle up the stairs, nearly falling, and had stepped up and gripped the handlebars herself. "Let me keep it for you," she said, carrying it back down and wheeling it into her apartment. "We'll park it in my foyer, and you can just knock when you need it."

The arrangement worked well, because someone was always home at the Russos' apartment. Now Francesca heard voices within, mixing like soup. A baby cried, a toddler squealed, and when the door flung open, a ten-year-old boy blinked up at her.

"Your bicycle?" little Roberto asked, and she nodded. He disappeared for a second, returning with the bicycle while she propped the door wide. She dropped her laundry bag, heavy with papers, into the basket.

"Wish I had one," he murmured, bending to examine the chain and the spokes.

"How's your mamma?" Francesca took the handlebars. Signora Russo's voice echoed from within. It sounded like she was breaking up a brawl between children.

Roberto straightened, looking at her with a gaze that always seemed older than ten. "Cross. There's never enough to cook with, you know?"

She did know. The Germans had interrupted Rome's food supply, and the city was quickly running out of everything. These days, most people existed on rationed black bread, a hundred grams a day, which was merely a slice. There was no milk for children. People concocted broths, learning to cook with anything edible, and the wild cats peppering the forum were slowly disappearing. They needed the Allies to liberate Rome soon, before winter set in.

Roberto brightened, echoing her thoughts. "It'll get better when the Allies come. Papà says we only have to hold on a few more weeks."

She nodded, but doubt clung to her heart. "I hope your father's right. Give your mamma my best, *sì*?"

She bade the boy goodbye and stepped into the weak morning light, tightening her coat, worrying that Roberto's father wasn't right at all. The Allies seemed to be stuck in the south, far from Rome. She listened to illegal radio broadcasts whenever she could, piecing together the news, and she'd started to believe the worst: There would have to be another invasion in Italy. The Allies needed to land on closer beaches, above the German lines, to reach Rome and the north. But would they?

The early-morning streets were quiet. She swung her leg over her bicycle, glancing backward before pulling out, and her gaze hinged on someone standing at the corner. Their eyes met long enough for Francesca to hesitate, and then he turned, vanishing behind a building.

She shivered, staring at the place where the figure had stood. Had she imagined it? A blackness welled in her chest, like deep water. Was that stranger watching her? Perhaps he'd only been looking up the street. She shook her head and pushed on the pedal, wobbling into motion. She couldn't let paranoia creep in.

But as she bumped along, gaining speed, the fear in her chest deepened.

★   ★   ★

FRANCESCA PEDALED TO a kiosk selling Fascist newspapers. She dismounted and made eye contact with the gaunt, one-armed man who ran it, a veteran of the war in Ethiopia. He nodded once and, whistling softly, stared out into the quiet street. Quickly, she pulled a pile of leaflets from her laundry bag and bent over the newspapers. Hands shaking, she flipped the papers open and slid a leaflet inside each one. Her heart in her throat, she went through the stacks while the man in the kiosk whistled and watched.

"*Buongiorno!*" he said loudly, followed by two coughs. Their signal. Francesca tucked the remaining leaflets under her coat and stood, pivoting, her breath rattling in her chest. A uniformed SS officer strode across the street, heels clicking, raising a hand. Had he seen what she was doing? She forced calm into her face, but her pulse throbbed in her skull. The officer stopped, bent to retrieve a paper, and rummaged in his pocket for a billfold.

She nodded her goodbye to the man in the kiosk, who began to talk with great animation, distracting his customer. *Please don't open the paper yet*, she prayed. She swung her leg over her bicycle seat, willing the leaflets to stay put where she'd jammed them in her waistband. The waistband was loose; she'd had to safety-pin it in place this morning. *Madonna.* If a single leaflet fluttered to the ground, she could start to count her last breaths.

She pedaled, holding her torso as still as possible, feeling the papers shifting. When an intersection appeared, she veered right, escaping from the kiosk's view. She exhaled, dizzy.

Next, she slipped into apartment buildings, following people through doorways and hoping there wouldn't be doormen. When she got safely inside, she looked up and down hallways and foyers before stuffing leaflets into letter boxes.

She was exiting her fifth building when she nearly ran into a man lighting a cigarette.

*"Scusa,"* she stuttered, and he looked up under a pair of heavy eyebrows.

It was the man from Carlo's building. The Fascist, the true believer, with the teenage boy, pimple faced and wary. She held her breath while he muttered, *"Di niente,"* staring at the basket on her bicycle.

She mounted, still unable to breathe, and pedaled away. She was at least a kilometer from Carlo's building. Was it a coincidence? She pictured the man, the snap of the flame burning his cigarette, and the way his eyes flicked up. Did he recognize her? Was he surprised to see her? *Or was he following her?* She pictured the figure she'd seen leaving her apartment earlier, standing on the corner until their eyes met, and her heart jumped. Was it the same man? She'd only caught a glimpse of him before he vanished. She could be sure of nothing. There were only two possibilities, she reasoned, pedaling faster and pushing her dizzy fear down. She was either being watched by *Fascisti*, or she was becoming unhinged by her own nerves.

Either way, she still had a stop to make.

A few minutes later, she was ringing a bell in yet another apartment building. A man's voice called through the door. "Who is it?"

"L'Allodola."

The door swung open, and she wheeled into a narrow foyer, blinking to adjust her eyes. A man, the age her father would be if he'd lived, stood before her. Wordlessly, she reached into her basket, feeling for the remaining documents.

They were identity cards, forged in a basement across the city late last night. The man stared at them in Francesca's hands, and then he was weeping. He wiped tears as they ran down the creases under his eyes and wet his mustache.

*"Grazie. Signorina, grazie mille."* He used the heels of his hands

to press the tears away. "Please excuse me. It means the world, you see. You've brought my family freedom."

An ache welled in her chest, and she pressed the cards into his palms and met his stare. His eyes were the color of dark honey.

"You mustn't thank me. I wish you luck, signore."

IT WAS NEARLY curfew when she landed in Carlo's apartment, as planned. She hadn't seen anyone worrisome when she entered the building; the man and his son were not in the courtyard, but still she'd tensed as if watched. Was it paranoia? She told Carlo upon arrival, and he darkened, muttering, "The kid just joined the Fascist Brigades. We'll have to start monitoring them."

"Someone may have been watching me this morning," she added, standing in his living room and tightening her arms over her chest. "I can't be sure. But if it has anything to do with your neighbors, we need to be vigilant."

Carlo nodded. "The new Fascist *squadristi* are following and pestering people all over Rome, often with little cause. They might not know we're actually resistance." He sighed. "I'll send out some eyes and ears of my own to try to figure out if we're being watched, *si*?"

Francesca nodded, shelving her worries and moving on to the topic that brought her here: Lucia. She took a deep breath, waited for him to meet her gaze, and prepared to say it all at once.

"I didn't tell you everything about Lucia. After I visited her the first time."

Carlo's gaze swung to meet hers. "What do you mean? Did you see her a second time?"

Francesca had reported on her first visit, assuring Carlo that Lucia was safely distant from the Fascists and, in fact, seemed to hate the Nazis. She'd kept the rest to herself, waiting to be sure Lucia was serious about joining the resistance. After yesterday, she was certain. And it was time to tell him.

"I met her a second time in the park, and a third time yesterday, which showed me who she really is, Carlo. We'd planned to meet on the Lungotevere De' Cenci, near the ghetto, and she saw what was happening there. So we went to warn her friend Lidia and help her hide with her family, though we didn't find them all . . ." Francesca paused, clearing the pain from her throat before continuing. "Lucia wants to join the resistance, and I think she should. She's already working on a plan to infiltrate Nazi social circles and listen for information. She's made a connection with someone named Hauptsturmführer Hans Bergmann."

Carlo stared at her, speechless, his mouth hanging open. After a long, uncomfortable moment, he spun, rubbing at his unshaven jaw. "You can't be serious. I never would have thought—"

"She can provide eyes and ears where nobody else can," Francesca interrupted, staring at him as he slumped down onto a chair. His hands hammocked his head, and he gaped at the floor, silent. "You're cultivating handfuls of spies for the CLN, Carlo. Rome's full of eyes reporting back to you. Why can't she join them?"

"She's not a spy, Francesca. You were supposed to be doing me a favor, keeping her out of danger, not *recruiting* her. *Dio mio . . .*"

"She recruited herself. She wanted to participate before I ever stepped through that door. And why should you insist she stay out of danger? She can make up her own mind, just like the rest of us. We're *all* in danger."

"Do you realize who her parents are? They're zealots—"

"Which makes her all the more valuable." Francesca puffed air through her lips, tamping down her frustration. "I trust her," she persisted, casting around for the root of his objection. "I was wary at first, but I saw something in her during the raid yesterday—"

"It's not a matter of *trusting* her." He raised his gaze, shaking his head in the dim light.

Why did Carlo think he could make decisions for an old girlfriend? Her life had clearly gone on without him, but apparently his heart stalled with her.

"What about her husband?" he said, as if finding a new argument. "How can she join German social circles as a married woman? And don't they have a small child?"

"She's a widow, Carlo."

He tented his hands over his jaw, digesting that. "But she does have a kid?"

"A five-year-old boy. But she's going to keep him separate from her evenings out. They don't have to know—"

"Wait." Carlo stared at her, stricken. "How old is the kid?"

"Five."

The color drained from his face. He began to shake his head, as if he couldn't make sense of anything she'd said. "You're sure the child is five years old? Could he be four? He looked so small . . ."

He leveled his eyes on her, and she struggled to make sense of his reaction. "He does seem small for his age," she conceded. "But Matteo is five."

"*Gesù Cristo*." Carlo stood, raking both hands through his hair. "*Matteo*. It's my father's name . . ." He began to pace.

Francesca fought to keep up. His father's name? She thought of Matteo, picturing his little face, and the dots in her mind connected like constellations. Her mouth dropped open on its own.

"*Madonna mia*, Carlo," she whispered, stunned. "*You're* her husband."

He nodded, eyes wide with shock, and she exhaled.

"And Matteo is your child."

"But she was never pregnant." He shook his head. "I thought she'd remarried. I didn't know. I didn't know he . . . that she was . . ." He paced back and forth, traversing the narrow floor. His voice cracked. "Is there any way to stop her from spying on Bergmann? What if I give her another job? There's a hairdresser on Via

Veneto who works for me. He needs someone to pass him the news, someone he can pass information to—Lucia can do that. Instead."

Francesca stared while he cast about, trying to make sense of this new reality, and her own mind sped ahead of him. Carlo still loved Lucia; that much was clear. But he wasn't a part of her life. He hadn't even known he had a son. He had no right to interfere with her now.

"I'll offer her the hairdresser," she said quietly.

"Does she know who sent you?" He stopped pacing and looked up, newly stricken.

"Of course not. She knows I'm resistance, but I've never mentioned you. I did say I'd speak to our cell leader, Gianluca, but she has no reason to make the connection. I won't meddle with your personal life, but I will facilitate Lucia if she wants to proceed. I saw her integrity yesterday. Her courage. She'll be valuable as a partisan." She caught his gaze and held it. "Carlo? She's more than your past. And we need her."

# SEVENTEEN

## ❧

## Lucia

*November 1, 1943*

Nonna Colombo glanced at Lucia as they approached the door to Salon Borghese, smiling with pursed lips. "I'm impressed you thought of this," she whispered, threading her arm through Lucia's. "Fabrizio works wonders. Even the wives of German officers see him now." She winked. "But there are plenty of *unmarried* officers. Like Hans."

Lucia nodded, but a storm whipped up in her interior as they stepped inside. She glanced at the half-dozen women before her, in various stages of beautification, and forced herself to smile. Did they realize that the rest of the city was hungry? Did they know how their lovers terrorized people, shooting and beating and arresting whomever got in their way? She touched her curls, as if contemplating a hairstyle, and inside she seethed. She thought of Lidia, running from the Nazis while her entire community was captured. Of Lidia's husband, parents, and father-in-law, whom she and Francesca had been unable to find. The trouble with these women, well fed and content in their salon chairs, was that they didn't care.

"Is everything all right?" A woman with a German accent stared at her. Lucia blinked, shaking herself from her anger. She met the blue-eyed gaze of the woman who studied her under a head full of curlers.

"Everything is lovely," she replied in German. She adjusted her mood like someone might straighten a crooked picture on a wall, forcing it even. For the next several hours, she would pretend she was the girl she'd once been. Carefree. Charming. Able to play a role.

A wide-shouldered man strode over, extending his arms to his new arrivals. "Frieda and Lucia Colombo?" He paused before them, pulling each inward to kiss their cheeks. He smelled of vanilla and cigarettes and carried himself like a dancer.

"I am Fabrizio. *Benvenute*." He looked at Lucia for a second too long, eyes bright over his arched nose.

She stiffened.

"I understand you're going out tonight?" he continued, smiling gallantly. "Where to? The Hotel Bernini? The Savoy?"

"The Excelsior," Nonna Colombo said, drifting to an empty chair, her satin gown shushing as she walked. She settled before a mirror, appraising her reflection. "My Lucia is just getting back into society. Make her look splendid, won't you, Fabrizio?"

"*Sì, sì*, it's what I do." He cupped Lucia's elbow to steer her. "If you'll come with me, *per favore*. There's a seat in the back, preferred by clients who wish for quiet. I'm afraid it's the only open chair at the moment."

"Quiet sounds lovely." She allowed him to steer her away from her mother and the other women wafting about the salon. They rounded a corner to a narrow alcove with a chair and a mirror. It wasn't exactly a separate room, but set apart enough for her purposes. Lucia dropped into the chair, and Fabrizio leaned close, shaping her curls while he spoke in a low voice.

"We have Gianluca in common, *sì*?"

She nodded, her heart in her throat. It was official: she was part of the resistance.

Fabrizio stared at the mirror, meeting her reflected eyes. His voice was so low she could barely discern his words. "Come each week, and I'll pass along what I hear. The wives of Nazi leaders multiply daily, and they love to talk to their hairdresser."

"Fabrizio!" a woman called from the main room. "My curls are set!"

"*Brava!*" he called back, his expression transforming from solemn to animated, as if someone had poked him with a pin. "Just one moment!"

He lowered his voice again. "When you come, you must insist on this alcove. *Sì?*"

She nodded. "*Capisco.* And I have this for you." With shaking fingers, she pulled a copy of *Italia Libera* from her purse. He lifted his shirt and stuffed it, without comment, into his undergarments.

"*Grazie, signora.* Now listen." He placed a hand on her shoulder, squeezing as if to underline his whispers. "The people you're circling are dangerous. *Capisci?* Befriend who you must, but look over this shoulder"—he squeezed once more—"always."

"*Capisco,*" she whispered again. She pictured Bergmann, with his dead eyes, and cringed. What had she gotten herself into? Matteo's face replaced Bergmann's in her mind. He was giggling, freckled nose scrunched with mischief, and her heart clutched. Was she endangering him by being here, playing a role? The thought made her panic a bit. *No.* She'd keep her boy out of all this. He'd be her carefully guarded secret.

Fabrizio's black eyes caught hers again in the mirror. She was struck by the idea that he understood somehow; that he sensed her divided heart.

"I'll be back in a minute to do something *magnifico* with your hair," he said in a regular voice. "Let's get you ready for a night out."

* * *

"YOU DON'T SEEM yourself tonight," Hans Bergmann said from his lounge chair on the other side of the coffee table. They were in the Excelsior, angled toward each other under the glittering light of a chandelier, struggling through a third encounter and their first real date.

Lucia shook herself from the words echoing in her mind. His words. *I'll enjoy Rome nonetheless, particularly once we've cleaned it up.* Had he meant the Jews? Was he involved in the raid on the ghetto? She met his stare and found his blue eyes locked on her face, examining her. He sniffed, as he did a hundred times a night, and she hardened. What would she give, right now, to ask him why he sniffed all the time—was it a cold? Allergies? A nervous habit? Was he so absorbed with himself that he didn't see how repulsive he was?

She tipped her wine, glancing at the liquid, and gave him a full smile. "I'm just a little tired. But I'm thrilled to be out, and to see you again."

He nodded as if she'd checked a box, and she sipped her wine. *Was* he repulsive? If she'd stumbled upon him, knowing nothing, would she think so? No. He just looked like a man, square, tall, and very blond, with a restrained manner. But she knew now that he didn't always restrain himself. He'd had something to do with arresting the Jews—she smelled it on him, like rot. She blinked, recalled the women and children huddling in the rain, and struggled to swallow her wine. It was why she was here, doing something. What she was able to do wasn't yet clear, and that irritated her, too.

He leaned back, examining her.

"You know?" she said, crossing one slim leg over the other, "I'm not sure what I've eaten today. Perhaps I'll feel more myself with a little something."

"Ah yes." He sat up. "You must keep up your strength."

He stood, and she reached out to squeeze his hand as he passed, murmuring, *"Danke."*

With the seat across from her empty, Lucia exhaled. She'd take a few bites of whatever he brought, and when he wasn't looking, she'd tip the rest into her purse for Matteo. Satisfaction pinged her heart. She hadn't foreseen it, but this position would allow her boy to eat good food once in a while. For a child who seemed to weigh half what he should, it was a gift.

She lifted her eyes to the chandelier. Did Bergmann like her? She needed to make sure that he did, but tonight her heart wasn't in it. And yet, perhaps she didn't have to work too hard to secure his interest. Bergmann stared at her as if adding up her parts: long legs, slim waist, breasts, dimples, curls, correct lineage. It all equaled one satisfactory woman. She dropped her gaze to the chair across from her and stilled.

His briefcase. She'd seen it with him last time, too. What did he carry in that slim leather case? *I've been procuring labor for the war effort, managing subversives—things like that,* he'd said. She thought of the many Jews in hiding across Rome. Did he have files on them, to hunt them down? And the labor sweeps were happening with increasing frequency. Just last week, the Germans had cordoned off a neighborhood outside the city walls, gathering all able-bodied men, aged fifteen to seventy, to build their fortifications. What if people could be warned?

Bergmann appeared, weaving through a cluster of people across the room. She smiled up at him as he neared.

"Hauptsturmführer Bergmann, would it trouble you if I called you Hans?"

He grinned as he sat, and for a second he seemed surprised. "Not at all." He met her stare. "I'd be pleased to think our acquaintance is progressing."

"Oh, Hans." She leaned forward and placed a hand on his arm. "I feel exactly the same."

They shared a long, smiling gaze, and one thought rebounded in Lucia's mind: she would find a way to steal that briefcase.

WHEN BERGMANN WALKED Lucia home, it was dark. He breached the gap between them, taking her hand, and she had to force herself not to pull away. At least her parents' house was close. Their footsteps echoed. It was after curfew, but she'd be unquestioned walking home with him. Yet he was only going as far as the home he thought she inhabited, her parents' apartment, the place she'd be expected to live as a single woman. It was difficult to say which was worse: walking the rest of the way alone after curfew, or walking with him.

He stopped before the building's door and turned, staring into her eyes. She held his pale gaze, fighting nausea. He expected her to kiss him. She thought about the briefcase dangling from his right hand and reached up on tiptoe, grazing his cheek. At the last second he turned, pressing his lips to hers like a hungry leech. She forced herself to hold still. He let go, and she dropped away. How long before he'd expect more? Could she convince him she was a traditional woman, chaste until marriage? Of course, he knew she'd already been married.

He smiled stiffly. "Can I see you next week?"

She mustered a grin. "That would be grand."

"Perfect—meet me at the same time and place. Until then, good night, my dear." He tipped his head, pivoting abruptly, and strode away.

Lucia wavered in the street, catching her breath. *Santo cielo.* Had she ever liked a man less? She watched him turn a corner before hurrying off herself, spitting his taste into the bushes.

The city was quiet and dark, all of its light smothered by the blackout. She slunk through it, threading along alleys and narrow streets toward home. The unrelenting fall rains had actually relented for a bit, and clouds skated over the moon, dropping shafts of pale light. When she crossed open streets, she could see her breath.

She was eager to return to Matteo. He'd be asleep when she got home, in his own bed thanks to her mother, who'd had an uncharacteristic flash of kindness after the salon. "I'll take him home and fix him something to eat," she'd said, and a strange smile climbed all the way to her eyes. "It'll be better for him to sleep in his own bed, *Liebling*. He was afraid the last time he stayed over with us." She'd winked, adding, "Heaven knows your father can fend for himself and make his own dinner, once in a while."

It was strange with Nonna Colombo lately. Lucia gripped her handbag, heavy with precious *antipasti* smuggled out for her child, and glanced up and down another moonlit street. It was almost as if her mother loved her. Her dates with Bergmann seemed to have thawed something in her, which only made Lucia freeze harder. If her mother knew the truth, that fragile love would evaporate like mist on a hot day.

A noise broke into her thoughts. She tightened, stepping again into a strip of shadow. Had she imagined it? She didn't turn or alter her pace, but she stopped breathing. Listened.

There it was again. The soft echo of a step.

Lucia's heart pounded as she walked faster, staving off panic. All she could hear now were her own footsteps, her own sweeping breath, but she knew. Someone was following her. Could it be Bergmann? *Oddio*. Or what if it was someone he'd sent? Was he suspicious of her? She replayed his kiss in her mind, his abrupt goodbye, and fear flooded her soul. She had to find a way to escape. To hide.

Despite herself, she glanced back at the dark alley. It appeared to be empty. Could she have imagined it? She pulled up a map of the city in her mind, zeroing in on where she was. She saw the entire alley, its exact contours snaking between wider streets. She would take the next left, away from home. Whoever was trailing her couldn't know where she lived. Should she hide and try to see who it was?

Up ahead, another moonlit street unraveled, and she strode toward it. Faint steps, intermittent, sounded in her wake. It was nearly nothing. In normal times, it could have been a cat, slinking along a wall. An echo. But now, in Rome after curfew? It was someone, after her.

Lucia crossed the silvery street, walking quickly, and ducked into the shadow of a narrow alley. She turned, pressing against the building, watching the open expanse. If whoever was following her thought she hadn't noticed him, he'd pass through the moonlight momentarily.

Two more shaky breaths, and there he was. A long figure looked up and down the empty cobblestones, ducked, and jogged across. As he neared, the moon cast its light on his face, tracing his brows, shadowing under his jaw, falling on his shoulders.

Lucia dropped her handbag. She was staring at a ghost.

# EIGHTEEN

୨୨

## Francesca

*November 1, 1943*

F RANCESCA FLIPPED OFF the late radio broadcast, frustrated. She'd caught the ten o' clock news from London, and it was bleak. The American Fifth Army had yet to capture Isernia. At this rate, they'd never reach Rome. The Germans had the advantage of well-prepared defenses in Italy's rocky southern mountains. Francesca thought of her hometown, perched on a Tuscan hill, built to withstand ancient invasions. From its walls, hills and valleys dropped into the distance, every approach visible. Southern Italy was the same, only the mountains were higher, the passes narrower.

She stood, tottering on aching legs, and made her way across the apartment to her armoire. As she passed the bed, her heart ached, as it did every night. She blinked and pictured Giacomo warming the sheets, the mess of his hair, his goofy smile, the way he tapped out a rhythm on a book as he read. She swallowed the pain in her throat, shaking out her nightdress.

A knock sounded on the front door. She stilled, the nightdress gripped in her whitening knuckles. Who could be knocking now? It was well after ten o' clock.

"Francesca," a voice called through the door, urgent. She exhaled, dropping the nightdress. *Signora Russo.* She hurried across the apartment, relieved but no less confused. Her neighbor wasn't seen after dinner, ever. With a houseful of kids to put to sleep, she vanished into her noisy apartment as if on cue. Why was she here? Was she all right?

Francesca opened the door, and Signora Russo stood there in her robe, pale faced and frantic. She grabbed Francesca's hand, tugging her into the hall.

"The Germans," she whispered, her voice harsh. "They're pulling up outside. Roberto saw them. *Madonna mia*, Francesca. We have to get you out before they surround the building."

"Surround the building?"

The older woman towed her, like a tugboat, and Francesca's mind spun as they started down the stairs. "Why do you think it's me they're after?" she managed as Signora Russo threaded her arm into Francesca's, bearing her weight down the final flight.

"*Cara mia*, I know you've been up to something."

Francesca was about to protest, but Signora Russo held up a hand to stop her.

"You don't have to pretend. I admire you for it. You're a brave girl, Francesca. *Andiamo*—we'll check the back exit of the building. I'll make sure it's clear."

They hurried, wordless, down a dark hallway while shouts erupted at the building's front door. Something started to bang the locks, hard. Metal clanged on metal while they wove deeper into the belly of the building, toward an obscure back door. Signora Russo stopped in the complete darkness, and Francesca sensed her hand rising again. *Wait*. Signora Russo sidled forward, and Francesca could make out her shape, feeling for a door that led to a narrow alley. She found it, and the handle turned without a key, *grazie a Dio*. A wedge of moonlight fell into the hallway as Signora Russo poked her head outside, looking up and down. She beckoned Francesca forward, eyes wide in the faint light.

Before Francesca slipped outside, Signora Russo leaned in, kissing each of her cheeks in the dark.

"Thank you," Francesca whispered over the ache in her throat.

"*Di niente*. Now get somewhere safe. In three days, I'll send Roberto to school with your bicycle and some clothes. Meet him there to fetch it. And to let us know you're all right."

Francesca squeezed the older woman's hands, nodded once, and detached, ducking through the opening.

The alley was dark, and she scurried down it, away from the building while its door swung closed, sealing off the shouts erupting from within. Would her neighbors withstand the search unharmed? Had she put them all in danger?

She wove through moonlit streets all the way to the Tiber, swallowing the throb of uncertainty. She'd find a place to hide by the river, in trees or an alcove, until morning. And then she would figure out what was next.

# NINETEEN

ᖇᖇ

## Lucia

*November 1, 1943*

CARLO STEPPED INTO the alley and nearly fell backward when he saw Lucia there, pressed flat in the darkest shadow. She stared at him, blank inside. It was as if a wave had crashed through her soul, sweeping her bare. She couldn't think. She couldn't move.

"Lucia. I'm sorry . . ." He stood before her, traced in moonlight, clearly at a loss.

She shook her head, equally lost. But with the movement, her thoughts whirred to life. *It was Carlo.* How could it possibly be Carlo? Tears thickened Lucia's throat, coming from nowhere. She found herself collapsing over her own knees like a rag doll, as if her bones had liquified in the shock. "I thought you were someone else," she managed to gasp. "A Nazi . . ."

His hand landed on her arm, and he hoisted her upright, keeping his body at a polite distance. But his hand stayed on her elbow, helping her stand.

"I'm sorry," he said again. "I shouldn't have followed you. I was just worried about you walking home alone, after curfew—"

Her mind swung into focus, alert.

"How did you know?" She shook him from her elbow, straightening on her own. "How did you know I'd be out here alone?" Her questions multiplied, yet unspoken. Where had he come from? Why was he here, standing before her in a dark alley after six long years? Where had he been?

"I'm Gianluca." He dropped the words like stones, waiting for their impact.

"L'Allodola's contact?" She started to shake her head again, stunned afresh. The girl worked for him? She'd known about Carlo all along? Betrayal seemed to lap at Lucia's feet like an ocean, returning again and again.

He guessed what she was thinking. "None of this is her fault. I sent her to check on you because I was worried about you, with your family's background. I was terrified that you'd be persecuted after the war. She didn't know our history. She thought you were married to somebody else. And that your son . . ."

"Our son." Anger flared in Lucia's heart, giving her strength. "Though he's never had a father. How long have you been following me? What gives you the right?"

He slung his hands in his pockets, sheepish, and shook his head. His eyes caught the moonlight. "You insisted on joining up, Lucia. I didn't see that coming. And now you're in such a precarious position, and I feel responsible. So I've been shadowing you when I can, to make sure you're safe—"

"*Sì?* When you've never wondered if I was safe for the past six years? When you never once *felt responsible* for me or your son? Save your worry for someone else."

He slumped a little, and the smell of him drifted through her, knocking her off-balance again. He smelled the same as she remembered, of soap and smoke and something warm, like spice. She tightened her arms over her chest, glaring at him, though suddenly she wanted to fall into him. She wanted to beat his chest, to wail.

Somewhere beyond the city walls, a plane droned, its noise

expanding. They both froze. The Allies continued to bomb the outskirts of the city periodically, taking out railroad lines, stations, and bridges. They had no reason to hit Rome's center, but Lucia still held her breath, waiting for the bombs to fall somewhere else and dispel her fear. Carlo cocked his head, listening. An explosion thundered in the distance, followed by several more. His eyes stilled, two dark pools, as if measuring thuds and concussions and drawing up coordinates. She squinted in the moonlight, taking him in, while somewhere, not far off, the world burned. He looked the same, though thinner than she remembered. His dark hair seemed to be flecked with gray, but maybe that was just the moonlight. He wasn't yet thirty.

"Where have you been all these years?" she said when the roar of bursting bombs died. The drone of motors faded from the sky.

He hesitated, pushing his silvered hair back with his wide hands.

"Answer me," she whispered. The words cracked as she said them, and an ache expanded around her heart.

His voice was gravelly when he found it. "I went to Spain at first. After I came back, I was arrested for being a dissident and sent into *confino politico*—three years ago. I got out of political exile just before Mussolini fell."

She nodded, as if this was explanation enough, but fury boiled in her chest. He'd gone to Spain. When she was struggling to nurse a baby and keep the money coming from her father for the apartment and maintain her dignity while neighbors whispered . . . *he'd been in Spain.*

During the civil war there, she realized. Had he fought in it? Like her brother Marco, but on the opposite side? He'd left her to fight another country's war? Every realization felt like a new bomb, detonating in her soul.

"I can see that I never really knew you," she said at last. "I don't know you at all."

"Please, Lucia—I didn't realize you were going to have a child. I can explain everything. I never would have left—"

"It doesn't matter." She stepped out from the shadows, staring right into his moonlit eyes. "We will go on as if this never happened. You will continue to be Gianluca, and nothing more. I will continue to do my bit until the war ends. And then we'll part ways for good."

Carlo pushed the hair from his forehead, clearly struggling for words. The ache in her heart was unbearable, but she straightened her spine and lifted her chin. She'd suffered enough sorrow to know how to hide it, even from him.

He cleared his throat to find his voice. "I want to meet our child. Matteo."

"It's too late."

She stepped away, turning to continue on down the dark alley, alone.

# TWENTY

## ‹›‹›

## Francesca

*Mid-December 1943*

CURFEW WAS CLOSING in, and the streets in the Ponte neighborhood, flanking the Tiber, were quiet. Francesca walked arm in arm with Tommaso toward Piazza di San Salvatore in Lauro. She'd been living with him and his grandparents for a few days, but only because she needed a couch to sleep on. His grandmother, plump and solicitous, welcomed her, which made Francesca miss her own mother. From Tommaso's, she'd go to Lucia's, then to Alberto's, looping around Rome as she had for the past month. If she moved often, the Nazis wouldn't be able to track her.

They ambled and whispered like lovers in the darkening streets, keenly aware of every passing pedestrian. Francesca hoisted her shopping bag, which was heavy, but not with groceries. They rounded a corner, mere blocks from their destination, and a trio of German infantrymen approached. The soldiers wove, tipsy, but she knew enough to be wary. Tommaso carried a false identity card claiming he was seventeen to avoid being arrested for desertion. He could no longer secure an exemption from fighting as a medical student, so he'd ignored the latest military draft and procured false papers instead. So many boys and men did the same, but few had the audacity to walk around the city; most hid in forests, convents, and attics. Would Tommaso's papers hold up under scrutiny?

Boots echoed as the soldiers neared, and Francesca reached for Tommaso's shirtfront under his open coat. She grabbed a fistful of fabric, pulling him to her, ignoring his startled face and kissing him. They needed to seem like nothing more than strolling lovers, unremarkable and benign, and by hiding their faces, they ensured they couldn't be identified later. Understanding, Tommaso softened, kissing her back, long and slow. His embrace was warm, but her heart split. He was different than Giacomo; taller, with ropy arms, and he tasted of cigarettes. Would she ever kiss the man she loved again?

The Germans passed, and he pulled slightly away, eyes flicking up to follow the backs of their uniforms. With his breath hot in her ear, he whispered, "When we get there, remember to climb the steps of the church right away so you can keep watch. After it's done, we'll get out fast and play lovers on our way home."

She nodded. They'd already discussed the plan. He must be nervous. He straightened, and a flop of hickory hair fell in his eyes, but he didn't brush it away. She reached for his hand, squeezing cold fingers.

"It'll go well, Tommaso. I promise—you won't be caught."

They started forward, and he glanced at her. "How do you stay so calm?" he murmured. "You're legendary for it. Do you know that? When the CLN needs someone with cool nerves, they send L'Allodola."

For a moment, the only sound was her uneven walk. Was that true, or was he trying to flatter her? What he couldn't see now was her rapid heartbeat, her overactive mind. "I just think about what they've taken from me," she said finally.

They came to the end of the street, and a modest piazza stretched before them in the twilight, encircled by connected buildings and a towering white church at its end. Only months ago, this square was an expanse of cobblestone, full of people and neighborhood kids kicking balls, but now it was something different altogether. German command, betting on the Allies' reluctance to bomb Rome's historic center, had begun parking their vehicles in the city's piazzas. This one now housed a dozen trucks and two tanks, fueled for the front, parked in tight formation with open space separating them from the ring of buildings. Francesca scanned the vehicles, calculating. Tonight they would destroy more than Nazi property. They aimed to hinder the way the enemy used their city as a staging ground, while simultaneously sabotaging their confidence.

Tommaso met her gaze, and she nodded, handing him the bag. She hurried away, scaling the short stairs of the church as quickly as she could. The doors were bolted tight against the darkening city. *Perfetto.* She sidled up to one of the two columns flanking the stairs and gazed out from her vantage point. Tommaso stood in the center of the parking lot, ready, and she studied the incoming streets and shadows. All was quiet. The sky stretched overhead, purple, and the shutters of every building were clamped tight against the cold.

She caught Tommaso's figure in the center of the piazza, wedged between the tanks. His silhouette was stiff, his eyes on her. She gave him the signal.

He reached into the bag, and she held her breath. He picked up a cylinder, fumbled with it, and threw it into the crowd of vehicles to his left. As soon as it was aloft, he ran down the path between trucks, pulling out another *spezzone* as he skidded to the end of the lot, lit it, and threw it hard to the right. Tommaso sprinted and fell against a truck at the very end of the row, huddling beside its tire just in time for the bombs to go off.

A roar engulfed the piazza as the first truck exploded, belching a hot plume of fire. A second thunderclap followed, deafening. Francesca pressed behind the column, her hand on her racing heart, leaning out to glimpse the exploding vehicles and the buildings ringing the piazza. Several windows burst, raining glass onto the cobbles below, but there seemed to be no other damage to the buildings. She exhaled in relief. Firelight leapt against pink stucco, and the church at her back glowed orange. Another truck, parked close to the one engulfed in flame, caught fire. Its canopied bed erupted in a chaos of pops and cracks, building into a crescendo of small explosions. *Ammunition.* It was better than they'd planned. The fire jumped between trucks, and she hugged her elbows, jolting a little with each new burst. The vehicles were packed close together, loaded with fuel. With any luck, they'd all be ruined. She grimaced in satisfaction and prepared to leave.

Tommaso appeared from his crouch and ran across the open space flanking the church. He was nearly there when a word shot out over the roaring fires.

"HALT!"

He skidded, wheeling in the firelight, and Francesca looked frantically around the piazza. Two Germans in uniform came running in from a side street, skirting the burning trucks and screaming at Tommaso, guns raised.

Seeing the barrels of their weapons, Tommaso froze. He lifted his arms but glanced at Francesca, still behind the column. The Germans rounded the bend and sprinted toward him. He bent his head sharply, urging her to disappear. She stepped back, concealed in the shadow of the column, but she didn't run. Giacomo hung in her mind. She saw him standing in the sunshine on an empty road, hands in the air while an armored car bore down. She saw him stepping into it, glancing back to implore her with his deep stare. Pain, familiar now, split her heart.

She tucked her hand inside her coat, feeling the weight in her breast pocket. The Beretta was cold on her fingers. She closed her eyes, governing herself, and pulled out the gun just as the Germans reached Tommaso. His plump grandmother laughed in her mind. She pulled air, heavy with smoke and burning rubber, into her lungs. She wouldn't let them take another person. Not while she watched.

The soldiers shouted, gesturing with their weapons, spittle flying in the firelight. She raised the Beretta, breathing hard. They weren't far. Just down the staircase. She aimed, waiting a second for her focus to settle. The fire leapt, the Germans gestured for Tommaso to pivot, and a quiet fell over Francesca. She pulled the trigger.

The first soldier fell, and Tommaso stumbled back, hands still over his head. The other soldier wheeled, raising his weapon to the shadows among the columns. He squinted, searching, and she inhaled. She pulled the trigger.

The second German fell, screaming, and she tucked the gun away. Her pulse gathered, bounding again, and the noise and chaos flooded back in. Tommaso turned and sprinted down a side street heading farther into the city, leaving her. *Bastardo.* There was no time to think. She took the stairs as fast as her legs would allow, hairpinning right and down a narrow alley that wound to the Tiber. It was only a block away. She coughed out soot and smoke, running toward the shapes of trees and the dark, open sky.

She scrambled up to the Lungotevere and breathed the fresh air coming off the river. She looked up and down for bridges. Somewhere behind her, sirens erupted. *There.* Two blocks away, the Ponte Sant'Angelo spanned the water, the statues lining its railings bright in the twilight, promising escape. The farther she got from the burning trucks, the safer she'd be. Her legs hurt as she hurried down the dim street and started across the bridge, her breath shaking in her lungs. Where had Tommaso gone? She frowned. He'd panicked. He'd probably backtracked to his grandparents' house, their planned hideout, but she couldn't reach it now. The area would be swarming with Germans. Instead, she'd walk along the other side of the Tiber and cross back into Campo Marzio, aiming for Lucia's house.

The sky over the river deepened, and Bernini's ten marble angels rose like white sentinels guarding the bridge. She took a deep breath, pacifying her heartbeat and forcing herself to slow across the span toward the looming Castel Sant'Angelo. It would be best to appear calm, as if she'd been out for an evening stroll before curfew when the sirens erupted nearby.

"HALT!" The word rang out over the bridge, flung from the road.

She froze. An engine rumbled, and she turned, taking in a truck bouncing along the Lungotevere above the riverbank, under the skeletal trees. A soldier leaned from the window, shouting again.

"HALT!"

Everything in Francesca stilled. She glanced up at the nearest angel, carrying its crown of thorns, its face forever startled by human betrayal. She stepped forward, counting on the figure to block her from view, and pulled the Beretta from her pocket. She stared at the gun for a half second, calculating, and dropped it over the side of the bridge. It fell like a rock, vanishing in the currents.

Boots started across the bridge, clicking fast. She pivoted under the statue. Two German soldiers strode toward her, hands on their holstered guns, and she stood as still as the angel while her pulse thundered. When they neared, she saw their faces, tight with suspicion, scrutinizing. They both appeared to be younger than her. One was lipless with lidded eyes, and the other dark and handsome. They studied her, and their faces fell in disappointment.

The first soldier glanced away with his lidded eyes, murmuring to his partner, who seemed to tighten all over. They argued back and forth, and Francesca balled her hands into fists and crossed them over her chest. Would they let her go? Why weren't they getting out their flashlights and asking to see her papers? She took a few steps from the angel, letting them see her limp, and they paused and looked at her leg. *Please*, she pleaded silently. *Let them think I'm weak. Incapable.*

She looked at the murky river, the darkening sky, and the white dome of Saint Peter's fading in the distance. Curfew was near. Was that why they seemed at odds concerning her? Perhaps one thought she was nobody, that they were wasting their time when they should be searching for the partisans who'd bombed the piazza. And the other couldn't shake his suspicion. It was the one with lidded eyes, who gazed at her for a long moment, then motioned for her to come.

*"Kommen Sie. Schnell!"*

The darker soldier raised his gun, gesturing her toward the truck. His eyes were troubled over its barrel, but he shouted, nonetheless. *"Schnell!"*

When Francesca started to walk, it was with a stagger. Only then did she feel the panic, coursing through her chest and limbs, paralyzing. The dark-haired soldier came alongside her, hooking his arm in hers. He hoisted her toward the truck gently, murmuring things in German as she limped on her tired legs.

They were arresting her. It came over her in a wave. She caught sight of the river coursing under the bridge and saw herself swirling down it, away. If only she'd jumped.

*Madonna mia*, she prayed. *Help me.* She climbed into the truck with a boost from the kinder soldier, who nevertheless locked her in.

# TWENTY-ONE

ℵ

## Lucia

*Mid-December 1943*

IT WAS EARLY evening when Lucia and Hans Bergmann walked from the Hotel Excelsior, elbows brushing, down the cobblestones. She glanced at people in the street as they passed, fighting off the desire to hide her face.

"You wouldn't prefer to stay at the hotel, Hans? The rest of Rome's rather dreary, lately." He'd insisted on having drinks out, followed by dinner and dancing at the Excelsior, and she'd been trying to talk him out of it ever since.

He walked with a straight back, eyes forward. "Dreary, yes. But there's an excellent little trattoria just a few streets over that caters to us. They have a nice appetizer menu. Good desserts, too, and I'd fancy a piece of cake."

Lucia forced an untroubled smile to her lips, avoiding people's eyes as they passed. A nice menu for Germans, stolen from starving Italians. Yesterday she'd stood in line to fetch water from a public fountain to bathe Matteo. With Allied bombs hitting reservoirs, aqueducts, and water mains, water rationing was in effect. The plumbing no longer spit out enough to bathe, and Matteo had shivered in the tub. Every knob on his little spine showed under his pale skin. She'd poured water over him, heated in the kettle during the few hours the city turned on the cooking gas. Just the memory of it brought on a wave of sickening panic. She saw her hand on his back, his toothpick limbs. The war had to end soon, for Matteo. He was too fragile, too thin. And if something happened to him, she'd simply stop, like a frozen clock.

Hans reached for her hand, and she let him take it, ignoring her reddening cheeks. She was good at hiding her true self, but her blush told another story as she sauntered in the open air with what appeared to be a Nazi lover. The few people in the street paused, eyes both widening and narrowing as they took her in. Shame burned in Lucia's chest, but she lifted her chin. Let her countrymen stare. If they knew what she was really doing, they would applaud. Wouldn't they?

She pushed the shame aside, and thoughts of Matteo immediately replaced it, sliding back in like a hand over her heart. Her mother had come over to babysit, something she was always willing to do if it meant Lucia was going out with Bergmann. What if Matteo said something suspicious to her mother? About Francesca, who'd stayed in her house twice now, or about an overheard conversation, or his feelings about the Nazi monsters? Would Nonna Colombo chalk it up to his age, his limited understanding? Or would she bristle? Would she put them in danger?

"I'm happy to see you happy," her mother had remarked earlier, watching Lucia take in the waist of a dress.

She'd looked up, still startled by these bursts of warmth. "I've always been happy," she lied, dipping her needle into the fabric.

"No. You've languished, my dear, which none of us could have seen coming. You once had so much potential. Maybe some of that can return to you now."

Nonna Colombo meant before Carlo. Lucia frowned, glancing at Bergmann to make sure he couldn't somehow sense her thoughts. She hadn't seen Carlo again, of course. Not since he'd dropped into her life a month ago, ambushing her on a dark street. But he'd hung in her thoughts plenty, heavy as the moon.

"Here we are," Bergmann said, jarring her back to the present. She glanced at the restaurant before them and mustered a smile. They were turning into the trattoria when a tiny, middle-aged woman stepped directly in their path, stopping them mid-stride. Her hair was wild, and her eyes caught the light of the fading sky. She looked first at Hans, and then at Lucia, tightening a battered shawl around her shoulders.

"Can we help you?" Hans asked, and the woman's face pinched in fury. She scrunched up her mouth, working her tongue, and spit. The glob hit Lucia's cheek, warm and wet. It started to slide down before she could wipe it off.

"*Collaboratrice!* How dare you?" the woman hissed, crouching like a cat. "Dining with the enemy while your fellow citizens starve? Disgusting."

Lucia opened her mouth, struggling to muster a response, and Hans detached from her side. In one swift movement he reached into his belt, pulled out his pistol, and whacked the woman across the face with it. She stumbled back, cupping a bloodied cheek-bone, and fell. He stood over her, glaring down.

"Do that again, and you'll be shot."

There was no emotion on his face as he returned to Lucia, picking up her hand. She stumbled as he tugged her forward, his spine straight in his uniform, and Lucia glanced back at the poor woman shielding herself on the cobblestones. People in the street gaped and gathered around, whispering as Lucia and Bergmann disappeared inside.

Over drinks, she made all the right faces while the candle flick-ered between them. She laughed and smiled and made a show of enjoying her wine. But his words fell into her like bricks. She gathered them up, numb, storing away the useful bits.

"I'm afraid I must cancel our plans for Friday," he said, sipping his fourth negroni. His gaze swam a bit, knocked loose by cocktails. "I'll be occupied. Saturday as well."

Lucia's distraction fell away. Bergmann was drunk and, for him, talkative. She hinged closer. "Now you have me worried. You're not going on a trip, are you? Not with the bombers . . ."

"Don't be foolish. There's plenty of work to be done here." He set his glass down, and Lucia reached across the table, touching his hand. So far, they'd rarely touched aside from his hungry good night kisses, something she regularly thanked God for. Hans Bergmann was restrained in his courtship. Yet, sometimes when he looked at her, she saw fever in his stare, and it chilled her.

She chose her words carefully. "I hope you won't be in danger, nonetheless. I know the types of people you're forced to manage—"

"No, you don't." He shook his head, draining his drink. "And you should praise your good fortune for not knowing those beasts. We have the Allies on one side and the damned Italian rebels everywhere else, blowing up our supplies and murdering our men."

"Awful." Lucia's mind buzzed behind her wide, innocent eyes. "Thank heavens you're here to put a stop to them." Was he planning raids on partisans? Did he know where they hid? She thought of the homes and convents concealing so many. "I hope you catch them." She sipped her wine, hedging. "I imagine they're well hidden."

"It's what I do every day." He leveled his gaze on her, and she stilled. Her heart beat faster even before he said the words, "I hunt them."

She swallowed, forcing an approving smile. It was Wednesday. She'd tell L'Allodola first thing tomorrow. Francesca would tell Carlo, and he'd spread warnings, neighborhood to neighborhood. Triumph burned in her chest while desserts appeared before them. Because of her, Rome's partisans could prepare for a raid on Friday.

They'd both dipped forks into slices of cake when they paused, synchronized. An explosion burst somewhere across the city, then another. Lucia lowered her fork, and Bergmann met her stare. His blue eyes narrowed. Then he stood and quickly walked from the table and out the front door. She followed, finding him in the street outside the restaurant, scanning the darkening sky.

"Not from planes," he muttered. He sobered up on cue, firming his jaw and shaking his head. "It's those cursed partisans. *Scheisse.*" He wheeled in the street, swearing under his breath. But when he reined in his anger, it was abrupt; his face regained its cold composure. "Excuse me, Lucia," he said, his voice perfectly controlled. "I fear I'm needed."

Without further explanation, he fetched his coat and left, striding fast down the street in the direction of the explosions.

Lucia hovered outside for several minutes, pursing the satisfaction from her lips. Could it be someone she knew? Probably not, but she savored a bloom of pride, nonetheless. She ambled back into the restaurant and asked the waiter to wrap up the two desserts. Tomorrow, she would give Matteo cake for breakfast.

Then she started toward home, hurrying through streets emptying of people and filling, quickly, with the chill of a winter evening. As always, she took a circuitous route. She clutched her purse in one hand, her cakes in the other, and turned onto a narrow street wrapping uphill. A trio of boys still played on the cobblestones ahead, kicking around a clump of knotted rags that served as a ball and whooping as it took flight, arcing into the ribbon of darkening sky between buildings. Their footsteps echoed in the alley as they took off after the ball, elbows pumping, and reconvened where it landed against a dry fountain. Lucia was nearly upon them as they turned, about to lob the rag-ball back downhill.

"*Scusa,*" the tallest boy exclaimed when he saw her, freezing his kick. He grinned, all messy hair and cheeks red from the cold, and she matched his smile as she passed. She breached the hill, turned onto another alley, this one empty, and listened to the fading chatter of the boys with their ball. It would have been easy to miss it, but somehow she didn't. The voice of the tallest boy sifted through the near darkness as he spoke up again. *"Buonasera, signore."*

She stopped walking. The boys had addressed a man just now, somewhere in her wake. Was someone following her? She shrank against the wall and stared at the corner behind her, heart thumping, but somehow she knew who would appear there.

*Carlo.* He rounded the corner and stopped, eyes latching on to hers across the space between them, mouth falling open with unspoken surprise.

"I hope you never follow Nazis," she said, exhaling as her fear dissolved into irritation. "If I can catch you this easily, so can they."

He slung his hands in his pockets, hunching his shoulders as he covered the final steps to meet her. "The Nazis aren't as clever as you. But no. My job rarely entails following anyone."

Lucia crossed her arms over her chest, careful not to pinch the cake in its wrapper. "But this *isn't* your job. I don't need you to escort me home." She glanced up and down the empty cobblestones, making sure there was nobody to listen, deflecting the truth she wouldn't admit to: it was actually comforting to know she wasn't alone in the darkening streets.

"Have you followed me every time I've gone out with Bergmann?"

"No. Only when I knew where you'd be. This is the third time." He hesitated, meeting her gaze, still sheepish. "How'd it go tonight?"

She pursed her lips. Was he suddenly her supervisor, ordering reports? Of course he was, in a sense. *"Benissimo,"* she relented. She lowered her voice to a whisper. "I learned that the Nazis have planned a raid on Friday and Saturday, hunting partisans." The triumph of this intelligence swayed her for a moment, and she had to suppress a grin as he raised his eyebrows in appreciation.

"Well done." He nodded, mulling it over, his mouth curling into a half smile. "I'll get the word out."

"Those explosions tonight," she ventured. "Were they ours?"

He nodded again but gave nothing else away. His breath hung in the cold air.

Lucia glanced up at the twilit sky. "Listen. If you want to escort me home, you'll have to walk alongside me. Nobody will see us at this hour." She caught his eye and started to walk, her stride long. Carlo matched it, hands in his pockets.

For a moment, the only sound was the echo of their shoes hitting stone, out of sync. Then Carlo cleared his throat, raking his hair from his forehead, and spoke in his measured way.

"I apologize for following you. I have no right to do it. But it's dangerous after dark, and that asshole you're involved with is beyond dangerous. I lie awake at night, worrying over it."

She glanced up at him, but his eyes were fixed straight ahead, bobbing with each step. She'd forgotten how he moved. With grace, and assurance. She took in his face, and a tiny piece of her heart gave way, despite herself. Everything about him—the shape of his lips, always suggesting a smile, the warmth of his eyes, the tufts of his hair—it was all so intimately familiar. Stubble shadowed his jaw, and in a flash, she remembered the feel of it, the sense of his bones and muscles beneath his skin, the weight of his forehead tipping toward hers to share her breath. She inhaled sharply, jostling the memory away.

They turned onto a wider, tree-lined street. Over their heads, branches rose naked in the purpling sky.

"But what would you do if I was caught?" She tried to picture it: the Nazis apprehending her while Carlo lurked somewhere in the shadows.

"I'd kill them." His voice was clear and low, and he glanced at her, holding her stare. "I wouldn't hesitate."

Lucia's breath hitched. She stopped under a tree, shadowed by its reaching, twisting limbs, and he turned to face her. She could just see the brown of his eyes in the cold twilight, and there was something in them. Trouble, and grief.

"Why did you come back after all this time?"

"Isn't it obvious?" He took one step closer to her but stopped short. They were like two magnets, flipped to their negative poles, hovering around each other's field.

"It's not obvious, Carlo. Nothing about you is obvious anymore."

"I never stopped loving you." His gaze rested on her for a moment before lifting to the skeletal tree.

She chuckled, on reflex. "Interesting claim, considering how you left me with no more than a note and a pregnant belly. For six years, I couldn't bear to think of you. I didn't know if you were dead or alive, if you hated me, if you were in love with another woman—"

"Never. I've never loved anyone like I loved you."

She glanced up, seeing the fervor in his eyes.

"Then why did you leave?"

"I was compromised." He looked away, as if ashamed. "I'd been organizing the underground in Rome, in secret. The police were tracking me, and I feared what would become of you. I left because I loved you, Lucia. I hoped you would move on with your life—"

Her anger surged. "Move on, with a baby at my breast?"

He shook his head. "I didn't know—"

"That doesn't change anything. You should have trusted me.

You should have told me the truth and let me have some say in my own life. Instead, you made decisions for me, and I've been living with the consequences for six years. And so has Matteo." Tears came from nowhere, and she pressed them away, taking a deep breath, suddenly exhausted. She didn't want to do this. She didn't want to talk about the past, to crack open her heart in this darkening street, to dredge up all the pain. She didn't want to hear declarations of love. She resumed walking, and he followed, uncertain.

"You can see me home, but leave the past where it belongs. The past is dead." She'd keep the unspoken truth to herself: he couldn't talk about loving her, because she couldn't risk forgiving him. He'd inhabited her soul once, too long ago, and when he disappeared, he left her hollow.

"Can you tell me what he's like?" Carlo asked eventually. They'd turned onto her little elbow of a street, passing Noemi Bruno's vacant apartment. Lucia glanced at its shuttered windows, her heart swelling with grief. The Nazis hadn't requisitioned it, probably because it was too small, too humble. If only she could talk to Noemi now.

"Matteo?" she managed, her eyes on Noemi's forlorn, unswept stoop.

"I can't stop thinking about him." Carlo didn't smile, exactly, but something flashed in his eyes as he looked at her. Was it hope? Pride?

Surprised, she cleared her throat. "He's wonderful. Clever, imaginative, gentle. The war has been hard on him, though. I worry constantly."

"Could I help? I could try to find food for him, somehow . . ."

Lucia's apartment came into view, and Carlo looked at it, troubled, as if he could see their son through the stone and curtains. Reality swept over Lucia like a brisk breeze, and she grabbed his hand, pulled him backward, and lowered her voice.

"You have to go. My mother's watching Matteo. If she caught a glimpse of you . . ."

He nodded, stepping into the shadow of a building without further prompting. His voice was so low she could barely hear him. "I understand. Can I see you again?"

She sensed his hope, glittering in the darkness. She hesitated.

"I don't know." She glanced back toward the windows of her house. "Carlo. Please go."

He nodded, holding her stare for several breaths before turning to stride silently away.

She watched him until he vanished.

# TWENTY-TWO

༂

## Francesca

*Mid-December 1943*

WHEN THE TRUCK pulled up alongside an ocher building, night was falling. Francesca understood, immediately, where they'd brought her. Via Tasso. The dark-haired soldier helped her down; without him, she would've collapsed. The barrel of a gun nudged her back, and she began to move, haltingly, toward an entrance trimmed in red flags bearing swastikas. She stepped into the building that had become notorious among partisans as an SS prison. And, according to rumors murmured throughout the city, it was also a torture center.

Francesca struggled up the stairs, weak with fear. They ushered her to a room, and its door opened like an eye, then all was black.

"There's a bit of space over here," a female voice whispered after locks had clicked. A pair of hands reached through the darkness to guide her. The hands switched as she moved forward, changing in shape and texture. It took a moment for Francesca to understand what surrounded her. She was stumbling through a crowd of seated women, their hands taking turns guiding her to a vacant spot.

When she lowered to sit, her weak leg buckled, and she landed in a heap of limbs. A wall of bricks, crudely set, scratched her back. She strained to see it as her eyes adjusted to the gloom. She could make out a brick patch, sealing up what was once a window. They'd walled off the window? She managed a question.

"What should I expect?"

The shapes of women shifted around her. It was too dark to make out faces.

"Depends on what they brought you in for," someone answered eventually. A pair of hands fumbled to her, finding her palm and squeezing.

"Gather your strength," a tired voice said.

Francesca's thoughts began to race. What would the Nazis do to her? She couldn't see the faces around her for clues. "How long have you been here?"

"A long time, some of us," someone croaked from the far corner. "Best you can do is convince them that you're nobody. They let the nobodies go sometimes—no space for them."

Before Francesca could ask another question, boots clicked down the hall outside. The locks turned in the heavy door, and everyone in the room shuffled. She shrank back instinctively. A guard waded in, walking through the crowd of women huddling on the floor, his flashlight bobbing over their faces until he found Francesca.

"Come with me," he barked in accented Italian. *"Adesso, adesso."*

They led her down a stark hall, a gun in her back and two men gripping her elbows. She staggered into a room similar to the other, but brightly lit and empty. Its window, too, was sealed over with bricks, and the walls were covered in busy wallpaper. In its center sat a wooden chair. A light shone over it.

She stumbled to the chair, and when she sat, every part of her trembled. She squinted into the light, and memories flashed in her mind: hospital beds under bright bulbs, other inspections and questions, the promise of pain.

"Why were you out tonight?" a man barked, invisible on the other side of the glaring lamp.

Francesca shaded her eyes, speaking with forced calm. "I wanted to go for a walk—"

"At curfew?"

"It wasn't yet curfew."

"Where do you live?"

She hesitated. An empty apartment appeared in her mind. It had been a meeting place for partisans, but nobody lived there now. She rattled off the address, squinting to see past the lights. Her questioner was nothing more than a dark silhouette. An armed guard stood at the door.

"Do you know any partisans?"

"No."

"Do you have a job?"

"I did. In a bookshop. But it's closed now."

"Have you heard the name 'Gianluca Falco'?"

Her interior shuddered, but she maintained an impassive face and steady voice. "No."

"Do you know anyone called L'Allodola?"

Again, she spoke without a flinch. "No."

The figure behind the lights stepped forward, and his face came into view. He had bright eyes, glacial blue, and angular cheekbones. He knelt, sniffing in a quick breath, examining her as if she were a pinned butterfly.

When he spoke, it was with a smile, but his eyes remained cold. "I do believe you're lying, my little lark. You know how people hunt larks, don't you? They hang tiny mirrors in a tree, very pretty little mirrors, and skylarks fly right into the trap. Perhaps they're confused when they see their own reflections. Interesting, *ja*?" He stared at her for a long moment, then stood to his full height. Before she saw it coming, he cuffed her, hard, across the eye.

"Where is Gianluca?"

She held trembling fingers to her eye. "I don't know any Gianluca."

Something hit her stomach, and she doubled over on the chair.

"Where is Gianluca?"

Francesca sucked air, heaving over her throbbing belly. She fought a wave of nausea. What would an innocent girl do? She released tears. "I don't know any Gianluca," she sobbed. Her left eye warmed and swelled under her cupped fingertips.

"Which partisans *do* you know?"

"None."

The club hit her shin, and she yelped. The skin around her eye throbbed, and she began to weep for real. Would her eye be damaged? Her good leg? She inhaled and tried to corral her bucking thoughts. *She couldn't say anything.* She was nobody. She knew nothing.

The Nazi knelt again. For a long moment, the room was quiet. She didn't open her good eye but touched the damaged one. The skin was puffy, like dough. The sweep of his breath was inches away. She sensed the weight of his stare.

"I can beat you all night, if you're stubborn," he murmured. "Or, you can tell me now and I'll take you back to the cell and we can all get some sleep. Wouldn't that be nicer? To lie down and rest?"

She didn't move, but she opened her good eye. She met his stare with her uneven gaze, unblinking. "My name is Francesca Gallo." Her voice came out rough. "I worked in a bookshop. I have no friends in Rome. I'm nobody important."

He stood, spinning on his heels and looking at the bricks as if contemplating the view. "Interesting," he said quietly. "Do you know we arrested a man this week who was printing illegal documents in a basement? Such terrible disloyalty." When he turned, he thumped the club in his open palm. "Guess what he mentioned, here in this very room? A *girl* picked his documents up. *L'Allodola*, he called her. And what a coincidence that you were out taking a stroll so close to the site of a crime tonight!"

Her heart hammered. Had the forger described her? He'd have tried not to, she was certain. She forced her words out. "I was only out for a walk. To see the sunset."

He stepped closer, and his voice dipped in anger. "It's too bad we had to beat that man to death, *ja*? If you want to avoid his fate, you'll tell me where your friends are."

"I have no friends."

She saw the club before it crashed into her temple. She gasped, folding in on herself, and something bright bloomed in her head before the club slammed down on her bent back. She fell from the chair, collapsing to the floor. Orange flashed behind her eyes, little explosions of light and pain. It hadn't subsided when someone heaved her to her feet, forcing her writhing body to straighten before the lights. She staggered, and the glacial eyes appeared in front of her, shifting like a mirage. Her head throbbed while she tried to focus.

"Where's Gianluca? Tell me, and we'll be finished here."

Her voice was a croak. "I've never met anyone named Gianluca. I'm just a bookshop clerk. I know nothing—"

The arms holding her up let go. She fell, hard, on her tailbone. The Nazi stepped over her, staring down.

"You'll stay here and think about your options. You have only one, signorina." He chuckled. "I will kill you, if I have to."

With that, he pivoted and strode away, heels clicking, and the door swung shut behind him. Francesca managed to glance around the room, her vision swimming. She might die here. She thought of her mother, waiting in her little farmhouse, and sobs came on their own. Francesca had been angry since her father vanished, but her mother carried her grief alone. And now her mother would grieve again.

She blinked through her tears. The world seemed to spin around her, faster with every turn. Her gaze hinged on the guard, still standing at the door, staring blankly at the brick wall. Then the world narrowed, dimming, and it all fell away.

She was with Giacomo in the orchard. She sat in a tree, daylight on her face, legs dangling over the stream. It glistened, shining like a thousand prisms in the sun. Giacomo perched beside her. His hand rested next to hers on the clean bark.

"You have to be brave." His eyes flicked up, dark and lively. His hair fell over them, and he smiled faintly, reaching up to touch her cheek.

"Mino. I'm trying." She hesitated, confused. "I've been fighting them, all this time. I'm fighting, so hard, to find my way back to you."

"I know." He leaned over and kissed her eyes. The olive leaves rustled, like petticoats in a breeze. "Francesca, my love. I'm already with you."

She looked up. She sensed the warmth of him, the pulse of his heart. She'd yearned to touch him, to hold him, for so long. Was he really with her?

A swallow dipped overhead, skimming the stream, and they glanced at it in unison. Its wings arced like arrows, and it rose past the trees, evaporating. Francesca's breath caught. Something was happening. The edges of the orchard darkened, as if a storm surrounded them on every side, but the ribbon of water was bright.

"I'm with you. I'll be with you always." Giacomo reached for her chin, turning it toward him. *"Coraggio, amore mio."*

Courage, my love.

Darkness blurred the edges of the orchard, creeping like fog. His eyes remained on hers, black and steady, while the darkness slipped over the stream, closed over the silver leaves, and climbed up his legs. Francesca let go of the tree limb, reaching for Giacomo's hands, but they disintegrated under her grip. She was losing him again.

"Giacomo," she wailed. His eyes stayed on her, even while the rest of him faded. "Don't leave me again," she wept.

But all that was left of him was a word, spoken into the darkness. *Coraggio.*

She lay, somewhere between sleep and consciousness, sobbing. A voice broke into the fog of her mind.

"Who's Giacomo?"

The voice was soft, and her thoughts jumbled with confusion. Mino had just been here, with her, hadn't he? The words fell from her lips.

"My fiancé."

"Where is he?"

She sobbed the words while her mind cast around, trying to make sense of things.

"Taken. By the Nazis."

Her questioner was gentle. "What's his last name?"

"Lombardi." Who was she talking to? She struggled to open her eyes but couldn't.

"Where is Gianluca Falco?"

She shook her head instinctively, fighting to climb out of her jumbled dreams, to remember where she was. Her head throbbed with a steady beat.

"We can find out where your Giacomo is," the voice coaxed, returning to a gentle cadence. "I only have to make some calls."

She found herself nodding, dipping again into the current of dreams, and everything faded away.

\* \* \*

"Wake up."

Francesca shifted on the cold, hard floor, struggling to surface. She tried to open her eyes, but one pair of lids was stuck shut. Light broke into her other eye, too bright, searing her pounding skull.

"We know where Giacomo is."

For a moment she couldn't move. Giacomo? How did they know about Giacomo? It was as if someone threw cold water over Francesca and her mind sharpened, gaining clarity. How long had she been unconscious? The words hung in the room as she scrambled to pull herself up from her heap on the floor. The lights were on. She touched her swollen eye, and then her pulsing head. Every bit of her ached. The world she'd escaped from assembled around her, cool and bright.

She was still in the room.

"I can tell you where he is, but you must answer my questions first."

She blinked her good eye and turned to the chair, using it to wrench herself up. She clawed her body onto its seat, and the chill of fear settled in her chest. She looked up to meet her interrogator's cool, measured stare. *He knew where Giacomo was.* Her heart skipped faster, propelled by wild hope, yet she knew what she had to do.

"I can't answer your questions," she sputtered, tasting blood. "I know nothing."

His face was impassive, as if carved from stone, giving nothing away. "We can save him. Bring him back to you. All you have to do is cooperate."

Everything in Francesca stilled, as if she were walking a tightrope spanning a gulf. One false move, and she'd plummet. She inhaled slowly.

"I'm nobody. I know nothing."

Fury lit her questioner's eyes. He stared at her for another moment, calculating, and then he let the words drop. "You're too late to save him anyway. Giacomo Lombardi is dead."

It felt like falling, wind whipping around her, the impact quickly approaching. "He's not dead," she hissed, but her chest flooded with something cold. "He's a medic, working on the front lines."

The Nazi laughed softly. "Is that what you think? No. He was a *laborer* on the southern front. Like all the other Italian men we've caught deserting Germany, their greatest ally, in its hour of need. We took him from Rome on September 10. Transferred him to Bracciano, a labor camp, and then south to build fortifications." He shrugged, glee in his gaze. "He tried to escape."

She couldn't breathe. He stared at her, aware that she hung on the fishhook of his words.

"We shot him."

And then she knew. This Nazi wasn't lying.

She blinked up at the bright lights and saw Giacomo, not from life but from moments before, when he'd dropped into her mind. She saw the swallow dipping over the stream, the tree, his dark eyes fading. And she knew what he'd been trying to tell her: he was gone from this world. But he was still with her.

Fear calcified in her chest, hardening into something formidable. She looked up at the Nazi, with his amused smile, and without thinking, she gathered saliva in her mouth and spit. A glob of bloody liquid landed on his polished shoe.

"Is that how it's going to be?" He cocked his head. "Or would you prefer to answer my question? Who are you?"

"I'm Francesca Gallo," she croaked. "And I'm *nobody*."

"Ah." The Nazi turned, nodding. "You very well may be nobody. But I have to find out for sure. We must know for sure, *ja*? In these dangerous times?"

When he pivoted again, there was something in his hand. Francesca's head throbbed, the pain like an ocean pulling back and crashing forward, again and again. She tried to see through it, to make out what was in his fingers.

"Oh, you're wondering what this is?" He ambled over, kneeling before her, turning a tool in his hands. It flashed in the light. "Just pliers. Good for removing things."

He nodded to the guard, who strode over like an automaton. The guard holstered his gun and stood behind Francesca, threading his arms through her elbows. He tightened his grip, and her chest thrust out. She tried to think through her pounding skull. What were they doing? She looked down with her good eye, thoughts humming, electric. Giacomo's voice echoed in her soul as she saw the Nazi fit the pliers over her middle fingernail.

*I'm with you.*

She closed her eyes just before he yanked. Pain engulfed her hand, snaking up it like flames. She screamed, and the sound echoed through the room, otherworldly. Agony pulsed through every part of her body, and she heaved, somewhere between vomiting and gasping while the guard pinned her tighter to the chair. The flames continued to roll through her while the interrogator's voice spoke over them.

"Now would you like to answer me, or will you lose another fingernail?"

She gurgled instead of speaking, riding the waves. But her mind began to work on its own as she struggled. *She'd known pain.* An image floated to her: polio, as she'd pictured it in childhood. She'd imagined her disease as a growing thing, its roots plunging through her body, multiplying until her seven-year-old limbs were paralyzed and wracked. *But her mind.* She breathed. Her mind was another thing. Giacomo hid there, in her memories.

And she could hide there, too, separate from her body. After all, she'd had to do it before.

"I'm nobody," she croaked again, and the pliers latched on to another fingernail.

This time when the pain crashed over her, she retreated into her mind. She heard herself screaming, she felt her body shuddering and heaving where it was pinned to the chair. And she saw herself in a hospital bed, immobilized and tiny. She saw the arch in her young neck and the whites of her eyes, and she remembered herself then: a small child, finding a way out. Polio's roots twisted through her, the tall tree that had grown through her life. And, somehow, those roots strengthened her now.

"Who are you?" the German shouted again, latching the pliers to another fingernail. Francesca sucked in a deep breath, found Giacomo's eyes in her mind, and readied.

The door flung open. The pliers paused.

*"Was machen Sie?"*

Someone strode into the room, but Francesca couldn't see him.

*"Das ist nicht dein Ernst. Dieses verkrüppelte Mädchen?"*

The guard released her elbows, and she slid into a heap on the chair, breath rattling. The men convened in the corner. When she could see straight, she shifted enough to view the man who'd come into the room, moments ago, as if he owned it. She studied him with her good eye, taking in his uniform and stature, while her body shook through waves of pain. The newcomer glanced at her, rolling his eyes as if exasperated. She tilted to the side and closed her eyes. Perhaps this high-ranking man wanted to go home. Perhaps he felt that his colleagues were grasping at straws, interrogating a crippled girl in the wake of a bombing.

Their voices rolled from the corner of the room, and she tried to make out words, but it all seemed very distant. Perhaps she'd succeeded, like the imprisoned women advised her. She'd convinced them she was nobody.

An argument broke out, and Francesca slumped beneath it. She thought about how she looked, collapsed there, with her shriveled leg and bloodied hands. The high-ranking Nazi glanced at her again, disdain in his glare, and barked something at his subordinates.

She drifted. Something flashed before her, but she didn't look to see what it was. Barely conscious, she clung to her last hope: that nobody in the room could see what she'd become.

Unconquerable.

# TWENTY-THREE

རྒྱ

## Lucia

*Mid-December 1943*

L UCIA SHUDDERED AWAKE, pulled from a dream she couldn't remember. She glanced at Matteo, curled in her armpit and breathing softly. But when she relaxed, closing her eyes, she heard something. A faint clatter, coming from the parlor. She stiffened, listening hard. The house was quiet, then something pinged against the window again, hitting the balcony.

She stumbled out of bed, tightening her robe around her night-dress, and walked across the cold floor. She opened the bedroom door, blinking in the darkness. *Ping, clatter.* Someone was throwing pebbles at her window.

Lucia hurried across the apartment. Was it Francesca, in need of a place to sleep? She pulled the blackout curtain back and looked down over the narrow balcony, squinting at the figure in the street. He raised a hand, waving, and her breath caught. She'd parted ways with Carlo at the corner hours ago. Why had he come back?

When he stepped inside, quiet as a cat, she gestured toward the parlor, and he followed her across the apartment, tiptoeing past the bedroom door. *Please let Matteo stay asleep*, Lucia prayed. She glanced back at Carlo as he passed a bookcase they'd bought together. In a flash, she saw them, years ago, hoisting the bookcase up the stairs, laughing. He'd righted it against a wall and pulled her into a kiss, his hands on the small of her back. She frowned as an ache rose in her belly. She *would not* long for him. She was done yearning.

She checked the blackout curtains, sealing the window, and lit a candle. When she set it on the table in front of the couch, Carlo's eyes caught the light. They were full of fear.

Lucia lowered onto the chair across from him, perching on its edge. "What's happened?" Again, she glanced toward Matteo's bedroom door.

"They caught L'Allodola."

Her mouth dropped open on its own. They'd caught Francesca? *Santo cielo.* She pinned her eyes shut, and there was the girl, with her solemn face and wide, determined eyes.

"Where? When?" she stammered.

"Earlier tonight. Tommaso came to warn me. He's running now to everyone L'Allodola knows in the CLN." He scrubbed his stubbled jaw with one hand. "People talk under torture. Even the strongest people . . ."

"Torture?" Lucia could barely breathe. She wanted to throw up.

Carlo nodded, biting his thumbnail while his gaze traveled the floor. "We're all in danger, Lucia. I had to warn you."

His words crashed over her like an avalanche. She understood. *Matteo.*

"Should I take my boy and go to my parents? What should I do?"

He shook his head. "Bergmann thinks you live there. If she says anything about your position, they'll check there first."

"She knows where I live, too. *Oddio.*" She glanced again at Matteo's closed door, as if she could see him through the wood. What could she do?

"With any luck, you won't even come up. They'll question her about sabotage. They'll expect to hear about male partisans—I don't think they'll lead her down a path that would reach you, and she'll volunteer nothing. It's safest to stay here, at least overnight. I'll wait with you until we know you're secure."

She found herself nodding, but her mind veered back to Francesca. The explosions she'd heard with Bergmann—those must have been connected to her. She pinned her eyes shut. *Santo cielo*—he'd rushed off to deal with the aftermath of the attack. Could he have had anything to do with her arrest?

"Bergmann might be with her," she whispered.

Carlo nodded. "I've thought of that. I won't sleep tonight—if anyone comes, we'll run."

Run where? She lifted shaking hands to her head, breathing deeply. Again, Francesca rose in her mind. How would that slip of a girl survive *torture*? She pictured Francesca, her frail body concealing a soul as strong and clear as a diamond. Lucia hadn't realized, until now, how much she admired L'Allodola.

"Poor girl," she whispered.

Carlo shook his head. "I can't bear to think about it." He stood and stepped over to the window, lifting the blackout curtain a bit to peek out. Then he dragged a stool up to the sill and sat, head resting on the pane. For a long time, neither of them said anything. They sat on opposite sides of the room, riding their own waves of fear.

Would Francesca survive this? Lucia swallowed a surge of nausea. Would any of them survive the unending catastrophe? Fascism, occupation, deportation, resistance, the war? She closed her eyes and saw Matteo, with his freckled nose and hopeful stare, and her heart capsized. Her mother's earlier words rose out of nowhere, somehow connected to the image of her own child's face. *You once had so much potential.*

Piero had thought so, too. Growing up, he'd watched over her, delighting when she dared to keep up with him, shielding her when she couldn't. "Mamma," he'd say in the grass of a summer day, "Lucia's a fast runner for a girl." Or at the dinner table he'd interrupt their father, speaking around his fettuccine. "Papà, did you know Lucia passed her exam?" Her parents had looked on, seeing only Piero's swift intellect. Piero's lengthening limbs. Piero's future.

But, her long-dead brother had seen hers. *Piero,* she whispered, *help us now.* Matteo slept in the other room, a tiny copy of her brother, and still, his future wasn't his own. Would anyone she loved ever be free? Why had all of their lives gone so wildly wrong?

She raised her head in the dim apartment, glancing toward her estranged husband.

"Carlo," she ventured, pulling his gaze from the window. "What happened?"

She hid the pain welling in her chest.

"She was with Tommaso, striking—"

"Not that." She cleared the pain from her throat. What would it have been like if he'd stayed? What would it have been like to raise Matteo with a father? To have help, and love, and someone to share him with?

"Why did you leave me? Really?"

He sat very still for a long time, legs bent under his stool, hands in his lap.

"I was a fool." He croaked it.

She couldn't respond. She looked to the ground while he found his voice, speaking quietly from across the room.

"I was so taken with you, Lucia. I thought nothing mattered. Not our different backgrounds, our parents' different political beliefs . . ." He heaved a sigh, raising his eyes to the ceiling as if he might find answers there. "But your parents thought those were *all* that mattered. And I was tearing you away from them. You recall?"

She did recall. She could still hear her father shouting over the dinner table the night before Carlo vanished. Both men had risen from their chairs, her father hollering something about pride and sacrifice and loyalty to country. Mussolini's commands shot from his lips with a burst of spittle. *"Credere, obbedire, combattere."*

"How can I believe, obey, and fight for Mussolini?" Carlo had stood to his full height, gesturing widely. "Il Duce's aligning us with Germany! He's impressed by Hitler, *a madman—*"

"He's not a madman."

"You've seen how Hitler treats the Jews, *si?* Have you been paying attention?" Carlo narrowed his eyes, holding the older man in the heat of his stare. "Think of your own neighbors, your friends, Signor Colombo."

Her father's fist pounded the table like punctuation. "Sometimes the few"—another pound—"must sacrifice for the whole! Our country comes first, before our own ideals—"

"I will fight for my ideals. *Fight* is the one command I can manage."

That argument went on and on. Lucia's mother sipped her wine, her gaze icy, waiting for the storm to pass like all the rest. The only reason that particular dinner was remarkable was because it was the last Lucia had shared with Carlo.

She turned to face him. "But my parents didn't matter to me. I loved you regardless of their disapproval."

He shrugged, his limbs loose on the stool. "I didn't see it that way. What I saw was myself, and my inability to stay neutral. And I saw a family grieving their son, a son who'd died for a leader my family fought against. That I was fighting still. I couldn't be a different person, Lucia. I couldn't pretend that Mussolini's war with

Ethiopia was anything but immoral, that his dominance over his own people was forgivable, that all this endless war was anything but tragedy . . ." He held her stare in the candlelight, swallowing hard. "So, I spoke my mind. And I tore you away from them, bit by bit. And I saw how they looked at you when they realized who you'd married."

Lucia remembered that look. Her mother could still flood her with shame in one hot stare. She pursed her lips and glanced away. "Do you remember when you held me after I told Marco not to fight in Spain? How you said my family didn't deserve me?"

"They don't deserve you. But what if I'd become a reason for them to disown you?" His voice was grave. "I began to imagine your life without me, and I believed it would be easier, that you'd be happier. We'd only just married—I thought I could slip away, and you could carry on along the path I'd interrupted. You were so bright and beautiful, Lucia. I was sure you'd find someone else, someone who wouldn't sever you from your family. And then I got word that my branch of the underground was compromised. I feared what would happen to you if I was arrested. I wanted you to hate me, to think I was gone, maybe dead, so you could move on. Because how would your parents have reacted if I'd been arrested, *exiled*, when we were newly married? Would you have kept a single friend?" He searched her face. "I thought I'd ruin you."

"You did, Carlo. You did ruin me."

He nodded. "I see that now. And I see that I underestimated you, Lucia. When I left, it was because I only saw you in relation to myself."

WHEN LUCIA WOKE up, it was to anemic morning light. She was spread out on the couch, the candle a puddle of wax, and the blackout curtain partially drawn. Carlo still sat next to the window, slumped on his stool, his forehead against the pane as he watched the street. Lucia sat up. Someone had covered her with a blanket.

"Nothing?" she asked, and he shook his head. Relief flooded her, tailed closely by worry. Nothing *yet*.

"Maybe we should go out? We could spend the day walking the city . . ."

He shook his head again. "I sent Tommaso to watch Via Tasso last night. He'll have spied on the front door to see who's coming and going. I expect him to report here soon, and then we can talk about whose house might still be safe—"

"Mamma?" Lucia spun on her seat bones. Matteo hovered in the doorway, shivering. Carlo sat up straight, a ridge on his forehead from the windowpane. His brown eyes widened.

"Who is that, Mamma?" Matteo asked, padding across the parlor and climbing into her lap. He stared at his father for a long moment, studying his face with his own serious gaze.

"A friend," she managed.

Carlo stood, glanced at the street again, and walked tentatively across the apartment. He folded his long body into the chair across from Lucia, never taking his eyes off Matteo.

"You look like your mamma," Carlo said, clearly unmoored.

Matteo nodded his head. He scrunched his freckled nose, thinking, then reached down to scratch his knee under his pajamas. "You're very tall. What's your name?"

Carlo swung his eyes to Lucia, clearly unsure of the answer.

She hesitated. "His name is Gian . . . carlo, *piccolo*. Giancarlo is visiting Rome."

Carlo may have sat there forever, adrift, but a knock at the door down below made him jump. Lucia stopped breathing, widening her eyes. Carlo leapt up and loped back to the window, craning his neck to see the street below.

"It's her, Lucia."

"Who?" Matteo asked, cocking his head.

Lucia stood while Carlo swept by them, out the front door, and down the stairs. Her heart started to pound. She bent before her little son, staring into his eyes. "Matteo, can you please go to your room and draw me a nice picture? Something extra special. *Sì?*"

He nodded, eyes wide, catching the urgency in her voice.

Not a minute after Matteo had vanished to his room, the front door creaked open. Tommaso and Carlo appeared with Francesca slung between them, struggling to walk.

"You're sure you weren't followed?" Carlo asked, lowering Francesca onto the couch.

Tommaso answered. "I'm sure. I took every precaution."

"Boil some water," Carlo barked, and Lucia scrambled to the kitchen. She'd stood in line at the public fountain to fill containers yesterday, thank goodness. But cooking gas was rationed, too— would it be on? She hurried to fill the kettle, then turned to the stove, willing the burner to light. It did, and she raised her eyes in relief.

The relief, however, was short-lived. There was only so much hot water and clean cloth could do. L'Allodola was bruised and beaten. A purple mass bloomed around one eye, her scalp was split, and her shoulders shivered in spasms. Worst of all, her hands sat in a bloody heap on her lap. Lucia sickened. What had happened to them?

She left the water to boil and went to the girl, kneeling at her feet. "*Cara mia*, what have they done?"

For a long moment, Francesca stared at her with her one green, unharmed eye. "They tried to break me," she whispered, her voice rough. "But in the end, I convinced them that I was nobody. They couldn't conquer me." She lifted her good eye to Carlo. "But *maestro mio*, you have to hide well. They're hunting you, too."

# TWENTY-FOUR

## ☙❧

## Francesca

### *January 1944*

Francesca stood at the window, as instructed, staring at the unfamiliar street below. She ran her two bandaged, nailless fingers over her lips, a new unconscious habit. The rest of her was, more or less, healing. Her ribs ached; Carlo thought they were broken, and only time would mend them. Her gashes were turning to scars. The only part of her that was irreparable was her heart. It beat like an echo of its former self, scoured of hope that she'd see Giacomo again.

"How do you *know* he's not alive?" Lucia had asked, over and over. "They might have been lying. You can't be sure until the war ends."

"They knew the date he was taken from Rome," Francesca maintained, shaking her head every time Lucia insisted she rekindle hope. "And Giacomo *would* try to escape if he had even a sliver of a chance. They weren't lying, Lucia."

She merely had to close her eyes to see Giacomo in the orchard, his gentle presence disintegrating, his last words fading in the wind. *Coraggio, amore mio.* He was gone from the world, and nurturing false hope was too painful. She wouldn't do it. She swallowed the ache in her throat, which expanded to an unbearable wedge, and stared at the street below. She would continue on, to avenge Giacomo. Fury alone drove her now.

The last man stepped into the apartment, and they bolted the door. Francesca glanced from the street to the spartan room. She didn't know who lived here, just that Carlo had asked her to serve as lookout for a meeting. A quick glance around confirmed what she suspected: this meeting was important. She maintained a blank expression, re-pinning her gaze on a man standing at the street corner directly below. The man shifted his newspaper-wrapped submachine gun to look up and down the street. Then he glanced at the window, nodding once.

*Va tutto bene.*

She stole another look at the room behind her. Men settled into an assortment of chairs, faces serious, all of them leaders of the CLN. Carlo stared at his hands as if thinking hard, rolling a cigarette between thumb and forefinger. The ring of resistance leaders formed around a wiry American who had just arrived in Rome. He was an OSS agent—a real spy.

Satisfaction burned in her chest, and she looked back to the guard in the street. The Americans had sent an agent to form a partnership with the resistance. It could only mean one thing.

"There will be an invasion," the American began when everyone quieted, speaking perfect Roman dialect. Francesca held her breath to listen.

"When?" another man asked.

"I can't say when or where—you understand the need for secrecy. But I can tell you that Allied landings are imminent, and that we need the help of the underground."

Francesca glanced back in time to see men nodding around the circle. One bent his head to light a cigarette, spurring a chain reaction in the group. The room filled with the acrid smell of smoke born of nervous men.

The American sat with his elbows on his knees, brow gathered, and continued.

"The most dangerous time post-invasion will be during the German retreat. Our primary objectives will be to disrupt their communications and routes of retreat, while protecting the city from destruction. The Nazis have mined all the bridges . . ." The American spoke on, describing the ruin he'd witnessed in Naples in the wake of the German retreat there. Francesca watched the road and pictured buildings and bridges exploding, catching fire, crumbling. Naples, he said, was left devastated.

A member of the CLN interrupted. "We've organized plans to safeguard public utilities—"

"And what about the radio station and its transmitters?"

The American nodded vigorously. "It's critical to protect them. When we have news to spread to the population, we'll need radios . . ."

Francesca's attention moved from the discussion to the guard with his newspaper package down below, pausing to stare up the street. He walked the other way, craned his neck, and then nodded once toward the window.

"We have plenty of volunteers." Carlo's voice drew Francesca's focus back to the group. "But we don't have nearly enough detonators. And we have no anti-tank weapons to barricade roads, if it comes to that."

The American spoke quickly. "I'm already planning to ask for an airdrop from the Allies. I'll request detonators, fuse cord, and anti-tank weapons, but I can't guarantee anything. For now, we need to focus on reporting German movements and locating the mines, especially on bridges. The trick will be to disable them at just the right moment, so the Germans don't have time to re-mine before they retreat. I'll send a courier as soon as I have more information."

Francesca glanced back as the men nodded all around. *Retreat.* Anticipation swelled in her chest. Without Giacomo, she couldn't feel joy, not even when the Germans finally left Rome. But the satisfaction would run deep.

She glanced back as the American stood, looking each man in the eye. "Freedom is imminent, my friends. But we'll all have to walk a fine line to get there in one piece."

The men stood, shaking hands through the haze of smoke. The guard on the street corner nodded up at the window again, and Francesca ran her damaged fingers over her lips.

"You ready?" Carlo asked, coming up behind her. "This is it. The start of the end."

She subdued the urge to smile.

"If I've learned anything, *maestro mio*, it won't be so easy." She took his arm, walking toward the door. "We have a road to travel yet."

# TWENTY-FIVE

૭૨

## Lucia

*January 22, 1944*

MATTEO COUGHED WHILE he walked, his old leather shoes slowing on the cobblestones, cheeks brightening in the cold morning air. His hands balled into fists as he struggled for a clean breath. "Mamma?" he sputtered in the wake of the spasm. "I still want to go to the park. I'm *not* sick. I promise, Mamma."

Lucia hesitated, studying his face, pale as a shell under an old cap that sat crooked on his head. A few dark curls escaped around his ears. He swiveled to stare toward the grounds of the Villa Borghese, just across the piazza, emphatically repeating, "I *promise*."

She crouched and placed a hand on his forehead, feeling yet again for heat, her heart constricting with worry. *Nothing.* The cough had developed over the last week, starting as a tickle and building into something deeper, something that filled her with dread. But he didn't seem sick otherwise, and Francesca had weighed in this morning after bending to inspect Matteo where he waited in the kitchen, begging to go out.

"Fresh air might be good for him," she'd said, giving him a smile as she stood. "It's terrible to be cooped up when you're little. Take him to the park and let him stretch his legs."

Now Lucia reached for his hand, hoping Francesca was right,

and they set off toward the promise of paths and trees. She smiled at the thought of the girl. Francesca had slept in the guest room for a month now, recovering from her injuries, and despite having to stretch her nearly empty cupboards, Lucia liked having her around. Francesca taught Matteo to play checkers, and she talked with Lucia in her serious, straightforward way about all kinds of things. And, though Lucia wasn't ready to admit that she welcomed it, Francesca gave Carlo an excuse to stop by. He popped in often, on his way to wherever he was hiding in Rome's cellars and attics. He'd started when she was first recovering, bringing ointments and making her giggle until her solemn face transformed, as lovely as a swan. But even as Francesca got better, Carlo kept coming. Just three nights ago he'd brought them meat, bought on the black market, for dinner.

"What is it?" Lucia had asked as she unwrapped the limp chunk of flesh, mouth already watering. He'd come just in time for the gas to turn on, and her hands shook at the sight of the meat, red and raw—she didn't actually care what it was. But she was still guarded around Carlo, still terse.

"Who knows?" He flashed a grin, and Matteo giggled across the room, eager to please his tall, new friend.

"Matteo," Carlo said, pivoting. "Want to play checkers? Except I know you'll beat me—you're far too clever." Lucia glanced up to see him move across the room and settle on the floor, long legs crossed beside his little son. Matteo grinned, hugging his knees with enthusiasm, and Carlo hummed a tune as he set up the board. It occurred to Lucia—he was happy. They both were. She'd turned away and bent to light the stove, hiding her warring heart. She was still angry. Perhaps she always would be. But watching her son with his father made it hard to keep the other feelings at bay. There was joy, seeing them together. And fear, because she already knew she'd never keep them apart again. If Carlo wanted to be a father, she would let him, for Matteo's sake. When the war was over, they could tell Matteo the truth and find a way to share their son.

Now, she and Matteo arrived at the terrace flanking the Villa Borghese grounds, and she let go of his hand. He skipped ahead, another cough rattling his little body, his hands stretched out as if he might lift off into the January sky. A bird dove before him. He chased it, spinning to watch it rise.

"Lucia!"

Her heart nearly stopped at the voice. She instinctively touched the scarf on her head, her mind racing. She always feared running into Bergmann with Matteo, so much that she'd taken to wrapping her hair in kerchiefs, shopping far from Via Veneto, and devising stories to explain her son if she had to: he was a neighbor's child, a nephew, a friend. She told Matteo to say nothing, not a contradictory word, if they were stopped. But surely, Bergmann wasn't at the park?

"Lucia!"

She turned, her pulse slowing slightly as understanding caught up with her reflexes. It was a voice she knew well, and she spotted the figure who matched it, silhouetted against the backdrop of Rome spreading beyond the Pincio Terrace. Carlo hurried across the terrace toward her, his hands stuffed in his pockets and shoulders hunched against the cold. A wild grin lit his face.

"What are you doing here?" she whispered as he drew close. She glanced around the empty grounds, spotting Matteo where he crouched in the gravel, his hand stretched toward a hesitant squirrel. "How did you find us?"

"Francesca said you'd be here. You'd just left when I stopped by your place." His eyes danced with something, as if he could barely contain laughter. "I had to track you down to tell you. It's happening."

"What's happening?"

"The invasion." Carlo's grin was like punctuation. He seemed unable to contain himself. He stepped close, took Lucia's hands, and tugged her from her stunned stance. He whirled her into a little jig across the gravel before she could protest. "It's happening!" he laughed, lifting her from her feet.

When Lucia's shoes hit the gravel, she found herself laughing as well, bewildered. She sought the right questions, her mind darting. "The Allies? Where?"

He grinned gallantly. "The Allies landed in Anzio. I heard it this morning through our contacts on the coast. I'm sure it'll be all over the city in no time."

"Anzio," Lucia echoed, trying to take it in. "Over the Alban Hills—it can't be more than sixty kilometers away, can it?"

"Less than that." Carlo seemed to vibrate. "The Allies will be here before we know it. Rome will be free within a week."

Lucia was dumbstruck. She glanced again at Matteo, who was still focused on the squirrel down the path. She'd been to Anzio, many times. She pictured its sandy beaches and found herself laughing.

"Mamma?" Matteo rose, noticing their visitor. He cocked his head in surprise and called out, "Giancarlo!" as he started to run.

Carlo loped over and picked the little boy up, twirling him until he shrieked with laughter. "It's a lovely day, Matteo!" he said, grinning. *"Un bellissimo giorno!"*

Matteo giggled when his feet hit the ground, and then he doubled over coughing. Lucia put her hand on his back, feeling his little lungs spasm and fill, until they calmed.

She frowned. "We should walk farther into the park." She glanced around the exposed, empty terrace. "Run ahead, Matteo."

When their son was safely out of earshot, Lucia whispered the questions multiplying in her mind. "What happens next, Carlo?"

"The partisans need to plan for Rome's liberation. I have a meeting in a couple of hours to organize our next steps."

Her gaze flashed to him. "Will you be in danger?"

He shrugged but met her question with his warm, brown stare. "I don't know."

"When will the Allies reach Rome? Will it really take a week?" They were only sixty kilometers away, after all. "Will the Germans put up a strong fight in the Alban Hills?"

"Too early to tell. An American contact confirmed that the Allies landed without much difficulty early this morning, but that's all I know. We think they could be here as early as tomorrow, or as late as the end of the week."

Rome would be free. In mere *days*. It was breathtaking news. Everything would change. Countless people who'd been forced into hiding would be liberated. All across Rome, disbanded soldiers and Jews waited in attics and cellars and convents, avoiding deportation. Partisans hid from the SS, always fearful, always moving. Young men, having dodged the draft, hid from deportation or execution for refusing to fight any more Fascist wars. Lidia and her family would be free now, too. She was still at the Fatebenefratelli Hospital, protected by the fictional Syndrome K disease. Lucia had only seen her once since the *razzia* in the ghetto. Was there any chance Lidia's husband, parents, and father-in-law, whom Lucia had never found, hid somewhere, too?

Lucia watched Matteo run toward a tree. A flap of newspaper stuck out from under his trouser leg. Matteo hated the feel of paper under his clothes, but it was all she had to warm him. Rome was out of textiles. If the Allies arrived within the week, would cloth and food and gas return soon after?

"Carlo," she ventured, her thoughts turning. "I'm supposed to go to the salon tomorrow, to see Fabrizio. Should I stay home?"

"If we're still waiting for the Allies tomorrow, you should keep your appointment." He nodded, decisive. "You might hear something about how the Germans are reacting to the news."

They slowed on the path while Matteo warmed to whatever game he was playing, bending to collect pine cones. Lucia tensed, watching. His little hands must be freezing. A more immediate question rose. "Is it safe for us to be out here?" She pivoted, searching the quiet paths, suddenly afraid. Rome was on the verge of liberation. What would happen next?

But Carlo shook his head. "No need to worry, not today. The Germans have far more to fear than a young family out for a walk."

She glanced at him, and for a second everything within her stilled. Carlo gazed toward Matteo, thoughtful, something like joy lighting his eyes. His hair fell over his forehead, the same color as his son's, and the curl of his smile was calm. She remembered that confidence, so innate in Carlo's soul, and how it had once made her believe everything would always be all right. As long as they were together. She looked away, trying to clear herself of troublesome feelings.

"You still love him," Francesca had said a week before, her eyes on Lucia while Carlo disappeared out the front door. She'd flinched, suddenly aware of the way she watched her estranged husband's broad back. *With longing.* Was it that obvious?

"I could never love him again," she'd insisted, turning back to her mending. She pushed a needle through Matteo's sock, sealing a hole. Francesca had studied her, in that open way of hers, but she'd said nothing more.

Lucia sighed, tightening her coat against a cold breeze that swept down the path.

"I'm surprised by how much he looks like you," Carlo said, breaking into her thoughts.

"He looks like Piero." Her breath hung in the air. She didn't mention that he had Carlo's lighter coloring, his lively eyes. Matteo knelt, wobbling as he reached for more pine cones, making a pile while a squirrel chattered from a branch.

"I can't imagine not knowing him now." Carlo glanced at her, hesitant. "I wish I could tell him the truth. About me. I know we can't, but someday I want him to know that he has a father. A father who loves him."

She softened. "It doesn't have to be someday, Carlo. I've been thinking about it, too, and I think we should tell him soon. When Rome is liberated, and all this secrecy can finally end." Her voice cracked. "I will let you be his father, Carlo. I don't know what you and I can be, but Matteo deserves to have you in his life."

Carlo lifted his eyes to the sky, wiping at their corners. He cleared the sudden emotion from his voice before looking at her again. "Thank you."

"Mamma!" Matteo called. "Come see!"

Lucia closed her eyes and inhaled. When she opened them, she'd contained the explosions in her soul. "Coming, *piccolo!*" she called, forcing the tremor from her voice. They turned in sync toward their son, and Carlo followed her across the grass.

When they neared, Matteo blinked up with his lovely eyes, grinning. "I'm making a home," he announced. "For the squirrels. See this pine cone? It's a tiny door."

She bent to appreciate his pine cone house and tousled his hair. "*Santo cielo*, Matteo. You're so kind and clever." She wanted to gather him up, to never let go.

Carlo looked at the branches spreading over their heads. "This is a perfect climbing tree. See those low limbs? What do you say?"

Matteo's face brightened. He was as thin as a newly hatched chick but had always been startlingly brave. Lucia pinched back a smile. If he got regular meals, he'd be swift and strong someday, able to climb the highest trees.

"I say . . . I say yes," he declared. "But I don't know how."

"Don't know how? *Prego*—I'll teach you right now. I climbed trees every day as a boy."

"In Rome?" Matteo asked, and Carlo laughed.

"Not in Rome."

He put his big hands on Matteo's waist and hoisted him up, waiting for him to cling to the lowest branch. Then he followed, swinging onto a higher limb and reaching for his boy's out-stretched fingers. "I grew up in the hills," Carlo said, pulling Matteo up again. Lucia wandered across the grass, her fingers pressed against her lips. She settled onto a bench and watched them in a crook of the trunk, propped in the branches. Carlo talked on, and Matteo giggled through a wet-sounding cough. Then they were laughing, clinging to the bark side by side, and a trio of birds dipped into the branches over their heads. Carlo laughed like he might have as a child, before war, before regret.

"Mamma, look at me!" Matteo called out, and Lucia waved.

Could she ever laugh like that again?

THE NEXT DAY, after a lunch of wormy kidney beans and black bread, Lucia headed to her appointment at the salon, leaving Matteo with Francesca. When she stepped inside, the Salon Borghese was all but empty. Lucia's mother looked up from a chair, hair already in curlers. Her blue eyes were wide, and she held her head unnaturally still. Lucia batted down the nerves spreading in her chest. Soon Romans would rise up, united, forcing the Germans out while the Allies rolled in. But, until that moment, she had a part to play.

"You heard the news?" her mother whispered.

Lucia nodded. The Fascist papers had printed only a vague report of the Allied invasion, but rumors seeped from the coast into Rome, spread by partisan couriers. Gossip streamed from neighborhood to neighborhood, preparing the population for the coming insurrection.

"I don't know what will become of us," Nonna Colombo murmured as Fabrizio sauntered over. She shook her blond head, at a loss. "I suppose we can move north, to Bavaria . . ."

Lucia had an unexpected pang of sympathy for her mother. "One thing at a time, Mamma," she said, patting her shoulder as she walked by. Was her mother worried that she'd finally be held accountable for aligning with the enemy? Lucia, at least, had the partisans to vouch for her. They would tell her neighbors and acquaintances, when the time came, that she was not what she seemed.

She followed Fabrizio to her customary chair, though there was no reason to sit in the back today. The salon was empty, aside from them. But her mother seemed to be in enough of a daze that she wouldn't question it, and Lucia longed to whisper to Fabrizio. She wanted to hear his take on what was playing out in Rome and the beaches beyond the Alban Hills.

He leaned close, and in the mirror his gaze darted like a raven's black eyes.

"Many Germans are leaving Rome," he whispered, combing her curls. "But you should still meet with Bergmann as soon as you're able. Try to get information from him. We need it now, desperately."

"Desperately?" Confused, she turned to look at his face, inches from hers.

Fabrizio nodded, grave. "My friends in the Alban Hills report the arrival of many German divisions. Several farmers in the area have reported the same thing—Germans are blocking the roads to Rome. They're counting unprecedented numbers, but of course they're farmers, not—"

Fabrizio ceased whispering abruptly as a shape drifted into the mirror behind their joined heads. They glanced up in unison, the trance of their meeting broken, and stared into the startled eyes of Nonna Colombo.

"What have I just interrupted?" she asked, looking between them. Lucia's heart beat hard in her chest. Would her mother connect the dots? Would she realize that Lucia, and Fabrizio, had been working against the Germans all along?

Thinking fast, she reached for Fabrizio's hand, squeezed, and let her fingers drop back to her lap, brushing his thigh along the way. Her cheeks heated, and she used the blush to her advantage, looking down to her hands in her lap.

"Fabrizio and I . . ." she murmured, and he caught on. He stepped away, as if sheepish, and stumbled over himself leaving the alcove.

"Please, Mamma, don't tell Hans."

Would her mother believe this? The suggestion that they'd struck up a romance in this alcove seemed absurd, but Nonna Colombo blinked at Lucia for a long moment before shaking her head.

"You have such strange taste in men," she whispered, glancing away, embarrassed. "Forget him and focus on Bergmann, my dear. You want to win the affections of an officer, not a hairdresser."

Lucia bit back her response, stung by her mother's judgment. It was always there, simmering. And yet, deep down, satisfaction flamed in her heart, because Nonna Colombo had forgotten one thing: Bergmann would soon be gone.

# TWENTY-SIX

&

## Francesca

*January 24, 1944*

NEWS FROM ANZIO rushed through Rome like a spring wind. Francesca pedaled along streets more crowded than she'd seen in months. People huddled in the cold afternoon, smiling and laughing on every corner. There wasn't a German to be seen. How many had left? She bumped around a corner and pressed up the Lungotevere, cycling against a breeze coming off the Tiber. According to Carlo, a steady stream of staff cars had rolled north during the night, spiriting German officers out of the city ahead of the expected Allied approach. She filled her lungs and tried to feel the satisfaction she'd anticipated, yet her heart remained grim. She veered toward the bridge Tommaso had chosen as a meeting place. Perhaps, when the last German left Rome, she'd be able to welcome the relief she'd long sought.

Francesca dismounted at the lip of the Ponte Sant'Angelo, glancing across the cobbled span to the ancient castle rising over it. Bernini's angels stood guard over the bridge, forever stoic. She started across, passing groups of joyous people out for a stroll, shivering in their threadbare jackets. She looked up at the angels; the last time she'd stood under them she was being arrested. How different things were today, not a season later.

At the end of the bridge, she spotted Tommaso, seated on the ground against the railing. She paused. Nerves gathered in her stomach, followed quickly by anger. Tommaso was surrounded by a handful of other young men, undoubtedly partisans, though she didn't recognize them. Most of them looked like boys, barely old enough to fight. They sat cross-legged, passing a bottle of wine, laughing and talking loudly as the clouds rolled overhead and splashed them in winter sunlight. *The fools.* Francesca clamped her jaw and strode toward them, incredulous. She was leaning her bicycle against the railing when Tommaso saw her.

"*Ciao,* Francesca!" he called up, his grin sloppy.

"*Stai zitto!*" she snapped, widening her eyes to drive home her command to shut up. Anger bunched in her stomach: now everyone here knew her real name. She stumbled into the group and sat awkwardly down while Tommaso stared at her, stung. Someone across the circle snickered, and another passed the bottle.

"Loosen up," a boy said, stumbling over his words. He'd clearly had too many swigs already. She turned to glare, trying to place him. What were they thinking, meeting here, out in the open, when Germans were still in the city?

"I will not loosen up," she said, keeping her voice low. She had their attention somewhat, though she caught one man rolling his eyes. Tommaso seemed to have sobered. He looked at the ground between his knees, sheepish, and someone passed him the wine. He stowed the bottle and met Francesca's stare.

"Have you lost your minds?" She forced her voice to steady itself and held Tommaso's gaze. "The Allies aren't here yet—our job isn't finished. And you're meeting in the open for all the world to see? What if someone reports you to the Gestapo?"

A freckled man, younger looking than Francesca, shook his head. "The Gestapo are gone. They're all running away—haven't you heard?"

"Not all of them, you fools. And until they're gone, until you can reach out and touch an Allied soldier right here in these streets, you need to behave like you're in danger." She rounded back on Tommaso, who blew a chunk of hair from his eyes. "Didn't you hear anything Gianluca told you? The Americans warned us that this would be the most critical time. *Now*. This very bridge you sit on could explode at any moment—the Germans mined them. In Naples, they blew up nearly everything on their way out of the city."

The circle shuffled around her. A few of the young men looked down.

Tommaso squared his jaw. "What you missed, Allodola, is that we're not just celebrating here." He lowered his voice an octave. "Yes, we feel a bit lighthearted. *Gesù Cristo*, we've been hiding for months. Haven't we earned some wine and fresh air, at the very least? You, of all people, have earned that. You should take a swig. But we're also discussing our next actions—we're well aware that there's more to do."

The freckled man spoke up, Adam's apple bobbing. "I think we should hit the Germans on their way out. I saw streams of cars last night—easy targets."

Tommaso nodded, his gaze igniting with its old passion. "I've long thought we should take advantage of their movements. With the way they paraded up and down the streets of Rome, it would've been so easy. Why didn't we hit them every chance we got?"

"Because we weren't ordered to," Francesca interrupted. She weighted each word. "This isn't a game. Everything we do has consequences. Is your memory so short?"

He looked away, and she knew he understood. She'd never told anyone about the moments after their attack on the piazza, when Tommaso had run away, leaving her behind. But it hovered between them.

She cleared her throat. "You're to follow the instructions of your superiors, like actual soldiers. Every strike is designed for a specific reason—to meet a strategic objective with as little risk to civilians as possible. We're not meant to kill Germans just because we can."

One of the boys smirked. "*Oddio*. We should have expected the girl to be soft."

She rounded on him, pinning him down with the fury of her stare. "I'm not *soft*. But I'm no fool, either. I've seen the inside of Via Tasso—did you know that? Do any of you boys know what the Nazis will do if they catch you? They'll torture you, and you'll endanger everyone if you can't withstand it." Again, she looked at Tommaso. She knew who was likely to cave under pressure. "If you randomly strike, killing the easy targets, as you say, we'll all pay. You think you want revenge, *ragazzi*? I'll tell you who likes revenge: Nazis."

"But they're leaving," someone said, and she forced herself not to shout.

"They're not gone *yet*."

She put a hand on Tommaso's shoulder, using it to stand, and the boy who'd had too much wine snickered again. When she stood on both feet, she glared at them all a final time.

"Don't do anything you haven't been told to do." She controlled the fury in her voice. "And, for God's sake, stop acting like children. Get off this bridge. Don't gather in public. Don't use the telephone, even if it's working. Don't allow yourself to feel confident, or lighthearted, until the Allies roll through the Aurelian Walls."

# TWENTY-SEVEN

༚

## Lucia

*January 24, 1944*

LUCIA HURRIED DOWN the cobblestones, her mind moving at an equal clip. A bomb thundered in the distance, followed by heavy artillery. How incredible that here, in the streets of Rome, one could hear the battle in Anzio! That's how close the Allies were. It could have felt ominous, but instead it was exciting. Everyone, careworn and exhausted, knew that time was nearly up for the German occupation. She paused at an intersection on Via del Corso, waiting while a convoy full of German paratroopers rumbled by, heading toward the beaches at Anzio, no doubt. She smothered a smile. Was she imagining the shock in their eyes as they passed? The future, sodden and gray for so long, glowed bright.

The Hotel Excelsior was eerily empty. Lucia passed through the door with a heavy fur coat draped over her shoulders, given to her by Nonna Colombo. Earlier that day, her mamma had pulled it from her closet like a good luck charm, her wrinkled hands shaking a bit, and Lucia could feel the hope in her mother, the desperation. But what did she imagine? Hans Bergmann would soon be kicked out of Rome. Did her mother think he'd be so taken with her that he'd return someday? Or that his country

could still win this war, that he would offer her a victorious future
in Berlin? That a fur coat would snag Lucia the life her mother
had dreamed of all along? Her father, on the other hand, had seen
Lucia wearing the coat as she left the house. He'd tipped his newspaper, scanned her with his dark stare, and shaken his head. Perhaps he thought romance was far-fetched amid war. But then,
Lucia couldn't imagine he'd ever believed in romance. The only
thing he believed in was Il Duce.

Now she glanced around the empty tables, the spatter of people at the bar, the bored waiters, the quiet dance floor. Anyone
could see the truth. Her mother gripped the past so tightly that
she couldn't understand the present.

"Hans," Lucia called, spotting Bergmann across the way, seated
at a little table under a chandelier. She hurried over to him. His
briefcase leaned against the leg of his chair.

"I didn't know if you'd still be here." She infused her voice with
concern, lowering into a seat opposite him.

He stared at her for a long moment, expressionless. "Why did
you suppose I'd be gone?"

"I heard people were leaving. That the German forces might
relocate." She pulled her gloves off, finger by finger, and spoke
breathlessly to conceal her confusion. "The city's abuzz."

He dropped his pale gaze to his knees, nodding. "The military's moving toward the front, yes. They'll fight this new invasion, but I'll remain in Rome."

"Oh, thank goodness." *Damn*, she thought beneath her words,
reaching for his hand. His gaze bobbed up to meet hers. Was that
a trace of uncertainty in his face? He sat as stiffly as ever, but his
shoulders were hunched, his expression hesitant. On the table beside him, under a lamp, was a half-finished negroni, and the tablecloth had several rings on it. Had he already consumed multiple
cocktails? If he continued to drink, he might let down his guard.

"I've been talking with my mother about what we'll do if the Allies invade the city. Perhaps we'll flee north, to her family in Bavaria." She held his stare, frowned, and gambled. "Hans, what do you think will happen to us? Will German headquarters stay in Rome?"

He hesitated, sniffing, and lowered his voice. "The Allied invasion took us utterly by surprise, Lucia. We've been ordered to ready ourselves for departure if they march on the city. I'm not sure I'd have time to seek you out for a farewell, if it comes to that."

"Oh, Hans, that would be devastating." She squeezed his hand.

He hesitated again, casting his drunken gaze about before returning to her. "But a report has just come in that might buoy you, my dear. The Allies are shifting south, instead of marching directly on Rome, which will change everything. We have infantry there already, and several other divisions are on their way to the beachhead. If they hesitate much longer, we'll be able to defend the city."

"I certainly hope so." *Dio santo.* Her thoughts buzzed, and she smoothed her skirt to buy a second. Could it be true? Did the Germans still have a chance against the Allies? She tried to muster some tears and wasn't surprised when they came easily. She blinked so her eyes would glitter in the light of the crystal chandelier. "I've been desperately worried, Hans."

He sniffed, two quick uptakes of air. "We've all been worried. But rest assured." He lowered his voice yet again. "There are rumors that the 14th Army is to be transferred from the north and re-headquartered here. If that happens, we'll annihilate the Allies."

She nodded, trying to appear relieved when in fact she was panicking. Was this true? Was Germany sending such numerous reinforcements? She remembered what Fabrizio had said not twenty-four hours ago: *Germans are blocking the roads to Rome.* She caressed Bergmann's long fingers. She had to get the information to Carlo, and fast.

"I'm going to get us something more to drink," he said, patting her knuckles and rising to stand. He wobbled a little, and his face smoothed as he focused. Then he strode away, gliding like a tiger, and she watched the back of his uniform disappear around the corner. She held what she'd just heard in her mind. She yearned to get up, walk away, and never see him again. Could she? Her eyes landed on the briefcase. Surely, the Allies still had the advantage, regardless of how many German divisions were on their way. And if she got the information to Carlo immediately, perhaps he could pass it along to the American spy before it was too late. The time to march on Rome was *now*. Right now.

She thought, her eyes on the briefcase. She'd always imagined it carried information about people. Wanted people. Vulnerable people. If the Allies succeeded, she'd never have to see Hauptsturmführer Hans Bergmann again. But if they didn't? Whoever's names were in that briefcase would be in trouble. She hesitated, staring at the little gold clasp atop the leather. Surely, Carlo could pick the lock? She looked toward the bar—Hans would never again be this distracted. And that was her last thought. She ceased deliberation, and her body took over, as if mechanized. She reached down, gripping the case's handle and glancing around. There was nobody near, so she picked it up, set it beside her chair, and draped her heavy fur coat over the leather. Bergmann was striding back, carrying two drinks. She risked a glance down, checking that the leather was fully covered by the mounds and folds of her mother's fur coat.

"Oh, lovely," she said, rising. Bergmann slopped some of his drink on his sleeve as he rounded on her. She pretended not to notice. Instead she took her tumbler, stood on her tiptoes, and kissed him. He tasted of salt and gin, but despite his haze, he responded, slipping his tongue into her mouth. She played with it, pressing close before pulling away.

He stared at her with open hunger. She sipped her drink, grinning over its rim. She had to distract him enough to stow the briefcase somewhere before he realized it was missing.

"Hans," she murmured, leaning into his chest. She pushed him a little, maneuvering him toward the elevator. "With all this upheaval, all this uncertainty, we may not get another chance . . ." She brushed her fingers across his midsection, and his eyes widened.

"Would you like to come up to my room?" His voice was guttural.

"Very much," she whispered. "But first I need to duck around the corner to let my mother know I won't be home. Rome's in chaos—I wouldn't want to make her sit up all night worrying." It was a gamble.

"Can't you phone her?"

She shook her head. "Remember the lines? I'll have to run out and leave her a note." Her parents, and all of their neighbors, no longer had working telephones because the lines around the Excelsior had been cut off, months ago, to protect German headquarters from spies. She smiled at the irony while wrapping her arm around his waist and tucking her fingers into his belt. "Would you go and fetch us a bottle of something while I step out? I'll not be five minutes."

"Champagne?" He wavered a bit on his feet.

"To celebrate the annihilation of the Allies," she whispered, grinning.

She detached from him, heart hammering, and bent to gather her coat. She slipped her arm under the mounds of fur, gripped the handle of the briefcase, and stood. What would she do if he tried to help her into the coat? Everything in her gathered, like light in a diamond, all sharp angles and glare. She was being reckless. But he walked off, as she'd known he would in some subconscious corner of her mind. He'd never yet helped her into her coat.

She started toward the door, the fur draped over her clasped hands, the briefcase bouncing under it. *This is madness.* The words reverberated in her mind. *Idiocy.* What would Carlo say? Ten more steps, nine, and she'd be out. Her shoulders tightened as she expected his voice behind her, any second now, shouting to stop. It would be a death sentence. The sentries at the door would rush over, grabbing her arms, the briefcase falling out from under the coat . . .

But the shouts never came. A *portiere* opened the door for her, she flashed her dimpled smile, and she strode out into the cool evening air. She walked quickly, the snap of her heels loud on the cobbled street, the briefcase bumping her thighs with each step. At the corner of the hotel, the intersection was empty, but a convoy approached down the street, and she walked against its tide, hurrying to her parents' apartment. She'd stow the briefcase there, where nobody would ever suspect it, under Piero's bed. *Piero*, she thought, glancing at the clouds forming a lid over Rome. The sound of a distant bomb shook the air. *Watch over me, brother.*

Lucia skirted the remaining block, took the stairs into her building two at a time, and slipped into her parents' apartment unnoticed. She slid the briefcase under her dead brother's bed, stowing her purse as well, and ducked out again.

Back outside the building, she pulled the fur coat over her shoulders, and dread bundled in her chest, vying for space against the thrill of success. She had to return to the hotel, lest she fall under suspicion. Would he have already noticed that his briefcase was missing? She shuddered. Would he realize it was Lucia who took it, or would he blame himself for being drunk and careless? She walked quickly. She would use all of her charm, everything she had, to obscure the situation. *It could've been anyone*, she rehearsed as she walked. *Someone lingering at the bar, someone passing through . . . Are you sure you didn't leave it in your quarters?*

She rounded the corner, nearly upon the entrance. The other possibility was that he hadn't noticed, which was almost as terrible. Because if he waited at the bar with a bottle of champagne, none the wiser, she would have to sleep with him.

She swallowed her dread and strode into the Hotel Excelsior.

Across the lobby Hans waited, champagne in hand, by the elevators. So, it was to be dreadful scenario number two. She sauntered over to him, coat swishing, and grinned.

"How was your mother?" His voice was sharp, and she stiffened. The hair on her arms rose in warning.

"Already asleep." Lucia stepped close, spreading her fingers across his chest, and he wrapped his free arm around her waist. He bent to kiss her, and when his lips pressed fully on hers, he picked her up, swinging her around so her back was against the wall. He sucked on her, hard, and fear sharpened in her chest. He'd changed in the five minutes she'd been gone. *He knew.* She could feel the anger coursing through him, like electricity.

When he broke the kiss, his lips popped from hers, audibly, and he brought his hand from her waist to her neck. He spread his fingers around her throat, pushing gently on her windpipe.

Her heart stammered. Behind him, a waiter paused, tray in midair, mouth open.

"Where is it?" Hans hissed.

"You're hurting me!" She struggled to get the words around the pressure on her throat, the terror in her soul. "Let me go, please, Hans . . ."

His blue eyes locked on hers, and she reached up, scraping at his hands. He held her there for a long moment, examining her, applying just enough pressure to stoke her panic while allowing her to talk and breathe.

"Hans," she gasped, "I don't know what you're talking about." She saw it: for a split second, he was unsure. She let tears heat her eyes. His uncertainty could be used. She could still get out of this.

"Hans, I . . ." She wiggled under him, casting her gaze about as if something was just dawning on her. "My purse?" she stuttered. "I don't have it." She tried to look toward the table where they'd been sitting.

He froze, still glaring at her, and then he loosened his grip. He glanced behind them, taking in the waiter, who continued to stare with unmasked shock.

Lucia touched her neck, blinking through her tears. *Keep it going*, she counseled herself. *You can fall apart later.*

"I don't understand," she stammered through a sob. "How can you treat me like this? Don't you trust me?"

"I trust nobody."

He released his hand fully from her neck, and she slumped. She allowed tears to shiver up through her words.

"I'm utterly aghast, Hans. And I must have left my purse . . ." She patted under her coat, as if frantic. "My papers—everything. What am I going to do?"

"My briefcase is gone as well," he muttered. He glanced around, narrowing his eyes at the various staff. There were a few diners now, and a growing collection of people at the bar.

"You suspected *me*? Are you mad?"

He swiveled, and she blinked up at him, incredulous.

"I cannot believe you would think such a thing." She lifted her chin, sniffing.

"Lucia, I—" He stared at her, clearly still suspicious, but his suspicion was at odds with common sense. She could guess the contradictions dueling in his mind. She was a Fascist official's daughter. A lifelong Fascist, in fact. They were speaking German. She'd mentioned fleeing to Germany. But the briefcase was just there . . .

"It seemed the only explanation."

"The only explanation? You astound me, Hans." She sobbed. "I was going to spend the night with you. To give you a piece of myself, lest the battle sweep you up . . ." She choked on another sob. "And this place is swarming with people who might not be loyal. Haven't you ever noticed that?" She waved her hand as if batting away smoke.

He cleared his throat, chagrined. "Let's talk to the management at once, then." He held a hand out to her, but she shrugged away.

"Everyone in this room just saw that spectacle," she whispered, applying heat to her voice. "And despite what you obviously think, I'm a respectable lady. I'll not stay another minute. I've never been so humiliated." She sniffed, huddling under her furs. "I'll return for my purse whenever it's recovered. I'm certain they'll find it hidden in some cleaning closet."

She stalked off without looking back, her arms clamped over her chest. She made it through the double doors, heart hammering.

Out on the street, she touched her stinging throat and choked on real sobs. The sounds of the battle were distant, but continuous now. Artillery echoed from Anzio as planes droned somewhere under the cloud cover. She hurried toward home; it wouldn't do to be caught out past curfew. She'd have to fetch her prize from under Piero's bed another time. Her heels clattered as she went, nearly running through the city. Somewhere on the coast, a bomb dropped, brightening a slice of horizon. She imagined the light illuminating beaches, those sandy strips in Anzio full of Allied tanks, guns, and soldiers.

*Please hurry*, she whispered to the soldiers in her mind. *We need you. Now.*

\* \* \*

"Lucia—what did he do to you?"

Carlo rose from the couch and met her in two steps, taking her hands in his. He scanned her with troubled eyes.

"I'm fine," she managed. But then she touched her throat, remembered the waiter's stunned stare, and found herself collapsing into Carlo's arms, the edges of everything blurring. He held her tight, rocking her a bit until the waves of emotion slowed.

"How was Matteo?" she croaked eventually. "Do you think his cough is any better?"

"Still coughing. But who I'm worried about right now is you." Carlo had insisted on standing guard over their son while Lucia kept up her charade one last evening. He'd also begged her not to go, but she felt strongly that she should. It would be a chance to learn what the Germans were thinking, she'd argued. And she had.

She took a deep breath and told him everything: what Bergmann had said after his many negronis, the impending German reinforcements, her new fear that the Allies wouldn't actually break through. Finally, she told him about stealing the briefcase, and about Bergmann's reaction.

"You did well," he whispered when she'd finished, his eyes stilling while he digested her words, and all their ramifications. "I can't believe you got his briefcase—*bravissima*, Lucia. Francesca can help you fetch it, maybe in a day or two when things die down. And I'll sneak out later to see the American agent—I'd like to go in the middle of the night, if you don't mind me staying longer? It's too close to curfew now."

"Of course you can stay. I'd like you to." She heard the words as she said them, and realized that they were true.

His face brightened at that, then darkened. "I'd be lying to say

I wasn't concerned about this new intelligence. Bergmann used the word 'annihilate'?"

"Yes, he said the German reinforcements will annihilate the Allies if they continue to hesitate in Anzio."

His frown deepened. "The American will be eager to pass that along." For a moment, Carlo seemed lost in thought, but then his gaze swung up, and he pulled her slightly closer. "Lucia. Regardless of what happens next, you'll never see Bergmann again. Promise me."

"*Sì*, I promise. I'm done with him."

His eyes traveled her face, and he lifted his thumb to her cheeks to wipe away what remained of her tears. Without planning to, she sank into him. He wrapped her up, and a thought slipped through her mind. *He felt like home.*

But a memory chased that thought. She saw her own hands pushing a rolling pin over the counter, sweat and tears falling into pasta dough while the baby cried from his blanket on the floor and her breasts leaked. She remembered the hole in her soul that day, and every day since. A hole he'd gouged.

Her voice cracked as she whispered into his chest.

"Did you truly love me? When we were together?"

"Always." He tipped his forehead into hers. "I'll never cease loving you, Lucia."

She wanted to push him away and pull him to her, all at once. "I've hated you for a long time, Carlo."

"You had a right to."

Her heart beat like a river bursting its dam. What was she doing? She'd held Carlo at arm's length since he'd reappeared in her life, unwilling to let him slip through the cracks in her soul. And now, here he was. The world was changing. And she wanted him.

Without thinking, she pushed herself up onto her tiptoes,

slipped her hand across the back of his neck, and pulled him to her. When his lips found hers, her soul, dormant for so long, opened. She pressed toward him, feeling his warmth against her chest.

When she pulled back, she looked into his eyes. She could see, in the intensity of his stare, that he was hers if she'd have him. He held her, studying her, and then he bent slowly. He kissed her cheek, softly, and she let him. His breath mixed with hers, and the fist in Lucia's heart loosened. He was warm and familiar, even after all these years. Could she forgive him?

His breath was hot in her ear. "I'll stand by you until the day I die. If you want me to, Lucia. If you'll let me."

Like a balloon in the wind, she let her mind go. She tugged him toward her bedroom, nudging the door shut behind them. She stood close to his lean frame in the dim light, fingering his hands, his wrists, his arms. Wordlessly, she worked his shirt off his body. His hand found the skin of her waist and he bent to kiss her and she was gone, swept away. They blended together, two currents in the same stream, letting go of the separate banks that held them.

Later, candlelight flickered at their bedside, casting shapes like spirits whispering up the walls. Carlo's skin was gold against the sheets, and she ran her hand along his arm, feeling his muscles and bones. He was thin. He cleared a curl from her eyes, fumbling to tuck it behind her ear, and she giggled.

"Remember our first night here?" she whispered, and he grinned. "On the terrace?"

She pursed her lips to hold back another giggle. "It's how I always remembered you."

He cocked his head, running his hand down her arm to latch his fingers in hers, and laughed. "How inappropriate."

"That's not what I mean. When I yearned for you, I'd think of you up there, under the stars, holding me while Rome lapped at our feet like a dark sea . . ."

He bent to kiss her, lingering. When he pulled back, his voice was rough, his eyes hopeful. "You yearned for me?"

She nodded.

He leaned in close, pressing his forehead to hers. She listened to the sweep of his breath, the pump of his heart, so close after all these years.

"I yearned for you," he murmured. "When I was exiled, I'd try to remember your face. For hours. Your smile, your laugh. Us." He tipped back, holding her stare with his earth-colored eyes. "I never should have left you, Lucia. I'll never leave you again."

She burrowed into his chest, holding him tight. His skin smelled the way it always had, of warmth and soap and home. "We'll be a family, when the war is over." The truth of her words landed in her soul like sunlight.

"Sì, I'll be your husband." He kissed her forehead. "And Matteo's babbo. I'll honor you for the rest of my life."

For a long while, she watched shadows and light flicker on the walls, wiping tears from her eyes and marveling at the joy growing in her spirit. When she could speak, it was to say what she knew had to come next. She tightened her hand in his.

"It's well past midnight. Don't you have to find the American spy?"

He nodded, his jaw brushing the crown of her head. "I do have to go, but I'll come back tomorrow." He kissed her once more, gave her long look, and swung his legs off the bed.

Minutes later, he was pulling on his trousers, his rib cage rippling as he bent for his shoes. She swallowed a lump of fear. "In bocca al lupo, Carlo." She pursed a smile from her lips. "Remember when you said that to me? The first day we met?"

He chuckled. "Into the wolf's mouth . . . an apt saying for our time, *si?*"

She nodded, and the levity dropped from the moment. "Come back," she said as he stood.

"I will." He looked down at her tenderly. "Always."

# TWENTY-EIGHT

∾

## Francesca

*January 28, 1944*

Francesca pedaled home under a darkening sky. She shivered, and her stomach churned. Broth and wormy beans didn't keep flesh on a person's bones, and tattered clothing didn't keep out the chill. Nonetheless, she pedaled hard. Because buried in her laundry basket was a German officer's briefcase. Lucia and Matteo had fetched it from her parents' apartment after avoiding the area for three days. They met Francesca in a nearby alley, stowed the briefcase in the laundry basket, and left separately for home.

Getting home safely had taken on new meaning since the invasion. Francesca turned a corner, worn tires skidding. Nobody could understand why the Allies had paused on the beachhead in Anzio, giving the Germans time to build their defenses. But they'd done exactly that. Every day and night since, German columns rumbled through Rome, and now they were so thick in the Alban Hills that the Allies had missed their chance to take the city. The war, and the occupation, would go on.

And to make matters worse? The Gestapo, armed with more information than ever about the partisans, were on the hunt. Francesca glanced at the linens shivering in her basket, grimacing. Stealing the briefcase had been stunningly brazen. Foolish, even. But, depending on what was inside, Lucia's brazen act could save a lot of people.

When she stepped into the building, Lucia and Matteo were already on the staircase.

"You got here fast," Francesca said, taking Matteo's cold little hand while Lucia came down and hefted the bicycle.

"A trolley was running." Lucia hoisted the bicycle with a quick smile. "A stroke of luck." Trolleys rarely ran anymore. At the top of the stairs, Lucia set the bicycle down, slid her key into the door, and froze.

"It's unlocked," she whispered, glancing over her shoulder with startled eyes.

Francesca's heart quickened, but she nodded and tucked Matteo behind her in one swift movement. She stepped forward, leaning close to the door to listen. Footsteps sounded within, approaching. She lurched back and was reaching into her breast pocket for the Beretta that was no longer there, when the door swung open.

Carlo stood in the gap, face pale. He beckoned, wordless, and they went inside.

Lucia bent to Matteo, mustering a smile before anyone else could speak. "*Piccolo*, would you go to your room and do your big puzzle? Don't come out until it's finished, *sì*?"

Matteo nodded solemnly, trotting off down the hall, and sorrow nudged Francesca's heart. The little boy understood fear and secrecy all too well. His door closed, and she turned to Carlo.

"What are you doing here? I was going to bring the briefcase to you tomorrow."

Carlo nodded. His eyes darted from them to the front door and back again. "It can't wait until tomorrow." He reached for Lucia, reeling her in, his eyes bouncing again to the door. "Alberto and several of his men were arrested. The Gestapo raided their hideout this afternoon. They're arresting people all over town. *Grazie a Dio* that you're both safe."

Francesca's anger surged. "I knew it. Everyone was so foolish . . . leaving clues across Rome like bread crumbs for the damned Nazis to follow. Do you think they're on to us?"

"Don't know." Carlo frowned. "Let's see what's in the briefcase, and then we'll decide what to do." He strode toward the bedroom, still talking. "I don't think Lucia's cover has been blown. Nobody knows her. It may be safest to stay here—I'll stand guard."

He sat on the bed, picking the lock on the clasp. It popped open, and he riffled through it, hands shaking. "*Gesù Cristo,*" he murmured, loosening a paper clip. "They're planning another labor sweep." He thumbed through the papers, eyes tracking back and forth. "There's a map and everything." He read intently for a second, then flipped to the next page.

Francesca plucked a file folder from the bottom of the briefcase, setting it on her lap.

Lucia paced the floor. "Should I take Matteo to my parents' house?" she whispered.

"No." Carlo spoke while reading, brow furrowed. "If you're compromised, they'll look there." He glanced up, clearly caught in indecision. "I know a priest who could hide us. He's been stowing people in a convent—"

"*Mio Dio,*" Francesca whispered involuntarily. Her stomach tightened as she flipped through the pages on her lap. Faces and names blurred in her vision. "This is what we needed—it's everyone the Gestapo's been hunting. As of three days ago."

Carlo and Lucia leaned over, staring at her lap while she turned pages. There were over a dozen documents, some with pictures, listing activities, associations, and histories deemed suspicious by the Nazis.

Francesca's mind raced. She saw the people in her shaking fingers like branches on a tree: each of them led to more branches.
The Gestapo could take entire limbs of the resistance down if
people talked under torture. "We have to warn them," she said,
meeting Carlo's stare. "We can prevent their arrests if we get to
them first. They're all partisans—"

"I'll go out and find them," Carlo said.

Lucia shook her head. "No—Carlo, please." Her voice caught.
"It's too dangerous, especially now with the Gestapo—"

Francesca turned another page, and Lucia stopped mid-sentence.
"L'Allodola." Lucia read it aloud. "Given name: Francesca Gallo."
It was printed across the picture on Francesca's lap. The picture
was of her, slumped in a chair with a bloodied, swollen face. She
recalled the flash in Via Tasso, the way she'd squinted against the
light at the very end, drooping with exhaustion.

"They *photographed* me. During the . . . torture." She could
barely speak.

For a long moment, nobody moved. When Francesca looked
up, Lucia started to pace the room again. "Perhaps it was just a
precaution," she said, hand on her forehead. "This doesn't mean
they're after you for sure. They took the picture so they'd have a
record . . ."

"And then they put it in this briefcase. Because they realized
they were mistaken in releasing me. They know my code name."
The words were dry in Francesca's throat. Every cell in her body
began to tremble. *They knew who she was.* She remembered the
bright lights. The flash of pliers. She couldn't return there. They
all had to hide, somewhere the Nazis would never look—

A knock sounded on the front door. She stilled, panic suspended. The knocking continued, echoing down the hall. Lucia
met her stare before slipping from the room, wordlessly, to fetch
Matteo. Francesca looked to Carlo, whose eyes were wide. The

knocking didn't cease. Her heart echoed it, pounding against her breastbone. She lifted the papers, with a shaking hand, back into the briefcase. "Hide it," she whispered, sliding it to Carlo.

Lucia appeared in the doorway with Matteo at her side. "Matteo, I want you to stay in here while I answer the door," she whispered, looking from Carlo to Francesca. "It's probably just Signor Bianchi coming up to complain. But don't move a muscle."

Lucia strode down the hall, and Francesca sat as still as she ever had in her life.

# TWENTY-NINE

## Lucia

When Lucia reached for the door handle, she thought she'd faint. She knew it wasn't Signor Bianchi. He'd never once climbed the stairs and pounded on her door. Not when she was a new mother with a baby who cried through the night, not when Matteo threw tantrums as a toddler, not even recently, with all the coming and going. Whoever it was had already been waiting suspiciously long—she couldn't hesitate further. She turned the handle, shaking, and peeked through the wedge in the jamb.

Nonna Colombo stood on the threshold, her hair wet with rain. Lucia exhaled, waving her in without a word.

"Mamma," she breathed, latching the door and glancing back to the hallway. "I couldn't imagine who it might be after dark like this. What are you doing here?"

Her mother held her gaze in the foyer for a long moment, her eyes dull. Then she strode down the hall to the parlor, wordless, still wearing her soaking coat. Lucia glanced at the bedroom door as they passed, willing everyone to stay quiet.

Nonna Colombo sank into a sofa, and Lucia sat across from her, hands on her knees, face as blank as she could manage.

"They ransacked my house," her mother said, emotionless. "Just after you left."

Lucia's eyes widened on their own, stinging in the chill indoor air. "Ransacked? Who?" But she already knew. In the pit of her soul, she knew.

"What have you been up to, Lucia?" Nonna Colombo lifted her gaze, and now her eyes were piercing, the blue of deep snow.

"I . . . Nothing, Mamma. The Germans searched your house? Why would they do such a thing, with Father—"

"Why, indeed?" The words were stone-cold. Nonna Colombo cleared her throat. "That man, years ago, must have rubbed off on you. I wondered when I saw you whispering with Fabrizio. He's been arrested—did you know?"

Lucia shook her head. She couldn't breathe. Fabrizio, with his elegance and wit, had been taken? She covered her mouth with her palm, suppressing the feelings whirling within.

Nonna Colombo leaned forward, hinging over her knees, and her veneer cracked. Her eyes welled. "Lucia, I'm your mother. You must be honest with me, because there might not be much time. Are you part of the resistance?"

They held each other's stares for several intakes of breath, and Lucia's mind darted like a bird in a cage. Why wasn't there much time? What did her mother intend to do?

"I am," she whispered.

Nonna Colombo sat still for one rigid moment, and then her shoulders collapsed. She shook her head and stood. "All right. You need to pack, right now. Come with me." She strode toward the bedroom.

Lucia leaped to her feet, scrambling to get ahead of her mother. "Pack?" she managed, inserting herself before the bedroom door. "What do you know?"

"If they came to my house, of all places, they'll come to yours.

They could be on their way now." Nonna Colombo reached for her hands, squeezing, and her face filled with worry. "I'm no fool. I can see that you're hiding something in that room. I can see that you've been hiding from me all along. But I'm your mother." Her voice cracked. "I would never do anything but protect you, *Liebling*. I've lost one child. I'll not lose you."

She stepped around Lucia and pushed open the door. For one stricken moment she stood in the jamb, her gaze darting from Francesca to Carlo and back to Lucia.

"Nonna," Matteo said, rising from the floor. His eyes stretched with fear. "What's happening?"

The older woman took a breath and collected herself in one clean sweep. She marched into the room and flung the wardrobe open, speaking with authority. "Matteo, you're going on a trip to the countryside." She moved as if mechanized, dumping clothes into the suitcase she'd found at the bottom of the wardrobe. She glanced at Carlo, still speaking to Matteo. "How long have you known him, darling?"

"Awhile," Matteo said, drifting over. "Nonna? Giancarlo's nice."

"Yes," she said, her voice catching. "I'm sure *Giancarlo* loves you, child. Listen. Can you go and fetch some clothes and your little toy bunny? You'll want it on your trip."

Matteo obeyed.

Carlo rose. "Tell me what you know," he said, looking between the women. Francesca sat on the bed, eyes wide as if she was stunned dumb. But Lucia understood her well enough to know that she was thinking, and that she was probably already ten steps ahead of the rest of them.

Nonna Colombo hefted the suitcase to the bed, taking a minute to refold the clothes in it. She spoke to Carlo while she worked, and Lucia marveled. Her mother's self-possession was astonishing.

"Surely, you listened through the door. You've put my daughter in great danger, Carlo. The Germans will be here anytime, of that I'm certain. And they have so many of your other people already . . ." She straightened, meeting his gaze. "It's only a matter of time before they talk. You'll all be caught if you stay in Rome."

Matteo ducked back into the room, clutching his faded bunny and a bundle of clothes. He gave them to his grandmother. "Will Francesca come, too?"

Nonna Colombo handed the suitcase to Carlo. She addressed Lucia while glancing at Francesca. "Is this slip of a girl involved as well? *Mein Gott.*" She bent before her grandchild, cupping his chin in her wrinkled hand. "She'll go with you, Matteo. And, my darling, keep those lips sealed. Don't say a word to anyone—especially if they're wearing a uniform."

Then she left the room. Not three minutes had passed. Carlo glanced at Lucia, and she shrugged despite her panic. She went after her mother, finding her in the foyer.

"I'm going home to talk to your father, and then I'll be back. I'll find a way to get you out of the city safely, *Liebling.*" She reached for the door handle but hesitated. She turned back to Lucia, and her eyes glistened in the dim light.

"Mamma." Lucia swallowed hard. "I don't know how to thank you."

Nonna Colombo reached out and brushed the hair from Lucia's forehead, tucking the curls behind her ear as if she were a little girl. "You don't have to thank me. I'm your mother."

Minutes after Nonna Colombo had left, they gathered in the foyer. Carlo carried the briefcase. The packed suitcase sat at Lucia's feet, and Matteo clung to her torso.

"Do you think we can trust her?" Carlo asked, meeting her gaze.

"We can trust her." Lucia swallowed, squeezing Matteo to her chest, still stunned. Her mother loved her, despite everything. "She'll probably come with a car. I don't know what we'll do about the checkpoints leaving the city—"

"Maybe we shouldn't wait for her," Carlo interrupted. "She won't know how to get us out. We could get to a safe house, right now, and figure it out from there."

Francesca's voice was soft. "Are there any safe houses anymore? We need to give the briefcase to someone who isn't compromised, and then we need to disappear." She leveled her green eyes on Lucia. "Your mother might be our best chance. If we go on foot, so close to curfew, we could be questioned."

Lucia kissed Matteo's head. He curled tighter, frightened and confused. What had she done? Her child was in danger. And both of his parents were in danger. *Oddio.* What would happen to him if they were all caught? She was opening her mouth to agree that they should wait for her mother when a noise halted the words in her throat.

It was the rumble of a truck engine. Carlo met her gaze, and in a half second it all flashed between them: their time was up. The Germans were already coming.

"We have to go," he barked, frantic.

Lucia's voice was thin. "Go where? They'll see us in the street. *Madonna mia*—"

Francesca limped to the window and peeked through the slit. "A German truck. It's stuck behind some people down the way. The road may be too narrow for it."

"The terrace," Carlo said, striding to the door. "We'll climb across the adjoining rooftop and escape through the next building. When we hit the street, we'll already be blocks away."

Lucia followed him through the door while he was still talking, hefting Matteo and letting Francesca pass before her so Carlo could hoist her up the stairs.

"If we're separated, go to my friend, the priest," Carlo continued, speaking quickly and quietly as he took the steps. "He's hiding people all over Rome, on properties owned by the Vatican . . ." Matteo's shoes bounced against Lucia's hips as she scaled the flights, listening to Carlo repeat the priest's name and address twice. They reached the rooftop door when the pounding started three floors below. She ducked outside, buffeted by wind, and the pounding continued in the stairwell as the terrace door closed. It wouldn't be long until a neighbor opened it for the Nazis, or before they broke it down.

Lucia was hurrying across the terrace toward the adjoining peak, following Carlo, when she saw the lemon tree. She deposited Matteo and bent, scratching frantically at the soil. It took only a second to find the oilcloth, and she snatched it, pulling it through the lemon tree's roots. She stood, and the next task loomed. She hollowed inside.

"Carlo, how will we ever get across it?" She stared at the adjoining roofline, hearing the terror in her own voice. The peak fused to their terrace's wall at waist height, stretching across the darkness before hitting another terrace wall. The roofline slanted sharply on either side, shedding onto the pavement several floors below. Moonlight shone on its tiles.

"This is impossible," she whispered. Her heart pounded her breastbone as hard as the Nazis pounding the door downstairs. Would they be better off with the Gestapo, or the roof?

Carlo whispered while he took Matteo into his arms. "Listen, Matteo. You remember climbing trees with me, sì? Never look down, right? Only look where you're going. This is like climbing across a thick limb. Hold tight to the tiles. Your mamma will be right behind you."

"Carlo." Lucia wanted to be sick. Every cell in her body protested while she watched her boy, with his wide dark eyes, nod at his babbo in the moonlight.

"Like a tree," Matteo echoed, though his bottom lip trembled. He coughed a little, glancing at the peak stretching before him. "Mamma? I have good balance."

"No, Carlo. We can't—"

"There's no time," he whispered. "Climb up behind him. *Now.* I'll stand guard until you're all across, and then I'll come, too."

Lucia looked to Francesca, who hadn't yet said a word. The girl stared at the roofline. She leaned in, whispering quietly so Matteo wouldn't hear. "It's safer than being caught. Take him across, right now. They won't spare him."

*They won't spare him.* Lucia lost her breath. What would they do to a child? Shoot him? Send him off in one of their trains? Or would he watch his parents be arrested, killed? She imagined him in a flash, screaming over their bodies. She pressed a hand to her forehead. They were right. The roof was less of a risk than the Nazis. She helped Carlo shift Matteo up, where he straddled the roofline on his hands and knees, and Carlo boosted her up right behind him, speaking in her ear.

"*In bocca al lupo*, Lucia. I love you."

She swallowed her bounding fear, murmuring words to Matteo as they began to crawl, one hand over the other. "That's it, love. Go slowly. I'm right behind you." *Please God*, she thought, the words repeating in time with her breath. *Keep Matteo safe. Piero, help him.*

Matteo crawled forward, his movements small, and Lucia mirrored them. She pinned her eyes on his little ankles, right under her nose. If he slipped, she'd grab him. A bomb exploded somewhere in the distance, rattling the horizon. They moved mechanically, hand over hand. Lucia forced herself to think of nothing but Matteo's feet. She watched them, sliding forward one at a time. She pictured them hitting the surface of the adjoining terrace, safe.

The moon rose overhead, casting light on tiles still wet from earlier rain. They inched forward. Artillery rumbled from the distant beachhead, and Lucia listened under it for Francesca, breathing hard behind her. Matteo crawled like a baby, one palm at a time gripping the tiles, and then he was there, at the end of the span.

"*Bravo*," Lucia whispered, her heart in her throat. "Now lower yourself down. I'm right here with you."

His eyes caught the moonlight as he turned, gripping tight with his little fingers until his feet dangled over the terrace floor. He let go, thumping safely down.

Lucia exhaled, and in one breath thanked God, the Madonna, and Piero. Then she followed her boy's movements, turning and lowering herself down.

As her feet touched the terrace floor, a shuffle came from behind her. Francesca gasped, and Lucia heard a tile come loose, clattering across the roof and falling to the street below. Francesca was still on the pitch, gripping the peak while her body slumped unevenly across it. She'd slipped on her weak side.

Without thought, Lucia hoisted herself back up, legs dangling, and reached for the terrified girl. "Give me your hand," she whispered. Carlo's silhouette turned across the span. He put the briefcase handle in his teeth and climbed up onto the peak.

Francesca hesitated. She closed her eyes, inhaled, and shot one arm toward Lucia. Lucia caught it just as the girl began to slide. She held on with everything she had, yanking Francesca toward her, scraping her over the tiles until they both tumbled onto the terrace.

They untangled themselves on the terrace floor, pain bloomed through Lucia's hip, and across the rooftops a door banged open.

Lucia stood as if she'd been electrified. Carlo was still at the start of the span, his dark shape straddling it, the briefcase in his teeth. In one fluid movement, he lifted a hand from the roof tiles, gripped the briefcase, and flung it, hard, toward Lucia. It landed with a thud next to Francesca on the terrace floor. Then Matteo started to cough.

Across the span, Carlo jerked his head down, urging Lucia to disappear, and he began coughing loudly himself, obscuring Matteo's noise. Before Lucia could duck, he started backing up. She pulled Matteo into her lap, pressed a hand gently over his mouth, and rocked his heaving body. Why was Carlo going backward? Panic thrashed in her chest while she rocked Matteo. Why was he giving himself up? Carlo's booming voice rose over the expanse separating them, and it was met with German shouts. She pinned her eyes shut and kissed Matteo's temple as the last coughs spasmed from his chest.

Carlo was sacrificing himself. It washed over her like a heavy wave. If he'd kept coming across the roof, the Germans would have found them all. If he didn't make a noisy retreat, they would have heard his child's cough. She felt as if she were sinking, fast. She couldn't lose Carlo.

"Mamma," Matteo whispered, his voice snagging on mucus. "What's happening?"

"Hush," she whispered right in his ear. "Not a sound, *piccolo*."

She tightened her arms around Matteo's chest, wishing she could press his coughs away for good. And she wished she could stand up, shouting at Carlo to escape, to stay with them, to be her husband and her child's father. Matteo curled against her, and his eyes, so like his father's, glittered like stars in the darkness. German shouts rebounded across the span, and she listened hard, trying to make out what they were saying. Where would they take him? Via Tasso?

A shot rang out, shattering the night. Francesca reached for Lucia's arm, squeezing it tight, and a sob escaped from Lucia before she could smother it. What had just happened? She listened to the sudden quiet, panicking. Matteo started to tremble, his arms circling her neck, and it was only his frail weight that kept her from standing, from crawling back home. Francesca shook her head in the darkness. The questions multiplied in Lucia's mind, like a skipping record. Had they shot Carlo? They couldn't have—he couldn't be gone. *Not again.* She rocked her boy while new noises floated over the expanse: a shuffle, voices ricocheting back and forth, a door banging open. The sound of boot steps faded, and the terrace door thumped shut.

Lucia gasped, closing her eyes, but Francesca again squeezed her arm. "We have to go," she whispered. "They saw where he was headed. They might know we're here. *Andiamo.*"

Fury and grief and panic roared in Lucia's skull like a hurricane, but she lifted Matteo, and Francesca tucked the briefcase under her arm, heading for the terrace door. Just before stepping through, Lucia glanced back to her own terrace. She saw nothing but the shape of the stunted lemon tree, traced in moonlight. Her heart faltered, and she hugged Matteo tight, ducking after Francesca through the door. A stairwell dropped before them, and they descended, moving as if mechanized.

Matteo sniffed on Lucia's shoulder, and she kissed the hair above his ear as images appeared in her mind: Carlo standing guard while they crossed, listening to the thud of boots ascending the stairwell. Carlo crouched on the dark roof, urging her to go on without him. Without meaning to, she imagined Carlo slumped against the lemon tree in the moonlight, a bullet in his chest.

*No.* She blinked hard, sickening. It was only her imagination, conjuring the worst possibility. She'd seen no body in her hurried look at the terrace. He couldn't be gone. Not again. She stepped from the building into the fresh, cold air, clutching her boy. Francesca beckoned, and she followed, stunned silent.

They would vanish now. But even as Lucia ran away, a part of her yearned to return to the rooftop. To Carlo, and the lemon tree, and the life they'd once imagined together.

# THIRTY

ॐ

## Francesca

*Early March 1944*

MATTEO SAT CROSS-LEGGED on the floor in a stripe of fleeting sunshine, frowning at the chessboard. He pinched the top of his queen, started to move her, and then slid her back, brows furrowing as he puzzled. For a child of not quite six, he was good at chess. Francesca had taught him how to play the game herself, keeping him busy through long days in the convent.

She glanced around the cell where they spent so much time now. After escaping over the rooftop, they'd found Carlo's friend the priest at his address in Trastevere, and he took the briefcase to the resistance and brought them to a convent to hide. They'd hoped it would be for days, a week at most, but February had bled into March, and they still waited behind these thick walls. They waited for news of Carlo, who was either dead or imprisoned—nobody knew which. They waited for news of the war. They waited for the Allies to advance, for something to change, for the Gestapo to pound down the convent doors as they had other Vatican properties. They waited, in agony.

"Checkmate," Matteo said, looking up and flashing a triumphant smile.

"*Bravo!*" Francesca tousled his brown curls. "Matteo, when you smile like that, you remind me of someone."

"Who?" He began to gather the pieces and set them up for another round.

"I called him Mino. I knew him when he was your age—well, I knew him always."

"Where does he live?"

Francesca's momentary joy split with a needle of grief. She maintained her smile while Matteo studied her, rubbing at one of his eyes with his fist.

"He lives in an orchard, with trees, and birds, and a little stream that runs through the wild edges."

Matteo cocked his head, blinking as he imagined it, and the door to the room creaked open. In one movement, Matteo pushed himself off the floor, exclaiming, "Mamma!" and skipped the three steps to thump into his mother's waist.

Lucia wrapped her arms around him just as he began to cough from his meager exertion. He buried his head into her skirt, his whole body shaking with gurgling bellows. The cough had worsened lately, the sound of it deepening. Francesca frowned. When he finally heaved a clear breath, he was flushed in the cheeks, his eyes wet.

Francesca pushed herself up from the floor as well. She was due to go out.

Lucia, sensing her intention, stiffened. "I wish you'd stay in," she whispered, releasing Matteo from her arms. He flopped down by the chess set, murmuring to the pieces and moving them around. "Let someone else take over—there's a price on your head, Francesca. Every partisan in Via Tasso could compromise your contacts . . . How do you know you're not walking into a trap? I wish you wouldn't persist."

"I have to." Francesca met her stare. "If those of us who are free don't persist, who will?"

They'd had versions of this conversation, abbreviated by Matteo's listening ears, many times. Lucia couldn't leave the convent, not with a sick child and Hans Bergmann hunting for her. But Francesca could still take the risk. She'd been covering her hair and slinking through alleys, going to meet Tommaso for news and tasks. With the false hope of liberation gone, the insurrection was on hold, and she'd become a messenger.

Lucia lowered her voice. "Promise to be careful. And you'll ask again?"

"Sì, every time." Francesca took in Lucia's drawn expression, the way she'd become thin under the cheekbones, furtive, blinking away frequent tears. "I won't give up on him."

With Matteo in the room, they wouldn't say Carlo's name. The boy had asked repeatedly why Carlo didn't cross the roof, scowling at their vague escape stories. When Francesca went out, she sought information about Carlo from her contacts, and she'd even sent Tommaso to Lucia's old terrace to investigate. There wasn't a body, and there was no trace of blood. Nobody in the building had seen a body, which flushed them with hope and gave way to new questions. If he hadn't been shot, was he imprisoned? Had they shipped him off for forced labor? Francesca turned to the armoire in the little room, shrugging off the questions while she shook a garment over her head.

A chuckle sounded from one of the beds while Francesca worked the black folds over her shoulders. When her head emerged, Lucia stared up, her face lit with a rare smile.

"Where did you get it?" Lucia pursed the amusement from her lips.

"Raided the laundry." Francesca brushed the wrinkles from the dark folds of fabric. "I was afraid Mother Superior would say no . . ." She glanced down at the habit covering her from head to toe, disguising her as a novice nun.

Lucia nodded, decisive. "This makes me feel better. *Sì*, you need a disguise if you're going to insist on wading out into the fray." She rose from the bed. "Let me help you with that veil, Sister," she murmured, stepping to Francesca and smoothing the fabric around her face, long fingers poking at stray hair. When Lucia finished, she paused, her expression again pensive.

"Do you ever still hope? For Giacomo?"

"No. *Never.*" Matteo glanced up, and Francesca caught herself. She hadn't meant to speak sharply. She stepped close, whispering into Lucia's ear. "I won't live on false hope. It's different with Carlo—he could easily be in prison with all the other compromised partisans. But Giacomo's gone, Lucia. I feel it with every beat of my heart." She met her friend's anxious stare. "You can count on me. I'll continue to ask about Carlo. I'll ask until we know something."

FRANCESCA WALKED THE streets of Rome, her habit flowing as she slipped along without her cane. She couldn't carry anything so obvious as a cane; if the Germans were looking for a girl with a limp, she'd give herself away. Hopefully, they wouldn't think twice about a limping nun.

Though it was early March, the streets were coated in wet snow. Clouds gusted overhead, the sun blinking behind them like a watchful eye. Francesca slid on the slushy cobbles. Rome could go years without snow—why, this year of all years, did winter have to grip so tightly to spring? She turned toward the center of the city, moving as quickly as she could up the streets.

As she passed alcoves of any kind, beggars called out, stretching their hands in the cold air. Refugees had been pouring into the city in the wake of the Allied invasion, fleeing the bombs and battles that ravaged across Italy. Little did they know during their long trek to the open city: Rome had nothing to offer.

The street curved up a hill, and a woman, huddling against a building and surrounded by three small children, grasped at her robes. "Can you help me, *Suora?*"

Francesca paused, taking in the woman's tired stare. "*Mi dispiace,*" she apologized, reaching to squeeze her hand. "I have nothing to give you." She glanced at the children, pained by their forlorn eyes. She'd asked if they could take more refugees at the convent but was told they had all they could care for. There were Jewish families hidden in the basement and political fugitives, like Francesca and Lucia, tucked into spare corners. And while they could fit more bodies inside, they couldn't feed them. All Francesca could offer anyone was a pledge: she would continue to fight. She wouldn't stop until either the Germans were gone, or she was dead.

A trio of Allied planes shot over the band of sky between buildings. The woman looked up, glaring at their trails. "God help us if they miss their target," she murmured. "The damned Americans already destroyed my house. Most of my village, too."

Francesca dropped her gaze. "I'm sorry to hear it, signora. But the Germans brought them here. Remember that."

The woman continued to stare at the sky. "Forgive me, Sister, but I hate them all." Her voice cracked. "We live in the street, in the snow and rain, nothing to eat. We listen to bombs falling day and night, praying one doesn't fall on us. The Allies will never break out of Anzio and Cassino. Nobody is coming to save us." The rumble of distant artillery underscored her words. The woman met Francesca's gaze, her eyes the color of the storm clouds skating across the sky. "We'll starve before they get here."

Francesca reached again for her hand, squeezing. "People are fighting to save you. Right now. They're dying and suffering, too, but they're still fighting. Don't lose hope, signora."

The woman inhaled, wiping her eyes with shaky fingers. "Pray for me."

Francesca nodded. She let the woman's hand go and turned, moving on up the street, the eyes of dozens of refugees following her progress. The roar of another plane grew on the horizon, but she didn't let it slow her down now. She was on her way to meet Tommaso, and she had to hurry or she'd miss him.

She reached the nondescript alley they'd planned as a meeting point, off main thoroughfares and, with any luck, away from curious eyes. Even here, in a quiet corner of the city, the walls were plastered with propaganda posters. Francesca leaned against one building and stared at the other, waiting for the echo of Tommaso's step.

She read the words of a propaganda poster that had been smeared with something that looked like excrement. *Italy begs her sons, in this tragic hour of her history, to fight or to work.* Through the brown streaks she could make out promises of *good food and good pay.* And, *Our well-paid work will help your family; don't let them starve for another day. Join the labor service. Volunteers for labor in Germany are welcomed at headquarters in Via Esquilino.*

Francesca frowned at the poster. Who did they think they were fooling? Everyone knew there was no longer such a thing as a volunteer. Men who hid from the call to fight or labor for the Nazis were hunted. They could be kidnapped and shipped north for forced labor. Or shot, depending on which list their names fell on. And whichever way they were taken, their families starved. The only people who weren't starving in Rome were the Nazis and their collaborators.

Footsteps interrupted her fury, and she turned to see Tommaso coming, his long stride sliding a little every few steps. He drew near, sinking against the wall. If anyone saw them, a nun speaking with a young man, it would be immediately suspicious. And if the wrong person saw Tommaso at all, he could be raked up to serve Germany. He was exactly the type of laborer the posters sought. So he spent his time hidden in a cellar with a huddle of other fugitive men, or ducking around alleys, working to move intelligence and reconnect the fractured resistance.

"This is good." Tommaso gestured to her new disguise. "Feel like you can walk the city safely in this?"

"Safely enough. Have anything for me to deliver?"

Tommaso nodded. "*Certo.* Here's a stack of leaflets." He reached into his waistband, pulling out a warm bundle of papers. "And here's a message." He handed her a tightly folded tissue paper. She lifted the habit and reached into her blouse, tucking the message in her brassiere, and she stuffed the leaflets into the waistband under her robes.

Tommaso spoke quickly while she reassembled herself. "The message goes to the usual man on the Lungotevere. He'll be there at three o'clock."

"*Va bene.*" It had become clear that the messages, always written on tissue paper, were vital. The resistance had spread its eyes and ears all the way from Rome to Anzio, employing regular people to observe German positions and movements. They passed the intelligence through messengers, like Francesca, until it reached American spies who radioed it straight to Allied command.

"I'll give you addresses for the leaflets," Tommaso went on, "but first . . ."

She looked up, and there was a spark of something in his eye. Was it excitement?

"Ready for some good news?"

She nodded, heart accelerating.

"Giovanni has a friend who was released from Via Tasso two

days ago. I managed to meet up with him yesterday, and Francesca—Gianluca's there. He's alive."

She gasped, pressing her hands over her mouth as her heart dipped and rose in a wave of emotion. Lucia would be overcome. "You're sure it's him?"

"It was an exact description. Sounds like he's in rough shape, but alive. Just has to hang on until the Allies come . . ."

Memory came in a flash: the bright lights, the pliers, the blows to the head. Nausea replaced her relief. She couldn't imagine the suffering brought on by *weeks* in Via Tasso. How much longer could he survive there?

"We need this damn occupation to end," she breathed, holding a palm to her forehead.

"That brings me to some other news. We're organizing a strike, and I'm meant to ask if you'll join us."

"What kind of strike?" She dropped her hand from her forehead.

"A big one." Excitement lit his eyes again. "Some of the partisans I'm living with have been watching the Germans move through the city. They parade up and down the same streets every day. Same time, even. Always singing. Like the goddamn *Balilla* boys from our childhood."

"You're not talking about a strike on a column of men, traveling on foot—"

"Damn right I am. Even better—they're SS."

She hesitated, recalling the hotheaded boys drinking on the bridge right after the Allied invasion. One had spoken of striking Germans moving through the city, boasting of killing them like *easy targets. Santo cielo.* These boys needed Carlo's cool guidance. Francesca's heart dropped as she spoke. "Tommaso. What would that accomplish? How would that have any impact on the greater war?"

He straightened. "They'd lose men."

"Not enough to make a difference on the front lines. *Dio mio*, the Germans would be angry as hell after." An explosion rumbled in the distance, ominous as thunder. "It's an unnecessary risk. You could compromise what's left of our network, our ability to help the Allies—"

"It would prove a point."

"What point?" She glanced up and down the street, checking that they weren't being observed. "That we can kill people? You'd better believe they can kill more people than us, Tommaso. And they will. If Italian partisans do this, the Nazis will seek revenge." She shook her head, staring at the sidewalk as her thoughts raced. She didn't trust Tommaso and his cellar mates to think strategically, to put the good of the cause first.

"We have to show them that they haven't beaten us." He hunched his thin shoulders, glancing up and down the street. "With so many of our people arrested and dead, we need to show them that the resistance is still operating."

"Why? It's better if they think we *aren't* operating, that we aren't still aiding the Allies. This plan is juvenile." She looked right into his eyes. "When we struck convoys, it was to interrupt their supply lines—to force them out where the Allies could bomb their trucks and tanks. Our objective was clear. What's the objective of this?" She waved her hand, her voice rising. "To flex our muscles? Who has bigger muscles? Tommaso, if you don't stop this strike, we'll be in *un mare di merda*."

He glanced up and down the street again, glowering. "I can't stop it from happening. It's far bigger than my cellar mates now. The strike has moved up the rungs. The Gappisti are running it."

"*Dio mio*." She spat. "When is it happening?"

He shook his head. "Can't tell you that."

She crossed her arms in frustration, turning to look up the

street. They needed to get out of here. They'd been in conversation, out in the open, far too long. "Tell me the addresses where you want the leaflets to go."

He rattled off a half-dozen addresses, and they slid into her mind and stayed. She nodded.

"I don't know how you memorize things so quickly," Tommaso said, and she glared up at his sheepish expression. She wouldn't let him soften her disapproval.

"Try to stop the strike," she replied, holding his gaze. "And meet me next week."

She pivoted and walked away, veering around the first corner. The leaflets tucked in her waistband poked at the bone of her hip, and her hungry stomach soured with new worry. But alongside her frustration there was a shard of joy. She forced herself to focus on it, holding the good news in her mind like a bit of gold. She'd deliver everything as quickly as possible, and then she'd go home to tell Lucia the news: her husband was alive.

# THIRTY-ONE

⅊⅊

## Lucia

*Mid-March 1944*

*C*ARLO WAS ALIVE. Lucia repeated this to herself throughout the day, whispering it while doing chores, while playing chess with Matteo, while ignoring her rumbling, cramping stomach, and while falling asleep to the thunder of distant battles. He was in hell, but alive.

She whispered it now, two weeks after first hearing it, while stroking Matteo's hot forehead. Sunlight fell on his face, but his eyes didn't open. His breath came shallow and fast, nostrils flaring with each uptake of air, and she swallowed the fear closing her throat. In a bed across the room, in this makeshift infirmary, a slightly older child slept, but she couldn't see him. The nuns had barricaded Matteo from sight with a pair of sheets in case he was infectious. It was the best they could do in the overcrowded convent.

Lucia closed her eyes, fighting panic. This morning, Matteo had failed to fully wake. He'd opened his eyes, coughed weakly, and fallen back asleep. She'd run for help, they'd brought him here, and now she perched on a stool in this white-walled square, listening to each raspy breath in terror.

A soft voice interrupted her thoughts. "Signora?" The sheet

lifted, and a grandmotherly nun wearing a stethoscope dipped inside. "I'm Suora Chiara." She was tiny, with a sharp nose, narrow eyes, and quick, assured movements that defied her obvious age.

Lucia blinked back tears. "I'd like him to see a doctor."

Suora Chiara shook her head and leveled Lucia with a direct stare. "I've worked in several hospitals, *cara mia*, and I'll take good care of your boy. We'd rather not bring an outsider into the convent—the Fascists have spies of every kind."

Lucia looked from the nun to Matteo, and like a reflex, she felt his forehead again. He was hot, flushed, twitchy in his sleep. She watched his flaring nostrils while she spoke, hearing the desperation in her own voice. "Should I take him to a hospital?"

The nun shook her head decisively. "Conditions are terrible in the hospitals. They've nothing to give their patients, and I've heard of patients dying of hunger before their ailments take them. He'll do better in this quiet room, with you at his side."

At the word "dying," everything within Lucia rose to a frantic height. *Matteo couldn't die.* Her own breathing came fast, but the nun didn't seem to notice. She shuffled close, fitting the stethoscope over her veiled head.

"All right if I take a look?"

Lucia nodded, and the little nun bent to listen to Matteo's chest. *Carlo was alive*, she reminded herself. Miracles could happen. She needed another miracle now.

"Pneumonia . . ." the nun murmured, moving her stethoscope around. "*Sì*, I hear it in his lungs. How long has he had his cough?"

"Weeks." The word fell out as a croak. "He's always been prone to colds, but this one just took hold of him . . ." She couldn't speak. She looked down and twisted the ring on her finger. It was her wedding band, plucked from the oilcloth she'd hidden in the lemon tree's roots.

Suora Chiara sighed. "Lack of nutrition makes it difficult to fight off infection, especially for the littlest." She bent again, taking Matteo's temperature and frowning at the results, then counting off his heartbeats. "We need to keep him hydrated," she murmured, perhaps to herself.

"Will he be all right?" Lucia asked, grabbing the nun's hand as she tried to pass. Fear coursed through her like continual jolts of lightning, mixing up the rhythm of her heart.

Suora Chiara hesitated. She glanced from Lucia to Matteo, firming her narrow lips. "It's difficult to predict how he'll do. Sometimes children bounce back from an illness like this, and sometimes they don't. I'll do everything I can to turn him around, sì?" She reached for Lucia's hand, pumping it once. "Stay strong for him. Let him hear your voice. He needs his mother." With that, the nun turned and strode out, muttering to herself, her robes vanishing under the suspended sheets.

Lucia bent next to her little son, taking his hand and choking back sobs. "Please get better," she whispered. She couldn't fall apart. She touched his hot forehead again, his lashes fluttered on his freckled cheeks, and she cleared her throat to speak. "Matteo, would you like to hear your bedtime story? *Caro mio*, a boy once went for a walk in a green and sunlit forest. He saw so many beautiful things . . ." *Please God*, she prayed as she spoke, her tears darkening the sheets. *I can't live without my son.* The words of the story emerged on their own, and she studied his flushed face, willing him to take a deep, clear breath, open his eyes, and offer his usual, "Then the boy saw a *farfalla!*" But Matteo slept on.

"He saw a butterfly," she continued, "and it was all the colors in the world. The boy followed the butterfly farther into the forest, forgetting everything to run and chase it, but then the forest grew dark. The boy was lost, and he thought he was alone, and he was afraid. But then, he remembered the sky. He looked up, and there were stars looking down at him, and he didn't feel alone anymore. He started to walk, and he knew where to go. And as he walked, he saw the forest was beautiful, even at night. He just had to travel through it to find his way home." She squeezed his pale fingers. "Matteo, do you know how much I love you? As much as all the stars. And the stars are always with us, even when we can't see them."

She watched his labored breathing, unable to take her eyes from his flaring nostrils, and suddenly, air-raid sirens erupted outside. They pealed three times, bouncing through the city beyond the convent walls. Lucia set Matteo's hand on the bedspread, wiped at her eyes, and went to the window, lifting the curtain. For months, the sirens had been silent, quieted by the myth that Rome was an open city. But all pretenses had fallen away since the invasion in Anzio, and now they shrieked constantly. A hum grew in the wake of the sirens, and Lucia's pulse throttled to life. She scanned the band of sky over the convent. The droning expanded, filling the air. Were the planes as close as they sounded? She craned her neck, eyes darting, and her breath caught as the first dark shape lumbered over the visible sky. There was no time to react, no time to hoist Matteo and scramble downstairs.

Before she could even turn around, the bomber released its load. A thud and a blast roared outside the convent walls. The air vibrated, and Lucia sprang to Matteo, covering his body with her own. His eyes blinked open while another explosion thundered, sucking all sound from the air, drowning the screams in his lungs. The windows burst, and Matteo's weak arms circled Lucia's neck. She felt the ping of shattering glass on her back and pinned her eyes shut, whispering a prayer.

"*God, protect my child. Please God, protect my child.* I have you, Matteo. I have you."

The roar died down, replaced by screams in the streets, shouts

in the convent halls, and Matteo's feeble weeping. Across the
room, the other boy whimpered, and the door flung open. Footsteps crunched over the broken glass, and Suora Chiara's voice
called out to Lucia.

"You all right, signora?"

Lucia struggled to find her voice. She let Matteo sink back onto
the mattress, and his hot little hands slid from her neck to her
palms. He gripped her weakly, his eyes darting around the ceiling. "Are we all right, Mamma?"

"We're all right." She kissed his forehead and glanced at the
sheets surrounding them. Sunlight poked through new slits sliced
by exploding glass.

"Franco," the old nun murmured across the room. "Let me
look. Just the cheek, *caro*?"

An uncertain voice answered, "*Sì*, Suora."

"We'll stitch that right up. Did the glass get you anywhere else?
Thank goodness for curtains . . ."

Another voice, belonging to a young nun, called into the room.
"It was a hit across the street. Shattered windows all over this side
of the building, but nothing more. The curtains caught the worst
of it."

"*Grazie a Dio*," Suora Chiara answered, and the halls outside
the sick room bustled to life. Lucia stayed where she was, murmuring assurances to Matteo, watching him while he drifted
back into his feverish sleep.

A few hours later, the room had been swept, the other boy's
cheek had been stitched and bandaged, broth had been spooned
into Matteo's slack mouth, and Lucia remained on her wobbly
stool. The sun fell beneath the rooftops beyond the empty window-
panes, casting an orange glow over the room. The door opened
and closed, and Suora Chiara's footsteps crossed the floor to the
other child's bed. Lucia listened to the nun's melodic voice.

"*Buonasera*, Franco. How are you feeling? Sleepy? At least with these open windows you'll hear the birds singing in the morning."

There was the sound of a stool dragging across the room, and then a quiver and a sigh as the older woman sat. "You know, I think you're almost well enough to join the other children downstairs. Maybe just another day or two. Ready to say your prayers, Franco?"

"*Sì*," a child's voice whispered. "But will we be safe tonight, Suora? No more planes?"

"No more planes. And I'll return to check on you, *caro mio*. Now, shall we?"

There was a pause before their voices joined together in a soft chant.

"*Sh'ma Yisrael, Adonai Eloheinu, Adonai Echad.*"

Lucia cocked her head, taking in the ancient words, her mouth falling open. She had no idea what they were saying, yet she recognized it. Lidia had said the same words every night before bed. Lucia held her breath to listen to the rest of the Hebrew prayer, spoken by a nun and a child, until their voices faded away.

The stool slid again on the floor, followed by the creak of aging joints. Lucia glanced at Matteo, smoothing his hair, before standing herself. She slipped through the sheet concealing his cot and looked at the other boy, Franco, his dark eyelashes already closed over his freshly bandaged cheek. She met the nun's gaze and followed her quietly from the room.

As soon as the door closed behind them, Suora Chiara turned and faced Lucia. She peered up with her small eyes, laugh lines crinkling around them. "You may think it was strange, what you overheard." She tipped her chin up, resolute. "But I believe the children hiding here mustn't forget who they are, so I learned their prayers when they first came to us. We pray the way their parents did with them, before bedtime. I trust you to understand."

"I do." Lucia had to clear the pain from her throat. "And I admire you for it, Sister."

Suora Chiara waved that away. "There's nothing to admire. Now, how is your little boy?"

"The same. Is there nothing we can give him?"

The old nun sighed. "In normal times, I'd prescribe sulfonamides, but there are none, you see. I'm so very sorry."

Lucia hesitated. "Could a person find it on the black market?"

Suora Chiara looked at her doubtfully. "I've no idea. But even if you could, you'd have to pay for it somehow. With the cost of black market oil and flour? *Allora*, I can't even imagine what they'd charge for medicine."

Lucia nodded, her thoughts running, her heart lifting. Because in her mind she saw an oilcloth bundle, full of jewels. She could indeed pay for medicine, if only someone could find it.

She bade Suora Chiara good night and turned on her heel, walking fast down the stone hall, on her way to find a nun who wasn't really a nun at all.

If the medicine still existed in Rome, L'Allodola could track it down.

# THIRTY-TWO

## Francesca

*March 23, 1944*

FRANCESCA PASSED A line of people, women mostly, queued up for water at an emergency public fountain. The line snaked all the way around the block, the waiting women toting an array of canteens and jugs, their dented sides glinting in the spring sunshine. Recent bombs had fractured the city's already damaged utilities, leaving Romans with even less of everything. Clothes hung off the people Francesca passed, standing propped against walls, shifting from foot to foot, squinting in the light. The nauseating odor of lice medicine wafted among them. As if being hungry wasn't enough, Rome was infested with lice. The scent of the ointments, ubiquitous now, seemed like the scent of despair.

Francesca's stomach growled, and she sighed. The latest bombs were obviously meant for the train stations flanking Rome, but a few pilots always seemed to miss. The convent's windows had been blown out by a bomb falling on a house nearby, terrifying Lucia and everyone else hidden there. Another had fallen on a queue just like the one Francesca left in her wake now. That bomb hit a line of people waiting for water, ripping through bodies like a machete in the brush. Rumors flew afterward: women had been beheaded, thrown up onto telegraph wires, buried in rubble. Fear darkened everyone's eyes, competing only with exhaustion.

Francesca was afraid as well, but not of bombs, not now. In a pocket under her robes, tapping lightly against her bony hip with each footfall, was a bottle of pills. She'd walked the city all morning, tracking it down on the black market in exchange for Lucia's jewelry, her own heart constricting at the thought of Matteo in his bed. He wasn't her child, not even related, but when she looked at him, the world seemed to narrow, reassembling its hierarchies until questions rang in her mind. What was most important? What had she been fighting for, these many months, if not the future? This morning she'd touched the future's own forehead, listened to the feeble inflation of his lungs, and left in a hurry with pearls in her pocket.

She passed the steps of a church, and as always, refugees called out to her. She clenched her jaw and walked on, wishing they understood. They saw a nun ignoring their desperation, but what they couldn't see was the message written on tissue paper crinkling against her chest. She had this last errand to run, and then she could hurry home with the medicine for Matteo.

She turned off the main road onto a narrow alley. Glancing up and down, she fished the tissue from her brassiere. The paper was thin enough to be eaten should she be stopped, but up ahead a gray-haired man in black materialized from an alcove, and she knew it would be another successful pass. She walked straight for him, exchanged a nod, and slipped the tissue into his waiting hand. He bent, tucked it into his shoe, and walked the other way. Francesca barely broke stride. She spilled out on the opposite side of the alley, job done.

She heaved a sigh, allowed herself to close her eyes for a second, and savored the sun on her face. She never read the messages, but she had an idea of the information she carried: the number of German vehicles someone had counted on a strategic road, the position of troops, the location of supplies. The tissue paper messages would help Allied bombers find the right targets, hastening their victory, hastening liberation. Francesca glanced at another huddle of starving refugees. Liberation couldn't come soon enough.

Revived a little, she turned up Via del Tritone, aiming for home. It was the second day of spring, and the weather had finally warmed. The pill bottle tapped her hip, and she felt lighter than she had in some time, nearly optimistic. She was about to turn another corner off the main road when a bang sounded, freezing her step. It grew exponentially, the thud and thunder of an explosion. She spun in place as the air shook with the concussion, the cobblestones vibrating underfoot. Had a bomb dropped? She wheeled again, scanning the sky for planes. It was a cloudless day, the kind people had begun calling, *"una giornata da B-17,"* optimal for lumbering American bombers. But there was nothing. She listened, cocking her head and stilling her body so she could hear the sweep of her own lungs. Gunfire burst to life, somewhere close.

Questions came to her in a jolt. Why had today's message drop been arranged for *this* neighborhood? Why hadn't they intersected at their usual meeting place? *The strike.* No sooner had the words slid through her mind than another series of explosions shook the streets. Her contact must have had reason to be in this neighborhood, playing some other role, and in an instant she understood.

Screaming and gunshots split the air over the neighborhood, and Francesca wheeled again, trying to locate the source of the noise. She couldn't think. Blood pounded in her brain as the shooting continued. People began running toward her, civilians streaming down Via del Tritone, their hands holding hats to their heads, bags thumping hips, eyes wild. *What had the partisans hit?* She tried to think, to command her mind to focus, but instead it skipped off in a frantic whir, and before she'd harnessed a single coherent thought, her legs were moving. She trotted into her limping run, one fist holding her robes aloft, the other pumping in time with her feet, her breath coming fast. Tommaso had spoken of a column of Germans. "*Madonna*," she said aloud, running faster. "*Madonna mia*."

She turned onto Via del Boccaccio, a narrow road connecting others, black robes flapping. She moved at a mechanical clip, devoid of thought, following sounds like a bat tracking a scatter of insects. A shot rang out. Another. Still, people streamed past her, ducking into doorways of shops and apartments, veering up side streets, faces feral. Gunfire spit, growing closer, and finally, her mind snatched at questions, holding them before they streamed on by. What would she find at the scene? Did anyone need help? What could she do?

It wasn't until she was nearly under the gunfire that her mind fully caught up with her legs. What was she doing, running into the scene of an attack? She slowed so quickly her robes tangled around her ankles, heart hammering in time with the shots. The road she paused on intersected with another, not ten strides away. She crouched, crab-walking the final steps toward the intersection, careful to stay hidden between a building and a trash can. *Just see if anyone needs help*, she told herself, holding her breath. The scattered shots died out, replaced by German shouts, and she took a final step to glance up and down the street.

She sickened. Bodies littered the narrow lane, thrown like heaps of dolls. Blood spattered buildings up and down the street. It ran downhill in trickles, slicking the cobblestones. A woman hung from a three-story window, shot in her bathrobe and caught on a railing. Francesca blinked, looking among the corpses for partisans, trying to hold on to some scrap of coherence, and her eyes fell to a blond head and shoulders, not far away, rolled up against the curb. It was a boy's head, a little older than Matteo, blown clean off its body. Vomit rose in her throat so fast she had to bend over and retch against the stucco wall she clung to. Her empty stomach heaved, its meager contents splattered at her feet, and she fought a wave of dizziness. *She had to get out of here.* Her eyes moved on their own, once again skating over the bodies, the surviving SS soldiers wandering among them a little way up the street, shouting. Gunfire shattered the synapse of quiet, ricocheting out of nowhere, and her senses flooded in like cold water. *Get out of here*, a voice whispered in her mind. There was nobody she could help. *Run.*

Francesca took off, slipping in her own vomit before catching her uneven stride. Shouts rang out behind her, but she scurried on, tensing for the bullet that was most certainly coming for her spine, sobbing through her bellowing breaths.

A side street appeared, and she careened up it, struggling to run, struggling to push the image from her mind that hung there now, like an omen. A boy's head, severed. Dead eyes, so young. Forever staring up at a cloudless day.

She collapsed against a wall, heaving. She couldn't breathe. Her own words came back to her, spoken on the first warm day of the year.

*Tommaso, if you don't stop this strike, we'll be in* un mare di merda.

But it was so much worse than a sea of shit. She saw the dead boy's eyes, held them in her mind, and bent to retch again. She already knew she would see that poor boy for the rest of her life.

# THIRTY-THREE

✿

## Lucia

*March 25, 1944*

T HE NEWSPAPER TREMBLED in Lucia's hands. Light from the low-ering sun streamed past her, landing on Matteo's bed. He slept on, each of his breaths merely a wheeze, unaware that the world was turning, unaware that Lucia's heart was shattering. Beyond him, Francesca leaned against the glassless window frame, looking at her feet.

The German response to the strike on Via Rasella was printed on the front page of *Il Messaggero*. Lucia read it again, trying to muster strength for the question she needed to ask.

*On the afternoon of March 23, 1944, criminal elements executed a bomb attack against a column of German Police in transit through the Via Rasella. As a result of this ambush, 32 men of the German Police were killed and several wounded . . .*

Lucia's eyes skipped down to the final paragraph.

*No one will be allowed to sabotage with impunity the newly affirmed Italo-German cooperation. The German Command has therefore or-dered that for every murdered German, ten* comunisti-badogliani *criminals be shot. This order has already been executed.*

"Already been executed," Lucia whispered, blinking fast as she reread the words. She formed the crucial question just as Francesca looked up, green eyes wide.

"Three hundred twenty people." Lucia's voice edged out of a whisper. "The Nazis shot three hundred twenty people . . . It says criminals. Where did they find their criminals?"

Francesca stepped over to Lucia. She couldn't seem to produce words.

"Carlo?" Lucia managed.

Francesca cleared her throat, nodding. "We think Carlo would have been among them. The Nazis haven't published a list of names, but they emptied Via Tasso, for some of the . . . I'm so sorry, Lucia."

Lucia's heart stammered, its rhythm faltering, and her knees gave out where she stood. She collapsed in a heap of angles, the paper crumpling in her lap. Had they murdered everyone imprisoned in Via Tasso? She heard a strangled sound coming from her own chest, but her mind seemed to detach from her body like a cloud on the wind. Could he have been spared? Her head began to shake on its own.

Francesca knelt beside her, pushing the paper away and taking her hands. Lucia couldn't think, couldn't process what she'd just been told. *Carlo was dead.* She stared into Francesca's eyes, shining in the last trickle of sunlight, as if trying to comprehend them.

"Where?" she managed.

Francesca wiped at her own tears. "Nobody knows for sure. Rumors are growing about the Ardeatine Caves. Outside of Rome. After seeing the news today, I walked the city to hunt down partisans, to learn what I could. I needed answers, I needed to know . . . Lucia, I didn't want to tell you, not with Matteo so sick, but I also didn't want you to hear it from someone else."

*Carlo had been murdered in a cave.* Lucia looked away, trying to grasp it. Had he been slaughtered like an animal? She closed her eyes and, like a reflex, imagined it: Carlo's eyes, bright in a dark cavern. The thump of his heartbeat, the smell of him, the smell of death all around him. A gun rising to his neck—

The floor hit her temple before she realized that she'd fallen. Whatever had held her up this long gave way, like a riverbank into a stream, and swift sorrow coursed through her. Francesca's voice murmured in the background, a hand rubbed her back, and her cheek pressed against cold marble, but Lucia felt as if she were floating away on a current and leaving her body. Drowning.

Behind her closed eyes, the darkness of caves rose again. Carlo's face hung before her, wild with fear, and he spun into the shadows. She saw them together on a beach, years ago, holding on to each other while the wind whipped at their clothes. *You*, he whispered, *you are exactly who I've been searching for.*

The light left the room in a slow retreat. Francesca huddled beside her, and Lucia wept long into the darkness.

MUCH LATER, WHEN the sky was black beyond a risen moon, Lucia balanced on her stool over Matteo's bed, and Francesca stood at the window. Lucia's throat was so raw she couldn't swallow, her limbs so weak she couldn't move. She watched her boy, asleep in the wash of moonlight, his breath coming in gasps, and her soul crumbled with every exhale. Carlo hung in her mind like a weight, and she couldn't take her eyes off her child. What if she lost him, too? Francesca had brought the bottle of sulfonamide pills two days ago, and at the right intervals, Lucia pushed them through his blue-tinged lips and poured water in after them, praying while she implored Matteo to wake enough to swallow. But nothing had changed. She'd heard Suora Chiara murmuring in the hall to someone she couldn't see. "He's just so weak. I don't see how he'll pull through . . ."

Now Lucia watched Matteo's chest rise and fall. What if he

pushed out the last of his breath, and failed to pull in more? She had to grip the bedsheets to keep from tipping over at the thought. If her boy died, her cherished boy, she'd simply cease to exist. There would be nothing left for her.

Lucia wiped at her stinging eyes and reached for Matteo's hand. She stroked his fingers, running her thumb over his perfect joints. Whatever hope had sustained her thus far was nearly gone. She prayed for Matteo's heart to continue beating, and she waited.

Even as she prayed, she sensed death seeping closer, like lengthening shadows at the end of the day. Was it fate? Matteo was carved from her brother's mold, with Piero's same beautiful face and sweet soul. And Matteo looked out at the world with his father's warm, steady gaze. Would he also share their fortunes? She reached for him, cupping the curve of his cheek in her palm. Did she dare hope for her child's future, while his breath faltered in his little lungs?

She tucked a curl behind Matteo's delicate ear, pushing an insistent thought away, but it returned like a tide to drown her again and again.

She was destined to lose anyone she loved.

# THIRTY-FOUR

ᴂ

## Francesca

*March 25, 1944*

FRANCESCA REMAINED AT the window, staring out, listening to Matteo's stifled breathing.

It was the end of everything. She swallowed the pain in her throat but stayed perfectly still. Silver light fell over the rooftops, spreading from the convent window, cathedral domes, and bell towers, all jumbled under a scatter of stars. She couldn't imagine moving her feet from where they were planted, ever again. Germany had just invaded Hungary, yet another defeat. The Allies were no farther up the peninsula, and no closer to Rome. Giacomo was gone, a dead boy haunted her thoughts, and Matteo was on his last breath. There was no reason to continue on.

A sob rose in her chest, and she smothered it, glancing back at Lucia and Matteo. Lucia had shifted to sit on the edge of the narrow bed. She held Matteo in her lap, her gaze unwavering. They were as still as the marble statues littering Rome, an echo of the *Pietà*. Lucia as Mother Mary, cradling her conquered son.

Francesca turned back to the window, overwhelmed by sorrow. She'd come to love the little boy, to see in him a reason to hope. There was a flicker in his eye when he smiled. And his giggle reminded her of Giacomo, years ago. When she'd imagined freedom lately, she imagined Matteo: a boy walking along the Tiber in the sunshine, free to laugh, free to grow up. Perhaps Lucia would buy him a gelato, and perhaps Francesca would walk with them. She'd tell Matteo a story about dragons and knights and courage, and when he ran in the wind, she would know he had a future. That, for the first time in her life, Italy's sons might grow old.

But now none of that would happen. And it was her fault. She wiped her stinging eyes. If Lucia had never met Francesca, the woman would still be safe in her house, unaware of her long-lost husband, uninvolved in the partisan war. If Lucia hadn't met her, Carlo wouldn't have been at her house that fateful night. He might still be alive. And maybe, if Lucia hadn't fought the occupiers, she would have access to a German doctor to save her child now. And why not? Was this better, this despair? Had they changed anything by following their own compasses? All they'd done, in their long fight, was lose anything they had left.

She sucked in her lips and stared out at the rooftops, tipping from shadow to light. Somewhere beyond them, hundreds of Italy's sons were newly dead. Francesca had trekked Rome all day, seeking contacts and asking questions, piecing together everything anyone knew. She'd learned enough to picture it. Men and boys were herded from prisons onto trucks, driven from the city they'd fought for, and maneuvered into caves, never to be seen again. And there were so many who'd fallen before them; the country was littered with ghosts. There was the ghetto, once full of families, now empty. And the Jews of other cities—had they met the same fate? And all the British and American sons, lost in the craggy south, who would never return to their mothers. She thought of Giacomo, her private tragedy, and tried to multiply the loss. The pain of it all was unfathomable.

What it all boiled down to, her whole life encapsulated, became clear: The enemy would always win. Ordinary people could resist, but in the end, the enemy had more fighters, bigger guns, fewer scruples. They would rip fathers from their families, rake lovers off the streets, empty neighborhoods of whomever they deemed undesirable. They would force boys to march, to load rifles, to learn how to shoot before they'd lost all their baby teeth. They would start wars, occupy cities, and starve the people until their children fell sick. And when the people fought back?

Murder.

Bells began to ring across the city, echoing from one church tower to the next, gaining momentum until the air over Rome reached a crescendo. It was midnight. When the bells ceased, the rumble of artillery replaced them, coursing along the horizon.

A voice from another star-strewn night murmured in her ear. *Marry me*, Giacomo had whispered. It seemed so long ago. *Marry me tomorrow.* Her eyes darted from star to star, tears cooling her cheeks. Why hadn't she said yes? She'd been foolish, all along. She should have married the only man she'd ever love, the moment he asked. She should have kept them both safe when the Nazis came. A bomb fell somewhere in the distance, fracturing the night, and for the first time since the war had come to Rome, Francesca couldn't imagine its end. For months, the city had lived on false hope. *The Allies are just around the corner*, people had whispered. *Our liberators are marching north*. Soon, soon, the city would be free.

What people had overlooked, in their desperation, was that there was always more to lose. She saw the boy's head in the gutter, rolling away from its body, and swallowed a surge of bile. Throat burning, she glanced at Lucia and Matteo.

What people had overlooked, all along, was that evil could win.

# THIRTY-FIVE

༚

## Lucia

*March 26, 1944*

L UCIA SENSED WARMTH on her face before she opened her eyes. She'd been floating somewhere, like a leaf in a stream, the world glittering around her. She held on to the dream as she sensed her own breath sweeping in and out. The memory of where she was, and all that had happened, trickled in.

There was a sheet under one of her hands, bunched and twisted where she'd gripped it. A small body lay under her other palm, a hand in hers. She felt Matteo's fingers, still and cool, and her dream fragmented in a sudden cold burst. She opened her eyes in a panic.

"Mamma?"

Lucia blinked, sitting up from where she'd slept on the narrow bed, and looked at her boy. Was she still dreaming? His large eyes were open, flicking around the ceiling before landing on her face in question. "Mamma? What happened?"

A sob and a laugh escaped her lips. Could it be? She reached for him, touching his forehead, feeling for heat. Nothing. She gripped his little wrist in her own stiff fingers, trying to believe it. He was real. She wasn't dreaming. Her beautiful boy had woken up.

"Matteo, *piccolo*," she sputtered, gathering his thin limbs in her arms. He shifted himself, resting his head on her shoulder. Not strong, but he was moving.

"Are you feeling better, my love? You've been very sick."

He shrugged, glancing up to study her. "Why are you crying, Mamma?" He held a shaky fist to his face, rubbing at his freckled nose.

"I'm just happy to see you awake, *piccolo*." Lucia wiped at her cheeks with her free hand. "Do you see the sunshine?"

He glanced toward the window, then took in the rest of the room. Francesca was gone; it was just the two of them. He blinked, his gaze hinging on her face. His eyes were so like Carlo's, bright and earnest, brown as warm earth.

She had to glance away as she remembered. She would never see Carlo again.

"Mamma? What's wrong?"

She looked back to her son, and when his lips curved into a hesitant smile, Carlo was there in her mind. But this time, she didn't imagine him in a cave. She saw her husband grinning at her under a pink sky while waves lapped at their feet, years ago. She saw him laughing with her on the rooftop, helping her spread dirt over the roots of a lemon tree. She saw him under the stars on that same rooftop, urging her to go. Urging her to save their boy.

Lucia smiled through her tears. Wherever Carlo was, he was still here. He was here in Matteo.

"Nothing's wrong, my love." She cleared the curls from her child's eyes. "We're going to be all right."

A FEW WEEKS later, Matteo and Franco sat on a bench together in the courtyard of the convent, perched like birds under an ornate crucifix, and Lucia and Francesca sat on a bench opposite. Lucia glanced up while folding linens, a giant stack produced by all the people sleeping in the convent's beds. Franco whispered some-

thing, and Matteo clapped a hand over his mouth, giggling. The
boys could be brothers. They both had dark hair and wide, brown
eyes. But Franco was nearly a foot taller at eight years old, and
thin, like everyone, and his cheek was sliced by a fresh, pink scar.
He had a sister downstairs, playing with the younger children,
close to hiding spots in case the Nazis came. Suora Chiara once
explained how their parents had saved them. On the day the Nazis raided the ghetto, they'd urged their children to run fast and
far, and, miraculously, they'd escaped. Lucia shook a sheet in the
sunlight, sorrowful.

The boys erupted in giggles, their bare feet pressed together on
the bench and clothes hanging loosely from their limbs. They'd
been held apart from the other children by their illnesses, and
now they stayed that way, lounging like little old men, gathering what strength they could. Lucia's stomach knotted at that
thought. They couldn't gather much strength, not with rations set
at a meager hundred grams of *pane nero* a day, the black bread
made of mysterious ingredients that never accomplished the task
of filling anyone up.

Francesca broke the quiet, echoing her thoughts. "They're so
thin they could blow away."

The knot tightened in Lucia's stomach. "So are you and I. But
soon—"

"What if they never get here?" Francesca turned, posing the
question like a challenge, her face a mix of solemnity and something like panic. "The Allies have been fighting the Germans in
Italy for nearly eight months. *Eight months*, and it's a stalemate on
two fronts. We keep saying things will get better when they
come, when they rescue us. But what if they don't? We could all
starve—that's what the Nazis want. If we live, our children will
grow up speaking German."

"No." Lucia glanced at the boys. They were still engrossed in their own world, leaning close for a thumb war while *Gesù* looked on over their bent heads, forever nailed to his cross. Francesca spoke quietly as a default; they hadn't heard. But ever since the attack on Via Rasella, she'd been like this. Hopeless. Angry.

"You need to find something to do," Lucia whispered, flicking out a pillowcase. "If you're not going out as a *staffetta* anymore, there are other ways to help. There are plenty of opportunities right here—the chores are innumerable."

"I cleaned the pots this morning. Though broth doesn't leave much to scrub off." Francesca picked at her fingernails, brooding. "They're saying Kesselring is unbeatable, you know. That the Allies are never going to break through at Cassino. That they'll never get farther than the beaches in Anzio—"

"*Stop it.*" Lucia pursed her lips, and Francesca quieted. L'Allodola had only left the convent once since the massacre in the Ardeatine Caves. She'd left for Lucia, crossing Rome to visit with an old neighbor named Signora Russo, and enlisting her boy, Roberto, to check Lucia's mail and deliver anything that came. The Germans had finally started notifying families of the men they'd murdered, and Lucia was desperate for certainty about Carlo. A week later, Roberto had come to the convent, letter in hand. She choked now at the memory of her husband's name in print, confirmed dead. It hadn't been a surprise by then, but the grief was overwhelming.

Now she cleared her throat, turning to Francesca. "You have to stop languishing. We're all afraid for the future. We've all lost people."

"I know." Francesca looked up, her stare suddenly naked. "Every day, I think of ways I could have prevented those losses. How I could have saved Carlo."

"Saved Carlo?" Lucia stared at her, puzzling. Did she hold herself responsible for what had happened? How could she? Lucia gathered Francesca's hands, squeezing, and understood: it was who she was, a person who unerringly chose right from wrong, who sought justice in the face of overwhelming injustice. Her father had been the same before her, and her Giacomo as well. The idea that the Nazis could win in the end? That evil might prevail, her fight meaningless? It was more than she could bear.

Lucia chose her words carefully. "Francesca, you must hear what I'm saying. None of this is your fault. You couldn't have prevented Carlo's death, or what happened in the Ardeatine Caves, or—"

"If I'd never met you, you'd still be safe in your house. And Carlo wouldn't have had to warn you the night the Gestapo came, because you would never have been in danger."

"No." Lucia said the word so firmly Francesca blinked. "You cannot take responsibility for the choices of other people. I *chose* to fight back. Carlo chose to find me. And the atrocities? The Nazis massacred all those men in the caves—not the partisans."

"But if I could've stopped the strike—"

"You tried." Lucia inhaled, holding Francesca's stare. "You always try, you always fight for what you believe is right, and there's power in that. What if everyone was more like you? Think of the difference you've made—all the papers you've carried, the identity cards you've delivered, the ammunition you've prevented from reaching the front and killing yet more Allied boys." She hinged closer. "You should keep on fighting, Allodola. It's who you are."

She held Francesca's stare, and the girl bent to weep. Lucia continued folding sheets, glancing over from time to time while Francesca sobbed through her private grief. When she eventually raised her head, her green eyes were glassy, but bright. The boys passed furtive glances across the courtyard, yet continued to play. They were used to seeing adults cry.

"Francesca," Lucia ventured. "It's nearly impossible for the nuns to feed all the people here. One of their tricks is going out individually to buy what they can, so nobody can trace the quantity back to this convent and calculate how many people are here . . ." She set a folded sheet aside. "You could do that. Put on those robes you used to wear and go out to fill rations."

Francesca squinted across the courtyard, wiping at her eyes, and she nodded. She appeared to be thinking still when a rumble grew outside the convent walls, starting small but gaining momentum. Francesca's eyes swung to Lucia, widening.

Lucia's heart began to hammer. She cocked her head, listening. It was the grind of truck engines. More than one. Were they coming to the convent? The sheet shook in her hands, trembling in the sunlight. She set it down, gesturing toward a line of rooms across the courtyard that looked out on the road beyond the convent, and Francesca followed her.

The Gestapo had amplified their raids since the attack on Via Rasella. Rumors flew through Rome, bouncing from neighborhood to neighborhood. In the last week, the Gestapo had searched houses for men and boys who could work, taking nearly eight hundred from southeast Rome and shipping them north. And the Nazis had doubled down on their hunt for Jews and partisans, sowing terror all over the city with surveillance and arrests.

Lucia swept into a dim room, blinking in the gloom. Could they be coming here? Did someone tip them off about the people hiding inside these walls? She rounded on the window, standing on her tiptoes to look out, and there they were.

Coming down the road, a pair of trucks tipped and bounced along. She narrowed her eyes, confused. What was that on their hoods? The trucks were covered in brush and mud, as if they'd been tearing through the sodden countryside. As they drew closer, she could make out olive branches lashed to the hoods, silver leaves fluttering. It took her a moment to digest that it was an attempt at camouflage.

Lucia didn't have time to dwell on the irony of olive branches in battle, because a long line of men followed the trucks. They were on foot, walking at a tired pace. Their uniforms hung loosely, as muddy as the vehicles preceding them. But Lucia's heart leapt. They were *Allied* soldiers. Prisoners or not, it was thrilling to see them. She exchanged an electrified glance with Francesca, whose green eyes widened. Francesca stepped quickly from the room to get a chair to stand on, and Lucia hoisted herself up a little and leaned out the window to get a better look. They propped themselves in the sill, watching as the Allied soldiers streamed beneath them, the first Allied soldiers they'd ever seen.

For prisoners, the men appeared strangely cheerful. Many of them had a bounce in their step, and they gazed around at the buildings towering over them with wonder on their faces.

"Not what I'd expect from prisoners," Lucia heard herself saying, voicing unfinished thoughts.

Francesca shrugged. "Maybe they're glad to be out of the mud, in a city? The Eternal City, at that. I wonder why the Germans are parading them through . . ."

Lucia followed their shapes, filing in an orderly cluster beneath the convent windows. "Probably so everyone will see them." She met Francesca's quick glance. "The Nazis love to boast, right? I'm sure they think parading Allied POWs around will smother anti-Fascist morale even more . . ."

Her words fell away when one of the soldiers glanced up. He was a young man with ruddy hair and a dirty face, and when his eyes found Lucia's, he did something that made her heart flip. He raised his hand in the air, his fingers forming a V, and grinned.

"*Vittoria,*" Francesca whispered. "Isn't that the sign for victory?"

Lucia held the soldier's stare, confused. "*Sì.* But he's been taken prisoner. Why is he flashing the sign for victory?"

Francesca stood motionless beside her. Lucia glanced at her

friend, whose face had gained a fierce intensity. "He's flashing the V because he thinks the Allies will win."

Francesca raised her own fingers in a V, and Lucia's soul leapt. The men below were prisoners, but they weren't beaten. They'd lost a battle, but they hadn't lost faith. She turned back to them, reaching out her own hand. The soldiers below erupted in cheers as they saw it: two Vs flashing on the outstretched arms of Italian women, hidden in the heart of Rome.

The next day, German leaflets fluttered down over the streets, and Lucia took a chance and ducked outside to fetch one.

She brought it into the courtyard, where she'd left Francesca sitting under the crucifix.

"Look at this." Lucia handed the leaflet over, sitting close so she could study it again. The German propaganda started with a photo of the Allied prisoners standing in front of the Colosseum. She scanned their faces, looking for the young man who'd held up the sign for victory, but the picture was too grainy to make anyone out. Beneath the photo, the Nazis had written a sarcastic message. *They said they would come to Rome: here they are!*

Francesca gripped the paper. Her jaw firmed, and Lucia's breath caught. Was there a bit of fire left in her yet?

"Little do they know," Francesca said, her eyes snapping up. "The men in this picture? They're merely the first. And the rest will come on their own."

# THIRTY-SIX

ನಲ

## Francesca

*April 1944*

F RANCESCA WALKED TOWARD the bakery, a basket over her elbow, her limp pronounced. She'd been working her body too
hard again, scouring the city daily for food that was nearly non-
existent, leaving her bicycle behind to disguise herself as a nun.
But she only had to think of the people in the convent, their features sharpening, their strength waning, to push herself on. She
was wasting away as well, but at least she had a purpose to drive
her forward. She would keep the people she'd come to care about
alive, for as long as possible.

People had started to die in Rome. Not from the usual culprits:
bombs, violence, disease. Now, as spring began to shine through
the seasonal rain with full force, people were dying of hunger.

It was very early in the morning, the sun barely up over the tile
rooftops, but the line at the bakery was already long. It fanned out
in an untidy stream, with women standing in the streets, baskets
and bags over their arms, desperation on their faces. She limped
into the ragged end of the line and glanced at a woman, frizzy
haired and frazzled, to her left. "*Buongiorno,*" Francesca murmured.

"Is it?" The woman looked at her, taking in her robes. "I haven't had a good morning for a very long time, Sister."

Francesca nodded her agreement, squinting up at the windless blue. For months, she'd scanned the sky throughout the day, like a reflex, but lately, the bombings had tapered off. There seemed to be a shift in the war, like a shift in the wind, but so far she couldn't sense which way it was blowing. She'd recently met with Tommaso again, reconnecting with the resistance, which had fractured after the reprisals in the Ardeatine Caves. It turned out that many partisans felt as Francesca had in the wake of such horror: divided. Only now had they begun to pick themselves up and regroup.

"Do you think we'll ever get bread today?" the wiry-haired woman murmured, flicking her gaze to Francesca.

"Eventually, I'm sure."

"Don't be so sure. Yesterday I waited here into the afternoon, and they never served a single person. I've never been so angry." The woman's voice cracked, and she took a second to recompose herself, wiping a frustrated tear from her cheek. "I have four children at home. Used to have five, but we lost the littlest over the winter. I'm terrified we'll lose another—they're so hungry."

Francesca turned to the woman, taking in her troubled eyes as they skipped nervously to the bread line and back. "I'm very sorry to hear of your loss," Francesca said, placing a hand on her shoulder. "You'll get your bread today."

"How can you promise such a thing?"

Francesca didn't know, but she felt the truth of her words glowing in her heart like a lit coal. She glanced around the line of people, shifting on tired feet, and firmed her jaw. All of these women should get their bread today.

Without thinking, she raised a fist in the air. "We want our rations!" she shouted, and the women in line jumbled and turned to look at her, stunned. They took in her habit, traced the black fabric up to her raised fist, and widened their eyes. Then another woman hollered.

"Give us our rations!"

"*Pane!*" the frazzled mother at her side yelled, eyes feral. "Give us our bread!"

The crowd began to move, shifting and bubbling toward the building, as more women picked up the chant. The women called out scattered demands before joining together, finding one another like clasped hands, and rising in unison.

"Bread!" they chorused. Francesca cupped her hands around her mouth, shouting in time with the women. "We want our bread!" She pumped her fist in the air, and everyone around her did the same. In one swift minute, they'd became a battalion of mothers, demanding that their children eat.

When the crowd began to surge forward, an armed Fascist police guard appeared on the steps of the bakery. He gestured over the angry women, raising his Beretta in warning, but terror glittered in his eyes.

"Bread!" the women screamed, and before the guard could pull the trigger, a stout grandmother grabbed his gun and flung it into the crowd, her white hair catching the sun. The crowd cheered wildly. Francesca watched the weapon's arc, her heart thumping. It landed somewhere off to her left. Clutching her basket, she shoved her way past the frizzy-haired woman, who now screamed, with rage in her eyes, and pumped her fist. The crowd edged forward as Francesca fumbled farther left, scanning the tightly packed women for the gun.

There. The sun edged through a nest of arms and legs and glinted off a metal barrel. Francesca shoved her way toward it. She neared and saw that a tall woman in a floral-print dress held it to her side, her eyes panicky and her mouth drawn tight. The woman looked from the bakery to the edges of the crowd, clearly unsure of her next move.

Francesca pushed close, and the tall woman glanced down as they bumped together on the last step, shoved from behind.

"Give it to me," Francesca said, her voice rising out of a whisper as the women around them shouted, "Bread!"

The tall woman scanned her up and down, caught in indecision. She glanced around the crowd again, the line of her mouth clamped tight, and nodded. She passed the gun through the gap. Francesca lifted her robes and, in one swift movement, tucked the Beretta into the waistband of her skirt. When she dropped the robes and looked around, the two women closest to her gaped, scanning her habit, stunned. She held their stares for one sharp moment, holding her breath as well. They could turn her in. They merely had to drag her out to another guard, showing what she hid under the robes, and she'd be back in Via Tasso before noon. Francesca felt heat rush to her face, and she braced herself to fight, but then the women nodded, one after the other. One winked, and the second raised her fist in the air, hollering, "Bread!"

Not a minute later, the crowd was surging forward again, and the wide windows of the bakery shattered. Objects continued to fly at them, taking out any remaining glass, and the door flung open. Women streamed inside, shouting and cheering. The bakers sidled up to the wall, out of the way, their faces stricken with fear.

Inside, the bakery smelled of dough and crust, and the women settled into an almost orderly ambush on the storeroom. Someone passed sacks of flour through the storeroom door to the people crowding the bakery, arms out. Women filled their baskets and bags and, with faces both triumphant and terrified, hurried through the door and broken windows. Francesca took two sacks, piling them into her basket and clutching the weight of it close.

When she stepped out through the bare windowpane, a middle-aged housewife reached up to help her down. *"Grazie,"* she murmured, wading back through the uproarious crowd.

At its fringes, a small lady with a bobbed haircut met her gaze, hoisting her dress up into a makeshift hammock, her knobby knees showing under its faded fabric. "Can you believe it?" she said conspiratorially, merging alongside Francesca. "The damn Fascists were hoarding white flour in there, all along. Have you looked in your sacks, Sister? It's *white flour*—while we've all been eating pitch."

Francesca nodded, saying nothing, and hurried off up a side street. She passed through two more alleys before allowing herself to slow, smiling a little. Inside, triumph burned to her very core.

The women of this neighborhood, at least, would eat today. And tomorrow. And tucked into the waistband of Francesca's dress was something she needed if the insurrection ever actually happened. She sensed the familiar weight of the Beretta against her navel, and suddenly it was all there again in her mind: the Germans retreating, the Allies advancing, the resistance finally shaking off the scourge of the occupation.

If Roman women could still find the strength to fight for their families, Francesca could fight again, too.

# THIRTY-SEVEN

ตน

## Lucia

### June 4, 1944

*I*T WAS HAPPENING.

Lucia's hands shook as she hooked them into her elbow creases, pacing the dim room, her calves warming each time she passed through a square of early-morning sunlight on the floor. While everyone else gathered in the courtyard at the heart of the convent, full of joy, she'd remained in her room. Her heart swung between elation, relief, disbelief, and guilt. Was it really happening?

The news had been everywhere for the past two weeks: all over the wireless, on the lips of every person on every street corner, worming its way into houses and trams and stores and hideouts.

The Allies had broken through on both fronts.

They'd mounted a heavy offensive on the Gustav Line in the middle of May, and soon after the news had thundered in that the German line was broken. After that, Rome came alive, crackling with energy, brimming with hope. People filled the churches to pray for peace, while others walked the streets, smiling but whiteknuckled. After all, they'd hoped before. Could this really be the beginning of the end?

Now on this bright morning, the end had clearly arrived. The city brimmed with noise as a river of metal churned through it. German tanks, trucks, and armored cars crossed bridges onto ancient roads in an endless procession, fleeing north. Lucia stared out the convent windows, frowning with nerves, unable to see the source of the noise, though she knew what it was.

It was the first sound of liberation. The Germans were leaving.

She inhaled, marshaling her feelings and moving to the armoire to run a comb through her hair. It was time. She couldn't avoid it any longer. She blinked, tugging the comb over her limp curls before dropping it and gathering her handbag. Good enough.

"You're not going out?" Francesca appeared in the door just as Lucia turned toward it.

She cleared her throat. "A quick errand."

Francesca leaned against the jamb, her sharp hip angling her skirt, her hair long on her back. She looked Lucia over, contemplating her, before speaking quietly. "You shouldn't leave the convent. Not now."

"But you said they're retreating without a fight."

"Mostly." Francesca nodded. She'd been gone for two days, having been called by leaflets dropped from Allied planes. *Stand shoulder to shoulder*, the leaflets implored. *Do everything in your power to prevent the destruction of the city*. So Francesca had spent a day and a night guarding and demining the city with bands of partisans, bracing for violence that so far hadn't come, and she'd only just returned to the convent to rest for an hour or two.

Francesca looked toward the window while she spoke. "The Germans will be moving through Rome for most of the day as their divisions retreat. I watched their tanks and trucks stream over the Ponte Milvio all night. It was like an endless river. There are others stealing cars, handcarts—whatever they can find. It's not safe until the last German leaves, Lucia. There could still be snipers. Or saboteurs. Or just desperate, angry soldiers."

"I can't wait for them all to leave. I might already be too late."

"Your mother?"

The air left Lucia's lungs. "*Sì.*" She glanced around the empty room. "When the Allies landed in Anzio, my mother spoke of following the Germans north. She wanted to take my father to Bavaria to avoid the Allied advance, and whatever might happen afterward . . . I can't let her do that, do you understand? I can't let her travel deeper into danger, where bombs fall every—"

"Don't." Francesca shook her head. "You can't rescue your parents. If they followed fascism this far, they'll follow it to its end."

Lucia hesitated, her thoughts scrambling. She hadn't seen her mother since the night she came to warn them, months ago. Was Francesca right? Should she leave her parents to whatever fate they chose? They had, after all, chosen Il Duce her whole life, over everything. Even over their sons. But just as Lucia was about to put down her handbag and relent, a different face appeared in her mind. She saw her old friend, Noemi Bruno, blinking up at her on her front stoop, her silver hair speckled under fluttering bougainvillea. *We can all be strong*, she'd said, gripping Lucia's hands with her bony fingers. Her kind eyes stared through the memory. Lucia sighed, brushing the wrinkles from her skirt with a shaking hand. If Noemi were alive, she would tell her to help her parents.

"I have to see my mother." Lucia turned back to Francesca. "It's the right thing to do. She came for me. She came for me and Matteo, when we were in danger."

"But will she even be safer here?" Francesca dropped her voice to a whisper. "They're *collaboratori*. How will people respond to Fascists like your parents when their protectors are gone?"

Lucia wavered again. Would her parents be safer up north,

away from their history? Her father would probably go without her mother, if he had a choice. He'd follow Il Duce until he died. And if he stayed, he'd face the wrath of all the neighbors and citizens he'd watched be arrested, persecuted, and starved. Her mother deserved that wrath, too. But Lucia thought of the bombers flying low over the convent, weeks ago, the windows exploding while a building was leveled across the street, and guilt raked her soul. The bombings were worse in the north, with entire cities pummeled and leveled. She had to tell her mother to abandon her dying ideology, to remain in Rome, to change. She would have to face whatever wrath she'd earned when peace came, but she didn't have to run.

"I'm going. I won't be long."

She was nearly out when Francesca's urgent whisper pulled her back into the room once more. "*Wait.*"

She turned, and Francesca motioned for her to close the door. Then Francesca unbuttoned her blouse a little at the navel, reaching around to pull a dark object from her own waistband. A gun glinted in a shaft of yellowing sunlight. "You should take this," she murmured, passing it to Lucia and giving her a quick tutorial. "This lever is the safety, but we'll leave it off in case you have to act quickly. If you need to fire, you'll pull the slide back to load the chamber. See here? This pulls the hammer back, and then it's ready. Here, tuck it into your underwear—turn around, against your lower back—in case something happens." Without preamble, Francesca fiddled with Lucia's backside, stretching the waistband of her garments to tuck the gun in place, fluffing her blouse, and reassembling it all.

Lucia patted the back of her skirt, which now held a solemn weight.

"If you need to shoot, it's quite accurate at close range. Easy to use."

"I won't need to shoot."

Francesca came around to her front, her face grave. "You might. If it means coming back to your little boy, do it without hesitation. Now go, while it's still early."

IT ONLY TOOK a second, as Lucia followed her father into her parents' apartment, to see that they were indeed packing. Her mother stood over a pile of clothes, her earrings swinging when she turned to see Lucia appear in the doorway. A sob burst through Nonna Colombo's habitually pursed lips. She dropped the skirt she'd been folding and stepped across the marble floors, arms out, face stricken, and pulled Lucia in close. But after a volley of sobs, she tidied up her emotions, sniffing them away and releasing her embrace.

"I didn't know what had become of you," Nonna Colombo whispered. She moved her hands down and gripped Lucia by the wrists, holding her still for inspection like she'd done years ago, when Lucia was a little girl. She cleared her throat. "When I came back to your house that night it was ransacked, and you and Matteo gone . . . Nobody could tell us anything. None of your father's contacts—" Her voice hitched. Her eyes searched Lucia's, startled and pained at the same time.

"We've been in hiding, Mamma. But we're safe." Lucia pulled back a little, casting her gaze over the empty suitcases and stacks of clothes. Piero's photo sat on top of the nearest stack. He laughed out from the frame, forever jaunty in his airman's uniform, forever young.

"What are you planning to do?" Lucia managed.

Her father drifted to the sofa behind her, settling down with a groan. "We're leaving," he muttered. "Il Duce still has a firm grip on the north. The Germans will establish another line now that they're abandoning Rome, so we'll go north of it—"

"No." Lucia said the word with more force than she'd intended, stopping her father short. "When the Germans leave, Rome will finally be at peace. Papà, Mamma, why would you choose to follow the war? Where would you even go?"

Nonna Colombo's voice was unsure, but she answered. "I managed to get through to a cousin, in Bavaria. They'll take us in, though we're also thinking about going to your father's relatives in Vicenza . . ." She pivoted, looking around her living room as if she were lost.

Lucia stepped into her gaze. She took her mother's hands, sensing her father's stare as she spoke. "Mamma, you've lived in Rome most of your life. You don't want to go to Germany, do you? Stay here. Matteo needs a grandmother. He's lost . . ." She inhaled, subduing a surge of sorrow. "He's lost his father. And Mamma, I need you. I don't have anyone else now."

Nonna Colombo's bony fingers tightened. She blinked quickly, expelling tears from her eyes as fast as they came. They coursed down her pinched face, glittering in the afternoon light like the jewels dangling from her ears.

"We can't stay," her father interrupted from the couch.

Lucia turned to look at him, her palms gripped in her mother's, and everything within her stilled. He stared at the floor, head hammocked in his hands like an old man. Why couldn't he stay? Everything she knew of her father swam into her mind, all at once. She saw his boots, which he'd stacked by the front door every day of her life. He'd polished them himself on Sundays, and she could conjure the scent of bootblack even now. She blinked, and there she was as a little girl, sitting quietly at her father's side, legs swinging, while he buffed his leather to a deep shine. She'd studied him while he worked on his boots, wondering why they were so important, wondering why he was so important, wondering what he did every day. He'd always been a mystery, and as children do, she'd accepted it. When she'd grown, she understood that he was a mid-level government official, a paper pusher with his feet planted firmly in family money. What more was there to ask? But questions occurred to her now. What paper, exactly, did her father push? And what had he done since the Germans came to Rome?

"I know you cooperated with them, Papà," she ventured. How bad could it be? She thought of his tidy desk at work, with its pens lined up and files neat in a drawer. "But lots of people cooperated with the Germans. Do you think they'll all run away? Surely, we can move forward after the war ends, rebuild—"

"I didn't just cooperate with the Germans, Lucia. I worked for them."

Nobody spoke for a moment. He worked for the Germans? The floor of her stomach opened like a trapdoor. For the first time, it occurred to her: she didn't know her father at all. He'd moved like a shadow in the background of her life, providing for his family, but she'd never thought to ask how. He stood, smoothing out his pant legs with shaky hands.

"You and I, Lucia, we're on opposite sides of a wall now. You're my daughter first, but second? You've made yourself my enemy. Your mother and I are leaving. We'll let you know how Marco is doing, if you care anymore. Last we heard, he was still on the Russian front, God be with him." He paused, shifting his dark stare to the open window off the balcony, where noise from the departing army thundered like a constant storm. "At this point, all I can say is good luck to you. Take care of my grandson."

With that, he strode from the room, shoulders back in defiance.

Nonna Colombo still gripped Lucia's hands, and she tightened them now. "I'll write when I'm able," she croaked, nodding as if that settled everything. Lucia's lips trembled, and she tried not to cry. Questions skated through her mind, and she guessed at the answers. Her father was not just a loyal follower of Il Duce. He was a collaborator, a betrayer of his own people, a man who had something to hide. And her mother?

"I should have thought for myself," Nonna Colombo said, lips pursed. "He's not that important in the scheme of things, Lucia— I can see what you're thinking. Your father is several rungs down from the top. Yet he's on the ladder. And that worries him with a change in government upon us." She cast her hand around the room, gesturing at the waiting bags, despair in her face. "I never had much to say about any of it. I didn't follow the news really, didn't care for politics. Even now: I don't want to go, but I'm going. Learn from my mistakes, *Liebling*, and follow your own mind." She laughed a little, lifting her liquid eyes and a trembling hand to Lucia's face. "What am I saying, darling? I know you will. You're far braver than I've ever been."

LUCIA HURRIED THROUGH the heat of oncoming summer, ducking along her parents' street, her pulse underscored by the continual rumble of engines somewhere to the north and intermittent gunfire. Her back and the fabric under her armpits were sweaty, but whether from nerves or the strengthening sun, she didn't know. A bell tower rose over a corner, casting its shadow, and Lucia glanced at its dark shape. German snipers could very well be watching these streets. Her shoulders tensed. Even now, a rifle could be trained on her silhouette, ready to shatter her spine. She thought of Matteo's beautiful face, and fear lurched in her stomach. Maybe Francesca was right. She shouldn't have come here. She'd achieved nothing, and now she was out while Germans were yet in Rome, with little left to lose.

She came to Via Veneto, which was eerily quiet in the brightening day. Somewhere in an adjacent neighborhood, gunshots burst out at sporadic intervals. Lucia glanced toward the stately hotels a few blocks down, and bile rose in her stomach as she jogged across the street. She suddenly felt too alone, too exposed. Had German command left yet? Or were they still here, packing their things into black staff cars, preparing their retreat? Her gaze dropped from the hotels to the few silhouettes on the sidewalks, all of them ducking and hurrying. She turned onto a narrow street, her cardboard heels slapping cobblestones as she strode onto a yet narrower alley. It was empty, and she fought the urge to run.

The walls on either side of her were scrawled with graffiti; people had left traces of their anger and desperation all over the city's stone. She glanced at the looping messages. Some were unreadable, having been scrubbed out or overlapped with a more recent scrawl. The largest letters simply proclaimed, *Bread!* Her eyes slid over it as she passed, nearing the next intersection, and when she swung her gaze forward, all the air left her chest in a horrified gust.

Hans Bergmann strode around the corner, boots clicking stone, legs swinging, and his eyes nailed to her with furious intensity.

She pivoted to run, but it was too late. In one swift movement, Bergmann grabbed her from behind, raked her across the ground, and pinned her up against the wall, her legs pedaling.

"You," he growled, his voice like the tremor before an earthquake. "I've been looking for you for a long time, you piece of partisan shit."

His hand was on her throat, and he pushed in, narrowing her windpipe.

"You thought you could get away with everything? That you're invincible? You almost were, darling. My scout was *just* about to leave his post outside of your old building. If you'd waited a few more hours to visit your parents, you would have gotten away clean."

Her pulse throttled, and she tried to look up and down the alley, searching for help, but he pressed her head harder against the graffiti and grinned.

"Do you think someone is coming to rescue you? Don't you realize I've killed off your friends, one by one? We filled the prisons with them, the goddamned traitors, and then we emptied those prisons."

Lucia opened her mouth, trying to scream around the pain in her throat, trying to scramble her way out of a trap that was quickly closing. She dropped her purse and clawed at his hands, filling her fingernails with his skin, but he just laughed. Terror trundled through her soul, and one word repeated in her mind, timed with the laborious pumps of her own blood.

*Matteo. Matteo. Matteo.*

"I thought about killing you here. The second I was alerted to your presence, I thought I might just shoot you in an alley and leave your body to rot, like all of your friends rotting away in those putrid caves. But then I realized: You've never seen the land of your ancestors, have you? Bavaria, wasn't it? How about you come along to our northern lines, and I'll throw you into a cattle car that's passing right through Bavaria on its way north?" His voice was sharp, derisive, and he smiled over her weakening breaths. "Yes, I think that'll suit you well. I'd rather not kill you yet, darling. Dying slowly, with plenty of time to consider your mistakes—that's an appropriate fate for a traitor like you, Signora *Moretti.*"

He let go of her throat but grabbed her left wrist, tightening his grip as she fell in a wheezing heap. "Stand up, bitch."

He threw his leg back and kicked her, hard, with his steel-toed boot. When he dropped her wrist, she fell, her spine hitting the ground, wheezing and whirling with pain. She pinned her eyes shut, trying to breathe, and despite her smothering fear, she sensed a metal object digging into the small of her back, pressed against the cobblestones. Bergmann laughed over her curling body, and she looked up in time to see him wind up for another kick, his expression hardening. His boot hit her in the stomach, and the air left her lungs, replaced by bile rising into her burning throat. The sky fractured behind him as she choked back pain and acid. She reached behind her back, sucking in air and shaking, as if she was going to push herself up from the ground.

He was laughing when her fingers found the Beretta, feeling for its grip beneath her underwear and clamping down. He glanced up the street, checking for onlookers and readying another kick, and she brought out the gun. With a trembling hand she squeezed the slide and pulled it back. Bergmann's gaze fell to her and he froze, eyes widening as he stared down a loaded barrel.

"Don't move a fucking muscle," she breathed, her words coming out in cold, fluid German. Propelled by some inner force, she stood smoothly, ignoring the pain in her stomach. She kept the gun level with his head.

"You wouldn't," he spat. His eyes darted around in small movements, the rest of his face still, and he took a careful step backward. "You don't even know how to shoot."

"I'm a partisan, you Nazi pig. I'll put a bullet in your Aryan brain if you move another inch."

He froze again, hands up, but she could see it in his eyes. He was planning, calculating. She should do it. *Shoot him now*, she commanded herself. *Shoot him while you have the advantage.* But what if she missed? She held his stare, and he held hers, his pale eyes icy with hatred, and she felt the same cold hatred rise up on a swell in her chest. Her finger tightened on the trigger.

*But no.* Her heart pulsed between her ears, her finger loosened slightly, and she knew: she wasn't a killer. She would never again pretend to be something she wasn't. And if she shot this devil, she'd see his face in her mind for the rest of her life.

"Run." She flicked her chin minutely, gesturing up the street.

He hesitated, glancing at his own shadow.

"Run away, you Nazi bastard. Get the hell out of my city."

She aimed the gun slightly to the left and pulled the trigger. The bang was tremendous, and her hand jerked back when the bullet left the chamber, leaving a whiff of white smoke as it sliced past Hans Bergmann. In an instant, all the fury fell from his face. Fear widened his eyes instead. He stared at her for a half second, shocked wordless, and then he turned and ran up the lane. His steel-toed boots slipped a little, and he stumbled to his hands and knees on the cobblestones, scrambling back up. He ran on, never looking back, until he skidded out of sight and away from the aim of Lucia's Beretta.

# THIRTY-EIGHT

❧

# Francesca

*June 5, 1944*

Rome was uproarious with joy. Francesca glanced at the band of fabric on her bicep, her heart swelling every time she saw its green, white, and red stripes. Over the colors of the Italian flag, letters stitched together to form *Comitato di Liberazione Nazionale*. She couldn't smother the surge of her smile. She was out in the open, wearing an armband of the National Liberation Committee, looking toward the future.

Lucia walked beside her, bouncing Matteo a little on her shoulders, and he gripped her chin with curled fingers and laughed into her hair.

"I see them! Mamma!" he shouted, voice high over the whoops and cheers rising all around them, like mist in sunlight. Allied soldiers had rolled in during the night, but so far, few people had laid eyes on them.

Francesca squinted up at Matteo, her hand wobbling on her cane as the crowd jostled past. "Where, Matteo?"

He pointed toward the Colosseum, and they all turned in the direction of his finger, staring at the stone amphitheater glowing orange in the morning sun. The crowd turned with them, as if the same question rippled through everyone at the same moment.

Could it be true? Had the Americans finally come to Rome? For a moment, the crescendo dipped as thousands of people waited in the hush, listening. Hoping for a first glance.

"Yes, Mamma!" Matteo shrieked, "I see tanks! Tanks with flowers on them!"

Francesca's joy struggled amid her strumming heartbeat. She couldn't believe it, not until she saw it with her own eyes. She began to walk, and Lucia followed, Matteo bouncing on her shoulders, and they wove through the jubilant crowd. Shouts and cheers rose again, like a wave crashing through the masses. She pinned her eyes to the ancient stone curving over them all, growing steadily larger as they progressed toward it.

*"Viva l'Italia!"* an elderly man shouted as they passed, pumping his knobby fist in the air. A woman, flanked by children, answered, *"Americani! Viva gli Americani!"* At her elbow, another young mother, toddler in arms, wept into a bouquet of wildflowers. Francesca firmed her jaw and pushed onward through the euphoric crowd, pulse still bounding and one thought in her mind: she had to see it for herself. Only then could she welcome the relief waiting to flood in, like sunlight held back by the shutters in her heart.

She stepped onto the road circling the Colosseum, and Lucia stayed next to her, pinning Matteo's little knees tight where they hooked over her shoulders. They wedged themselves through another cluster of whooping people with hands held high, fingers pinned in the shape of Vs. *Vittoria.* The word rolled amid Francesca's thoughts as she found a gap in the jostling bodies, emerging on a clear band of cobblestone.

"See, Mamma!" Matteo shrieked from Lucia's shoulders. *"Gli Americani!"*

A tank idled directly before them, inching along in the shadow of the Colosseum, the tide of people zippering around it. On its gun turret, a wreath of roses swung, and children had clambered up to sit with a half-dozen sunburned GIs. The children and the American boys waved, grinning, and the people of Rome cheered and wept as they passed. Matteo laughed, incandescent. A truck followed the tank, draped with soldiers in steel helmets and olive uniforms. They smiled down, rocking through the crowd. A slow line of tanks and trucks and marching men followed, pushing carefully through a population drunk on joy. Francesca gripped her cane, barely blinking, trying to let it all sink in. Someone threw handfuls of petals in the wake of a passing jeep, and she looked up at them, swirling and drifting under the blue sky. Lucia's face shone with tears, and she took one hand from Matteo's ankle and reached out to catch a petal.

Francesca threaded her free hand through Lucia's elbow, her mind running ahead. She could go back to being Francesca, finally. But who was she now? Giacomo's face appeared in her mind. His eyes found her behind the glint of his glasses, and he nodded. His image vanished as quickly as it came, but she felt him as though he were with her. A flock of swallows swooped over the crowd, skimming the line of American tanks. *The Germans are gone*, she told herself. War raged on in the north, but here the Allies were so close she could touch them. And petals drifted down instead of leaflets, landing on everyone like hope. Francesca wondered: *What next?* She watched the swallows turn, diving again toward the crowd, and she knew only one thing for sure.

She would not hide again.

# THIRTY-NINE

❧

## Lucia

*June 5, 1944*

WHEN THE SUN sank toward the horizon that evening, Lucia stood alone on her terrace. Rome, spreading before her, was alive. Church bells rang, pealing from hundreds of towers, filling the city with a jeweled crescendo. In the streets below, people still walked, laughing and crying in fevered joy. Rooftops and bell towers glowed in the setting sun, pink as a blush.

Lucia turned from Rome to the lemon tree. It grew on in its humble pot, fighting heat and drought and neglect, persistent in its reach for the sun. Drawing a deep breath, Lucia stepped across the terrace and knelt before the tree, sitting on her heels. She reached out to touch a tear-shaped leaf.

"Carlo," she whispered. "I wish you were here."

The wind murmured, bending leaves on the lemon tree. Lucia touched the wedding band on her finger.

"I loved you, always. Do you know that? I miss you so much." Her voice cracked, and she paused. Hanging high over the terrace and all the rooftops of Rome, the first stars winked in the sky. She lifted her eyes to them, pulling words from her soul.

"I wish we'd had more time together. I no longer blame you, Carlo, for anything. The world got in the way. Yet every night I yearn to hold you in my arms one more time. To talk to you. I wish I could put my hand—" Her voice left her for a moment. "I wish I could put my hand on your beating heart."

She folded slowly over her knees, her forehead bumping the terra-cotta pot and resting there, like a pilgrim at journey's end. Grief rolled through her, endless as waves, while the sun dipped below the distant hills.

When Lucia sat back up, pulling in long, shuddering breaths, the stars shone brighter. She stared at them, knees numb, her wet face lifted to the deepening night. He wasn't coming back. She'd hoped, despite everything, that he might. That there had been a mistake, that he would appear in her life once more, warm and alive. But the truth of it settled in her soul like a soft rain. He was gone this time. Forever.

She spoke again, her eyes on the stars. "Thank you for giving me Matteo. He's the gift of my life. And when he looks at me, Carlo, I see you. You're there in his eyes. Someday I'll tell him about his father. About your bravery, and integrity, and the way I loved you. The way I always will."

She paused, glancing from star to star, piecing together constellations of her own design.

"I've been thinking about what I'm going to do next." She turned the ring on her finger, eyes on the strengthening stars. "When I first knew we'd lost you, I thought I'd also lose myself. To grief. But then Matteo nearly slipped away as well, and things became clear. I can't give in to my private pain. So many people have lost everyone they love to this war, but I still have Matteo.

And the two of us have a future." She looked from the stars to the tiny, struggling tree. When she found her voice again, it came out whole.

"Today I watched the Allies arrive, finally, and I knew: We can't forget. We have to keep fighting for the world we want to see. I'll never hold my true heart back again, Carlo. I'll step forward, however I can, and build a better world for our son."

# FORTY

&

# Francesca

*Early July 1944*

The noonday sun pressed heavily on their shoulders. Francesca sat on a bench on the terrace, sweating in her blouse, watching Lucia and Matteo.

"Like this?" Matteo asked. He swung a full watering can up toward the lemon tree's pot. The water sloshed as he poured it, and Lucia bent beside him, steadying the canister. "*Sì*. Exactly like that, *piccolo*. And if you help me water it once a day, it will give us fruit. Now, can you make a design over its roots with these pebbles?"

He blinked up at his mother, eyes lively. His freckles had darkened in the sun, splashing his nose and cheeks. "Just to make it pretty?"

Lucia tousled his curly hair. "Just to make it pretty, love. Later on, when it cools down, we'll go see Lidia and you can play with Rosa, *sì*?"

Matteo nodded and knelt at the pot's rim in his short pants, his little fingers moving rocks around, busy so Lucia could take a rest. Francesca smiled, but her heart smarted at the mention of Lidia. Lucia's childhood friend had still heard nothing about her husband and missing family members, but she carried on as well as she could. Because what other option was there? Lucia visited her often, taking Matteo so the children could play and the mothers could talk.

"Is it too hot?" Lucia asked, moving to the bench. "We could go back downstairs."

"No." Francesca pulled her hair over one shoulder, cooling her neck. "It feels good to be out."

Lucia nodded, sitting back and closing her eyes. A companionable silence descended as Francesca lifted her gaze to the sky. She'd been living with Lucia and Matteo since liberation. They'd never discussed it, really. She'd just drifted home with them, taken the spare room, and settled into the rhythms of their lives. It seemed the entire city was trying to find new routes forward. Battles still raged up the peninsula, and Rome rocked like a ship in a storm, charting its course in changing seas. The day after liberation, the Allies had launched another, more distant invasion, entering France through Normandy. They fought now on French soil, and Francesca and Lucia listened to their progress each night on the wireless, breathless. The war was far from over in most places, but Francesca had found her faith. It would end, and it would end with Germany's defeat. She believed this now.

And she'd just decided what she'd do with her life when it was all over. "Lucia," she ventured, breaking the silence, "I made some inquiries yesterday."

Lucia rolled her head sideways, squinting. "What kind of inquiries?"

Nerves tightened Francesca's stomach. What would Lucia think? She inhaled, plowing forward. "I went over to the university, to see about classes. I'm planning to enroll."

"You absolutely should." Lucia straightened. "What would you study?"

Heat flooded Francesca's face, but she maintained a steady voice. "Law."

For a second, Lucia stared at her, thoughtful, her smile spreading. "*Sì.*" She reached out, taking Francesca's hands in her strong grip. "An attorney! *Certo*—it's a perfect fit." She gave another squeeze. "Live here while you go to university. Will you?"

"I'd love to. You don't think it's too bold, a young woman studying law?"

"*Santo cielo*, Francesca. You were born to be bold. Anyway, I have a similar confession." Lucia blinked, pursing the grin from her lips. "I've been thinking about the future, too. Promise you won't laugh."

"You know I won't."

Lucia glanced at Matteo, lowering her voice. "Rumor has it people are already talking about the new government. It'll be a while yet—when the Allies leave us to our own devices, I suppose—but I've heard women are interested in leadership roles. Especially women who were active in the resistance. Things are changing for women, and I just thought . . ." Lucia looked down at her knitted hands.

Was Lucia considering a role in politics? Francesca smothered a bloom of surprise. She tried to picture it, and images rose in her mind. Lucia, with her charming smile, shaking many hands. Lucia, clever minded, studying the issues and crafting strategies. Lucia, speaking with the people, playing the right roles at the right times, maneuvering them toward a better future.

Francesca spoke decisively. "You'll be perfect."

"It feels so audacious to even think it. You're not just saying that?"

"You know I never just say anything. It's exactly what you should do, Lucia. We've shown that women are just as capable as men. Why shouldn't you help rebuild Italy when the time comes?"

Lucia laughed. "Well, look at us." She laughed more, and Matteo turned, examining her before bending back over his pebbles. "A single mother like me, and a country girl like you, shaping the future."

Francesca grinned. She was about to ask more when footsteps sounded in the stairway, pounding up toward the terrace. Her heart started to pound as well, a reflex, and she pushed up to stand.

"Who could that be?" Lucia murmured, rising and cocking her head in concern. But before they had a chance to investigate, the door to the terrace creaked open.

A boy stood in the doorjamb, all limbs and tattered clothes, and it took Francesca a second to find her voice. "Roberto! What brings you here? Is your mother all right?"

"My mamma sent me. *Si*, she's fine."

Francesca exhaled with relief. She'd visited her old neighbors several times, bringing Signora Russo flour from the market, a pair of hands to hold a baby, and conversation.

Roberto rummaged in his pockets. He pulled out a white envelope, smudged and crinkled. "Mamma said this came for you."

Francesca froze. "It came to my old letter box in the building?"

"*Si*. The new neighbors brought it to Mamma."

Her pulse bounded in her chest, filling her with something like fear as she stared at the envelope, bright in the sunshine, suspended in Roberto's hand. Francesca crossed the terrace, and she managed to murmur, "*Grazie*, Roberto," retreating to her bench.

Her fingers shook as she flipped over the envelope, examining the handwriting, warding off hope. Lucia ushered Roberto over to play with Matteo, and the hum of their voices melted away as Francesca studied her previous address on the envelope, written in an unknown hand. The return address, printed out in blocky letters, was the American 23rd General Hospital in Naples. What did this mean? Her heartbeat stuttered, and she ripped open the paper.

*Francesca, my love.*

It was like being hit with a wave. She rocked on the bench, dizzy, pressing a palm over her lips. She tasted salt from her tears before she even realized she was weeping. Across the terrace, Lucia looked up, but she continued to occupy the boys.

*Giacomo.* The next wave to hit filled her with urgency. She blinked through her tears, eagerly reading the blurring words.

*I've written you so many letters, despite not being able to mail them through the chaos separating us. I had the inspiration to send this one with an American friend who was headed to Rome on leave. I pray it finds you.*

*I'm sorry, so deeply sorry, for the agony I've undoubtedly caused. Ever since they took me, I've fought to come back to you. I fought, and lost.*

*In September, I refused to enlist alongside the Germans, so they sent me to a forced labor camp along the southern lines. I was lucky not to end up in Germany, but it was hell, nonetheless. They worked us from sunup to sundown with little rest. We were hungry all the time. But even more unbearable was the fact that they were using us to build fortifications against the Allies. Eventually, my friend Sandro and I resolved to escape. We were working on a hilltop, building bunkers, when we slipped away, but we were seen and shot at. Sandro and I fell as we ran, dropping down a rocky incline so steep it was almost a cliff. Our guards, likely assuming we were dead, didn't come after us. By some miracle, we both found ourselves alive at the bottom of the cliff—battered, but alive.*

*We waited until darkness, and then we walked south. By morning, we stumbled upon a remote farmhouse, and there we found friends in an elderly couple who had refused to evacuate in the face of the war. They hid us in their cellar, helping us heal and gain strength until we were ready to offer our services to the Allies. I have many to thank for my life.*

*Later, Sandro and I volunteered with the Italian Liberation Corps, the Italian army formed to fight alongside the Allies. I worked in field hospitals along the Gustav Line as a surgical assistant, and Sandro was among the many, many men killed in that unending battle.*

*Since late May, I've been hospitalized, but please don't worry. I'm recovering. I was both lucky and unlucky in taking a bullet to the leg. It hit my femur, shattering some bone, so I found myself evacuated to an American army hospital near Naples. Francesca, I count myself among the most fortunate. It all could have been so much worse for me. Still, my recovery has been slow and bumpy, probably due to the poor state of health that bullet found me in. Please don't worry, my love. I'm nearly ready to come home.*

*I think about you every minute of every hour. Last month, they brought us newspapers here, and I saw pictures of Rome on liberation day. Like a fool, I studied the photos for you. I don't know if you stayed in Rome or went back home. I'm terrified that you're unwell, or unsafe, or worse. Because, Francesca, I can't imagine my journey ending anywhere but with you.*

*Not long ago, I was afraid all the time, and many nights you visited my dreams. Always the same dream. Do you remember*

*sitting in the olive trees when we were kids? In my sleep I'd be*
*there, with you. We'd sit in those trees, over that feeble stream*
*where I was always trying to catch a fish, and we'd talk. Your*
*voice in my mind—it's what got me through.*
        *Soon as I'm able, I'll travel north. Be safe. Wait for me.*

FRANCESCA WAS DIMLY aware of Lucia across the balcony, looking
at her questioningly. But she couldn't respond. She sat motionless,
shocked through, afraid to blink, afraid to shatter this new, fragile truth. Giacomo was alive? She hadn't dared to hope it, not for
months. She lifted the letter, reading it again. And again. It took
several reads for reality to sink in. *He was alive.* And he was coming home.

When Lucia finally crossed the terrace, she waved the boys
downstairs. They tromped through the door and disappeared, a
whir of elbows, knees, and thumping feet. Lucia stepped to the
bench and sank down. Francesca was unmoored. She blinked at this
woman who had become her dear friend, trying to govern her
thoughts.

"I'm so sorry," Lucia whispered, reaching out to grip her
limp fingers still holding the letter. "It must be about your Giacomo."

Francesca found her voice. "He's alive." She offered the letter,
too stunned to elaborate.

Lucia bent, reading quickly. Her expression changed as she
read, loosening from grief to surprise.

"*Santo cielo*, he's in Naples?" She shook her head, laughing even
as tears wet her eyes. "He says he'll be able to come home soon.
*Cara mia*, I'm astonished."

Francesca found herself smiling, but as Lucia wiped her own
cheeks, bending to read Giacomo's letter again, sorrow poked at

her joy. Lucia pursed her lips, tears beading her eyelashes, and Francesca's heart ached.

"My friend, I'm so sorry. You deserved such a letter, too."

Lucia's dark eyes swung up, startled. "What do you mean?"

"Just that I understand." Francesca cleared the pain from her throat. "I know you're happy for me. But perhaps it's difficult, with luck and life being so arbitrary, to see one man return and not another."

Lucia was already shaking her head, eyes shining. "No. Your happiness doesn't erode mine, *cara mia*. Quite the opposite. I'm overjoyed. To see you continue your life as it always should have been, with Giacomo by your side? How could such a thing sadden me?" She glanced down at the letter, folding it. "I'll always grieve for Carlo, but I can be happy for you at the same time."

They sat in silence, the sun high over their heads, hands clasped, before Lucia spoke again. "The spare room is still yours, if you want it. I understand if you and Giacomo would prefer privacy, but housing is so hard to find right now."

"We'd be honored to stay with you." Francesca's mother rose in her mind, never far from her thoughts. "Eventually, we might bring my mother to Rome, if she's willing to leave home to live with us. But for now—"

"You'll live with me," Lucia interrupted, grinning.

Francesca returned the smile and found her feet, standing. "But first I'm going to Naples, so I can bring him home." The words emerged before she had time to contemplate them. And yet, the moment they left her lips, she knew it was what she had to do. She would leave as soon as possible.

Lucia stood with her, laughing a little. "I thought you'd go and find him. You're not one to sit idle, waiting for things to happen."

It was true: she'd rather not perch if she could fly. Francesca turned, looking around as though the world were new. Her eyes fell on the lemon tree, striving in its pot, then traveled past it, to the rooftops and bell towers spreading all the way to distant hills. Rome shimmered and birds floated over it, rising and falling in an eternal dance.

When Lucia spoke again, her voice was strong. "Go and find him, Allodola. Bring Giacomo home."

# EPILOGUE

✼

## Matteo

*May 1957*

Matteo hoisted his books and thumped down the steps, jaunty despite a long day of classes. His suit coat flapped as he loped toward a bicycle chained to a tree.

"Matteo!" Federico called, emerging from the heavy doors in his wake. "Aren't you joining us for drinks? It's Friday, *amico!*"

Matteo pushed his hair off his forehead, pivoting but still walking backward, and flashed a lopsided grin up the steps. "Going to meet my family, Fede," he called up. *"A più tardi."*

*"Ci vediamo!"* Federico called with a resigned wave, and Matteo tipped his chin and turned back to his bicycle. He dropped his books into the basket on the handlebars, and moments later he was pedaling hard, leaving the university, filling his lungs with cool evening air. He'd just claimed this bicycle, changing out its tires, lifting the seat, and oiling its chain, happy to take it over for now. It was too big for his cousin, but someday he'd fix it up again and gift it to her. After all, it should stay in the family.

He sailed through Rome's streets, weaving into the ever-more-crowded *centro storico*. Sunlight slanted over buildings, and doors opened and closed as people emerged for *la passeggiata*. Matteo careened around a corner and jumped the curb, narrowly missing a boy eating gelato in an impossibly white shirt. Matteo grinned. That kid was one stumble away from ruining his clothes. He himself had been lovingly teased throughout childhood for dirtying clothes, ripping through knees, and scuffing elbows with alarming frequency. His aunt used to take him for long walks, sometimes buying him more than one gelato along the way, which would invariably drip down his shirtfront in the hot Roman sun.

It took a long time to arrive at the trattoria along the Tiber; the streets were packed with people laughing, chatting, and sauntering along in their finest as the sun hung low. Finally, he pumped up the Lungotevere, the Tiber glittering at his elbow, and spotted tables spilling out from an awning onto the sidewalk. His family sat in dappled shade, drinks in hand.

"*Ciao*, Matteo!" Uncle Giacomo called, seeing him first.

As he swung off the bicycle, his uncle stood, stumbling, and Aunt Francesca reached up to steady her husband. Giacomo had been shot during the war, fracturing his femur, and he'd used a cane ever since. In his characteristic way, he laughed about it, declaring that he and Francesca were a matched set.

Giacomo pressed Matteo's hands in his. "Took you long enough." He chuckled. "We've already finished half the carafe, kid." Matteo steadied Giacomo as he lowered back into his chair, straightening his tie and draping an arm around his wife's shoulders. He was a lighthearted man, attentive and kind, more like a father than an uncle.

Francesca rose a little, smoothing her tailored jacket, and Matteo bent to kiss her cheeks.

"How's the bicycle working?" she asked.

Matteo opened his mouth to answer, but little Giulia interrupted. "When will you take me for a ride on Mamma's *bicicletta*?" His cousin stared up, glasses magnifying green eyes, eight years old and serious as she chewed bread.

Matteo laughed. "Tomorrow? We can go for a trip to the park, *sì*?" He ruffled her hair, and Giulia shrugged, suppressing a smile.

"How was class?" his mother asked, rising as Matteo neared. Her gaze found his, with its usual blend of concern and love. He told her daily not to worry so much. Yes, he was getting enough to eat. Yes, he was studying hard. No, he wasn't cold. Of course, there was plenty he wouldn't tell her. There was the girl he'd started seeing. And the party he'd find with Federico later. And the fact that he was treading water at school, completely at sea.

"*Va tutto bene*, Mamma." He bent, kissing her cheeks, and finally took his seat at the table.

"And the biology exam?" Giacomo asked, pouring a glass of wine from the carafe and passing it across the span. Matteo took the glass, wincing internally. Biology had been catastrophic this week, despite his uncle's help. Giacomo, a surgeon, had inspired Matteo to take an advanced biology class. It was a mistake.

"Terrible," Matteo admitted. "Looks like I can cross medical school off my list."

"*Allora*, you didn't really want to be a doctor," Giacomo said, batting away any unspoken disappointment. Aunt Francesca smiled, reaching to pat his elbow.

"It's too early to cross anything off your list, Matteo. Don't be so hard on yourself—there are lots of things to be."

Matteo took a gulp of wine in lieu of saying more. It was true— he *was* hard on himself, but how could he not be with such a family? He glanced at his mother, her graying hair swept up, her poise unbreakable. Lucia was an important woman. She'd been elected to parliament in 1953, and because she still held a seat, her life was a flurry of meetings and networking. Her occupation fit her, sliding on like a well-made suit. When Lucia spoke, rooms quieted. And Aunt Francesca, currently clipping her daughter's wild hair back, was a lawyer. She was also something of a firebrand, known for championing the weak and taking on labor cases. Matteo swallowed more wine and looked away from the table. The sky was bright as fire over the Tiber's bridges, the sun nearly down.

"Matteo." His mother's voice pulled him from his thoughts. "It's all right. Don't worry about the exam."

He nodded, trying to clear any unease from his face. Did she know the pressure he felt to become something? Did she know how he worried about letting her down?

She held his stare. "You'll find your way. We all had to."

He nodded again, Giacomo passed the bread, and Matteo was relieved as the discussion turned away from his studies, and his future. But his mind wandered as he sat back, listening to his family chat. He hadn't told them about the nascent feeling he'd had lately, something he could barely articulate. When he thought of his future—stripped of university classes and exams and his expectations for himself—what he saw was his family's past. Their story vibrated within him, as if yearning to get out, as if it wasn't quite finished with him yet. And it seemed like more than an account of Matteo's own childhood, or of his family, or even of his country. The people pouring wine and laughing around this table were connected through a past of extraordinary courage, conviction, and profound love.

Theirs was a story of humanity. Could he tell it, somehow?

Matteo glanced at his uncle, who winked at Giulia as Lucia leaned over to talk with Francesca. They weren't blood relatives. They'd met during the war, forging ties that bound them together for life. And because Matteo had no father, Giacomo had stepped in.

Matteo looked out over the Tiber again, purpling under its bridges. He barely remembered his real father. His mother spoke of Carlo sometimes, but Matteo could only pull up pieces of the man from his memory: long legs, fingers moving over a checkerboard, an unshaven jaw. A pair of arms swinging Matteo up into a tree. Wide palms. The flash of eyes in the dark, catching moonlight. A voice whispered alongside those eyes, fossilized in his memory. *"In bocca al lupo, Lucia."*

Matteo looked back to his family. *In bocca al lupo.* His uncle, his mother, his aunt, and the father he'd lost—they'd all been in the mouth of the wolf, once. And they had survived. His stare fell to the bicycle, propped nearby. And maybe that was all you could do. Keep on pedaling, despite the wolf at your heels, despite fear, despite uncertainty.

The first stars pricked the deepening sky, and Matteo smiled to himself, recalling the words of his mother's bedtime story. *He looked up, and there were stars looking down at him, and he didn't feel alone anymore. He started to walk, and he knew where to go.* And, Matteo realized, he did. Perhaps he hadn't decided which degree he would pursue, or what line of work he'd eventually occupy. But he understood, suddenly, that the past would shape his future. That someday, he would find a way to share his family's story.

"You all right, Matteo?" Francesca studied him, eyes bright in the evening light.

He shook himself back to the present. *"Sì, sto bene."* He managed a grin. "I'll be fine."

# AUTHOR'S NOTE

୬ଓ

THE BEGINNINGS OF *Courage, My Love* were first sparked, long ago, by my grandparents. Both of my grandfathers fought in World War II, one in the Pacific and the other in Europe. But it was my grandmother, a military nurse in the war, who spurred my imagination with her stories. She would fold laundry, or chop vegetables, or pair socks—her hands always busy—and talk about her life in the army. She described nursing under canvas in the fields of France, setting up hospitals in bombed-out buildings, and caring for patients in the wake of now-famous battles. Eventually, she'd pause, a contemplative look in her eyes, and say, "Just remember: the world is a lot bigger than your own backyard."

Coming from her, this meant something. My grandmother grew up during the Depression in rural Canada, and despite limited opportunities available to women, she attended nursing school. When Canada entered the war, she looked far past her own backyard and enlisted alongside the men, shipping overseas with the Royal Canadian Army Medical Corps. The war took her first to England, then to France in the wake of D-Day, and on to Belgium, where she witnessed V-E Day. There, she met my grandfather, an American captain, and they married in a cathedral in Ghent.

My grandparents' home was full of relics from the war. In the den, a pair of steamer trunks served as coffee tables. If you were cold, you'd be handed a scratchy, olive-green blanket that had once graced an army cot. On the walls of the bedroom where I slept, an embroidery hung, stitched by one of my grandmother's patients in Normandy. Sometimes I'd slip into their bedroom to study their wedding photos. In them my grandparents stood, smiling and impossibly young, on the cathedral steps in Ghent, both uniformed, grinning with the combined joy of their union and the war's end. Everywhere, the past echoed.

My grandfather rarely spoke of the war, but my grandma did. If I asked about the photos, she'd tell me what came before and after the camera's snap. If I sat down on an old steamer trunk, she'd tell me where it had been, weaving a history I'd never have guessed belonged to the object under my seat bones. Her stories captivated me then, and captivate me still. Over time, this propelled me to seek others like them: accounts of women in history, often serving in unsung, overlooked roles, their bravery and skill and defiance of societal expectations inspiring.

*Courage, My Love* arose from my grandmother in this way, and also from her encouragement to see the world. Due in part to her insistence that we look far afield in life, I traveled to Europe during and after college, living in Italy for two extended periods. During one of those experiences, I had a professor who was interested in World War II, and so we visited many of the landmarks connected with the period in Tuscany and Rome. As an avid history lover, I found Italy utterly compelling. Whenever I wandered Rome, with its copper light and a past centuries deep, I would

imagine all the feet that had walked the cobblestoned roads before me, and their stories. I've had a love affair with Italy ever
since.

When, years later, I started to learn about the role of women
in the Italian resistance, the idea for this novel fully ignited. I read
everything I could find about them, from diaries to research papers to history books, resulting in a tower of dog-eared, high-
lighted volumes. I was fascinated by the story of these brave
women, who resisted both the Italian Fascists and the Nazis to
fight for the future of their country. Women who, like my grandmother, stepped beyond the expectations placed upon their gen-
der and, later, were largely forgotten for it.

Of the approximately 200,000 Italians formally recognized by
their government as members of the resistance, some 55,000 of
them were women. Like Francesca and Lucia, they served in a
variety of roles. Many started as *staffette*, or couriers, transport-
ing everything from documents to weapons between partisan
groups. Women also engaged in sabotage, hid vulnerable people
from the Nazis, spied on the enemy, and fought in battle. As
females, they could capitalize on the fact that the Nazis overlooked them, consistently underestimating their strength and
cunning.

Also like Francesca and Lucia, women left the resistance
changed. Prior to the war, women could only vote in local elec-
tions in Italy, and they were pressured to conform to Mussolini's
narrow view of females as homemakers and mothers. After the
war, Italian women took on new roles. In 1945, they were granted
the right to vote, and the general election of 1948 saw forty-one
women elected to leadership positions. Learning this, I gave my
characters a similar future: law school for Francesca, to suit her
sense of integrity and justice, and politics for Lucia, who'd stood

with her feet in so many spheres, surviving on charm, intelligence, and wit.

While the characters in this story are fictional, the events unfolding around them were inspired by what actually occurred in Rome from 1943 to 1944. As it happens in the novel, Mussolini was ousted in July 1943 following the first Allied bombing of Rome, one of only a handful. Unlike many European cities, Rome was generally spared heavy bombing because of its exceptional history and its importance to Catholicism. After Mussolini's fall, a tense, forty-five-day period of confusion and rumor ensued before an armistice with the Allies was signed. The result was German occupation, and a country divided by its Fascist past and the promise of the future.

Rome suffered under the occupation, and the circumstances in the novel spring from history. Notable events, which actually occurred, include the bombing of San Lorenzo, the battle at Porta San Paolo, the deportation of the Jews, the false hope of Anzio and subsequent hunger and despair, the attack on Via Rasella and the reprisals in the Ardeatine Caves, and finally, liberation by the Allies. I've endeavored to portray an accurate account of occupied Rome, seen through the eyes of fictional characters.

Throughout the novel, I used real excerpts from radio broadcasts, newspapers, and leaflets as often as possible. This includes text from the Allied leaflets dropped on the city, the Action Party's *Italia Libera* paper responding to the raid on Rome's Jews, and *Il Messaggero*'s reaction to the massacre at the Ardeatine Caves. The graffiti and propaganda posters also appeared, as described, on Rome's city walls.

During the war, approximately eighty percent of Italy's Jewish population survived, with over sixty-five percent hiding to avoid deportation. In the novel, Hans Bergmann, a fictional *Hauptsturm-*

*führer* inspired by real historical figures, searches for hidden Jews and partisans. He voices the common sentiment that "half of Rome was hiding the other half." Vulnerable people did, indeed, find refuge all over the city, stowing away in private homes, convents, and churches. The Fatebenefratelli Hospital, where Lidia's family hides, still exists on Tiber Island. The doctors there really did save dozens of Jews and anti-Fascists by inventing a fictitious, dangerously contagious disease called "Syndrome K." It was named for the German commander Kesselring and the chief of the Gestapo in Rome, Colonel Kappler.

Another group requiring refuge were military-aged men. Boys who came of age after Mussolini's downfall in 1943 were generally disillusioned, and therefore many ignored conscription notices and went into hiding. Furthermore, soldiers who'd been disbanded from the Royal Army in 1943 were left without leadership, often far from home, and in grave danger. Falling into German hands meant a return to the battlefield or, more likely, deportation and forced labor. Many chose to resist and go underground. Noemi Bruno, while fictional, was inspired by regular Romans who hid young men from the Germans.

The site of Francesca's interrogation, 145 Via Tasso, is also a real place. Approximately two thousand men and women passed through the Gestapo headquarters, enduring torture and imprisonment. Today, it houses the the Museum of the Liberation of Rome. Among the extensive documents, memorabilia, and displays recounting wartime struggles and resistance in Rome, visitors can view an example of the four-pointed nails used by partisans (and fictional Francesca) to puncture the tires of German convoys.

If any liberties were taken with historical events, I've attempted to keep them minor, perhaps adjusting the curfew time on a particular date (curfew frequently changed in Rome, at the whim of the Germans), or omitting what the characters couldn't yet know about events as they unfolded. An important example of this involves the massacre at the Ardeatine Caves. The Nazis mandated that for every German killed, ten people would be shot in reprisal. This leads Lucia and Francesca to assume that 320 people were lost in the caves, when actually 335 men and boys were murdered. Because this wasn't understood until much later, Lucia and Francesca can't mourn the true number of people massacred on that terrible day.

Though fictional characters populate this story, their circumstances are rooted in historical truths. For example, Carlo Moretti and Giuseppe Gallo (Francesca's father) were subjected to *confino politico*, or political exile, which was the fate of vocal anti-Fascists during Mussolini's dictatorship. Giacomo was swept off the street during the occupation, which indeed happened to countless men of all ages, who then became forced laborers for the Nazis. They built fortifications near front lines, worked in factories, or toiled for the war effort in Germany or Poland. In Chapter Twenty-Four, Francesca and Carlo attend a meeting with an American spy to prepare for the invasion at Anzio. A real OSS agent, named Peter Tompkins, infiltrated Rome in January 1944, and he held a similar meeting with the leaders of the CLN. Finally, like Francesca and Lucia, the Italian resistance brimmed with ordinary women—housewives, students, factory workers, and matriarchs—fighting in every capacity for a future they could believe in.

Lately, I've pondered my interest in World War II. Why do I return, again and again, to the stories of such a devastating period? This is where my grandparents, and the women in the Italian resistance, fully intersect: By and large, the heroes of World War II were ordinary people living through unthinkable events.

They provide a powerful example for how we might navigate our own lives in uncertain times. The courage of such people, who sought light amid the darkness, who kept faith in the face of tragedy, inspires hope. May the unconquerable Francesca and Lucia, and all the real women behind their story, do the same.

# ACKNOWLEDGMENTS

Ever since I learned to read, I've wanted to write books. I have been so fortunate not only for the opportunity to realize this long-held dream, but also for all the people who have made it possible. Behind every book there is a team of dedicated, talented people, and I'm profoundly grateful for every one of them.

Thank you to my incredible agent, Kevan Lyon, for believing in me from the outset, and for providing unflagging encouragement, advice, and support every step of the way. Much gratitude also goes to my fantastic editor, Kate Seaver. Throughout the editorial process, I've benefited from your insight, guidance, enthusiasm, and warmth. I am so lucky to work with you both.

Many thanks to the team at Berkley, including Ivan Held, Christine Ball, Claire Zion, Jeanne-Marie Hudson, Craig Burke, Fareeda Bullert, Brittanie Black, and Jennifer Myers—with a special call out to Vikki Chu and Rita Frangie for the gorgeous cover design.

I'm beyond grateful to two of my brilliant first readers, who are also my parents, Lois and Hugh Judd. Thank you for always being ready to read first drafts, hash out plot tangles over the phone, and celebrate when life calls for it. I love you both, so much.

Thank you to Carrie Kwiatkowski, my talented and perceptive critique partner. I'm so appreciative of both your friendship and your red pen. Here's to many more writing adventures! I'm also lucky to have the tireless support of early readers and dear friends, among them Sasha Smith, Michelle Campbell, and Alicia Rule. Thank you for reading, commiserating, and cheering with me throughout this long journey.

Many thanks also to the Lyonesses; I'm honored to be among you, and endlessly grateful for your fellowship, advice, and support.

For help with languages, many thanks to my lovely friend Julia Hofmann for correcting my German, and to Katharina Künzel-Giacobini and Luigi Giacobini for checking my Italian. *Grazie mille!*

Finally, this book would not have been possible without the love, encouragement, and patience of my family. For years, they've given me the time, space, and support necessary to pursue this wild dream. So, an enormous thank-you is owed to my husband, Jeremey; your steadfast love keeps me going. And Finn and Lily, thank you for the joy, laughter, and love you bring to our lives. You two are my reason and inspiration in all things.

# COURAGE, MY LOVE

KRISTIN BECK

# DISCUSSION QUESTIONS

1. At the start of the story, Lucia and Francesca appear to lead very different lives; it seems they've had opposite upbringings, fostering contrasting perspectives and positions in society. In what ways are they, in fact, similar? Do these commonalities grow as their paths intersect?

2. Every character in the story is tugged between personal responsibilities and a moral call to action. Discuss how this works for Francesca, Lucia, Giacomo, Carlo, their parents, and Noemi. What does each person risk by taking a stand? How do they navigate this conflict? What sacrifices do they make? Have you ever faced this kind of tug in your own life?

3. Discuss how both Lucia and Francesca are shaped by loss. How would their lives be different if they hadn't faced hardship?

4. How do you feel about Carlo and his justification for the past? Do you think he deserves forgiveness? Why do you

think he made the choices he did, both in the past and during the war?

5. Throughout the story, the parent-child relationship is complex. Lucia has a challenging connection with her mother, and she herself is raising a child in difficult circumstances. Nonna Colombo, impossible as she is, often acts out of love for her children. Francesca is deeply affected by events involving her parents. Discuss how parent-child relationships impact the characters and their decisions.

6. At one point, Francesca views herself as unconquerable. How is this true? Is there ever a point in the story when she feels defeated? What gives her strength when she struggles to carry on?

7. In Chapter Fourteen, Lucia angrily declares, "But I'm a woman, and all the women I know hold back, quieting their ideas." How does this realization affect her path? Is her statement true for other women in the story? Does it still resonate today?

8. The lemon tree appears throughout Lucia's life, and she seems to feel its significance at the end of the story. What might it represent for her?

9. In what way are the characters in this story unlikely heroes? What makes them heroic?

10. What legacy have Francesca and Lucia passed along for their children? How would you expect them to lead their lives? Do you think family lore has a lasting effect on children?

**Kristin Beck** first learned about World War II from her grandmother, who served as a Canadian army nurse, fell in love with an American soldier in Belgium, and married him shortly after V-E Day. Kristin thus grew up hearing stories about the war, and has been captivated by the often unsung roles of women in history ever since. A former teacher, she holds a Bachelor of Arts in English from the University of Washington and a Master's in teaching from Western Washington University. Kristin lives in the Pacific Northwest with her husband and children. This is her first novel.

Ready to find
your next great read?

Let us help.

**Visit prh.com/nextread**

Penguin
Random
House